A LONG TRAIL ROLLING

A LONG TRAIL ROLLING

BOOK ONE OF THE LONG TRAILS

LIZZI TREMAYNE

Lizzi Tremayne / Blue Mist Publishing

Franklin Road, RD 2

Waihi, New Zealand 3682

www.lizzitremayne.com

Cover design by Safeword! Author Services, Elliot J. Thompson and Lizzi Tremayne

Photos and cover design by Lizzi Tremayne

Author photos by Kajai Lang | Artwork by Made by B 4 U

Printed in New Zealand and United States of America

Book One of The Long Trails series

A Long Trail Rolling/ Lizzi Tremayne 3rd Edition 2016

Draftt2Digital Paperback Edition 2022-09-06 -V19

ISBN 978-0-9951157-6-7

DEDICATION

To my three men: Elliot, Matthew and Stuart
You complete me.

To my mum: Kirsten
You gave me so much, every day:
—the belief I could do or become anything,
—the sky as my only limit,
and
—Sourdough.

CONTENTS

LIZZI'S BOOK LIST AND SERIES ORDERS

The Long Trails Series
A Long Trail Rolling (Book One)
The Hills of Gold Unchanging (Book Two)
A Sea of Green Unfolding (Book Three)
The Long Trails Box Set: Historical Western Family Saga: Books 1-3

Multi-Series Samplers
Lizzi Tremayne First Chapter Sampler

The *Once Upon a Vet School* Series
~Vet School 24/7~
Fifty Miles at a Breath
Lena Takes a Foal
~Practice Time~
Greener Pastures Calling

Boxed sets with Bluestocking Belles
Follow Your Star Home

Sign up for Lizzi's VIP Club to hear about new releases and specials, plus get your free sampler gift here:

www.lizzitremayne.com/VIPLong

PRAISE FOR LIZZI TREMAYNE

With this debut novel, **A Long Trail Rolling,** *Lizzi was:*

Winner 2016 True West Magazine
Best Western Romance
Winner 2015 RWNZ Koru Award
Finalist 2015 Best Indie Book Award
Winner 2014 RWNZ Pacific Hearts Award
Finalist 2013 RWNZ Great Beginnings

"vivid, light and fast-paced… a ripping good read. " *–Deborah Challinor, #1 bestselling author and historian*
    "An authentic, emotional story of one woman's fight for survival in an unforgiving landscape." *–Leeanna Morgan, USA Today bestselling author*

"An impressive debut…a romance, a western, and an adventure story, all rolled up into a compelling read." *–Booksellers NZ*

The Hills of Gold Unchanging:
    "The pace is fast, there's plenty of action and adventure and a few twists I didn't see coming. Good characters plus excellent history

equals a great read." *–Deborah Challinor, number one bestselling author and historian*

"...superb storytelling." *–Judy Knighton, editor*

"I particularly liked the attention to historical detail... an author who does her homework... a cracking good yarn." *–Shelagh Merlin, NetGalley Reviewer*

A Sea of Green Unfolding:
"the historical research is excellent...well-integrated into the narrative." *–Deborah Challinor, number one bestselling author and historian*

"A lovely combination of historical accuracy and adventure...[a] beautifully researched and engrossing story." *–Shelagh Merlin, NetGalley reviewer*

"Loved this book. The characters draw you in on a story filled with interest and suspense." *–Kate Le Petit*

Fifty Miles at a Breath
"Lizzi Tremayne is a born storyteller. The...characters...[are] three dimensional and you can feel Lena and Blake's emotions." *–Lori Dykes*

"a wonderful series about the path to becoming a veterinarian, the love of horses and sweet romance. Lena and Blake will grab your heart." *– Teri Donaldson*

Lena Takes a Foal
"This book is for anyone with a passion for horses... or anyone who loves a story about strong, independent young women finding love!" *–Stacey*

"The story... displays Lizzi Tremayne's ability to develop strong characters... with a nice strong black moment to challenge our heroine and prove her worth." *–Shelagh Merlin, NetGalley Reviewer*

"...the perfect blend of sweet romance, horses and real emotions with fascinating information woven in about the medical care of horses." – *Teri Donaldson*

Greener Pastures Calling
"A young female vet, in rural NZ, tell of the trials and tribulations of being the first female [horse] vet in the area... The romantic aspect... runs hot and cold. Outside interference doesn't help, but it all comes to head on Christmas day... Good story, with interesting look into rural New Zealand." *–Rosemary Hughes*

"I adore Lizzi Tremayne's writing and in this Once Upon A Vet School series, it gets better and better... even though it was a novella, it packed a lot into every word and I highly recommend this story as I do anything written by this author!!" *–Lori Dykes*

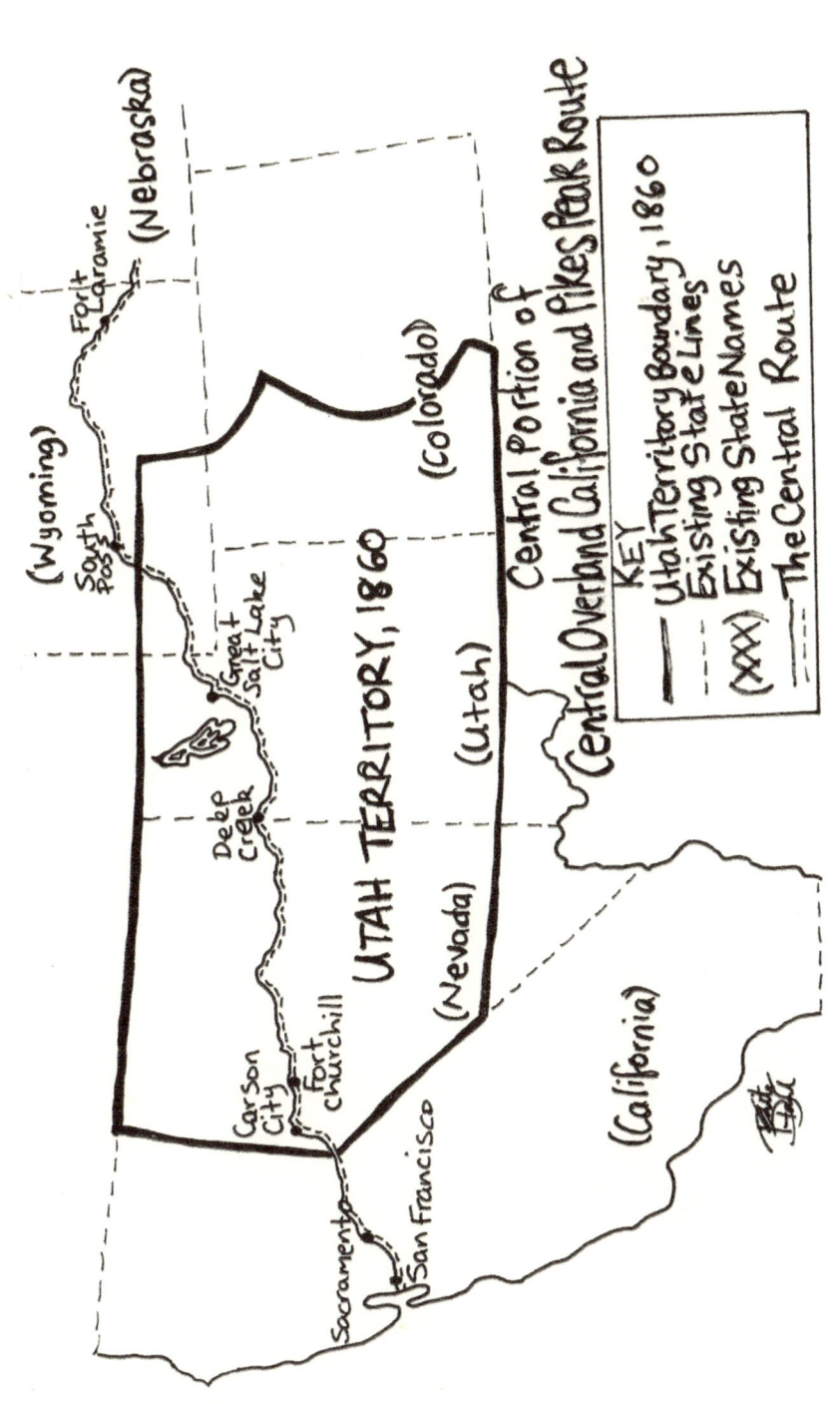

Central Portion of
Central Overland California and Pikes Peak Route

KEY

— Utah Territory Boundary, 1860
- - - Existing State Lines
(XXX) Existing State Names
—— The Central Route

UTAH TERRITORY, 1860

(Wyoming)

(Nebraska)

Fort Laramie

South Pass

(Colorado)

Great Salt Lake City

Deep Creek

(Utah)

(Nevada)

Carson City

Fort Churchill

Sacramento

San Francisco

(California)

Stations of the Pony Express
of Utah & Nevada, 1860

Pocatello

Krzysztof's ✕ Cabin

Weber
Dixie Hollow
Bachmann's
Hanks
Salt Lake House ✱
Travelers Rest
Rockwell
Joe's Dugout
Camp Floyd

Great Salt Lake

Great Salt Lake Desert

Rush Valley (Faust's)
Point Lookout
Simpson Springs
Riverbed
Dugway
Blackrock
Fish Springs ✱
Boyd's
Willow Springs
Canyon
Egan's Deep Creek
Prairie Gate
Antelope Springs
Spring Valley
Schell Creek ✱
Egan
Butte
Mountain Springs
Jacob's Well
Diamond Springs
Sulphur Springs
Roberts Creek ✱
Grubb's Well
Dry Creek

Ruby Mountains

Great Basin

KEY
✱ Home Stations

1

April 1860, Echo Canyon, Utah Territory, U.S.A.

S *he smelled blood.*

Its metallic tang assailed her senses before it was overshadowed by the stench of death. Stepping back to scan the sheer wall of the bluff rising before her, her breath caught in her throat and a sob escaped.

Finally, she'd found him.

A scuffed black boot and fur coat showed through the snow, his body wedged into the bottom of a crevice three feet above her head. She looked up to the top of the cliff, from which he must have fallen, but saw no one.

Finding handholds where there were none, Aleksandra Lekarski scrambled up the wall as her heart constricted in her chest. She tugged her father's cold, stiff body free and down onto level ground, giving thanks he'd been out of reach of the wolves whose tracks abounded in the snow where she now stood. Her world blurred as she dropped to her knees and cradled his lifeless head in her lap, rocking him. Ceaseless tears flowed down her doeskin tunic.

With a numbing pain in her mind, she ran shaking hands over him, seeking answers. What could have made an experienced trapper like Krzysztof Lekarski fall off a bluff and succumb to a death more suited to a greenhorn?

This couldn't really be happening.

Just seven days ago, he'd kissed her goodbye with glowing eyes.

'Keep the fire going in the smokehouse this time, will you, Aleks?'

'Of course, Papa, my promise. Be back soon, I'll miss you.'

'I'll return before you've missed me, then we'll go sell last winter's furs at the trading post.'

We'll never go to town together again.

Aleksandra sat back on her heels and gripped her swimming head in her hands, fingers pulling her hair until it hurt, then whimpered and returned her attention to her papa.

She shrank from what was left of his eyes… and was glad he'd been in the narrow gap, too small for large predators. Beetles had been there, or some rodent, maybe even a hawk. The scent of decay was a sharp contrast to the clean bite of fresh snow. Trying not to breathe through her nose, she swallowed hard, stomach rolling.

Aleksandra's hands froze as hard-crusted blood met her fingertips. Her heart stopped altogether at the sight of the inch-long, bloodied cut in his buckskin jerkin, repeating into his chest wall. She turned him over. A laceration of the same size exited the soft leather covering his back.

Papa hadn't simply fallen off the bluff. Nothing but a sword made such a wound.

Aleksandra's ears began to ring, her world narrowing to a small gap, as she fought the rising panic.

It couldn't be…Vladimir couldn't have found us. Not over two decades, two continents and the Atlantic Ocean.

The ground swayed as she hunched over her father's still form. Squeezing her eyes shut to stop the motion, she recalled the words Papa had endlessly repeated, so she would always remember:

'He *will* seek us out. Vladimir will come for the secret and we must be prepared to keep it from him—at all costs—always.'

But what a cost.

Despite her entire being screaming to fall apart for the loss of her only remaining family, years of Papa's training to protect their secret stopped her in her tracks. Struggling to draw air into her lungs, she looked around the bottom of the cliff. Her clearing vision now showed more wolf sign: scrapings on the wall below his body and white snow darkened by blood beside stinking yellow patches.

Leaving his body here, knowing the scavengers would return, would be the hardest thing she'd ever done—but Aleksandra knew what her papa would have required of her.

Heart sinking, she slumped to the forest floor beside him and took a deep breath of the wind whistling cold up the valley. Closing her eyes, she touched her lips to the top of his head. With shaking hands and tears flowing anew, Aleksandra lifted the leather thong of the beaded *Shoshone* medicine bag from about his neck and pulled the signet ring from his finger. Kissing her papa once more, she covered him with dead leaves and snow, beseeching the forest spirits to care for him with love, if she couldn't return.

She rose and turned to leave, but through the brain-fogging misery, she remembered to check for the tools of Papa's trade. The trapper's sword scabbard was empty and his rifle missing. The firearm was nearby, half covered by a snowy branch, but even after searching for precious minutes, his *shashka* was nowhere to be found. With a twinge of regret, she gave up seeking her father's Cossack sword. She shouldered the rifle and stared back at the man she loved beyond life, her heart in a vise, with a promise and a prayer for his soul. Tears dried cold and tight on her face as she stood gazing past the putrefying corpse to the heart of her papa. She returned once more to brush back the frozen leaves and kiss him goodbye.

Her eyes scanned the aspen glade in the brilliant morning light. No one watched. With the silence and speed of the *kwahaten*, the antelope, her name with the *Shoshone* people who had welcomed her family into their own, she ran for her pony.

'It's you and me now, Dzień,' she choked out as she untied him and slung the rifle on her back. Vaulting on as he struck off into a lope, they flew back toward the cabin, the Indian pony seeming to sense the urgency and single-mindedness of his mistress. Slowing him to a stealthy walk as they neared the cabin, she slid from Dzień's back, signaling him to wait. She crept closer to the cabin. Before its open door, papers lay scattered beneath a light dusting of snow, fluttering in the chill breeze. The open barn doors slowly swung back and forth.

By now Papa's stallion should have been tearing up the stable and his field, but Rogan was gone. She waited, straining every muscle for any sound, but only silence met her ears, save the creaking hinges. She tiptoed around the perimeter of the yard in soft deerskin moccasins, keeping to the tree shadows as she'd done with her *Shoshone* friends in play. Hidden in shadow, Aleksandra stole to the window at the back of the cabin and peered in.

Her breath caught at the destruction. An intruder had turned the cabin upside down and must have set-to the place with a sword. The white softness of sliced feather-tick mattresses covered every surface and bedclothes were ribboned and strewn over the floorboards, but there was no movement. She eased the door open and slid inside, hand on the hilt of her own *shashka*.

The doors of the oak secretary, Krzysztof's gift to Aleksandra's mother just before her death two winters ago, lay open. She nearly cried to see its drawers flung helter-skelter and papers scattered.

Utensils danced amongst broken crockery and cast iron pans. In some dim recess of her mind, she noticed the *zakwas* and sourdough pots still stood on their shelf behind the cook stove, high above the chaos.

She broke into a sweat at the sight of the stove lids lying in deep, black grooves in the wooden floor of the cabin. Lids hot enough to burn themselves into the cedar planks meant she'd narrowly missed the visit of the intruder when she left the cabin to find her pa.

She froze. Nothing of value seemed to be missing. This was only a search. Her heart sank further at the sight of the sun-bleached muslin dress on its peg in the corner by her bed, doubtless informing the unwelcome visitor, by now almost certainly the Russian Vladimir, that someone besides Krzysztof lived here.

Aleksandra climbed onto the table and peered up into the eaves. Papa's velvet-lined boxes were still in their places. She lifted the lids and nearly smiled, then hopped down and slipped out the door. Skirting the yard again, she noiselessly opened the back door of the barn and peeked in. The summer smell of new hay assailed her nostrils as she entered and surveyed the damage. The trespasser had been busy here too.

Harnesses and building tools were scattered about the dirt floor, the contents of the feed room and hay pile scattered.

Well, that accounts for the scent.

The buckboard wagon and dogcart were still there, but the gate rails of Rogan's loosebox lay where they'd been dropped. The manure in the stall was dry, several days old.

She glanced around the darkened corners of the barn and the yard outside once more before returning to squeeze her hand into the secret cache behind the colt's feed bin. As her fingers chilled at the touch of the dozen or so frigid glass vials and the box next to it, her lips twisted into a bittersweet smile. For the first time in days, the leaden melancholy lifted from her shoulders, if only a little. Despite the destruction, Vladimir had missed what he came for.

What now? Aleksandra ruminated, shaking her head, then took a great lungful of air.

Dzień trotted up at her whistle and she resolutely wiped her tears onto his mane, then hugged him around the neck with the hint of a smile.

'Papa's secret is safe, Dzień. We can bring him home,' she murmured, pressing her face into his furry neck. Reaching around, he nuzzled her derriere in reply and Aleksandra twisted to kiss him on his white star. She pulled the bedroll and bags from her saddle, then led him to the travois just inside the barn. She adjusted the two long poles, bound together with woven rawhide strips, then covered the widest part of the litter with a buffalo rug. Her papa's conveyance was complete.

On the long walk back to the bluff, she thought of her father's loving touch, his constant presence in her life, his sweet smile, his twinkling eyes. She would have them no more. Spiraling downward again, the thought of drowning in the emptiness was almost welcome, but she gritted her teeth and mentally shook herself. The focus was now on survival. Aleksandra suspected Vladimir didn't know the exact nature of what he sought, but nonetheless, he would return. She needed to be ready. Better yet, gone.

Aleksandra didn't fool herself. Her father, a survivor of Austro-Hungarian-occupied Poland, spent countless hours teaching his children self-defense. Unfortunately, Aleksandra's skills with a *shashka* were a fraction of those of her papa's… and even less than those of *his* own teacher, Vladimir. The Russian was, according to Papa, unsurpassed with the short Russian Cossack sword.

'You're a good swordsman, Aleks, but your impetuosity gets you into trouble,' Papa always said, shaking his head as he disarmed her, yet again. The last time, he'd added: '…whether you're sparring at *shashkas* or trying to knit for the memory of your mama, God rest her soul, who tried to reconcile you to your femaleness.'

Aleksandra grinned through her tears. Knitting that always ended up as a wad of uneven and dropped stitches—inevitably thrown in fit of temper onto a set of antlers high upon the sitting room wall.

ROUNDING the bottom of the bluff, Dzień picked up his head and pricked his ears, sniffing the breeze, then headed for the pile of leaves covering Krzysztof. He stopped dead six feet away.

Aleksandra gave him a pat on the neck and tried to smile, but failed. She left the pony's head to adjust the travois. Breathing deeply through flared nostrils, Dzień stepped towards Krzysztof. He shook his mane, then nuzzled the lifeless body, knocking off the leaves as he checked the man's full length. Dzień tapped him with a front hoof, then snorted and turned away, showing the whites of his eyes as he stared at the motionless man from the corner of one eye. Aleksandra's gut wrenched.

Blood pounded in her head as she struggled to drag Krzysztof's six-foot frame onto the makeshift stretcher. Dzień craned his neck around to watch, his muzzle and the skin about his eyes tensed and strained.

The pony responded to Aleksandra's gentle urging and took Krzysztof home one last time. She would bury him with his beloved wife and sons in their overpopulated graveyard, then determine how to elude Vladimir and survive.

'Can't protect our secret if you're dead, *moje drogie córki.*' Papa's words came back to her, in his thickly accented but precise English.

"*My darling daughter.*" Gulping, she clutched her father's medicine bag and choked back more tears, realizing she'd never hear those words again.

Her body strung tight as a bowstring, Aleksandra kept a close lookout of the woods around them as they neared home, and their burial ground. Gritting her teeth, she tugged her father from the litter, then begging her papa's forbearance, followed Dzień to the barn and stripped off the travois. In his stall, she slipped the bridle from his head, then rubbed the tired horse down as he relished his oats and tore into last summer's sweet meadow hay. He'd worked hard for five solid days in search of Krzysztof. Halfway through his meal, he threw up his head, looked towards Rogan's stall and whickered softly before shaking his head and returning to his feed. Aleksandra left him to his rest and strode to the house, snow crunching beneath her feet, to assuage her own hunger for food and solace.

The meat, suet and berry mixture the Indians called *pemmican* had kept her alive on the trail this past week, but she gave thanks the corn pones were still where she'd left them when she left to find Papa. Dry and stale after five days on the cooling rack, they were ambrosia with maple syrup and sliced *kielbasa*. Hunger sated, Aleksandra stared with longing at the woodstove, but the thought of lighting a fire in daylight with a killer somewhere near sent a shiver up her spine. Night would fall soon enough. She rubbed her icy hands together until they began to thaw. Taking Pa's rifle, pick and spade, she left to bury him with an aching heart.

Hacking at the frozen ground, memories of her papa, mama and brothers flooded her mind, but she kept her head down and went on digging.

There's something I'm forgetting, something important.

The thought recurred as she added a rough cross to the mounded earth and slumped beside it, tears, sweat and unbound hair flowing over her father's last resting place.

I'm sorry there are no flowers for you, Papa. They've returned to the earth, too.

She sat motionless, barely noticing the drifting flakes of snow until her nose and hands were too cold for her to remain.

Entering the barn to check on Dzień, Aleksandra's mind rolled on, inexorably…water and feed Dzień… take the skins to the trading post soon…

But for what?

As long as she could remember, every year's work culminated in a wagon full of exquisitely soft, tanned skins to trade for tools and seed, stock feed, dry goods, fabric, thread for clothes and harness as well as treats for the family. Things were different now.

No kin.

She hugged herself tightly, shoulders hunched, as the bands around her heart tightened further. Drawing a ragged breath, she glanced around the barn at the furs on their elevated platform and stopped in her tracks.

'Oh, my dear Lord, *the furs.*'

Covering her face with blistered hands, she rubbed her eyes. Struggling to remember the date, she counted the days while her heart plummeted. The Hudson's Bay Company Agent on his annual purchasing trip would have already left the trading post. If by Providence he'd been delayed, she might still catch him. Running to the house, she shed her filthy buckskins and dragged on her muslin dress, a woolen everyday over that, then her long fur coat. She bolted for the barn, remembering at the last minute to yank her bonnet from its peg.

'I'm sorry Dzień,' her murmur almost a caress, 'but we need to get to the 'post, *now,* my darling.'

Wrinkling his muzzle and tilting his head, he gazed at her as she threw the harness saddle over his back and nimbly did up the bellyband and the crupper. The pony obliged when she offered the bit, though he scrunched up his eyes at her, then looked back at his supper when she led him between the shafts of the hastily-loaded wagon, full of furs and a nosebag of feed for the beleaguered pony.

THE SOUND of hoofbeats and creaking wagon wheels brought Xavier Arguello to his feet. He reached for his rifle, braced for an attack. Running feet sounded on the porch and the door flew open, slamming against the wall as a golden haired girl flew into the trading post. She stopped like she'd been shot, then wildly glanced around the room.

'Is he *gone*?' she blurted out.

Xavier released a breath as he lowered the muzzle of his gun and set it on the counter, watching the girl. Tears rolled down her reddened and dirt-smeared face.

'Have I missed the agent?' She was all big eyes and trembling mouth, wisps of unruly curls escaping her long braid. A crumpled bonnet hung by its ties down her back.

She bolted past him into Scotty's embrace and clung to the trading post's proprietor like she'd never let go.

'Nay lass, *dinna fash*.' The big Scotsman chuckled, giving her a fatherly hug, then held her at arm's length. 'He's out back harnessin' his horse, but what's the matter, *a nighean,* my darlin'?'

She mutely shook her head and stepped away a few paces, eyes wild, breast rapidly rising and falling.

'Why the tears, *mo nighean bhan?*' He reached out a hand to wipe them from her dusty cheek, then looked behind her and frowned. 'Where's yer da?' At that, the color drained from her face and she grew white as death. Both men reached for her as she slumped towards the floor.

'I've got her, Scotty.' Xavier lifted the unconscious girl and considered her pale visage as the older man threw a buffalo robe over the countertop. He lay her down on the thick pelt and placed his fingers over the rapid and thready pulse at her throat. His brows narrowed. 'Does she normally faint?'

'Wouldn't have thought it possible. She's usually a tough little hellion,' he called over his shoulder as he walked out the door. He returned, shaking his head, lips pursed. 'Her da's not here. She's alone.' Scotty's eyebrows nearly touched.

'Who is she?' Xavier glanced sideways briefly at Scotty from the girl's side.

'Name's Aleksandra. She and her da are trappers, 'bout an hour into the Wasatch Mountains. They've lived out there fer years.' Scotty's brows were lowered, lips tight beneath his mustache, as he absently wiped up the whisky he'd spilled on the counter when the blonde whirlwind blew in the door.

Xavier felt her pulse again and reached for an Indian rug to cover her. 'Whatever could've happened to her pa?'

Both men fell silent, looking down at Aleksandra. Plenty could've happened to a trapper on the Weber River in Utah Territory. If an accident or sickness didn't get him, hostile Indians or a highwayman could.

'Yer guess is good as mine, Xavier. Her pony's nigh exhausted and I've never seen Dzień ever break a sweat.' He closed his eyes and rubbed a forearm against his sweating brow. 'I don't like the look of this.'

'When did you last see them?' Xavier's gaze slid from Aleksandra's face to Scotty's.

'They were here 'bout a month ago. Fer supper,' he said, returning his attention to the girl's still form. 'Ain't she a sight?'

'Shall I take care of her horse, what did you say his name was?'

'It's "*Dzień*", something between "gin" and "jean". It means "day" in Polish.'

'Polish, got it.' Xavier raised a brow and started towards the door.

'Thanks, Xavier, I'll do it.' Scotty took a deep breath and walked out the door, shaking his head. 'Not like 'er to push a horse like this. Ain't never seen the likes,' he muttered, clomping down the steps to where the fur buyer stood staring at the wagon with its stacks of furs, steam rising from the pony's dripping body.

The tension in Xavier's jaw subsided as Aleksandra's pulse slowed and strengthened beneath his fingers, her color returning to a healthy pink. Shaking his head, he took a deep breath. He kept his distance from people for a reason. This girl, for all her charms, was not going to change that. He brushed his hair back with his fingers as his thoughts spun.

Xavier sat nearby to keep her from falling off her perch if she should awaken. As the hour passed, the wall around his heart began to crack open just a little. Aleksandra looked like she'd been through hell. Her face and neck were sunburned and when he turned over her grubby hand, its underside was reddened and blistered. Young, too. Couldn't be more than seventeen, five years his junior. Her curves were ripe, her lips full. He breathed out hard. He'd stayed far away from women for a long time. Maybe too long.

Get a grip, hombre. She's out cold.
Closing his eyes, he shook his head as he kicked himself.
I have no need for this girl, nor any other, in my life.
Still, something about her tugged at his heart.

SCOTTY RETURNED after seeing the agent off and putting Dzień away. Raising his eyebrows, he smiled at the sight of Xavier still sitting on a barstool near her, oiling his rifle while he sang under his breath in Spanish, his muscular torso dwarfing her. Waking up to Xavier might be just what the doctor ordered for the wild young Aleksandra.

When this quietly confident young Californio rode in last week from the west on his magnificent gray Spanish horse, Scotty gratefully accepted his offer of work. His timing was perfect, fortuitously coinciding with the Hudson's Bay Company agent's visit. Trappers from miles around converged upon the trading post for this yearly event, bearing great stacks of furs to trade for next year's supplies.

Normally run off his feet, Scotty enjoyed the fur buyer's visit for once. Six-foot-plus Xavier did his share, and *then* some, handling the heaviest sacks of coal like they were stuffed with cotton. Scotty wondered about the courteous young Spaniard, who spoke a cultured English rarely heard in these parts. He seemed to lack a history or a plan. It didn't take long for the Scotsman to learn that sharing confidences wasn't in Xavier's vocabulary.

No matter. Ever'body's got secrets. Least out West, here, folks let people keep 'em!

VLADIMIR CHABARDINE LOOKED up from the mesmerizing nod of his chestnut mare's ears.
There was someone else living there. Perhaps I should have waited longer—Krzysztof's secret yet eludes me.
The letter in the secretary addressed to Mr. K Lekarski said he was in the right cabin, but for three days he'd waited there and ransacked the place, finding nothing. He sighed deeply and ground his teeth.

A smaller horse's hoofprints showed in the barn. They could be from a mount of Krzysztof's, still tied in the forest somewhere, or they could belong to a woman's horse, by the tattered dress hanging in the cabin and the general tone of the place. There were three graves behind the orchard, so who knew if she were still alive in this God-forsaken wilderness.

Death—it seems to be all around me.

He shuddered. Finally finding Krzysztof after nearly two decades, and then killing him, was something a Cossack arms master should have managed to avoid. He squeezed his eyes shut and forced his jaw to relax.

After having come so far, it was unconscionable to lose his life's goal, and everyone he loved along with it, by the slip of a foot.

A FEW HOURS LATER, Xavier's patience was rewarded as Aleksandra stirred, slowly opening eyes the color of a clear, blue sky. Too soon, they clouded over and flashed as she reached toward her hip. Thinking she would fall off the bench, Xavier dropped his rifle and grabbed her, speaking to her as he would a frightened filly. 'Steady, *mi querida*, steady.'

He stilled as cold metal, sharp and glittering in the sunlight from the window, indented the skin of his neck.

2

'*Sguir! Aleksandra, stop!*' Aleksandra heard Scotty bark, and then continue in a low, steady voice. 'Wouldn't move, 'f I was you, Xavier. Her da's Cossack-trained and it 'pears she is too.' Scotty chuckled beneath his breath.

Xavier eased his hold on her, but didn't let go, despite the blade at his neck.

'Now *a nighean*,' Scotty admonished her, 'Xavier's *a charaid*, a friend. He's been watchin' over ye for the best part of the afternoon.'

She relaxed the death-grip on her *shashka*, removing its point from Xavier's throat. Her gaze met his smooth cocoa eyes fringed by long, black lashes, crinkles of laughter showing at their corners. Aleksandra's bronze-skinned benefactor had the look of a dark Spanish lord.

'The vixen has teeth,' Xavier said with a grin.

Aleksandra gave him the ghost of a smile, then frowned at his hands still upon her. White scars crisscrossed his right one, and his knuckles. He let go of her and stepped back from her side.

'Well Aleks, feelin' better after yer little rest?' Scotty approached cautiously and removed the sword from her shaky grip. 'How 'bout a drink of water?' He reached for a filled mug. 'Ye ready to talk yet?'

She nodded slowly, eyes on Xavier.

'Where's yer da, Aleks?' Scotty's brow wrinkled, his voice tender.

Aleksandra's heart sank as she struggled to sit up. Reaching for the proffered cup, she drank slowly. The liquid's coolness soothed her cracked lips and parched throat. Handing the vessel back, she wrapped her arms about herself tightly, chin to chest. When she swayed again, she dimly noticed Xavier moving closer.

And she didn't mind his all-too-familiar closeness.

How odd…

She shook her head, then concentrated on Scotty's words and her eyes began to fill.

'Papa is at rest,' she said, so softly and with such hesitation they had to move in close, tilting their heads toward her, 'with Mama and my brothers.' Tears blurred her vision before they ran cold down her cheeks.

'Oh, Aleks,' Scotty murmured. His arms were welcome around her, warm, holding her tight until she was ready to speak again.

'He left a week ago to check traps along the Weber River. He was only going to be gone for two days, but when he didn't return after three, I went searching. Felt like I covered all of Utah and half of Washington Territory over the next five days.' She shook her head. 'I never expected to find him only two valleys from the cabin. I didn't even think to check the little bluff canyon.'

'Poor darling.' Scotty blotted her tears with a grimy handkerchief.

'We were to come here and sell the furs when he got home.' She let out a sob, then took a deep breath and continued.

Aleksandra looked down. She was clinging to Xavier's hand for grim death. When she glanced up at his face, the deep pools of his eyes caught hers and she stopped speaking. His smile flowed all the way to her heart, warming a little spot in her very cold soul. She gulped and closed her eyes.

'Papa said Vladimir would find us." Aleksandra swallowed hard and went on. "He made me promise.' Her voice rose to a wail at the end.

'Who? *Who'd* find you? *Promise?*' Scotty's look of confusion would've been comical if this weren't such a nightmare. 'Who would want to kill yer da?'

Aleksandra clamped her mouth shut tightly and shook her head, feeling she might explode.

I nearly revealed Papa's secret. After all this...

'Aleksandra, do you know who killed your papa?' Xavier's words came to her softly, words edged with steel.

Aleksandra took a deep breath, her mind racing for an explanation, and sat up straight. 'Many years ago in Poland,' she finally said, 'Vladimir Chabardine vowed to find my father. It *must* be him. He's destroyed the house, searching...' She stopped, her heart clutching in her chest.

No, take care.

She looked at the men, then started again. 'He slashed up anything he could find with his *shashka*,' she said, then glanced down at the ground, silent for a moment again, not meeting Scotty's eyes. 'Oh yes, and Rogan's gone,' she added quickly and looked straight at Scotty.

'Rogan?' Xavier looked at her sideways, eyebrows drawn together.

The corner of Scotty's lips twitched in a reluctant grin.

'Krzysztof's young stallion.' Scotty's eyes sparkled as he shared an amused glance with Aleksandra, despite everything.

'He'll be gettin' a run for his money.' She half-chuckled, half-sobbed.

'The colt's a terror,' he murmured to Xavier. 'I bet he's wishin' he'd left 'im behind.' He glanced at Aleksandra and sobered.

'Where's Krzysztof now, Aleksandra?' Scotty touched her cheek with his gnarled knuckles and she leaned against him.

'Buried in our graveyard.'

Xavier stared at her, mouth gaping. 'You buried him yourself? In this frozen granite?'

'Needs must when the Devil drives.' Aleksandra quirked an eyebrow at him. 'Not very *deeply* in the ground, but yes.'

'Aye, no wonder yer hands are blistered!' Scotty rolled his eyes. 'Ye could've come fer me, *a nighean*, y'know I'd have helped ye.'

'I had Dzień to help me.'

'A nice pony, I'll give you that,' Xavier smiled at her, 'but I'm not sure how good he is with a spade.'

Narrowing her eyes at him, she gritted her teeth and pulled her hand from his.

Scotty looked up from where he'd been perusing the floor. 'I'm sorry y'had to face this alone. Yer da was as fine as man as I've had the pleasure t'know.' His voice quivered and his eyes glistened, not quite running over.

Xavier began murmuring condolences, then snapped his mouth closed when she glared at him.

'What now then, Aleks?' Scotty said, after a long silence, his brow furrowed. 'Yer welcome here. Y'could help me mind the shop. We'd do jes' fine.' He nodded vigorously and smiled at her.

'Dearest Scotty,' she touched his cheek, 'thank you for the offer. I appreciate it, but I can take care of myself. I'll go to the *Newe*. The *Shoshone* are my family now and I'll be loved there as a daughter.'

The men exchanged glances over her head.

'Aleksandra, is that safe? You know about the unrest between the *Pah-Utes* and the settlers' army, don't you?' Xavier brushed his hair back from his face with his hand, the light reflecting off the signet ring on his middle finger.

She scowled at the dark Californio. 'My father is blood-brother to the *Shoshone* chief.' She tossed her head at him. 'Of *course* I'll be welcome in their village.'

Xavier's face shadowed and his lips tightened to a fine line. 'It's your funeral.' He turned from her and moved to stand just outside the door, staring off into the distance.

'Children, children,' Scotty muttered under his breath and shook his head. 'Aleks, I'm sorry to remind you of him, but who's this "Vladdie"? We need to get word 'round so we kin bring 'im to justice.'

She dragged her gaze back to Scotty from where she found it, perusing the handsome stranger's broad shoulders and trim hips in snug leather leggings.

'That's the problem, Scotty,' she paused and looked back at Xavier. Despite her annoyance, she had to admit he was a fine figure of a man, with raven blue-black hair past the collar of his buckskin shirt and sparking brown eyes, nearly black when she fell into them as she awoke…

She shook her head and refocused, then turned back to Scotty.

'Vladimir Chabardine. Cossack arms master, servant of the tsar—armed and extremely dangerous. Papa's nemesis.' She looked down at the ground, pausing until her voice returned.

'Aye....' Scotty ventured, eyebrows raised. 'How will we know 'im?'

'Unfortunately, I don't know what he looks like. He's Russian or Ukrainian. Papa said he had blond hair, probably gray by now, and a strong accent. He's ten years older than Papa. He'll handle a horse and a *shashka* like a Cossack, but further than that, I know nothing,' she said, dropping her eyes to the floor.

OUT OF HIS element in this wilderness, the unaccustomed feeling of ineptitude was driving Vladimir around the bend. He was becoming incautious, and that was not wise.

From Krzysztof's cabin, he travelled down the mountain, joining a large wagon trail leading west when he reached the flats below. An hour later, coming upon a small hamlet, he pulled the brim of his hat low and surveyed it, chewing on the inside of his cheek. There was no way around the buildings, closely-packed as they were between the overhanging red cliffs and the river banks, so he walked the horses through its single street as quickly as he dared. He let out his breath when they passed the last hovel of the settlement and continued west.

Soon after leaving the village, the wagon trail crossed the river at a ford. A wagon, loaded to the gunwales with furs, was exiting the water and passed them as they entered it.

'Don't you know where you are, man? Why, you're on the Emigrant Trail!' the driver said, chuckling as Vladimir struggled to drag the bay colt into the deep water.

Unfortunately, neither he nor anyone else Vladimir met that day had seen a solo traveller with a small horse. Judging by the sideways looks and the speed at which they scurried away, his evasiveness about the name and gender of the one he sought must have made them think he'd been in the sun too long. He couldn't blame them. Frustrated by his lack of success in finding Krzysztof's companion, he wanted to run away too.

'SURE THAT'S ALL Y'KNOW?' Scotty raised his eyebrows at Aleksandra.

Why do I get the feelin' there's somethin' she ain't tellin' me?

'Well, Rogan's missing,' Aleksandra averted her eyes and a blush spread over her cheeks, 'so I imagine he's taken him,' she mumbled, then hesitated. A minute later, she looked up again. 'He's an unusual horse for these parts, wouldn't you say?' Aleksandra's eyes seemed to hold a challenge and this time she didn't look away.

Scotty tilted his head sideways and pursed his lips. 'What else, girlie?'

Aleksandra squirmed silently tugging at her braid.

When Scotty finally shook his head and turned to finish cleaning up, she burst into action and spun toward the door.

'Well, Scotty, thanks for the rest, but it'll be dark before I get home as it is, so I'd best get going,' she said, then stopped short.

'*Oh no, the furs—and Dzień,*' she wailed and turned back to face him.

'*Dinna fash, mo nighean.* I kept the buyer here since yeste'day 'cause I knew ye were comin'. He's paid fer yer pelts 'n gone.' Scotty rumpled her hair.

She let out a huge breath and smiled her thanks.

'And that pony, he's got a heart o' gold. Ye *dinna* need to go, you know, yon wee man's in the stable, munchin' away with me old geldin'.'

Aleksandra hugged him again. 'What would I do without you, Scotty?'

'It's the least I kin do fer you and yer da, aye?' Scotty remarked, his voice wavering. His vision blurred as his eyes filled.

'Papa wouldn't have been pleased to see Dzień abused so, but there was nothing else for it. He never even slowed down.' She looked at the floor.

'Aye, but he's a bonny one.' Scotty smiled.

'It would've meant the world to Papa, knowing we made it on time and our year's work wasn't for naught.'

'Right ye are, missy.' Scotty smiled at the hint of the girl's normal glow showing in her eyes, albeit beneath her wet lashes. He raised his brows at her. 'Now, d'ye want me to hold some o' the money fer now so it *canna* be taken off ye by highwaymen?'

'Thanks, Scotty, please keep it all here. I don't need it yet.'

'Are ye *sure* ye need t'leave tonight?' Scotty was unconvinced. 'It's getting' mighty late and we could make you a bed o'sorts.'

Aleksandra's eyes narrowed at the dark man still standing in the doorway.

'I'd rather risk the highwaymen and the wild animals for tonight, thanks,' she said tartly. 'I've got my *shashka* and bow.'

There was a choking sound from the entrance, then Xavier mumbled something about checking the horses and disappeared outside. Scotty turned away and coughed to hide his chuckle from the pair.

XAVIER WAS HARNESSING Dzień to the wagon when Aleksandra came outside.

'I can do that,' she snapped, rushing to the side of the pony, her blue eyes icy and cheeks flushed pink. Xavier smiled at her back as she hurried around to the pony's other side to finish.

'I'm sure you can, *Querida*, but I'm happy to help,' he said, wrapping a breeching strap around the shaft and buckling it snugly.

'Thanks,' she said, tight-lipped, looking away as her hands slid down Dzień's rump towards the crupper.

'Any possibility you might tell me just why you went *loco* on me back there?'

Aleksandra's brows lowered as she stared at a strap she'd just buckled too tightly. Her lips tightened further as she readjusted it. She finally spoke. 'I want nothing to do with people who insult my friends.'

'*Como*, what?' He shook his head and blinked at her.

'My *friends*, Dzień, and the *Shoshone*. The only friends I have left alive, other than Scotty,' she said from between clenched teeth, and then slumped, sobbing, against the horse.

Cautious of her all-too-effective looking sword, Xavier slowly approached her. He slid his arm around her shoulders and pulled her against him, watchful for any fast moves on her part, not caring if her tears soaked his shirt. How long they stayed like this, he neither knew nor cared. Once her sobs quieted, he slipped his fingers under her chin, lifting her face to stare into the watery depths of her blue eyes. 'Okay now, *Querida?*'

'As okay as possible, I guess.' She dropped her head again. 'The *Shoshone* have been family to me, especially since Mama died,' she murmured into his shirt.

'Are you sure you won't stay here? I'll sleep in the stable, if it would make you happier.'

She closed her eyes and was still. 'No, it's fine. I'm sorry, Xavier. I'm upset, but that's no excuse for my rudeness. Thank you for this.' She nodded her head at his tearstained chest.

'*De nada*. It is nothing.' He smiled. 'May I at least accompany you to your home?'

'No, really, I'm fine, thank you again. I'd better go farewell Scotty. It's getting late.'

'If you're sure…' Xavier shook his head and followed Aleksandra back inside.

'SCOTTY, WHAT'S THIS?' Aleksandra blinked at the bill tacked to the wall beside the trading post doorway:

The Central Overland California and Pikes Peak Express Company seeks:

Young, skinny, wiry fellows not over eighteen. Must be expert riders, willing to risk death daily. Orphans preferred. Pay: 25 dollars a week.

'Ayer. Mr. Egan, the Area Supe'visor from Salt Lake House, came by last week to tell us 'bout their new overlan' mail service. They're proposin' gettin' messages telegraphed from the 'tlantic coast to St Jo' that'll be picked up by boys ridin' relay, all the way t'San Fran in ten days—'

'Ten days?' She stared at him.

'—*if* ye'll let me finish, girl,' he looked heavenward, 'each horse'll go 'bout 20 miles or so. Can ye b'lieve it? They're buyin' the 400 best horses they kin find.'

Aleksandra smiled. His accent thickened when he was excited. 'It sounds impossible, but yet—' Aleksandra's sadness lightened she read it again. 'I could do that," she murmured under her breath.

Scotty eyed her sideways. 'Don't ye go gettin' any ideas, missy. They only take boys and ye don't look like any boy I've seen lately, b'sides, your da would skin me alive fer even lettin' ye see that poster.'

'True.' She looked down at her rumpled overdress, her heart clenching again. 'Well, Scotty, I must be off.'

'Be careful, that scoundrel's still 'bout an' it's snowin' again. I'd not see ye caught in a late blizzard.' Shaking his head, he hugged her tight. 'I'll be thinkin' of ye 'n yer da.'

'Yes, I'll be careful. Thank you both for everything.'

Mounting the wagon box, she gave Dzień his head and he moved off. From her seat, Aleksandra looked over her shoulder at Xavier's furrowed brow and smiled. 'We'll see you both soon,' she called back.

Driving through Echo Canyon, Aleksandra scrutinized the sienna rock formations lining the steep sides of the defile high above her, outlined against the last of the evening's light, then turned off alongside a meandering stream into a big valley heading north. It was full dark by the time she reached the steep wagon track to their cabin.

Aleksandra stood listening at Dzień's head for long minutes when they neared the home clearing until she was sure no one waited. Exhaustion and misery caught up with her as she rubbed the pony down. She wrapped herself in a blanket and sat in the straw at his feet, clinging to him for solace.

VLADIMIR WAS BEGINNING to doubt his wisdom in taking the massive bay colt. Knowing Krzysztof's taste in horses, Vladimir wasn't surprised to find the conformation and bearing of the young horse were second to none he'd seen in this country. Looking at the piles of furs in the barn, he guessed Krzysztof hadn't been to town for a while. Hopefully long enough that no one they met would recognize the growing three-year-old colt.

He roused himself.

Your mind wanders Vladimir. The fact remains that in this harsh part of the world, taking what you need to survive is acceptable.

By his actions, however, he'd turned himself into a horse thief as well as a murderer.

Please God, let me find Krzysztof's companion and his secret before whatever passes for the law out here finds me.

SHE AWOKE from a dream of shining brown eyes and jet-black hair to Dzień's warm breath on the back of her neck... and memories of the devastation that was yesterday. Despite it, she almost smiled at the morning sun streaming through the open doorway. Her blessed pony hadn't moved a muscle all night. Both of her arms were still wrapped around his fuzzy forelegs.

The Mustang's inquisitive nuzzles and the steam rising from the sun's rays on the frozen ground warmed Aleksandra's heart. She stood and stretched, then turned Dzień out into the orchard to graze the early spring shoots. Her throat tightened and tears began to flow again when she passed the newly heaped soil in the graveyard. Pulling her eyes away from the new crosses, she somehow dragged herself back to the house.

Entering the cabin, she made an effort to put it to rights then made a snack of *kielbasa* and the last of the petrified corn pones. She packed some gifts of food and the barest essentials into her saddlebags, then saddled Dzień and left for the Indian village.

Winding her way into the mountains, the cleansing peace of the pristine, crisp morning air and the abundant life around her soothed Aleksandra's soul. As they climbed, a browsing doe turned to watch her, accompanied by the glorious cacophony of birds and squirrels overhead.

The stream tumbling down its rocky bed reminded Aleksandra of the snowy March day she'd first met Dancing Wolf. She and Papa had found an Indian boy clinging to a tree branch in the frigid, swollen river while running trap lines many years ago. They searched out the Indian village and returned young Dancing Wolf to his father, Chief

Golden Hawk of the *Shoshone*. On that day, a friendship was forged between Krzysztof, the Chief and their two children that spanned a decade.

'*Kwahaten! Kwahaten!*' Shrieking children raced toward her as she entered the big meadow. The faster dogs, bowing and grinning, were the first to greet her, followed by the children, all wriggling fingers and dear little round faces, who dragged her by both hands towards the cluster of dwellings.

Women working outside stopped their tasks and waved at Aleksandra. She lifted her hand in reply, but was preoccupied, torn between the children's enthusiastic welcome and her memories of the times she'd spent here with Papa.

Tall and regal, Dancing Wolf strode to her. His beautiful brown eyes were shadowed with sorrow.

'My heart is glad to see you alive, *Kwahaten*. Yesterday I found the new grave, but no one at your cabin.' He wrapped his arms about her and hugged her close.

'It's Papa.' Her hands clutched at his buckskin shirt and tears flowed anew.

'I was afraid of that. I followed your travois tracks to the bluff. There were old bloodstains and signs of a struggle on the cliffs above. I feared for you.'

She remained silent, heart in her throat, not knowing what to say.

'We were leaving just now to find you,' Dancing Wolf said, leading her to his father's hut. 'Our warriors have gathered to search.' He glanced at the huge group of waiting men.

'Please give them my thanks, Dancing Wolf.' She stared at the assembled band in awe and nodded her thanks to the warriors.

Dancing Wolf waved at them again and they dispersed in silence. The usually-familiar men looked massive and fierce in their armed warpath finery. She turned and ducked her head under the brush arch of the doorway, then stepped down into the sunken dwelling.

Aleksandra recounted her saga to Chief Golden Hawk and his son as they shared a meal around the fire. The leader was stricken at the death of his blood-brother.

With downcast eyes, Aleksandra untied the thong of her papa's *Shoshone* medicine bag from about her neck.

'Papa would want you to have this.' She handed it to Golden Hawk.

'No, Aleksandra, it is for you.' He closed his eyes and sighed deeply. 'May it protect you better than it did your papa.'

She clutched it to her breast, breathing in Pa's scent. The deerskin bag, with its familiar aroma, was a part of her papa she could still hold and her heart lightened for having it returned. She'd placed her papa's signet ring inside it and was glad to keep it. Papa had always said it would be hers someday.

A someday far too soon.

The beadwork on Golden Hawk's chest rose and fell with each deep breath. He nodded toward his son: 'This young brave asked your father for your hand last year, *Kwahaten,* but Krzysztof believed you too young to marry.'

Aleksandra started and glanced across the fire at Dancing Wolf, who gazed at her with intensity. The room swam around her for a long moments until she remembered to breathe again.

Why hadn't Papa told me?

'He still desires you for his wife. As you are the daughter of my brother, I wish for you to live with our people, now the rest of your family is gone...' The wise old chief bowed his head in sorrow and motioned his son to continue.

Her spinning world crashed further with his son's next words.

'However, my father has decided, Daughter-of-his-Blood-Brother,' Dancing Wolf continued formally, 'that he cannot allow you to stay with us, no matter how much we care for you. It would be an insult to the spirit of Krzysztof to keep you here, knowing our people will soon be at war with yours. The *Pah-Utes* are pressing the tribes to join them in making war on the settlers. We long to keep you here with us,' his voice broke for a moment, 'but our village cannot keep you safe when the other tribes come.'

Aleksandra clenched her shaking hands together. Emptiness and desolation threatened to overwhelm her, but she gritted her teeth and closed her eyes, trying to control her whirling thoughts.

Now I truly have no one.

She wanted to scream and tear at her hair, but she bowed her head in acquiescence. They truly could do no more. Golden Hawk would see her protected as best he could, but they all knew her life would be forfeit if she stayed in the village, whether married to the son of Golden Hawk or not. The chief held his arms out to her and she moved into his embrace for one last hug before she left his fireside.

HOPE WAS FAR from Aleksandra's reach, her heart in tatters somewhere lining the bottom of her empty chest, as she and Dzień wandered down the mountain toward their cabin.

How could I have missed it?

She understood how the deepening rift between the settlers and the indigenous people wouldn't let her safely live in their midst, but what of Dancing Wolf? How did she miss his deepening feelings for her, when they were close as brother and sister? Aleksandra had been attracted to him, but accustomed only to the overt displays of affection in her family, his increasing reservation toward her as they matured had blinded her to the truth. She shook her head to clear it and smiled as she thought of their leave-taking.

Dancing Wolf had accompanied her from the village and stopped at their old halfway meeting point. The tall young man dismounted from his pinto Mustang and for only the second time since they were children, wrapped his arms around her and held her close as she sat her pony, silent, for long minutes.

'*Kwahaten*, you have been the most special part of my life and a large piece of my heart leaves with you. For your safety, I cannot have what my heart desires most, you by my fireside, beneath my furs,' he stopped, flushed, and then cleared his throat, 'riding by my side, forever. You need to go to your own people,' he finally managed. 'I will be watching for you. If you are ever in need, you know how to find me.'

Aleksandra nodded. 'I understand, though I feel the rest of my family has truly died now. With you, I also leave much of my heart. May we meet again soon, my special one.' She kissed the top of his head, bowed against her breast. He lifted his face to hers, his eyes deep pools of darkness, searching into her soul. Their lips met in their first kiss, the intensity of his touch shocking Aleksandra, and she drew back for a moment. His lips continued warm and insistent against hers as he wrapped his arms around her. She sighed and melted into him, her arms moving about his neck of their own volition as she breathed in his musky scent. A gripping tension fired in her belly as he deepened the kiss and she inhaled sharply. He pulled back slowly, his eyes darkened to black, then smiled at her, while he shook his head slowly and let his breath out. Brushing the stray strands of hair from her face and taking her hands, he kissed her softly on the lips once again, and looked down at her hands between his.

'What we might have had—' he started, then paused.

'—cannot be, my special one,' Aleksandra said into the silence, 'but I will always remember.' She tried for a smile, looking at him through bleary eyes. Her hands still shook, but at least her heart felt as if someone had kindled a small fire inside, and it was warm.

'Go now, dear one of my heart, my *Kwahaten*. You cannot be mine, but I will always be here for you.' Smiling at her, he swung onto his pony as Aleksandra turned her own Mustang and rode back down the mountain.

DZIEŃ WALKED FASTER as they entered their home clearing and headed for the barn. Sliding wearily from the saddle, Aleksandra stumbled as she hit the ground. Slipping the cinch and pulling the saddle off, she unbuckled the throatlatch and slid the headstall over his ears. He carefully stepped over the lowered rails of his loose box and investigated his feed bin, looking at her enquiringly when he found it empty.

'At least some things never change, Dzień.' She smiled. 'Thanks for your hard work this week—you've been wonderful,' she murmured against his velvet nose as she handed over his corncobs. He snuffled his thanks into her hand and disappeared into his feed bin. Leaning back against the rails, she watched him munch for a moment, and then turned to plan her next move.

She hesitated before lighting the fire. The thought of Vladimir finding her made her heart clench, but it was truly cold tonight.

Merely having to consider this choice told Aleksandra she was out of options.

It wasn't safe for anyone to live the life of a lone trapper in these mountains—especially a young woman with a murderous pursuer. More importantly though, not only must she survive, she had to protect Krzysztof's secret. Learning of Dancing Wolf's proposal and his feelings for her didn't help her confusion, but there was nothing to be gained there. She hardened her heart against the thoughts they raised.

She needed to survive, in any way she could. Realistically, her best option was to accept Scotty's offer and eat humble pie with Xavier.

Xavier...

Another reason to return to the trading post. Where might that lead? Her face heating, she brushed the thought away—it was warm, but disconcerting nonetheless. "I truly have no one", she'd thought as she left the Indian village. Maybe it was true, but then again...

Maybe it wasn't.

Laughing brown eyes, raven hair and a Spanish accent intruded on her thoughts. She swallowed and sighed.

Perhaps I just need to grow up and stop feeling sorry for myself.

Suddenly hungry, her heart and body craving succor, Aleksandra reached for the *zakwas* sour rye culture and started a pot of *żurek*. Similar to the wheaten sourdough starter used by pioneers to leaven their breads, *zakwas* gave *żurek*, the traditional Polish comfort food, a unique taste when stewed with grilled *kielbasa*, bacon, potatoes, mushrooms, and sour cream. She nibbled at crispy shreds of the aromatic sausage as it cooked and sighed with pleasure as she piled chopped vegetables into the Dutch oven. She nearly began to smile again as the partly-finished stew bubbled away.

Scanning the cabin with a mug of a restorative herbal tisane to hand, Aleksandra began piling up belongings to take. Papa's surgical kit and medicine box, then the kitchen utensils, cast iron pans, and bags of dry goods: rye, wheat, salt and *pemmican*. Scotty and Xavier would doubtless also welcome the stored fruits and vegetables from the cellar and preserved meats from beneath the eaves.

A few minutes with a needle and thread healed the least-damaged feather tick victim of Vladimir's *shashka* attack. This mattress, along with her bedroll, a warm buffalo robe and two Indian blankets, would keep her warm all winter. Aleksandra's bow and arrows, Pa's rifles and their skinning knives finished the pile. She tried to fill her lungs as she fingered Mama's most prized possession, the oak secretary, every pillar, slot and drawer so beautifully turned and finished. It had been her mother's only physical reminder of the *szlachta* way of life and the family she'd lost in Poland. Every time Aleksandra saw the desk, her heart ached. Her mother left her life far too soon.

Aleksandra couldn't budge the huge piece of furniture, which was just as well because she hadn't the heart to sell it.

Turning resolutely away, she packed her clothing and Papa's last gift, a bolt of lavender sprigged lawn, into her clothes trunk and then added her brother's old clothes and boots for dirty work. With a last look around the house, she headed for the barn.

Aleksandra chose the dogcart over the heavy wagon. Its light body and two big wheels would ease Dzień's work on the muddy and rutted roads. She and Pa had last driven it to a picnic with their Indian family in one of the high meadows last summer and her tears rose again.

It won't do to think of that now.

Aleksandra gritted her teeth and jarred herself back into action, thinking of Papa's words.

"Most carriage accidents are preventable."

She checked the cart over carefully, greased and tightened the axles, then gave an extra turn to a few loose screws on the shaft hardware, then loaded tools and equipment, shoeing gear, bags of oats and corn, extra harness and tack into the space between the seats.

IT WAS a mystery to Aleksandra how something as simple as food could comfort her, despite everything. She smiled as the hot, thick *żurek* filled her belly and soul to bursting. She was pleased with her efforts today, and sat down on the front step in the sun to consider the rest of the day. It might be a long time before she returned. She bit her lip and glanced out to the orchard, where Dzień grazed, then she grinned. They'd go for a ride.

At her whistle, the Mustang's head swung up and he pricked his ears, then meandered across the orchard. The pony happily took the bit she proffered and stood like a rock while she swung up. They spent a quiet afternoon wandering the trails and meadows that had seen them grow together from a foal and a young girl. The sun was long gone by the time she fed and rubbed Dzień down in his stable.

Aleksandra gazed around the walls of the solid log house Papa and Mama built, her heart in a vise. Wiping away tears with the back of her sleeve, she tended the fire and ate another steaming bowl of *żurek*, then curled up in bed for the last night in her old home.

THE EARLY MORNING sun shone on the last patches of melting snow in the yard as Aleksandra pulled the cart to the cabin door. She packed the traveling trunk beneath the wagon box with the house goods she'd gathered and left a rifle and knife within easy reach, then lashed a tarpaulin over the rest.

Breaking the ice on the washtub water, Aleksandra shivered as she washed, then drew on her muslin dress with a clean apron over the top of her doeskins. In deference to Mama, ever hopeful that her young ruffian would someday become a lady, Aleksandra tied under her chin a starched bonnet.

Finally, sad but resolute, she sat beside the graves and promised her mama, papa and brothers that she would care for herself and think of them always. Heart breaking, Aleksandra turned away and called softly to Dzień, who dozed in his meadow. The pony followed her to the barn, where she harnessed him to the dogcart, apologizing for its weight.

Checking the view from the barn doors and window carefully, Aleksandra returned to Papa's cache behind the manger. She squeezed five of the glass vials through the narrow gap and carefully wrapped them, then placed them into a buckskin pouch. She slipped its cord over her head, and the pouch slid down to fit snugly between her breasts. She started at the sound of a bird flying into the barn, then took a long breath as she concealed the hiding place again.

Dzień nuzzled her when she went to his head to adjust the blinkers.

'Well, Dzień, this trip should be a bit warmer than the last one.' Aleksandra smiled faintly as she pulled on Pa's big overcoat and driving gloves. Mounting the box, she sat on the buffalo robe she'd placed on the seat and rested her moccasin-clad feet on the hot bricks wrapped in their skins. They were away, headed for the trading post, to safety, and Xavier.

3

'What do you mean, he's gone? Gone *where?*' Aleksandra glanced around the trading post, then stared blankly at Scotty.

'Wouldn't ya just know it,' Scotty shook his head, his brow furrowed and lips pursed, 'our Xavier turns out to be a son o' one of them fancy Spanish Dons from a big *rancho* out in California.'

'He told you that?' Aleksandra raised one eyebrow at him.

'Nah, 'e was telling one of them guys from the Ove'land Stage Company, that Bolivar Robert's from Carson that Mr. Egan brought by, looking fer station keepers. Same Mr. Egan 'at put up the poster ye were readin' just b'fore ye left last time.'

'But where has he gone?' she persisted, tempted to keep searching the trading post.

' 'E went with 'em. Hired on as a station keeper in one of their Home Stations down the line. Camp Floyd Pony Express Station. Seems he knows all 'bout carin' for good horses 'n stock as well as bein' learned in accountin'. They've already started the route, but they were still short one station keeper.' Scotty sighed and aimlessly looked around the trading post.

'He's really gone, isn't he?' She sat down hard on a barrel and stared at Scotty.

'E's only been gone a day and I already miss 'em,' the Scotsman admitted, pulling at his mustache.

Aleksandra slumped. The emptiness deep in her gut made her want to curl up in a ball and hibernate, but she knew that wouldn't help. She forced herself to get up.

'Oh well, Scotty,' she turned to him, then started for the door. 'I've come to take you up on your offer. Apparently, just in time.' She grinned with more enthusiasm than she felt.

'Oh, have ye now?'

'But just so you know,' she frowned, 'I'll only stay if I can earn my keep. I don't want to be beholden to you.'

'Aye, that's mighty fine.'

'To sweeten the deal,' she said over her shoulder, 'the bits and pieces I've brought you from home ought to keep you satisfied for a good long while.'

VLADIMIR's uncomfortable feeling that he should've stayed longer at the Krzysztof's cabin kept recurring. He was keen to get back to the little cabin in the clearing. Their return trip was faster, once Vladimir gave the young stallion his head and let him seek the shortcuts he obviously knew, reducing their three-day outgoing trip to a one-day return.

From around the bend on the track to the cabin, he saw the barn doors no longer stood open as he'd left them. Tying up the horses, he crept around the back, made a quick dash to the entrance and slipped inside. Biting his lip, he clenched his fists in impotent anger. Blood pounded in his ears as he scanned the empty walls and the bare dirt floor, where he'd dumped piles of tools and harnesses on his last visit. Doubtless whoever emptied the barn was gone, for the dogcart and the furs had disappeared too. Vladimir slid out the door and back behind the building, keeping to the darkness beneath the trees.

Hearing no sounds, he whipped open the cabin door and threw himself back against the outside of the doorway. After listening again, he peeked in. Grinding his teeth at the sight, he aimed a punch at the door. The tidy interior, clearly not at all as he'd left it, said someone *had been* here, and for some considerable time. Half of the cabin's contents were gone and the ashes in the stove were stone cold. Nothing bigger than a rat could have hidden anywhere in the cabin by the time he finished looking. They'd left him no food, but there was plenty of firewood.

He added up what he knew…and that wasn't much. Small footed horse, he knew from last time, dogcart, what else? It appeared they weren't coming back, but one could never be certain. He had no idea which way to go next, so he collected the horses and put them in the barn after a long drink at the trough. The big bay hopped over the lowered bars of his loosebox and headed straight for his hayrack. From the loft, Vladimir threw big armloads of hay to the two hungry horses.

'Lucky beggers, at least they left you a feed.' He scowled at the horses as he finished filling their water buckets.

Entering the cabin again, he pulled the latchstring and sighed. Unreasonably pleased at the prospect of a full night's sleep in a real bed, he smiled for the first time in days, thinking about what Tatiana would have thought of the cosy cabin.

The most disappointing thing, he frowned at the empty shelf high above the stove, *next to not finding Krzysztof's companion, of course, was the absence of the zakwas pot. I must have lived in Poland too long.*

He'd seen it on his first visit, of course, but hadn't the heart to shatter the crock. He shook his head and pulled some dried meat from his saddlebag. Boiled with water and some dried onion tops he found still hanging from the rafters, it made a more than tolerable supper.

Settling himself on a feather tick, which seemed to puff feathers everywhere each time he moved, he grinned ruefully. *Shashkas* and feather ticks apparently didn't go well together.

The nervous tic in his jaw returned as he considered tomorrow's quest. He'd seek Krzysztof's companion to the east this time. He took a deep breath to quench his tension. For a man used to precision and correctness after a lifetime in Europe, the lack of roads and maps out in the place called the West drove him to distraction and made him feel a bumbling fool. What passed here for roads were, by European standards, undeveloped bridle paths. Often one that seemed to be a major track diminished to a deer or otter path after *far* too many miles of side-tracking. No one could say how far he'd traveled in the past week, but he'd retraced his path several times. As he drifted off to sleep, he once again sent grudging thanks to the bay horse, who'd taken him home.

WORRY MADE Scotty's stomach uneasy. In the five days since Aleksandra's arrival, she'd already squirreled away the goods she wanted to keep, reorganised the trading post and cleaned everything top to bottom. All good, except that she was starting to twitch and boss him around because there was nothing left to do. Accustomed to a life of activity, her unemployed attention began wandering. All too frequently, Scotty caught her surreptitiously eyeing the poster still on the wall.

'Scotty, would you cut my hair, please?' She looked at him, eyes big and beguiling, a smile playing on her lips.

'Eh?' He looked up from a yellowed *Deseret News*, eyes narrowing in discomfiture.

Just what she was up to this time? Her hair looked way too damned fine already.

'Yer hair... *mo nighean bhan*? Cut yer beautiful *hair*? The good Lord pertect me t' even think of it.'

'Scotty, it's just hair and it only needs a little trim.' She glanced again at the poster as she turned away from him.

'*Oh*, no. I *willna* be party to any o' *that*.' Slapping his newspaper onto the counter, he stared at her with lowered brows.

As if that would stop her.

'Well, I'll cut it myself then,' she spun on her heel, 'and it'll be a lot shorter than you would make it.' Reaching for her sheath knife with one hand, she grabbed her braid where it met her head with the other.

'*Sguir*! Okay, okay. Give it here b'fore ye cut yer damn self. Only to yer shoulders, mind. Some boys have it that length.' He stomped over to her, wishing he were 100 miles away. Well aware of the independent life she'd led, Scotty knew it was just a matter of time before she got bored and moved on, but as a *boy*? He'd never forgive himself if she got hurt, but he *did* know one person that just might be able to keep her in line. Beaming at his bright idea, he took up his sewing scissors.

VLADIMIR HEADED NORTHEAST up Echo Canyon after leaving the big valley below the cabin. The lofty red cliffs rising steeply on the north side of the canyon were the most awesome landscape feature he'd yet seen in this country. They continued for miles: box canyons, caves, outcroppings…it would be a fearsome place at night, full of faces and figures, where untold numbers of ambushers could hide. The Russian turned due east after exiting the canyon on a large wagon track, wishing again for a map.

Thinking back to this morning, he shook his head. In the dawn's early light, he'd pulled off his hat and wept over the new grave for the young man Krzysztof had been in Poland, the finest student he'd ever had. Someone must have found Krzysztof, brought him home and buried him—in the rock-hard, frozen ground.

His heart stopped again at the thought of the Pole dying on his own sword. He hadn't killed Krzysztof, but he still felt responsible for his death and his gut wrenched at the thought of what he might have to do to Krzysztof's companion to accomplish his mission here. He knew no one would believe he hadn't killed the Pole so he'd hidden him, sliding him off the top of the bluff into a narrow gap and hoping no one would find him. An action of which he was not proud.

Not at all.

THE END of the fourth day found Vladimir peering over the steep bank of a river. Two days of rain, soaking him and his belongings, had done little for his attitude or the traversability of the river. He glowered at the muddy waves, his hands red with cold.

As he searched in vain for a place to ford the torrent, the colt slipped beneath him, and he grabbed for the bay's mane. The mare's lead rein nearly jerked him from the saddle as she shied from his sudden movement.

Maybe this is a sign.

No one he met in the past three days, consisting of only two mounted men, had seen anyone driving a pony to a dogcart packed with equipment and housewares.

Where could they have gone?

East would make the most sense, unless maybe there was a trading post somewhere. He rolled his eyes and sighed, shaking his head.

What was I *thinking on the day I passed through the village near Krzysztof's cabin?*

There had to be one there.

Spinning the horses around, he headed back west. Someone in this hellhole would have to know.

Sure enough, there *was* a trading post, according to the old prospector who blessed Vladimir with the information. Seems it stood just outside the village of Echo, a mere hour or so from Krzysztof's cabin. Of course, the man hadn't seen a two-wheeled cart of any description either, but it was the first positive lead he'd had in weeks, so he managed a smile for the old man and headed on west.

'WELL DZIEŃ, Scotty says we ought to make Camp Floyd in two and a half days.'

The pony swivelled his ears at her comment as he picked his way down the trail just out of Echo, heading for Forney's Bridge. The dogcart and most of her belongings were stored at the trading post. She had with her only what she needed to survive and could comfortably carry strapped to her saddle or in her saddlebags. At a good walk, they could make forty miles a day unless it poured, in which case all bets were off on the quagmire trails.

Every time a traveller approached, Aleksandra's heart leapt into her throat for fear it would be a big bay colt that Dzień was sure to recognize. Luckily, no one looked twice at the little horse ridden by a scruffy boy with oversized frontiersmen's garb and bulging saddlebags who nodded shyly to them and kept on walking.

The closer they got to Floyd, the faster the butterflies in her stomach flew. She was following her dream of riding for the Pony, and seeking Xavier, but their upcoming meeting, and the scrap that would likely ensue, had her heart in her throat. How could she convince him to take her on as a rider?

As an excellent rider, and an orphan, she qualified for the position with the Express, other than the minor detail of her sex. These were good enough reasons to apply, yet to be truthful, Xavier was a part of the reason too. She pushed that thought away.

Keeping her head down and eyes wide open, Aleksandra watched all about her for a glimpse of Rogan and a silver-haired man. Given the fact that Rogan was an active young stallion, she clung to the hope Vladimir might not notice that Dzień was of more interest to the colt than any other horses on the trail. A chuckle escaped her. She only hoped he was riding a mare, then the Russian would be too busy dealing with Rogan to notice a grubby boy on his Indian pony.

The trail west along the Weber River was familiar from trips to Great Salt Lake City and beyond with Papa. Two miles north of Weber Station, she turned Dzień down a flinty trail towards Forney's Bridge. They'd been unable to cross it two weeks ago when the river was over the top of the bridge from snowmelt. Aleksandra smiled as they neared the river. The top of the bridge showed just clear of the swollen river and she sighed in relief. This week's cold snap must have slowed the snowmelt in the mountains above.

Snorting, Dzień stared suspiciously at the rushing brown water lapping over the edge of the bridge, but he moved forward at Aleksandra's urging, walking with muzzle low until he reached solid ground on the far shore. He shook his head and danced until she laughed and gave him his head. With an almighty great buck, he dashed up the trail, tail in the air.

'I'd be pleased, too, Dzień.' She chuckled at his antics as he slowed on the long uphill. 'That very bridge you disliked so much just saved you from an extra ten miles up around Henneforville.'

The Emergency Pony Express Station at Henneforville.

She choked back a sob, thinking of the last trip she and her pa made up there…

"The Express riders use this station," Papa had said, "when Forney's Bridge is underwater."

She sighed, trying for a smile, while her brow furrowed, then returned her attention to the trail ahead. With a furtive look around her, she checked her shirt again for the soft buckskin bags beneath, one with its well-wrapped contents. She tucked them down tightly.

'Scotty said old Ephraim Hanks at Mountain Dell Station would give us a hot meal, but the thought of him scares me a little. What do you think?'

The dun just shook his head, and continued along the westward trail of the Mormon emigrants and the ill-fated Donner Party. They rode up Bachelors Canyon, past Dixie Hollow Station, and on to Ephraim's station.

THE DROPPED BROWS, tight lips and menacing alertness of Ephraim Hanks standing before the station's log cabin made Aleksandra's mouth go dry. His index finger, longingly stroking his rifle's trigger was almost a caress, and her guts churned as she rode towards him.

'Good afternoon, sir.' She faltered as his face remained unchanged. 'I hoped I might be able to take a meal with you.' She gulped, shoulders hunched. 'If you please.'

They had met once, several years ago, on a trip with her pa. At the time, she couldn't believe the scary legends built up around the smiling, handsome bear of a man, who walked with the swagger of his younger sailor days.

This scowling man hadn't budged, other than his fingers on the trigger.

Today, however, I could well believe the stories.

The tales centered around Ephraim being the leader of a group of hit-men called the Danites—Destroying Angels.

'I'm a friend of Scotty's, from up at Echo.'

And I've met you before, but I hope you don't remember.

'I have a letter here from him.' She slowly reached for the letter inside the neck of her doeskin, careful to not make any fast moves.

'Why didn't you say so before? I might have shot ya!' He waved the letter away, a wide grin lighting up his face, and reached up to shake her hand with an iron grip. The man she remembered was back, blue eyes sparkling out from under his sandy forelock.

Aleksandra peered at him, suspecting she'd caught him in the middle of something, clad as he was in a grubby shirt with no suspenders. He led the way towards the L-shaped barn at a sprightly pace.

'Ephraim Hanks, at your service. And who might ye be, lad?' He looked at Aleksandra sideways. 'Ye look familiar and I say I never forget a face.'

'Oh no, sir, we've not met before.' She averted her face. 'I'm Aleks.'

One eyebrow lifted, he smiled. 'Hmmm. Righto, "Aleks". Ye can put yer pony in this pen and I'll throw him some hay. Water bucket's out by the trough.'

'Thank you sir, Mr. Hanks.' Aleksandra kept her head down. Fooling people she'd met before, even as a girl, mightn't prove as easy as she'd thought.

THE COLT DIDN'T SEEM to know the way home this time, so Vladimir's return trip to Krzysztof's cabin, en route to the trading post, took longer than he expected. More likely, however, the bay colt didn't particularly care about home. Since they'd turned around and headed back west towards the cabin, his mare had come fully on heat. He'd wondered if she was starting up over the previous few days, but there was no longer any doubt.

Vladimir now had a fair inkling why he'd been able to purchase this stunning, sound mare so cheaply this winter. He shook his head and closed his eyes. The constant presence of a stallion couldn't help, but doubtless the chestnut's previous owner knew how excitable she was for the sunny half of the year, when the longer days made her come on heat every three weeks. Vladimir's lips pulled tight across gritted teeth as he fought to keep his seat. Their little jaunt had become a trial. The young stallion was beside himself, travelling next to this winking, squealing hussy. Vladimir thought it safer to ride the green and horny colt, staying on top of him, rather than beneath him, if he tried to breed the mare.

He found the shortcut to the cabin—unfortunately, just *after* he rode the bay past the half-hidden trailhead. Catching Vladimir unawares, the colt looked back toward the trail, then jerked the reins from his hand and spun on a dime, nearly dropping him as the bay dived into the trees, headed for home. The mare meanwhile threw up her head and reared, ripping her lead rope from his grip as the colt bolted.

'You obviously knew *that* part of the way home.' Vladimir growled. He swore roundly at the beast in Russian, got him under control again and thanked whoever would listen that both horses hadn't left him stranded. It would be a long walk to anywhere and he didn't particularly want anyone to find him at the cabin with all the graves and none of the former occupants.

He needn't have worried he'd lose the mare. She couldn't get close enough to the colt as they made their way down the narrow trail. She twice smashed Vladimir's knee between her barrel and the plunging bay, but Vladimir eventually grabbed her trailing lead. A quick look around Krzysztof's yard gave no evidence of habitation, so he refilled two bags with hay, slung them over the mare's saddle horn and headed off down the wider wagon trail to find the trading post.

'So how's old Scotty keepin'?' Ephraim asked, after he'd served her supper and said grace. After a day on the trail, the wafting aroma of beef and gravy over sourdough biscuit made her mouth water. Aleksandra carried *pemmican* for herself and grain for Dzień on long trips, but a hot meal was always welcome.

'He's well,' she said, wrapping her hands around the warm mug of coffee. She nearly purred with delight at the warmth, almost forgetting to lower her voice. 'I've been helping him at the trading post for the past few weeks, reorganizing the place after the fur buyer's visit, but there's not much for me to do now, so I'm headin' west to meet with Superintendent Egan. I'm hopin' to get a job as a rider. I'm much obliged to you for sharin' your supper with me.' She smiled.

'It's nothin', always make plenty. Never know who'll stop by,' he said with a grin. 'Nice lookin' pony you've got. Tell me about him.'

An hour passed before she knew it.

'Well, I'd best be off,' Aleksandra said, and got to her feet. 'Thanks again for the meal, sir. How much do I owe you for that?'

'Not a thing, lad, happy for the company.'

Aleksandra's breath caught in her throat as she noticed him eyeing her suspiciously, as he'd done a few times before.

'Is there anything I can do to help you before I go?' she asked.

'Well, matter of fact,' he hesitated, 'I could use a hand to treat a horse with an arrow wound in his leg. We dug out the arrowhead, but it's festered and I'm all alone up here for now.'

'Be happy to help,' she said, as they left the cabin.

He grimaced at her over his shoulder as he entered the stable. 'It's my favourite Express pony, too.'

She turned her attention to the dispirited pinto Mustang as he raised his head a little way from where it hung near the ground.

'Hello darlin', not feeling so good, eh?' Aleksandra hunkered down and put her face against his muzzle for a few moments before moving back to his flank. She placed her fingers over the hot and swollen area near the jagged wound on the back of his gaskin.

'He showed up here with the arrow in him five days ago and he's gone downhill fast over the past two days.'

The smell of necrotic flesh overpowered any other scent in the barn. Aleksandra waved a hand at the flies settling on the wound, and on the blood-tinged yellow discharge beneath it.

'Is he eating and drinking?'

'Not much.' Ephraim glanced from the full water bucket to the untouched hay and frowned. 'Correction, looks like he's not doing either.'

'How did he find the arrow?'

'The rider never saw it, the arrow being around the back of his leg. Says the pony jumped when they rode through a ravine coming up from Salt Lake House, but he never missed a beat.' He gazed at the wound, deep creases dividing his brows as he rubbed the pony's withers with work-gnarled fingers.

'What have you done with it so far?'

'Just wiped it down with water and a bit of whisky. We're not well stocked up here, I'm afraid. Do you know a bit about healing?'

'A little, my grandpapa was a doctor and Papa nearly completed his physician training. He taught me everything he could,' her heart constricted and she swallowed hard, forcing herself to continue, 'about medicine.'

'Well, I'd be pleased for your help,' he said, looking at her sideways, one brow raised. 'What do you need?'

'To start with, a few pots of boiling water, salt and some sundried clean cloths. Later, some honey or sugar if you have it.'

'Can do, young man!' the station keeper called back as he hustled off.

From the medical kit in her saddlebags, Aleks produced the flushing syringe her father brought from Poland and took it into the station, placing it carefully into the smallest of the pots of nearly-boiling water.

She gathered up as many cobwebs as she could find from the corners of the room, after carefully allowing their occupants to escape. Moistening the pile of web with hot water, she crumbled onto it a piece of stale bread, then kneaded it together until it became a soft mass.

Ephraim watching Aleksandra from the corners of his eyes in silence while he gathered the rest of the requested items. She ladled a measure of salt into each pot of boiling water, then added the clean cloths.

Saying little, they carried the pots and medicaments back to the barn. The pony's muzzle was tight, his eyes surrounded by deep furrows. Aleksandra hooked a steaming cloth out with a ladle and held it in the air to cool, just long enough to be handled without burning. The pony flinched when she gently placed it against his inflamed thigh, then he stilled and sighed. She held it in place until it cooled, then swapped it for a new hot compress and repeated the sequence to heat up the inflamed tissue.

After half an hour of hot soaks, the pony's strained and anxious look was gone, his eyes softened. Aleksandra flushed the wound with boiled, salted water from the clean pot until the flush water ran clear. Drawing honey into her syringe, she filled the wound with it, followed by the web and bread poultice. Ephraim bandaged it snugly into place.

'I could have put in a drain, or stitched on a stent bandage,' she looked up at Ephraim, then turned back to the pony, 'but because the wound is directed upward, it should drain well enough on its own, and I wanted to use a poultice, so I thought we'd just bandage it. You'll need to keep it open, so it doesn't close up over infection, till it's healed from the inside.'

'You *do* know something about doctoring, don't you? Good call. The bandage might slip down, but since he's not moving around much, it might stay up until morning. That's a good job you've done there, Aleks, thank you. I'm sure the Express will be more than pleased to have you.' He nodded emphatically, his mouth turned up at the corners. His eyes glowed as he looked at the pinto, who seemed less tense.

Aleksandra was pleased to see the pony reach out his nose for a nibble of the hay he'd previously ignored and drink some water from the proffered bucket before they left him in peace for the night.

Aleksandra wanted to treat her patient in the morning, so she accepted the offer of a bunk for the night. Early the next morning, the pinto's supper was gone. Better yet, he nosed around the floor seeking more.

He must be on the mend, fever down, if he wants to eat again.

She nearly did a little dance, then remembered she was a boy, with a wry grin. The Mustang nodded his head at her until she fed him more hay. He'd left new hoofprints around the perimeter of his stall and his bandage was down around his hock, as would be expected, but most of the web poultice remained inside the wound. The skin surrounding it, and the wound edges themselves, were pink and cool to the touch.

She was reaching for the last cobwebs she could find when Ephraim arrived with a pot of hot water and clean cloths. They looked suspiciously like newly-torn bed sheets.

'He's much better this morning,' she looked up from the white cotton squares and grinned at him.

'Thanks to you.' He smiled. 'I know what to do with him now, if you need to be on your way.'

'No problem at all. I'm glad to help.'

'I wasn't sure you weren't an instrument of the devil when you started gathering cobwebs and breadcrumbs, but you've worked good magic on my favourite. I'm sending you off with a glowing letter of recommendation for Superintendent Egan to help you get that job.'

'I'd like that, thanks.' She beamed up at him and turned back to the pony. 'I'll flush the wound with my syringe, and then let you finish up while I pack my gear.'

Half an hour later, Aleksandra turned to Ephraim after she mounted Dzień. 'I look forward to hearing how the pony does. He's a great little trooper.'

'I sure appreciate your expert help.' Ephraim reached up to shake her hand.

'Thank you for putting me up. You should be able to find me at Camp Floyd, all going well.' She grinned over her shoulder, waving, as the pony began to move toward Great Salt Lake.

'No problem...*Aleksandra*,' he said, emphasized her name.

Her heart slammed into her chest wall and she broke out into a cold sweat, despite the early morning chill. She halted her pony and stood silently, still facing away from him.

Of course, he saw through my ruse.

Turning her pony, she took a deep breath and held it, mouth dropped open, having absolutely no idea what to say.

'Your secret's safe with me, girl. I heard about your pa, and I'm sorry for your loss. He was a good man and did me many a good turn. It's the least I can do.'

Aleksandra let her breath out slowly, her eyes closing for a moment. She sat up straight and closed her mouth, then looked at Ephraim again. A single tear traced its way down her cheek.

'I'm not sure why you're so keen to put your life in danger as a Pony rider,' he raised an eyebrow at her and shook his head, 'but you'll have your reasons. I stand up for what I believe and you have the guts to do so as well, so I support you in this.'

'Thank you, Mr. Hanks.' She met his eyes with difficulty as he approached her and stood at Dzień's shoulder. 'I think Papa knew his killer from long ago in Europe and yes, I don't want him to find me,'

'Well, if you get into trouble and need help, just send word and all will be sorted,' he said, his eyebrows nearly touching, his mouth a hard, firm line. 'I've got friends from one coast to the other.' Aleksandra glanced at his face, and her heart froze. She really could believe those old rumors about the man, and was mighty glad he was on her side. Before she rode away, she described Vladimir to him as best she could, but not the real reason for her subterfuge.

ALEKSANDRA'S first glimpse of the Great Salt Lake as she crested the last hill always took her breath away. She stopped to give Dzień a breather and gazed at the panorama, the lake and its surrounding flats running nearly to eternity, fringed by majestic mountains.

Dzień's ears pricked and she heard hoofbeats on the trail ahead. Aleksandra glanced about her, heart pounding in her chest, but there was nowhere to get off the trail.

Trapped!

With no escape in sight, she focused on slowing her breathing and heartbeat, trying for stillness, as two Indians appeared. After she spoke a *Shoshone* greeting in a deep voice, they nodded and looked at her in an odd manner as they rode past on their paint ponies.

They don't miss much, she grinned wryly. *They probably wondered why I'm passing myself off as a boy.*

Sighing, she let her pony pick his way downhill to the flats above the lake. She hopped off when the trail became steeper to save Dzień's legs, keeping an eye out for Indians, Russian accents and safe cover, especially after being caught out on the ridge. Tell-tale puffs of dust sent her scuttling off the trail where the terrain allowed and Dzień nibbled what grass and new shoots he found along the way. She let him graze in the stands of cottonwood and willow brush near the streams, for such greenery would disappear as they headed west.

Everything would become more rare, to the point of non-existence: settlements, water, grass. Everything except rocks, sand and salt. There were plenty of those, as far as the eye could see. Some of the rock formations *were* interesting, though, like the red bluffs back near her home at Echo.

Home…

Emotions swamping her, tears began to fill her eyes again. She blinked and changed tack before she melted down completely.

Think of something else completely—like what I'm going to say to Xavier—in too short a time.

Heat flooded her face. While longing to see him, she approached the anticipated battle of wills with trepidation. After another deep breath, she shook off her foolish thoughts with a crooked grin and prepared for battle.

THE CAMP FLOYD PONY EXPRESS STATION door swung open with a groan of hinges. Xavier looked up from his desk to see a boy in baggy buckskins walk in, tip his hat and mumble a greeting. His mind still on his pay slips, he stood and extended a hand.

'Good afternoon, what can—' He stopped dead and gaped, seeing familiar blue eyes and an unforgettable grin before him on the face of the "boy".

This cannot be possible.

He blinked and stared, his mind spinning, then spat out the first thing that entered his head.

'*Aleksandra, what have you done with your hair?*' His fists clenched as she rushed, scowling, towards him.

'Shhh! Someone might hear you!' Aleksandra reached up to clap a hand over Xavier's mouth but he grabbed it tightly.

'What in God's name are you doing? You were going to the *Shoshone* and now you're here, and you're...'

His face flushed as he pushed her back a step, still holding her hand, staring pointedly at her suddenly-flat chest. His jaw dropped.

'*Díos mío*, oh my God...give me strength,' he said, looking skyward for assistance. 'What are you *thinking*, Aleksandra?' His forehead scrunched.

'It's Aleks, and I've come for the job.' She lifted her chin and nodded.

Releasing her like she was a hot potato, he stepped back.

'Job—what job?' he managed, then stood shaking his head, his mouth open.

'The advertised job, you know, "wiry, under 18, orphan"? I'm here to see Superintendent Egan.'

'Not a chance!' He shook his head again, then gritted his teeth, counting to ten. 'It's lads only. Orphans no one will claim. Too dangerous.' Xavier said, when he could speak again, watching the pulse pounding at Aleksandra's throat.

'I'm here to see Mr. Egan. I ride better than any boy and besides, who cares whether I die? Even the *Shoshone* won't have me.' She looked down at the ground, then back up at him. 'Please,' she implored, her blue eyes soft, 'give me a trial?'

'Superintendent Egan isn't here. He's left me in charge. And *absolutamente*. Absolutely. No. I will not let you put yourself into the kind of danger an Express rider risks daily.' His eyebrows narrowed and then a thought occurred to him, and he looked her straight in the eyes. 'Does Scotty know you're here?'

'Yes.' She grinned at him, eyes sparkling with mischief. 'He sent me.'

'*¡Dios mío*, Scotty!' Slapping the handful of payslips onto the desk, he turned away from her, then faced her again. 'Look Aleksandra, I'm sorry, but the answer is still no.'

'Please tell me then,' she looked down her nose at him, 'how I am to feed and clothe myself? A mere, defenseless, woman?'

'Defenseless. Right.' He looked at her from beneath his brows, remembering all too well her *shashka* at his Adams apple. Through his anger, laughter bubbled out. 'You are anything but defenseless.' He shook his head. 'You can just go back and tell Scotty to put you to work at the trading post.'

'Stuck in a dress and bonnet, no hard riding, too many memories. You just don't understand. I need *life*,' she breathlessly rambled. 'I've seen too much death. I'm bad luck.' She slumped down the wall to sit on her booted heels. 'Everyone I love *dies*.'

'First off, you caused no one to die. Second, I—' Xavier stopped, eyes wide and heart racing, unwilling to say what he had nearly said to her. He scarcely knew her, how could he begin to think—

A flicker of emotion crossed Aleksandra's face, then she resolutely tightened her jaw, stood up and whipped open the door.

'Where are you going?'

'Where no respectable woman should ever seek employment.' She stomped out the door and down the dusty road towards the saloon.

He caught her in five long strides and grabbed her.

'Bad choice,' he growled through gritted teeth. 'You come right back here.'

As she reached for her hip, Xavier remembered their first encounter. Grabbing her wrist with one hand, he threw her over his shoulder with the other and made for his office door.

'Let me *go!*' she shrieked.

'*¡Cállate!* Before I'm tempted to spank you in the street!' he growled as he carried her into the station and dumped her unceremoniously onto the floor.

She bit her lip and looked up at him with huge eyes, their blue nearly black. Kicking the door shut, he ducked down to take her shoulders in a tight grip.

'*¡Basta*, enough!* Have patience. No wonder the Indians sent you on your way. They like submissive women.'

At this, her eyes bore into him again, sparks flying and cheeks blazing.

AT XAVIER'S LAST COMMENT, Aleksandra's fear fled, replaced by a burning anger. Never had a man touched her as Xavier just did—the memory of his hard body as she'd struggled against him burned into her mind, feelings tantalizing, yet frightening in their immensity.

His eyes glinted cold steel fire, one eyebrow raised. 'And did you stop to consider just what they would have thought of your applying for a position in their establishment dressed like that?'

The silence was deafening.

4

Aleksandra scowled, but gave it up with a little grin. 'Guess I didn't think. Papa always said I didn't think.' Eyes filling, she glanced up at Xavier, then a tear ran down her cheek.

'Look Aleks.' He tilted his head with a smile, reaching out to help her from the floor, 'I'd prefer you in a whorehouse even less than I want to see you riding.'

Frowning, she ignored his gesture and scrabbled to her feet on her own, wiping her tears roughly with a sleeve and rubbing her abused posterior.

'What do you say you help me run this office and cook for the Pony riders passing through here?' He seemed to be having trouble with his mouth, but his eyes glinted merrily.

'Nothin' doin,' she said from between gritted teeth, hands on hips. 'It's one or the other. You take your pick.'

'*Dios mío*, but you are a terror.' Raking his fingers through his hair, he stood silently for a moment, then looked her in the eyes. 'You drive a hard bargain, Aleks.'

He moved slowly toward her, his eyes soft, but then his face hardened and he stopped, turning his head away.

She finally took a breath in...relief? She wasn't at all sure about the fluttering in her belly.

They both looked at anything but each other for what seemed an eternity, then their eyes locked.

'Okay, let's say I give you a chance to show me what you can do.'

She jerked her head up.

'Now? Right now?'

'I give, Aleksandra.' Sighing, he held up his hands. 'Yes, now. Let me close up here and we'll go. The riders aren't due for hours.'

'It's *Aleks* now,' she said with a sideways glance.

'*Sí, sí, Aleks*, I'll try to remember that.' He raised an eyebrow at her. 'Get a move on, *Chiquita*, before I come to my senses and change my mind. Where's your pony?' Turning the key to lock the small adobe station, they headed for the livery stable.

SCOTTY LOOKED up from perusing his newspaper at the trumpet of a stallion.

Sounds like Rogan!

He glanced up at the new 'Wanted' poster tacked to the wall beside the door with Vladimir's name and details in large, bold typeface. The Pony Express Superintendent had sent out the Salt Lake Gazette's hastily printed posters with their Express riders along the trail in both directions, with orders to leave copies at every station or trading post they passed.

A powerfully built, graying man rode up to the open door on a chestnut mare. She kept trying to spin around, presumably back toward the indignant screaming of her mate. He must have tied the colt around the bend, knowing he would be recognized.

A little further away might have been wise.

Scotty shook his head, with the hint of a grin. Reaching beneath the counter, he checked his rifle, flicking the safety to off. The stranger clumped up the stairs and entered.

'Greetings,' he gruffly announced in a strong accent, as Scotty rose from his stool. This could only be Vladimir.

Red-faced and perspiring, the Russian sounded worn out, and he certainly looked it. Scotty stifled a grin, more of a grimace, as Vladimir walked to the bar.

'What kin can I help ye with, sir?' he called across the room, not quite trusting his voice with the potential killer of his best friend.

'Good afternoon, nice place you have here.' Vladimir scanned the room, only his rapid jugular pulse and the tension of his jaw evidencing his discomfiture at the sound of the screaming stallion down the trail, and the hysterical mare, even now trying to loose herself from the tie rail with her teeth. Glancing over his shoulder in the direction of the noise, he scowled.

'A whisky, please, unless you happen to have a good Russian vodka hiding behind that counter,' he said, averting his eyes from Scotty's gaze.

'Well sir, yer in luck, only it happens to be *Polish* vodka,' Scotty growled as he ducked under the counter to ferret out the bottle, not quite keeping the steel out of his voice. By the time the Russian caught his eye, he'd controlled his face and managed a grin. 'It ain't cheap, though, to git it here all the way from Europe!'

Vladimir smiled his thanks and downed it in one gulp.

'Ahhh, that helps.' He set down the glass, opened his mouth to speak, then hesitated. 'Why would you have Polish vodka way out here?' he finally blurted out.

'There's a Polish gentleman's been livin' near here fer years and 'e likes a drop 'r two o' his favourite, so I keep it in stock for 'im. He'll likely be down here any day.' Scotty busily wiped the countertop, risking a glance at the man, who had gone a rather pasty color.

'Polish, eh? I lived in Poland for some time many years ago. What did you say he was called?'

'His name is Krzysztof Lekarski.'

Vladimir flinched, then breathed and sat up straight. 'That sounds familiar, does he have a wife and children?' The Cossack eyed him sideways.

'His wife's dead these past few years and I heard tell 'e 'ad a daughter 'n some sons, but I think they died too.' Scotty looked away, crossing his fingers under the counter.

'That's too bad,' Vladimir countered. 'Would you know where he lives?'

'Ahh, 'bout an hour east o' here. Easy to find, if yer a friend.' Scotty looked him in the eye.

'Might have to catch up with him on my way back. I've just come from that direction.' Vladimir looked away. 'If I could just trouble you for another shot of that fine vodka, I'll be on my way.'

'Anythin' else I can help you with?' Scotty gestured to the wall behind him at the many items on sale, belatedly hoping none of Aleksandra's old goods were on display for sale.

'No, thank you, I must be off.' Vladimir didn't even glance at the shelves as he counted out coins and turned towards the door.

Halfway across the room, he suddenly stopped dead, then ducked his head and carried on, lifting his hand in a brief wave behind him. The 'Wanted' poster stared back at Scotty as Vladimir hurtled out the door. He vaulted onto the mare, already at a canter. He never looked back.

Sure can see where Krzysztof and Aleksandra got their horsemanship skills. He frowned, his lips tight. *Too bad he had to kill his student and orphan Aleksandra into the deal.*

The distant shrieks of the colt stopped abruptly. Scotty would have liked to capture Vladimir but he knew he was more useful to Aleksandra alive than dead. Even with a rifle, one old man alone does not easily stop a Cossack arms master. He could have held a rifle on him, but for how long, waiting for someone to come along?

Scotty waited at the cliff edge out the back of the trading post until the man and two horses came into view on the river bottom below. Watching the Cossack ride away on Krzysztof's plunging colt, trying to settle the squealing, kicking chestnut, his frown turned into a chuckle. Rogan would keep him occupied. He smiled when he saw Vladimir turn south, away from Aleksandra. Scotty had wanted to send him in that direction, but couldn't figure out how to do it without appearing obvious. Thankfully, the Russian did it himself.

Picking up a broom in agitation, he set about figuring out the best way to get word to his friends. He finally penned a note to Xavier, to be sent with the next fast rider heading west.

The trading post floor was cleaner than it had been in years.

'Ohhhh,' Aleksandra breathed at her first sight of Xavier's dappled gray. The dished face and long, curling mane and tail bespoke his regal Spanish blood. 'I saw a horse like this once, but he was black, ridden by a Spanish aristocrat travelling to the goldfields a few years back.' Her attention was captured by the stallion as he approached the stable door.

'*¿Le gusta?* Do you like him? His name is Charrolero. He's getting on a bit now, but he's been my companion these past many years.' The gray snuffled and lipped softly at Aleksandra's fingers, his liquid black eyes melting her soul.

She breathed into his nostrils and he breathed back, chewing softly as if recognizing a new friend.

'You must be pure of heart, Aleks,' Xavier murmured. 'Charro understands these things and consequently takes to few people so quickly.'

She glowed at this praise from a fellow horseman and dropped her head.

'I'm sorry about the scene back there, Xavier.' She looked at the floor with a faint grin, conceding the day. 'As I said, I just didn't think. Maybe it's time to start.'

'Well, if it's time for what you call "home truths", Aleksandra, I'm not so sure,' Xavier murmured close above her, 'that I can forgive you for cutting your hair.' She warmed under his gaze as he stared at the thin queue of her shoulder-length hair, tied back with a leather thong, peeking from beneath her hat.

'A boy has no need for hair he can sit on,' she said, spinning on her heel and placing some distance between her and the compelling attraction that was Xavier.

The stallion, startled out of his reverie, snorted at her in reply, his sculpted ears pricked.

'*Bien,*' he growled and took a deep breath as he folded his arms before him, his brow lowered. 'Okay, let's get going before someone comes and sees me quibbling with a smart alec—' He shot a sideways grin at her. '—a smart *Aleks* rider, one so young his voice hasn't even begun to change.'

Aleksandra took a playful swing at Xavier as she passed him, then dashed off to the pen where she'd left Dzień.

Half an hour's ride took them to the center of a flat, open valley of newly sprouting grass surrounded by pines and aspens.

'No one should be able to see us out here,' Xavier remarked.

Aleksandra slid to the ground and checked Dzień's bridle and girth.

'Instructions, Boss?' She tilted her head at him.

'Lady's choice, be my guest. Raising an eyebrow, he gestured with palm raised to offer her the field as he sat his big gray.

'Lady's choice it is then, sir!' Smiling, she looked him in the eyes, bowed, clicked her heels together and barked a brief command in Polish to Dzień.

Warmed up from his trek to the proving ground, he broke into an easy lope as Aleks vaulted lightly into the saddle and set him on an oval track around the inside of the circle of trees. Circling the makeshift arena twice, they increased speed on the long sides of the oval. She threw her red bandana to the ground as she flashed past Xavier and shook her head at him as he moved to pick it up. Retreating to his place in the center, he watched her make a return pass. Pulling both feet from the stirrups, she swung her right leg over the pony's head and pointed her toes at him, her body at right angles to the horse. After balancing on her bottom for four strides, she swung her leg back over, settling into the saddle for the turn.

On her third pass toward him, she again kicked out of her stirrups and this time, flicked her right leg up and over the pony's neck. Gripping the saddle horn tightly she slid from the saddle, took three quick steps beside her galloping pony and vaulted back on. Continuing at a gallop, the athletic pony never faltered, showing off her abilities to perfection.

XAVIER'S JAW dropped and he stood in stunned silence. He watched as she grabbed the saddle horn with her right hand, kicked her left leg over Dzień's back and disappeared from sight. All he could see of her was her hand on the saddle horn as the pony ran past, then she was suddenly back in the saddle.

'¡*Muy bien*! Bravo!' Xavier shouted. 'I want to see that one again!'

Aleksandra, cheeks pink with her efforts, flashed him a glowing look as she called to the pony and he increased his speed for the straight. She suddenly fell backwards next to Dzień's barrel, facing away from the pony, hands reaching for the ground.

Xavier rushed towards her to catch her, but stopped, grinning, when he saw that her left foot was hooked into the surcingle buckled around the pony's body, her head and arms only inches from Dzień's flying feet. Flashing past, she plucked her handkerchief from the ground and dragged her fingers through the grass for several strides before flicking herself back up into the saddle, jamming the scrap of linen into the neckline of her buckskin shirt.

On the next fly-by, Aleksandra repeated her 'disappearing act' for him. Speeding towards him, she held the horn in her right hand. In one fluid movement, she slipped her right knee under her stirrup leather and swung her left leg over the heaving rump of her mount, extending it towards Dzień's tail. After she thundered past, Aleksandra bounced up into the saddle.

Xavier's breath caught in his throat as Dzień took off at a dead run towards a pine tree just outside the track. As they neared the tree, she drew her *shashka*, gave a war cry, and lopped off a pinecone from a branch above her head, grabbing the trophy in her left hand. Easing back into a canter, she threw the cone into the air, catching it on the point of her sword and slid to a halt before Xavier, pony blowing. Bowing again from the waist, she presented the prize to the waiting man.

Xavier slowly removed the pinecone from the *shashka* tip and shook his head, gazing at her in admiration. Already flushed, she now blushed, probably to the tips of her toes, as his gaze devoured her.

'Your skill and affinity with horses far exceeds my expectations, exceeds even my wildest dreams, Aleks. Scotty was right, you're a horse-charmer and impressively trained by a master. What *was* that?'

'*DŽIGITOVKA*, Cossack military show riding. Practical as well as impressive, no?' Aleks pronounced the Russian name slowly and peered sideways at him with a grin.

She'd never known such praise from anyone, much less one for whom she felt such attraction. Never before had admiration of her skills mattered so much. He approached and she meet his eyes as he regarded her, shaking his head in wonder. Suddenly they were close enough to touch, but then a fleeting shadow passed over his countenance and he started and broke the reverie. Xavier was silent for a few moments, then he spoke distractedly, as if he couldn't quite believe what he was about to say.

'Aleksandra, although this doesn't change the fact that you're not a boy and I still don't see how we can make this work, I see you can care for yourself out there. I don't want to risk your neck and I'm not at all sure how you'll dodge bullets and arrows, but I imagine you'd do it better than most.'

'So you'll let me ride?'

He took a deep breath and looked her full in the eyes.

'I guess first thing,' he said with a sigh, 'is to teach you how to walk like a boy.' Then he grinned.

'Woo hoo!' she shouted, bending in the saddle to throw her arms around his neck in a quick hug.

AFTER THE HORSES were fed the next morning, Xavier followed Aleksandra into the station.

'That *dzig-*, *dzigit-*....' Xavier murmured from his position before the hot woodstove.

'*Džigitovka?*' She smiled.

'*Džigitovka*, yes. It sure was impressive. I'd like to learn more about it.'

'I'd love to teach you. You'll have no problem with it.'

'I'm starting to get hungry, maybe you could tell me more while we heat up some fresh *tortillas* and beans.'

'*Tortillas?*' Aleksandra's brows drew together quizzically.

'Mexican flatbreads, made from corn. They're a staple food for *los Mexicanos*,' he said, lifting a cast iron pan from its hook and placing it onto the glowing woodstove.

'Oh, sort of like *żurek* for me!'

'*Żurek?*' It was Xavier's turn to look confused.

'It's *our* staple and comfort food in Poland. It's the most—'

A shout came from the lookout posted just outside the fort. They both swung towards the door, then glanced at each other.

'Express rider?' She cocked an eyebrow.

'Not due until much later tonight,' said Xavier, his lips set in a grim line. Aleksandra whipped the skillet off the stove while Xavier ran for his pistol and rifle. The military men of Camp Floyd were turning out in droves, brandishing weapons.

5

Knuckles white on their rifles, the silent soldiers of Camp Floyd cheered as one when they recognized the oncoming horse as a Pony Express mount. Laughing nervously, they stood watching or slowly filtered back to the mess tent.

'He's *way* too early.' Xavier hurried down the steps, his jaw tight, and grabbed the bridle of the heaving chestnut. After one look at the travel-worn rider, he glanced back at Aleksandra.

'What's going on?' Aleksandra frowned at the pony.

'We need another horse saddled, *pronto*, now.' He nodded towards a pinto mare, staring at them over a rail, ears pricked.

'Afternoon, Boss,' the boy croaked in a gravelly voice and slid from the saddle, nearly landing in a heap. He tossed the *mochila* to Xavier and nodded at Aleksandra.

Glancing in the direction of the rider's gaze, Xavier spun around.

'Now!' he tersely quipped at Aleksandra, who had edged closer. 'Better yet, go find Murray. It's not time yet, but he's got to ride now.'

She bolted for the bunkhouse.

He returned his gaze to the grim, dusty face of the rider. The pony's head drooped from its dry, sweat-caked body. Xavier tried for a grin, but could only grit his teeth as he took in the state of the horse. It wasn't like James return a pony to a station in this condition. 'Not so good out there, James?'

'Bad news, sorry, Xavier.' He handed him a travel-worn piece of paper. 'Message from Superintendent Egan for you. The whole lot of 'em further west at Cold Springs and Smith's Creek have been killed 'n the horses and stock run off. Egan's shuffling men and horses along the route. He needs you and another rider at Fish Springs as soon as you can find a replacement for yourself here.' He wiped the top of his forearm across his eyes.

Xavier lifted the pony's lip. His gums were dry and tacky. Pinching the skin on the side of his neck to see how dehydrated he really was, he took a deep breath and closed his eyes. His guts clenched at the sight of the skin—it stayed exactly where he'd tented it.

'When did he stop sweating, James?'

'Had to be at least seven miles back, just a little way out of Boyd's.' The boy sighed and shook his head. 'There weren't any fresh horses to replace him and we needed to get this news out east. Egan's already been transferring horses, so this boy's had to go far more than his share, probably 50 miles, at a pretty clip. He's a good 'un, lots of heart. I know you'll take good care of him tonight.'

James limped towards the water trough and Xavier followed slowly with the unsteady pony, exhausted and dehydrated beyond sweating.

It'll be a long night taking care of this horse, if he's to survive this ride.

'Thanks James, we'll do our best.' Xavier smiled as the boy's head came out of the trough and he shook water everywhere.

'Aaaah,' he breathed. Xavier handed him the towel he kept at the water tank for the men, then gave the chestnut a small sip of water.

'How long have you been riding?'

'Started at Robert's Creek, but I had to go on at Schell, so I figure I must've gone about 180 miles, give or take a bit.'

'Why did you go on at Schell?'

'The rider at Schell Creek said he was injured, but with the news, I reckon he was just too scared to go out on the trail, so I went on.'

'*¡Dios mío!* Xavier's brows nearly touched. 'Not a job for the faint of heart, eh lad?'

'Ya got that right, Xavier.' The young man sighed in pleasure as he wiped the mud from his face while Xavier gave the drooping horse another small drink of water.

'If you can walk him for a moment, I'll saddle the next horse for Murray and grab you some grub to eat on the way to your bunk.'

Taking the reins, the boy gave the pony a pat.

'And James, not a word to the new boy when he comes back, please,' Xavier threw over his shoulder. 'Wouldn't want to scare off a Pony rider. Sounds like we need all the help we can get.'

The rider smiled his appreciation through the grime on his face and wobbled away with the weaving pony, stretching out his legs as he walked.

Leading out the excited pinto, Xavier slung the *mochila* over her saddle as Murray ran out the station door, stuffing a packet of *tortillas* and beans into his shirt. Aleksandra watched them, her brow wrinkled over narrowed eyes. She pressed her lips together in a line as Murray mounted the dancing pony, already pulling at the bit. The rider grinned at the mare and waved his thanks as he slipped the reins and she bolted away from them like a shot toward Salt Lake House.

'*¡Vaya con Dios*!' Xavier shouted after him.

Go with God.

His heartfelt wish for the riders in these dangerous times. Shaking his head, he couldn't believe he'd actually told Aleksandra she could ride. Especially now. His breath caught at the thought.

ALEKSANDRA TOOK the reins of the heaving chestnut and started to walk him cool, occasionally passing furtive glances at Xavier. He sat on the edge of the trough, reading and rereading a crumpled piece of paper. He finally lifted his eyes from the paper and stood, staring off into the distance towards the west.

What was going on?

After his last brusque command to her, she wasn't about to ask.

She offered the colt sips of fresh water every few minutes as they walked, alternating with salted water to rehydrate him slowly. As he cooled down, he began to move his jaw a little when she stuffed small handfuls of hay into his mouth.

There must be problems along the trail.
She flicked a quick look at Xavier.
This pony's gone a very long way today.
'Aleks.' Xavier heaved a great sigh and turned to her. 'I'd hoped to be able to tell you there was no work available, because though you're determined to be a Pony rider, I prefer you alive. However...' He shook his head and gave her the news.

She glanced up at him, not sure whether to be excited about being allowed to ride for the short-staffed Pony or sad for the dead men and their families.

'It's not a laughing matter, Aleks,' he said, through clenched jaws, and his brows narrowed dangerously. 'By the arrows, it's suspected that it was the *Pah-Utes*, some of whom have sworn to kill all white settlers, and those attached to the Pony in particular.'

'Yes, Xavier, I'm sorry.' She sobered. 'They can be aggressive. They've been inciting other tribes to retaliate for their losses from the settlers, as Chief Golden Hawk told me when I went to their village.' They were silent for a while, each lost in their own thoughts.

'I've been given leave to hire a rider and become Station Manager for Fish Springs. Guess it's time you were sworn in.' He shook his head and gave her a rueful smile. 'I could try to keep you as a stock handler, but I know you'd soon be off getting into trouble elsewhere.'

They walked the tired chestnut slowly for well over an hour before his pulse started to slow toward normal. Becoming gradually more alert, he began nosing at the proffered food.

Aleksandra peeked over the back of the pony at him. 'So, when do we leave?'

'A man from the Fort who's been relieved of his station is interested in becoming a Station Manager, so we can leave as soon as I let him know. I'll swear you in on the way to Fish Springs, "Boy".'

She couldn't stop grinning, despite herself.

'Will day after tomorrow be soon enough for you, Aleks?'

'As if you needed to ask.' Aleksandra laughed.

RETURNING EARLY the next morning from the feed merchant and grocery, Xavier found Aleksandra in the stable grooming Dzień.

'*Buenos días, senorita.*' He frowned at the revolting hat she refused to remove. It was all he could see of her until she peered around the buckskin's head with a wide smile.

'That colt's a toughie.' She nodded across at the chestnut. 'He barged at me against the poles of his gateway when I fed him breakfast. I think he'll be okay.' She grinned. 'How far is it between stations, anyway? He's gone a lot further than ten or twenty miles.

'Originally, it was twenty, but despite having the best horses they could find, the Superintendents soon found the horses couldn't maintain the speed they wanted for much more than ten miles, so they hustled to make more stations, every ten miles or so.'

'Guess it would depend on the lay of the land, no?'

'*Sí.* With the rough, dry terrain between here and Sacramento, the stations are closer together than they are back East, where it's flat and there's more water.'

She nodded, picking up a hoof pick and turning back to her pony.

'How long have you been up?' His gaze took in the four already-fed, watered and groomed horses. 'You've been busy, haven't you? You've always got a job as a stock handler, if you want it.'

'Nothin' doin. My gear's packed and I'm ready to ride.' Her voice came to him, muffled, as she picked out Dzień's hoof. She straightened up and stretched her back. 'Besides,' she continued, her impudent nose raised into the air, 'I've already got a job as a Pony rider.'

'Either way, you've done the horses proud.' He stroked the clean and glossy coat of his own horse, who whuffled about his pockets for a snack. 'Thank you.'

Aleksandra glanced at them over her pony's rump. Her already flushed cheeks flared under his approving perusal.

'We leave tomorrow morning. Everything is sorted.' His voice dropped low as he approached her. 'Do you even *sleep* with that disgusting hat? I haven't seen you take it off *yet.*'

'Yes,' she snapped, whirling away to pack her brushes and combs, eyes down. He moved closer. He was waiting for her, only a breath away, when she turned around, tears glistening.

'Don't, please,' she whispered as he reached his fingers toward her cheek to wipe off a tear. She dropped her head, ducked under his arm and was gone.

Sliding down the wall, he sat on his heels to contemplate her actions.

She draws me like a magnet, but I don't need the complications of a woman in my life. No female can be trusted. He frowned. *I swear she likes me, but why does she always run away?*

His thoughts swirled.

Sighing, he rose to his feet and rubbed the attentive Dzień about the ears for a moment. Packing up his own horse gear, he headed for the office, determined to avoid Aleks, if only for a short time.

Through the office window, he saw her ride away at a smart trot half an hour later. Fighting the urge to go after her, he turned back to his work. He might as well have followed. He never did manage to settle back to work. His jaw finally relaxed when he saw the girl return just on dark, but he was busy with the new rider and station keeper. When he was finally able to get out to see her, his heart sank to discover she'd already disappeared into the darkened bunkhouse.

CONFUSION WHIRLED in her mind as Aleksandra stood before her bunk. A six-hour ride hadn't helped her make sense of anything. She thought again with panic of her mother, long-dead. She never rose from her last childbed, from whence had come her younger brother. Both of her brothers joined their mother in heaven when Scarlet Fever devastated the population of Weber Canyon three years ago. Pain clutched in her chest as she thought of those she'd lost, and of Xavier. The thought of getting close enough to possibly become pregnant terrified her. Women often died in childbirth, especially from first births. Her whole family's lives would have been in vain if she died, and Papa's secret formula were revealed for Vladimir and his tsar were to find. Europe was a world away, but a real world, with many lives at risk if she failed in her duty.

Perhaps if I trusted in Xavier, he would help me protect Papa's secret, should anything happen to me.

A warmth invaded her heart for a moment, but then she shook herself and flopped onto the bed, whimpering into the covers. Her fear of letting him close overwhelmed her again.

The door to the bunkhouse swung open and she pretended to be asleep, not yet ready to face him.

Thunk! A bedroll hit the wall near her head and fell onto the adjacent bunk.

'Wake up, sleepyhead!'

Aleks turned in her bunk to see a young man about her own age stride through the door, as if he owned the place.

He thrust a hand at her and she shook it, raising her eyebrows at his forwardness.

'I'm Jake, I hear you're the new rider for Fish Springs? I was ridin' back East, but they needed help out here. I've always wanted to go West, so here I am!'

Aleks pulled her hat lower and closed her eyes again, not sure how to deal with this intrusion. At least she could forget about Xavier for a few minutes.

By the time Aleks could piece together a suitable greeting, he'd gone on for several minutes, sitting on the edge of the bunk opposite, and was looking at her askance.

'Sorry, I was sleepin',' she mumbled and closed her eyes again. 'I'm Aleks, what did you ask?'

'I *said*, are you comin' out tonight with me an' the other boys I met up with at the saloon?' He raised his eyebrows as if he thought she might be dense.

'Oh, no!' she squeaked, then lowered her voice. 'We're leavin' early in the mornin' and I told Xavier that I'd do the horses before we go, so I'm turnin' in early. Besides, I've got no money to speak of. Thanks, just the same.'

Jake stared at her, his eyes bugged out. His brow furrowed as he shook his head.

'Won't take no for an answer, Aleks, I'll bet you ain't never even been out before. Looks like we need to break in the new rider, so let's go!' He grabbed her by the elbow and tugged.

'Hey!' She pulled back, her hat nearly falling off. Ramming it back onto her head, Aleksandra looked up at the determined set of his jaw and reconsidered.

Maybe this will give me some time away from Xavier.

More importantly, staying in the background might be the best way to stay safe from Vladimir. Perhaps should go quietly and not raise anyone's curiosity. She'd be gone in the morning, with no one the wiser.

WALKING across town toward the chosen saloon, Aleks and Jake were joined by several other young men, some wearing army uniforms, and each looking rougher than the last. Her fists showed white, gripping the sides of her buckskins. She released them slowly, willing her heart to slow. Keeping her face toward the ground, she merely nodded as each new lad tagged onto their group. Her boy's garb gave her some protection, but she felt naked, as if everyone saw past the pert, sunburnt nose to the young woman beneath. She saw a few curious glances, but no one commented.

She'd never seen the inside of a saloon. The light from the gas lamps glittered off the rows of bottles behind the bar and the shiny dresses of the three ladies draping themselves about the room. The girls looked the young newcomers up and down with knowing smiles.

The brunette stopped short when her gaze met Aleks', one eyebrow raised. Aleksandra held her breath, and the woman's eyes moved on to the next lad. Aleksandra stepped out of her view behind one of the others and inched toward the door, feeling suddenly in need of air.

'Oh no, ya don't.' Jake laughed in her ear as he grabbed her by the arm and dragged her along to the bar. 'What'll you be drinkin' tonight, Aleks?

'Um, well, you see, I don't dr—'

'He'll have a whisky, Ned.' Jake grinned at the barkeep and tossed a coin onto the bar. 'We got us a virgin here,' he hooted and several of the boys lining the bar snickered loudly in reply.

Aleksandra flinched, her face heating as she tried to disappear into her boots.

They've no idea how right they are.

Aleksandra needed to turn this around before it got out of hand. Picking her head up, she inhaled sharply.

'No!' she squeaked, then continued in a deeper voice. 'Vodka, please, if you have it.' Jake stared at her.

'It was my father's drink.' She glared at him, daring him to correct her.

'Okay, then, get her a vodka, thanks Ned. Never did hear of anyone drinkin' that stuff.' He looked at her sideways.

When it arrived, Jake touched the rim of his shot glass to hers.

'Bottoms up!' He looked at her and drained his glass in one gulp.

Aleksandra stared at the clear, deadly fluid. She'd never tasted it before. What could she have been thinking? Knowing she wouldn't get away with spilling it, she went for a tiny sip.

Ready for her, Jake tipped the glass up with a finger so she had to drink it or it would have spilled down her front. Spluttering, she gasped as the fiery liquid burned its way down her throat, spitting half of it out in the process and attracting the attention of anyone who wasn't immediately ogling the ladies.

Jake kept a close eye on Aleksandra as the evening wore on, refilling the glass with vodka she desperately tried to avoid drinking. Most of it was poured out on the dirt floor when his back was turned. Even so, after a while, the room began to swim. A voice somewhere far off in her brain asked where Xavier could have gotten to, but everything became more unclear by the minute.

'Keep the new lad here while I'm gone, eh boys?' Jake laughed as he left on the arm of the redhead.

The blonde was sitting on the lap of an army officer when the brunette returned to the room from outside. She tucked something into her bodice as she entered the room, then straightened her dress.

With three of the young men still watching her, Aleksandra hadn't been able to escape, though she'd positioned herself in the seat closest to the entrance.

A couple of greasy-looking men slouched through the swinging doors. The shiftless gaze of the bigger one, a burly, yellow haired man, surveyed the room as he ordered a whisky. He barked a greeting at someone in Jake's party and walked toward them with an unsteady gait. His eyes lit upon Aleksandra and his face blackened. She shrank into her seat, gripping the half empty glass.

'What kind of manners do *you* have, young man?' His voice dripped venom. 'There are ladies present and you wear a hat indoors?'

Alcoholic fumes from his breath enveloped her as he reached towards her hat, the only one, she suddenly realized, being worn in the room.

Aleksandra froze, then ducked away from his arm, knocking her chair over backwards as she scrambled out of his way. She bolted for the door, but the blond's accomplice grabbed her from behind.

'My friend wants to talk to ya,' he menaced into Aleksandra's ear. He held Aleksandra by the upper arms, facing away from him. 'Hey Boss, the little mannerless boy is waitin' for ya! What d'ya want me to do with him?'

The big lout turned toward her, lost his balance and tripped over the chair abandoned by Aleksandra. By the look on his face, he got up angrier than he went down.

'You little, grrr...' He roared, brows lowered, and headed for her, fists raised. Aleks suddenly seemed to be outside herself, looking down.

There was a grubby urchin held by the arms, being rapidly approached by a heavy locomotive, snorting steam from its stack, arms waving like a windmill. The urchin cracked his shot glass on the table and waited for the onslaught.

The drunken train managed a few punches at the urchin's face. The other lads weren't game to interfere with the heaving brute himself, though one had the presence of mind to run from the room yelling Jake's name above the tumult.

Aleksandra's aggressor's aim wasn't all it could have been, nonetheless, he wasn't about to stop punching her. The red color of the blood flowing down his arms, however, must have penetrated the fog in his brain. He stopped short, staring at the cuts he was too drunk to feel, brows furrowing.

The blond's sidekick gripping her arms suddenly released her. 'He cut me, he cut me!' he screeched.

She ran.

Straight out the doors.

Straight into someone standing in the doorway.

6

The body held her fast, whispering roughly for her to keep quiet, while she was bustled into a darkened gap a few feet away. Aleksandra heard a bolt slide home, then her heart froze in her chest at the sound of shouting men, squealing saloon doors and heavy boots at a run outside the door. As they slowly faded into the distance, she took a deep breath and looked around her in the darkness.

The grate of a stove scraped open, showing a glowing bed of coals. Its light revealed her savior as the brunette from the saloon.

The woman set a twig atop the coals and lit the lamp. Its warm glow delineated the face of a woman not many years older than herself. Once she would have been a beauty, but already she showed the effects of too many years in her profession. From afar she was lovely, but close up, the pox marks couldn't be hidden by powder.

It was just a matter of time.

She shuddered, thinking of her impetuous dash toward the saloon upon her arrival in Camp Floyd, and of the man who stopped her.

'Are you alright?' The brown haired woman looked into Aleksandra's eyes, her brow furrowed.

'Yes, thanks to you, Madam,' she replied in her deepest voice, though it seemed to come from outside herself.

She chuckled under her breath. 'I am Desiree and you are certainly not a boy, but I won't let anyone in on our secret. Do you have a name?'

'Aleksandra.' She sighed and rubbed her stinging cheek.

'I'd imagine you have hair under that hat, no?'

'Mmmm… why did you help me?' Aleksandra hung her head, already pounding with pain from the blond's punches, despite the vodka fog.

'I saw you weren't what you seemed and knew you had reasons for your charade,' she said, then paused, considering. She dragged two chairs before the fire. 'Sit, please.'

Aleksandra wiped the blood off of her face with her sleeve, wincing when she touched her painful cheek.

Desiree took a deep breath and put a hand on Aleksandra's shoulder. 'When my family was taken by a fever on the trip west, I was raped and left for dead by an enemy of my brother. I survived and went on, masquerading as a boy, but when my girl's body was discovered beneath the boy's clothes, unfortunately I had not your skill with cut glass.' She raised an eyebrow and gave Aleksandra a wry grin. 'I was passed from hand to hand until I ended up here.' She sighed, elbows on knees, staring into the fire. 'Now I have enough to eat and God knows, a dry bed, though I rarely get to sleep in it,' she whispered, closing her eyes and shuddering. 'I didn't want the same to happen to you, so here we are.'

Aleksandra saw the pain in her eyes. Leaning forward, she wrapped her arms around Desiree and they both wept until their tears were gone. It was the first time since her papa's death that Aleksandra had allowed herself the luxury.

'Well, what now?' Aleksandra finally said, in a small voice, and sat up.

'Those bullies will hardly remember you tomorrow. They have few, if any, friends, but you'd best get out of town after the glass cuts. You could be in for some trouble.'

'Are you okay here, would you like to come with me? I'm to ride for the Pony…' Aleksandra hesitated, knowing it could never work.

'I'm living on borrowed time, Aleksandra. You see what I have become, I saw you looking at the marks on my face. I can live with this for a little longer.' Desiree gave her a brave smile, but tears brimmed in her eyes and her reddened fingers shook as they held Aleksandra's. 'I'd only slow you down, and then they'd have two victims.' Her voice trailed off as she looked at the dirt floor.

'I don't know how to thank you for saving me and talking with me,' Aleksandra said, gripping Desiree's hands tightly.

'Your safety is thanks enough. You've helped my heart, letting me cry with someone who cares. Perhaps Providence will let you help another in your turn.'

Hugging each other again, they moved to the door. Desiree unbolted it and peeked out. Exiting, she closed the door and returned a few minutes later.

'They've gone and the place is quiet. Your friends are back drinking in the saloon. You'd best disappear while you can.'

'Desiree, thank you from the bottom of my heart. I'll never forget you.'

'It was more my pleasure than yours. Take good care of yourself, little one.' She kissed Aleksandra's forehead and opened the door. 'Now, *run*.'

She ran as if her life depended upon it. Aleksandra's chest was heaving, her head pounding, by the time she pushed open the bunkhouse door. She lit a lantern with a splinter of wood from the woodstove, grabbed her already-packed bag and bolted for the barn. Dzień whickered to her as she entered his stall.

'Well boy, here go again,' she said, dropping the poles of his stall. He pushed his muzzle against her bruised cheek, then snorted at the blood while Aleksandra yelped in pain. Through her tears, she pulled his tack off the wall, bridled him and placed the saddle on his back.

Her injuries stung, but she knew the tears were mostly self-pity, for leaving a man she was beginning to like a great deal more than she probably should. One strong enough to withstand her moods and deal with her impetuous nature, but not constrain her for his own vanity.

Her loneliness was acute, but she couldn't risk letting herself fall for someone. Not now, not ever. She had Papa's secret to protect, and there wasn't room for anything else in her life. She reached under

Dzień, pulled the cinch around his barrel and whipped the *latigo* through the ring.

The pony's ears pricked as he swung his head around towards the doorway.

7

Xavier found Aleksandra in the stable saddling an already-bridled Dzień by the light of a shielded lantern, working like the barn was on fire. He leaned against the gatepost awaiting her attention, his brows drawn together and lips pursed. She'd never gone out after dark before.

Nothing could have prepared him for the sight of her face when Dzień swung his head around and Aleksandra startled, spinning to face him. Eyes wide open and cheeks glistening with tears, she stared at him, blood seeping from grazed bruises on her swollen cheek and nose. What he'd planned to say to her before she turned around just fell out of his mouth...at the same time as her hat fell off, golden curls tumbling down around her body.

'*¿Donde*—where the hell have you been and just where do you think—?' He stopped, shocked at his own words and at her disfigured face, contrasting sharply with her glittering locks, then rattled on '—and your hair?'

While he stood there gaping, the girl grabbed her kitbag, swung up and kicked Dzień straight towards him.

Recovering his senses as she tried to squeeze past him through the gateway, he grabbed the reins with one hand and her leg with the other, halting the skittering, wild-eyed pony in his tracks.

'Let me *go*!' She grunted and squirmed, trying to make Dzień move, but Xavier held them both tightly. He blinked at the alcoholic fumes drifting toward him and frowned. Aleksandra swallowed and went silent as she looked into his eyes. She shuddered and then seemed to soften, making no sound as he slowly drew her from the now-quiet horse and held her at arm's length, studying her face. He forced his tense jaw to relax and took a deep breath. Turning her face from side to side with the light touch of a finger, he glared at the bruises and abrasions.

'Who did this to you?' he bit out, word by word.

'No one of consequence. It's done. I need to leave.' Her chest heaving, she stared at him and tried to pull away again, but less spiritedly this time.

'I'll tear him apart, limb-by-limb. Who was it?'

'No! I've got to leave before they find…' She glanced towards the stable door.

'You're going nowhere, *mi querida*,' he said, brows narrowing. He'd never seen her hair unbound before, and the lamplight set the glorious tresses afire. Though nearly undone by the rare and abundant display of femininity before him, his overpowering thought was still of revenge against those who'd abused her. With an angry curse, he moved a step back and refocused his view on her face, then stroked her undamaged cheek.

She turned her head and looked at him sideways in fear, or dismay, he wasn't sure which.

She's hurt, vulnerable and now I'm pushing myself upon her. His mind raced. *I wasn't meant to get involved. What am I doing?*

Neither of them took any account of the dun pony standing guard at the stable door, but now he whuffled softly in their direction, nosing the man's shoulder as Xavier and Aleksandra stared at each other

'You're injured, I'm angry and I want to kill whoever hurt you,' Xavier murmured and brushed his hair back with one hand. 'We need to be on the road early, so it might be time for you to get to bed.'

'I need to go, I cannot be found here—'

Eyebrow raised, he waited.

'Ah…mmm…there was a wee bit of…an…altercation.' Her voice dropped to a whisper.

'Oh no, Aleksandra. What have—'

'—I cut someone.' She was barely audible. 'They made me drink… it was two drunken men against me…one was holding me…and I had a broken glass…'

Silence. He sighed and shook his head at his recalcitrant charge.

'*Dios mío*, Aleksandra. I guess we'd better make ourselves scarce. Are you really all right?'

Aleksandra's hands shook, but she gave him a wan smile and nodded her head. After scanning the surrounds outside the barn door, Xavier hurried her across the yard to his room to rest.

'We leave as soon as I've packed,' he murmured and slipped out the door into the night.

MUZZLE TENSED, Dzień peered around at Aleksandra when she asked him to walk out of the cozy barn in the wee small hours of the morning, but he moved off, carefully picking his way amongst the rocks on the narrow path skirting the sleeping town and fort. The moonlight through the bare branches of the tall cottonwoods showed their trail well, but it also made the two horses and riders more visible to anyone watching. They held their silence.

Xavier reined in to wait for Aleksandra when they reached the main trail west, then they rode abreast, Dzień settling into his strong walk beside Xavier's big stallion.

'*Digame, por favor*—, sorry, wrong language.' He shook his head. 'So how about you tell me what happened tonight?'

Silence.

Just where to start?

When she reached the part about Desiree taking her in, he smiled and shook his head.

'What?'

'Hmmm? What do you mean?'

'Do you know her?' Aleksandra scowled into the darkness, at the same time feeling guilty for her pettiness, especially in light of Desiree's kindness.

'She's a lovely woman who's had a hard time in life. I have spent time talking—'

'Is talking what men do with saloon women?' she interrupted testily.

'—with her. Talking, Aleksandra. Her history I am not prepared to discuss now, but suffice it to say I understand her past and was happy to talk with her. I have an aversion to abuse, which we will discuss another time. It's not safe to talk right now.' The finality of his speech kept her silent for some time.

'Xavier?' She looked down at her hands, barely visible in the moonlight upon the reins. 'I'm sorry, both to you and Desiree. She didn't need to help me and neither do you. I appreciate what both of you have done for me. I just wanted you to know.'

Riding closer to her, he reached out and gently squeezed her hand, then let go and kneed his horse away from hers again.

'*Está bien*, Aleks, it's all right. You're welcome.'

She smiled her own thanks into the moonlit night.

As they rode westward towards a pass in the low mountain range, Aleksandra kept peering north, looking for landmarks, and finally sighted the canyon she sought.

'Xavier, look.' She pointed north at a majestic mountain's snowy peak glittering white in the moonlight that towered above the others in the range. 'That's Flat Top Mountain, the highest peak in the Oquirrh Mountains, over ten thousand feet. Papa used to hunt on its slopes.' Aleksandra's voice seemed loud in the stillness of the night. She could almost taste the cool, fresh air from its lofty heights.

'Have you been up it?' His eyebrows shot up.

'Yes, Papa often took me hunting with him, and to Fairfield, which was a beautiful little village only four years ago. When Camp Floyd was built there, he didn't take me anymore. He didn't think a city of seven thousand men and seventeen saloons was an appropriate place for a young lady, no matter how wild.' She looked sideways at him with a grin, then sobered. 'Papa'd be rolling in his grave to have seen me there tonight, alone in a saloon.' She dropped her head and took a deep breath. '"All's well that ends well," as Mama always said.'

Xavier didn't answer, just sat tight-lipped. The silence lengthened.

His only movement was a careful regular scanning of the horizon in all directions.

Now I've angered him. He doesn't think a woman should fight for herself. I'll show him I can take care of myself. If he can give me the silent treatment, I suppose I can do the same.

She gritted her teeth, holding on to her anger to keep the anxiety at bay.

8

X avier's thoughts whirled. This young woman, trained to be as tough as a man—riding, hunting, fighting—and yet still so vulnerable. Where he came from, women were protected and coddled, other than his abused mother and sister, of course, but he wouldn't think of that now. He shook his head.

He'd more than once sworn to protect the helpless from those who would hurt them, and his guilt at allowing Aleksandra to become embroiled in the saloon fight overwhelmed him. And that was *without* allowing her to ride for the Pony. For half an hour, he rode with his mouth set in a grim line, straight as the trail they traversed.

'*Lo siento*. I'm sorry, Aleksandra.' He turned and reached out a hand to her.

Eyebrows raised, she looked at him.

'For not protecting you as I should have done tonight from the men in the barroom.'

Aleksandra stared at him as though he'd grown another head, then laughed. She laughed so hard, holding a hand to her bruised cheek, that he eventually had to join in, until tears ran down both of their faces and the tension melted. Glancing around once more to ensure no one followed, Xavier hopped off his stallion and hugged her.

'Whatever did I say to cause that?' He smiled, looking her in the eyes as he reached over to gently blot the tears from her swollen cheek, then wiped his own on a dusty sleeve.

'I am learning how differently two people can think. I was furious you thought I couldn't, or maybe shouldn't, look after myself in a saloon brawl.' She tipped her head and peeked at him through curling wisps of hair.

'You certainly gave them a run for their money,' he said with a crooked grin as he picked a piece of hay from her hair.

'And all the while, you were angry at yourself for not protecting me. We need to talk more, or we'll never understand each other.'

His answer was to take her in his arms. Holding tightly to each other, they clung together until Charro shoved his nose against Xavier's back and they fell apart, laughing.

'*Está bien*, Charro, it's okay.' He grinned at Aleksandra and looked westward. 'Let's go. That's Five Mile Pass ahead of us. There's a spot up on the ridge near the top where we can see the trail on both sides for miles. We can get some rest there.' Her smile stayed with him long after he mounted his gray and walked ahead of her down the trail.

'YOU SURE CAN PICK 'EM!' Aleksandra breathed up at him as she gazed around and leaned back against him. He wrapped his arms around her, standing on the edge of his cliffside tryst. The landscape shone in the moonlight in all directions, as far as the eye could see. A few pinpricks of light glimmered away to the east, all that remained to them of Camp Floyd.

'*Sí*, yes, I can,' Xavier slowly turned her to face him. When she shifted her gaze to meet his, his eyes glowed in the darkness.

How would she keep this man at bay when he attracted her as much as he did? He moved toward her, but she sidled away, cold fear gripping her heart.

'We'd better picket and feed the horses so they can get some rest,' Aleksandra said over her shoulder, picking up Dzień's reins. 'Would you like to take the first watch, or shall I?' She glanced at the closed look on his face as he tied one end of the picket line to a sage bush. It made her squirm, but she needed to keep her distance, even if he didn't like it. He'd just have to get used to it.

Spreading out their bedrolls, they made a meal of the *burritos* Xavier had carried from Camp Floyd, eating them in the deafening silence. Watching Xavier take his blanket to the vantage point, she shuddered to think they'd nearly embraced again. As much as she might want it, she couldn't have him. Xavier sat down with his back to her and wrapped his arms around his legs, chin on his knees.

'Goodnight, *Querida*.' He didn't even turn to look at her.

'Goodnight.' She curled herself into a little ball in her bedroll.

"What does that mean, "*querida*"?

"Dear one, lover." He said flatly.

She hadn't a clue what to say to that. Her heart was leaden, but she had no choice. She was exhausted, but after that, sleep was a long time coming.

'ALEKS...WAKE UP, *QUERIDA*.' Xavier's voice seemed to come from far away, though she felt a light touch on her cheek.

She turned onto her back, eyes opening to see the outline of the man she'd just left in a dream blocking out the stars.

'Can you take the watch for a few hours so I can sleep? We've got a long day ahead of us and I need to be alert.' His voice came more clearly now.

'Mmm...' She closed her eyes and reached out for him, grasping his hands.

After a few moments, Aleksandra opened her eyes again. Xavier sat beside her, quite close.

'You've had a good sleep, I can see.' He smiled down at her and glanced around them once again. 'As much as I'd like to sit up and talk, I need some rest.' His voice faded away again, but he was relentless. 'Aleksandra, did you hear me?'

'Mmm … mmhm … pardon?' She wriggled deeper into her bedroll and blinked up at Xavier.

'Can you watch while I get some rest?'

'Of course.' She sat up, rubbing her eyes. Yawning, she moved away a little when he dropped his *serape* next to hers and lay down and fell asleep instantly. Aleksandra reached out a tentative hand. He didn't awaken, so she gently stroked his luxuriant ebony hair while he slept. With a pang, she wished she were brave enough do it when he was awake.

The eastern sky began to brighten and the chill morning air held the promise of a bright, clear day. The aroma of sage, crushed beneath her bedroll, mixed with the musky scent of the man beneath her hands brought her fully awake. She glanced toward the horses. They watched her intently.

Dzień nodded his head and nickered softly at her. Rising, she wrapped her arms around his neck and rested the side of her face against his warm coat.

It was full light when Xavier awoke, but the dew yet remained on the wisps of dry grass near his head. Motionless, he watched as Aleksandra finished saddling his stallion. The horses contentedly munched in their nosebags, thick winter coats glossy from Aleksandra's early-morning ministrations.

She must have brushed out her own hair, as well. The golden ringlets flowed to her thighs and shone in the morning sun, swinging as she moved. He longed to run his fingers through it and pull her to him.

She disappeared around to Charro's near side. With a final tug on the cinch *latigo*, she gave the stallion a pat on his rump as she rounded his hindquarters and returned to Xavier's full view.

He followed the young woman with his eyes as she scanned the distant plains below them, taking handfuls of her own lovely mane to braid it up for the day. Charro noticed Xavier move and shifted his gaze to him, swinging his head around. Aleksandra turned.

Xavier looked into her eyes. They were soft this morning and she looked at him with a wistful smile as she came to him, dropping to her knees, still braiding.

'Leave be.' He took her hands from her all too rapidly developing braid. Eyebrows raised, she tilted her head sideways at him as he lifted the fine strands with his fingertips, watching the molten tresses spill over his hands as they slid from their bondage.

He'd never seen it down loose in the sunlight before. Imagination captured, he slid his fingers through it and around the back of her head, cradling her as he pulled her down on top of him. Her eyes snapped fully open and she began to pull away.

'*Querida*, shhh ...' He softly stroked her hair and she relented, still tense, but not yet in flight.

'Shhh. I won't hurt you. What are you afraid of?'

'I'm just afraid.'

'Of?'

'That I might want you too much, and...'

He waited.

'If I...If I...' Her face flushed and she held her breath as tears began to course over her bruised and battered cheeks. 'Oh, Papa.' She closed her eyes, then opened them again, biting her lip. 'I will fail him, I just cannot...he died for his secret.' She slid off Xavier and curled up in a ball, her head on his chest, and sobbed. He sat up and pulled her onto his lap, then looked down at her, brow furrowed. Would he ever comprehend her moods? One minute passionate, the next evasive, then desolate.

Perhaps it is for the best. I'll never trust a woman again.

Taking a deep breath, Xavier held her until her tears stopped and her breathing quieted. How he wanted to trust her.

'Are you ready to tell me what is bothering you, *Querida*?'

'Soon, maybe,' she mumbled against his damp chest.

'Very well, as you're not ready to speak of it yet, we'd best head off. The horses look lovely, thank you, Aleks...as do you.'

Her brow wrinkled slightly, but her smile still shone from under her lashes.

She sat up beside him and they shared the briefest of kisses.

'Okay now?'

'Yes, thank you.' She sighed and stood, her hands reaching behind her head to resume her plaiting.

'So how did you cut your hair, and—'

Aleksandra smiled as she lifted the heavy tresses above her head to show him the thin fringe of shorter hair beneath the rest.

'Ah, now I see, and I also see the need for the hat. I like it even less, now I know what it hides.' He grinned and kissed her again. 'You're an amazing woman.'

'That hat has its uses,' she said, cocking a single brow, and gave him a crooked smile.

'*Bien*.' Xavier said. He packed up his bedroll, tying it behind the cantle of his saddle. 'Doc Faust, the keeper at Rush Valley, makes the best breakfast you've ever eaten. If we trot a bit, we should be there in a couple of hours, just in time to eat.'

Her eyes lit at that. 'So Fish Springs is about 70 miles from here?' She tightened the cap of her canteen.

'Yes, there's about ten hours of trail after Faust's, at a walk—' He hesitated, then clamped his mouth shut.

Best to take our time and spare the horses, in case we need to outrun Indians... but I guess she already knows that.

'Where will we spend the night?'

'We need to get to the top of Dugway Pass tonight,' Xavier said, sliding his hand beneath Charro's cinch. 'I don't fancy sleeping out on the open flats with the *Pah-Utes* on the warpath.'

'Me either,' Aleksandra said, her jaw tense.

'All going well, we should ride into Fish Springs the following morning.'

'Sounds good,' she threw over her shoulder, swinging up onto her pony. 'Dzień should be able to handle the extra weight he's carrying on this trip at that easy pace.' She flashed a grin down at him. 'A bit different from Charro. I don't think he'd even notice if you filled your bedroll with rocks.'

Slinging a canteen over one side of the horn and his *pemmican* bag on the other, he checked his saddlebag ties and mounted the gray.

The trail sloped down gradually from Five Mile Pass toward the flats stretching ahead of them.

'How many Pony stations are there between St. Joseph and San Francisco?' Aleksandra cocked her head.

'180-odd stations over the 1900 miles of the trail, give or take a station on the day.'

She was silent for a moment. 'Umm … and there are Home Stations every seventy miles?

He nodded.

'Then there should be around … twenty-seven Home Stations?'

He glanced at her. 'You're fast. I thought you didn't go to school.'

'I didn't, but Mama and Papa had exceptional educations and they taught us. My mathematics were mostly learnt from Papa while we checked trap lines. Mama only had to chain me to the table for my written lessons.' She grinned at him, then sobered. 'They wanted me to go to a university someday,' she whispered, looking at the ground, before closing her eyes.

Xavier changed the subject before her tears flowed again.

'Yes, there were 157 Relay Stations and twenty-seven Home Stations at last count.'

She looked at him, brow furrowed, then she gave him the ghost of a smile.

Taking a deep breath, Aleksandra looked up, jaw set and eyes dry. 'Does the trail follow the California Trail along the Humboldt?'

'No, it goes along Captain Simpson's Central Overland Route.'

She was quiet for a moment. 'Bet I'll be pleased to see a Home Station bed and hot meal waiting after a seventy mile run.'

'When there's someone *there* at the end of the—' Xavier said, before he thought. His stomach clenched and he averted his eyes, thinking of dead keepers and run-off stock…and of Aleksandra's new position.

From the corner of his eye, Xavier watched her bite her lip and look down into Dzień's mane, all signs of mirth gone.

'I'm regretting I let you get yourself into this.' Xavier rubbed his eyes. 'It wouldn't be so dangerous if the idiots out at Williams hadn't kidnapped and raped those two *Pah-Ute* girls last week.' The blood began to pound in his head at the thought. He began to see red, but managed to stop himself before the anger took over.

Aleksandra spun to face Xavier, staring at him. 'What happened?'

'There was another letter in the envelope from Superintendent Egan. I only found it while you were out riding yesterday.'

She looked at him, eyes wide, and her mouth dropped open. 'The poor girls, are they back with their families or, or—' She fell silent, tears pooling in her eyes. 'Are they still alive?'

'*Ojalá que sí.* I hope so, but it's war now. You can't blame the

Indians for retaliating. Six days after the girls went missing, someone from their tribe heard the girls crying in a dugout at the Williams stage station.'

'Six *days*?' She wrung the fringe of her buckskins with her free hand as a tear rolled down her face.

'*Sí, Querida*. They rescued the girls, killed the stationmaster and two other men, drove off the stock and burned the station. One of the men from the station escaped and ran to Virginia City, where they put together a rag-tag, untrained militia of 105 men. They ran straight into an ambush and most of them died.'

'They would have been at the annual meeting of the tribes when the girls were found,' Aleksandra said, shutting her eyes. 'The *Pah-Utes*, *Bannocks* and *Shoshone*—'

'It's truly started this *Pah-Ute* War, into which I am dropping you,' he said, swearing under his breath with disgust, directed mostly at himself for not dissuading her from riding for the Pony.

Aleksandra sat motionless, wide eyes staring off into the distance, then went on as if she hadn't heard his last statement. '—and that was on top of a heavy winter, while the settlers took so much of the food and timber the Indians needed to survive.'

'Chief Numaga of the *Pah-Utes* was the only reason the Indians have waited so long. He fasted and argued for peace. This incident with the girls was the last straw.'

Aleksandra rode close to him. He took the hand she silently offered.

'It wasn't a Pony Express agent who did the deed at Williams,' he said, 'but the Pony, with so many riders and so much stock to support, wouldn't have helped the Indians survive this winter either.' Xavier looked down at Charro's mane and squeezed Aleksandra's hand.

'No.' Her brow furrowed. We're also an easy target, with solitary stations and predictable runs. My having grown up with the *Shoshone* won't make any difference to the *Pah-Utes*...and it certainly won't be much use against an arrow.'

9

Snatching at any grass within reach, the horses picked their way down the grade from the top of the pass. Aleksandra gazed out into the distance across the floor of Rush Valley, thinking of the tortured girls and the *Pah-Ute* War, wondering if she'd always have to be as watchful for blond Russians and hostile Indians as she was right now.

'Is that a station, Xavier?' She nodded west to a small square in the center of the huge, flat valley.

'*Un mommmennto...* just a seconnn ...' Xavier mumbled, tugging at a knot in the top of a pouch with his teeth. 'Got it. The slipknot turned into a knot.' He shook his head and grinned. '*Ahora, donde?* Sorry, where?'

Aleksandra pointed.

'Yes, East Rush Valley. It's only a small Relay Station, really just a dugout.' Loosening the top of the sack, he offered it to Aleksandra. 'Some *pemmican* to tide you over until breakfast?'

'I've had enough of it in the past month to never want it again,' she chuckled, 'but yes, please.'

Scattered wisps of fog remained when they reached the level plain, and the smell of sage permeated the chill morning air.

'Lonely place,' Aleksandra said, looking around her. The empty landscape went on forever—nothing bigger than hand-sized rocks, clumps of dry buffalo grass, and sparse sage-brush, with the trail cutting a straight line down the middle.

'It only seems that way, *Querida*. Look more closely.' He waggled an eyebrow at her and grinned.

'True,' she said. A small movement caught her attention. 'Lizards, sunning on that rock—' She whipped her heavy braid around and looked the other way. '—and rabbit pellets and owl scats,' she said with a laugh.

Xavier pointed out a hawk playing on the wind currents seeking breakfast, maybe even Aleksandra's lizards.

'Oh Xavier, the does and young bucks!' Aleksandra breathed and motioned with one finger at the frozen herd watching them from south of the trail.

'It's teeming with life. First perceptions are deceptive.' He raised an eyebrow at her.

She warmed beneath his perusal. Shaking her head, she took a quick breath. 'Yes, Papa said that, too.'

'It's easy to become complacent in the absence of threat, but there are Indians hidden in that landscape, make no mistake. We need to be watchful and pay attention to anything that doesn't seem right.'

'Papa always said "Listen to your gut feelings, they'll keep you alive."' Her eyes brimmed and she gulped, looking at Xavier. She reached for him as he rode up close beside her. '*Why* didn't they keep him alive?' The last came out on a sob.

They stopped, arms clasped about each other for long minutes, until her tears ceased.

Xavier gently detached himself and looked into her eyes, wiping the tears from her cheeks. 'You haven't really grieved yet, have you, *Querida*? You've had to be strong for so long. I'll shoulder some of your load when you wish it, remember that.'

She mutely nodded, wiping her nose on her buckskin sleeve. Inhaling deeply, she sat up straight and kissed his hand, which she still gripped.

'Here, we're nearly to the station. You'd best put your hair up into that disgusting hat,' said softly. 'Wouldn't want the station keeper getting any ideas about the new Pony rider.'

She smiled through her tears, but the sorrowful feelings still threatened to engulf her. 'I don't seem to be able to stop crying. I'm sorry Xavier.'

'If it helps, you're beautiful, even when you're crying. Now get that hair up, before I start getting ideas.' He shot her a lewd grin and sat back, watching her. 'That hat, wherever did you find it?'

She grimaced, then grinned. 'It was my brother's pride and joy. I wear it for him, and, of course, it's the only hat big enough to hide this great rope of hair.' She smiled as she rolled the thick braid and stuffed it beneath the cowboy hat.

'It's a big one, to be sure.'

'I'm not sure why it's called a "ten gallon" hat, though,' she said. 'You can't tell me it will hold ten gallons of water, so it *must* be something else.'

'I think it's an Anglicism of "*galones,*" the ribbons Spanish cowboys wear around their hats.'

'That makes more sense, a ten-ribbon hat.' Aleksandra nodded her head at the East Rush Valley Station, just visible ahead of them. 'Shall we announce ourselves, rather than become morning target practice?'

'Good idea.'

'You couldn't blame them for being a bit trigger-happy lately.' She raised an eyebrow.

'HELLO, ANYONE THERE AT THE STATION?'

A man peered around the corner of the dugout. 'Xavier, is it? Good morning!' he shouted. 'All quiet out there?' The gnarled stationmaster's brow furrowed and he pursed his lips as they dismounted and led their horses to the front of the dugout.

'We've seen no trace, but then we've just only come from Floyd. You'll have heard about Cold Springs and Smith's Creek?'

His face falling, he nodded. 'Bless 'em. Hope the Indians've done their dash fer awhile.'

Xavier made introductions and offered the man a quid of tobacco.

The man nearly danced a jig, holding the sticky plug before him.

'Thank ye much, Xavier, t'baccy's hard to come by!'

Xavier laughed. 'Great little stationhouse, this. Who built it?'

'Mr. Egan and his men brought in the poles and brush last summer and we started diggin'. Took five of us 'bout four days t' dig, lucky there wasn't too many big rocks. We dug it big enough t' make a room fer me 'n a stable fer a few horses 'n cows.' He chuckled. 'Bein' underground 'n havin' the animals inside sure keeps it warm when its covered with snow!'

Aleksandra repressed a shudder, thinking of the smell.

'How'd you roof it?' Xavier rested his hand on a log extending out from the top of a wall and peered underneath it.

'We put in a couple o' supports 'n laid logs over the top, covered 'em with brush 'n plastered mud over the lot. Keeps the water out 'n the heat in. Holds the snow okay, too.'

'I guess you'd—' Aleksandra grimaced, remembering too late to lower her voice. She continued in a gruffer one. '—you'd want to keep the building down low, with no trees to break the wind out here.'

'Yep, you got it, young man!' The station keeper laughed.

'Thanks for that, we'll be on our way. I want to make Dugway tonight, so we can shelter in the trees at the top of the pass, up off the flats.'

'Best o' luck to ye two, then. Lookin' forward t' seein' ye come flyin' through on yer runs, young man. Hold on tight to yer scalps, ye hear?' He nodded in emphasis.

'Thank you, sir, we will,' Aleksandra's best man-voice rang out.

Xavier grinned and waved back at the lone man in the doorway. Swinging up, they left the yard and headed west down the big valley toward the rolling hills.

'This meadow sure is green, and just look at the creek!' The horses eyed it, ears pricked, and increased their pace.

'I think that's Meadow Creek, fancy calling it that,' Xavier said dryly. 'Rush Valley Station is a mile after we cross it. It'll be good to see Doc. I haven't seen him in months.'

'Do you know him well?'

He nodded. 'He's one interesting man. I've stayed with him a few times.'

'Is he a doctor?'

'Sort of. He dropped out of medical school in Germany to seek his fortune in the California gold fields, then started raising horses for the U.S. Army. Now he's a station keeper and sometimes rides as well. He still raises horses and supplies quite a few of the stations with hay.'

'He's the best doctor we've got, whether you're white or Indian, and knows a lot about medicines and local history.'

After taking a long drink, Dzień stepped carefully through the rocky creek bed and up onto the opposite bank. Swinging his head up, ears pricked, he whinnied.

'He misses little, eh?' Xavier reached out to rub the dun's neck. 'He must smell the other horses on the breeze.'

'Yep, one smart Indian pony.' Aleksandra smiled at her favourite two males, the one with little dark ears pricked west and the one astride the stallion by her side.

Xavier beamed down at her, taking her hand as they rode. She smiled back, feeling her heart would burst, wishing her father could see her happiness.

Maybe he did, just maybe he did.

She turned in her saddle, once again, to survey the surroundings. The little horse kept a good lookout, but she needed to keep watch, else Pa died to no purpose. That didn't bear thinking about.

IN THE DISTANCE, Aleksandra saw a mixed bag of ten horses before a big log building with a low, pitched roof. They stood against a corral rail, staring at them. The horses whinnied, and more horses appeared, peering around the corner of the building from another corral behind it, while two men cautiously entered the yard and looked their way.

'*Hola*, Doc! Hello!' Xavier wasn't taking any chances.

'Is that young Xavier? Good to see you, Son!' A wide grin split the speaker's face as he strode toward them.

'Nice to be welcomed!' Aleksandra grinned at Xavier. 'You must have made a good impression on your last visit.'

Doc nearly jogged the last steps between them, grasping Xavier's hand and shaking it vigorously.

'Charro, my fine lad, you're looking well,' he said to the gray stallion as he stroked his neck. Glancing over his withers, he saw Aleksandra, then cocked his head and looked again.

'And this is …?'

'*Lo siento*, I am sorry, this is Aleks—'

'Hello, Aleks, nice to meet you.'

'Nice to meet you too, sir.' She extended her hand to him. He nearly rattled her teeth in his enthusiasm.

'Are you two just passing through, or have you come to stay and help run this place?'

Aleksandra's eyebrows shot up as she turned to Xavier.

'Aleks doesn't know I worked here with you summer before last.' He chuckled.

'I was trying to put this homestead together, all 160 acres of it, when this Godsend of a man showed up. I couldn't have done it without him.'

'Course, you could've, I'm sure I was just in the way!' Shaking his head, Xavier looked pleased all the same. He glanced into the open door of the station.

Doc saw the direction of his gaze. 'Righto, Xavier, yes, breakfast is ready. You always *did* know when it was mealtime.' He shook his head, grinning widely.

'We'd be happy to accept.' Xavier smiled sideways at Aleksandra.

'Sam will take your horses.' Doc turned to the young man. 'The gray has his own pen down the end.'

Sliding off their horses, they handed them to the waiting man, with thanks.

'So, how long are you two here for?'

'Not long, sorry, Doc. We're headed for Fish Springs. I'm to become station keeper, and Egan's moved Mr. Smith down the line to try to cover more stations. Young Aleks will be riding for the Pony out of there.'

Doc looked at her and shook his head, his brow wrinkled as he looked at her from beneath bushy brows.

Aleksandra froze and felt goosebumps on the back of her neck.

He knows I'm a girl.

'You must be the new rider that saved that Express pony up in Mountain Dell,' he said with a grin.

She let out her breath and the blood pounding in her ears receded.

'Old Ephraim sent a message for me to keep an eye out for you, and give you any help you need. So you got the job, did you?'

'Yes,' she replied faintly, her heart still hammering.

'Aleks is the best rider I've ever seen, Cossack trained. You should see he—, him ride.' Doc smiled at them, then pursed his lips, a slight frown creasing his forehead.

Sam entered the station as Doc stabbed a big fork into the crusty meat. He sawed away at it with his sheath knife.

'Sam, Xavier and Aleks are good friends of mine.' He waved his fork at them, by way of an introduction, then heaped eggs and slabs of salt pork onto their plates.

'Knew I had to come back for a reason,' Xavier said, inhaling deeply over his plate.

'So, Aleks, I hear you're a healer.' Doc sat down and looked at her squarely. 'Ephraim was a bit worried, at first, not knowing you and all, but he's pleased as punch now. Where did you learn your skills?'

He nodded appreciatively while she told him.

'Well done. The pony was trotting around his corral, last I heard.'

As Xavier raised an eyebrow at her, she remembered she hadn't told him about the horse.

Doc turned to Xavier. 'So you're heading straight on? I know Egan's been keen to have Smith's replacement at Fish Springs as soon as possible.'

'Yes, sorry we can't stay. I wouldn't miss the chance to see you, and of course,' he grinned, 'your breakfast.'

'Never a problem for you and yours, Xavier, you know that, but you'll need to see Charro's get before you leave.'

Aleksandra swung around to face Doc. 'Charro's foals? How old are they?'

'They were foaled in July, so about nine months old, Xavier?'

'How many?' Aleksandra practically bounced on her seat.

Luckily, I'm meant to be a boy, so I can wolf my breakfast and get out to the foals.

'Four colts and three fillies. Nicer foals out of my Canadian thoroughbred mares I've never seen. Xavier, you're sitting on a goldmine with that horse.'

Xavier glowed. He loved the horse to distraction, and it showed. Aleksandra smiled at him.

'We'll go see them after we finish what the good Lord has

provided.' Doc jerked his head at Aleks and proceeded to say grace, finishing with thanks for watching over his guests on their journeys.

'EVEN IN THEIR WINTER WOOLLIES, they're stunning. Doc, you're a master,' Aleksandra breathed, after one filly exchanged breaths with her. 'This is how all horses should be raised.'

'Sam and I did it together,' Doc said, looking at the ground with a crooked smile.

'I know the time and effort it takes to make a foal fearless and happy to leave its dam on a lead. You two are to be commended,' she said with a short bow, clicking her heels.

'These foals are worth the effort, but thank you, Aleks.' Doc raised an eyebrow and smiled at her. 'Xavier, I was going to give you one of the foals as fee for Charro's efforts, but with the quality of these horses, I owe you two.'

'Not necessary, Doc.'

'Oh yes, it is. They are worth that much more for me to sell than the others I've bred. They will be in high demand for army officer's horses, but I'll keep this colt for my own,' he said, rubbing the powerful-looking foal next to him, a black with white hairs already showing through. 'He'll be gray, like Charro. My new foundation sire.' Doc beamed. 'I appreciate the opportunity to breed with him and don't you ever forget it, Xavier.'

'I'm not sure what I'll do with two young horses right now.' Xavier raised a brow at Aleksandra.

'They'll be fine here until the end of the summer, when you might be heading home.'

Xavier's head dropped. 'Don't have a home,' he mumbled somewhere towards the floor.

Aleksandra stared at him, too shocked to breathe, as he seemed to shrink into himself, then the shadow was gone.

What is this?

It disappeared so suddenly she wondered if she'd imagined it.

'Well, you know where they'll be,' Doc's voice cut in. 'Which two do you want?'

'Aleks, you're a good judge of horses, you help me choose,' Xavier said, then took a deep breath.

She glanced at him, then moved amongst the foals and their good-natured dams.

'Fillies or colts?' She cocked her head at Xavier.

'What do you think?'

She pursed her lips and completed her appraisal of the youngsters, then turned to Xavier. 'It makes little sense to have a mare about, if you are to ride Charro, especially if I find Pa's colt. Two colts, perhaps? You could keep the best as a stallion for when Charro is older, that is, unless you plan to return home, and then you might want a mare to breed—' She stopped dead, staring at him, wide-eyed, as his shoulders hunched and his eyes glazed over, retreating behind a wall.

'Well, you don't have to decide now.' Doc filled the silence. 'We'll talk about this later, when they're a mite older. None of them will go before July and not without you making your choice.' Doc's forehead furrowed as he looked at Aleksandra behind the bowed head of Xavier and shook his head.

'So Xavier, how far do you plan to go today?' Doc brusquely moved to turn the foals free and Aleksandra followed suit.

Xavier shivered and sighed, then looked at them, his eyes seeming to clear. '*Perdón, repítalo*, I'm sorry, again please?'

Xavier slowly answered Doc's repeated question.

'Well then, as much as I'd like to keep you two here, I'd better let you get on.' Doc looked sideways at Aleksandra. 'Did he tell you he's the best worker I ever had here?' he said to her in a loud aside.

Glancing at Xavier out of the corner of her eyes, she grinned. 'No, I don't believe he mentioned it.'

'Well, he is that,' Doc said with finality.

'I wouldn't doubt that for a moment.' Aleksandra couldn't help shaking her head and smiling at them both.

'You'd best be off. It's a long ride to Dugway and I'd not see you sleep out there without shelter tonight,' Doc said, ushering them towards their own horses.

10

The track ran straight as an arrow across the flats for five miles, then rose toward General Johnston's Pass through the next mountain range.

'Amazing view.' Aleksandra looked back over her shoulder down toward Rush Valley. Dzień picked his way around the bigger stones on the wagon road.

'And it gets better. Have you been up here?'

'No, but Pa spoke of it.' Aleksandra peered around the sweeping bend in the trail before them.

'Some of the Express riders are calling it "Lookout Pass", maybe a reminder to "look out" for highwaymen and Indians.'

'I can see that.' The narrow pass was perfectly designed for ambuscade. During the mile-long ascent, they both continually scanned the close-in hillsides, watching their horses' ears for any hint of danger. Sparse mountain cedars, cheat grass and sage dotted the rocky slopes above them. Aleksandra shuddered.

Not a place to be riding in the dark.

Sliding off Dzień's saddle, she climbed the road beside him as it steepened towards the top of the pass.

Although she was warm from her climb, the cooler air at the

summit stung Aleksandra's lungs. Stopping for a break, she stared out at the panorama of desert and mountains

'This is Point Lookout. We're at just over 6000 feet.'

'Oh,' she said, 'the other reason for the name—Lookout Pass, what a view.' She smiled and took a deep breath to fill her lungs with the thin air, glancing at the rock-strewn descent of the trail ahead of them, then turned toward the north.

'Those are the Onaqui Mountains,' Xavier said, following her gaze.

'Aah. Pa brought me a fossil from one of those caves up there, then.' Pointing to the rocky ledges before her, she slowed her breathing with effort. 'South of this pass the range becomes the Sheeprock Mountains, if I remember right.'

Xavier stopped in his swing from the north to the south. 'Think you're right. Look back, Aleks, three matching summits!'

Smiling at his exuberance, she twisted to face the high peaks. 'There's still a fair bit of snow on them for May.'

'Yes.' He glanced around with wrinkled brows at the darkening skies. 'Now you mention it, the air feels like it could snow here, too. Let's get a move on.'

Turning, she led Dzień down the precipitous grade. The pony was negotiating a loose bit of trail as the first snowflakes fell. They hurried as much as they dared to get to Lookout Station before the snow worsened. Aleksandra giggled, sticking out her tongue to catch the falling flakes.

'You warm enough?' Xavier grinned and shook his head at her antics.

'Nose and fingers are cold, but the rest of me is warm.' She beamed at him, dancing sideways down the trail. Dzień ignored her and trotted on responsibly, keeping to his side of the trail. 'Soon we'll have numb fingers and slippery wet reins,' her grin turned to a grimace, 'and wet saddles when we get back on.'

Trotting down into a small, cedar-covered valley, Aleksandra's head shot up and she sniffed. 'Smoke,' she said, halting abruptly.

Xavier's brows furrowed as he handed his reins to her and disappeared around the next bend. A few moments later, he was back.

'All clear, it's Lookout's cooking fire.'

Heaving a great sigh, Aleksandra led both horses toward Xavier, then they went on. Smoke curled from the chimney of the station's log house.

'Lovely little cabin. I can't remember when I last saw golden timber.' She raised an eyebrow at him and grinned. 'Everything's usually sun-bleached out here!'

'It was only built a few months ago.' Xavier hallooed to the keeper, then wiped the melting snow from his mustache and forelock with the back of his rein hand, waving to the station keeper as he stepped out the door.

'We'll only stop for a moment here to speak with Mr. Jackson. The flurries are lightening, so we should be okay once we get out of the mountains.'

'The snow's still sticking, but it seems to be lessening,' Aleksandra said, glancing down at the white flakes on their clothing. It covered the horses' toplines and their saddles. She shuddered. Their seats would be wet and cold when they remounted.

'Mr. Jackson, this is Aleks. He'll be riding out of Fish Springs,' Xavier said, as they shook hands.

'Nice to meet you, Mr. Jackson. Excuse me, just one moment.' She turned back to him from where Dzień had just dragged her, trying to reach the new grass at the station's spring. 'Sorry, grass is the one thing he really likes.' Screwing up her face, she gave the keeper a crooked grin.

He laughed. 'Let him have it, it's okay.' He nodded at the grass.

They exchanged information, dusting the snow off their clothes and saddles, thankful it hadn't yet melted. Mounting up, they continued, stopping briefly just northwest of the station to gaze over the panorama of the great valley and desert spread out below them.

'That's the Great Salt Lake Desert?' Aleksandra breathed, awed.

'Yes, we'll be dropping down into Skull Valley soon. It's rapidly becoming known as *Pah-Ute* Hell.'

Skull Valley. Pah-Ute Hell. Ominous.

'I'd hate to be crossing it in a covered wagon.' Aleksandra shuddered, remembering she'd just signed on to race through here on an everyday basis. She started down the trail, dismounting once again to descend another rough grade.

The cedars became fewer and breathing easier as the snow flurries desisted to a wet drizzle, then stopped altogether. Reaching the flats of Skull Valley, bald patches of alkali soil showed amongst the cheat grass and rocks.

'Aleks, have you seen the salt out here?' Still leading his stallion after the steep mountain descent, Xavier pointed out some of the crystals, glistening like diamond-dust, then rubbed his foot over them to reveal oozy mud beneath.

'Mud? I thought it was mostly sand.'

'You usually find alkali dust underneath the crystals. I've never seen it wet before, but it must just be wet alkali dust.'

'At least we don't have to breathe it.'

'True.'

'Look back at the pass.' Aleksandra raised her eyebrows at him. 'Even this side is ambush material.'

'Let's get home,' he said. Mounting up, they trotted on, the sound of their horses' hoofbeats dampened by the wet earth.

'Pronghorns and jackrabbits at three o'clock,' Aleksandra sang out as they rounded the northern end of the Sheeprock Mountains.

'Golden Eagle above.' Xavier pointed at the raptor winging its way across the sky, playing on an updraft.

'Plenty of game out here. We may not see any Indians, but they're there, knowing we're crossing their traditional lands,' Aleksandra said, looking around.

'Mmmm.' he gazed about as well. 'Yes, you can feel eyes.'

Riding down a steep grade into the vast, sage-covered Government Creek Wash, a towering range came into view to the southwest.

'Oh, Xavier, look.' She nodded at it.

'The Simpsons,' he smiled. 'And those,' he pointed at the highest mountains in the range, 'are Indian Peaks. Luckily, the trail goes around their base. It's over 8000 feet to the top.'

'Good thing we don't need to go over.' She laughed.

Lost in their own thoughts, they rode through the sage-brush country in silence, until Xavier turned and looked at her askance.

'Just how many languages do you know, Aleks?'

'Hmmm … Polish, Russian, English and some *Shoshone*. Not a lot of each, but enough to get by.'

'Impressive.' Raising an eyebrow, he nodded.

'Of more importance to me, though,' she murmured, 'is knowing how other people live, like the *Shoshone*. I have a lot of love and respect for the tribes with whom we spent so much time. It can only get worse for them as more settlers come.'

Xavier reached for her hand and held it lightly. She nearly drew it away, but stopped herself, and glanced at him. His eyes searched her face before she returned her gaze to her pony's mane.

'I'm not sure what they're going to do in the long run,' she said, liking the feel of his work-roughened skin against hers. 'They've been moved nearly as far west as they can go. The settlers usually bring any Indian attacks upon themselves, like the fools at Williams.'

'It's the same in Mexico and California with the subjugation of the natives by *los conquistadores*, the Spanish explorers and conquerors.' Xavier shook his head. 'As with the Indians, there's been some inter-racial mixing, but for the most part, those of Spanish descent, my family included,' he grimaced, 'still hold power over the natives. It's changed with the influx of settlers pursuing gold and land, but it's just different people holding the reins. It won't help the *Ohlones* there, or the other Indians.' Xavier's brows lowered, his mouth set in a firm line.

'And therein lie the problems for the Indians,' she said.

'Mmmm. O'Sullivan's Manifest Destiny, the God-given right of the "Americans" to overspread the continent, implies natives are sub-human and of no consequence in his "great experiment of liberty and self-government".'

'So we force them off their lands,' Aleksandra said, her heart heavy, 'lands taken or "purchased" with trinkets, many times without the Indians understanding what was being traded, especially as they didn't consider land to be owned.'

'They are moved to reservations or just moved on. As you say, there is little for them now.' Xavier's eyes were downcast. Taking a deep breath, he looked at her. 'Why did your family come to America?'

She thought for a moment. 'How much have you heard about the European immigrants?'

'Very little, I'm afraid.'

'Papa wanted freedom for his family. In America, the "land of the free", he thought to find freedom from oppression, from a continent mired in discrete class divisions and serfdom as was Europe. Arriving in New York, he was stunned to see the hordes of hungry immigrants,' Aleksandra said faintly. 'They found themselves in a city which had been flooded by millions of immigrants for the preceding twenty years. Work was hard to find and available work approached vassalage. Many of these willing workers were treated as the lowest form of life by those seeking cheap labor. Worse, with no "*noblesse oblige*", as existed in Europe, the employers had little to no responsibility for the care of their laborers.' Aleksandra paused for breath, then continued more steadily. 'Papa's blood ran cold at the reality of slavery and racism against immigrants on that coast, so he took his family west. Luckily, he could turn his hand to just about anything. My grandfather was a physician in the great house of a *szlachta* family, so Papa was given an opportunity rare for one of his class: an education with the children of the house in the classics as well as in hunting and strategic warfare. He'd even begun his training as a physician under his father's tutelage.

'I suppose that's where Vladimir comes into it,' Xavier said, looking up from Charro's mane.

'Yes, he trained him in the arts of war. Although Mama was not trained in warfare beyond self-defense with a knife, she was given the best education money could buy.'

'Hence, your skill with languages?'

'Yes, Mama and Papa spoke Polish, Russian, English, French and German fluently. It was the norm in Europe for their class, or at least for the class of my mother.'

Xavier's brow wrinkled. 'Who was your mother, to have been provided with this learning?'

'Mama was a daughter of the Count, my grandfather.'

He closed his eyes for a moment, then stared at her. 'How did the son of a physician end up married to the daughter of a Count, and why did they leave Europe for this wilderness?'

'Do you know of Poland's history?' Aleksandra raised one eyebrow at him.

'No.'

'It's a long story,' Aleks said quietly.

'And one that will have to wait for another time,' Xavier said as the Government Creek station keeper called out a greeting. Briefly exchanging news, they watered the horses and resumed their way west along Government Creek, then circled north around the end of the Simpson Range.

'Papa spoke of Simpson's Springs.' She smiled wistfully. 'He said it always had plenty of fresh water, willows and even grass in the springtime.'

'The Express station was a stagecoach mail station for years because it has the most dependable water source in this desert.' Xavier grinned, 'It's also the last water for sixty miles, until Fish Springs.'

'How do they water the hors—' She stared at him, her mouth open. 'They *haul* it to the other desert stations?'

'*In* barrels, if you can believe it. Considering how much horses and cattle drink, not to mention people, just hauling it is a full time job.'

'Or two, I'd imagine.'

'And there's your real desert,' Xavier said, pointing west as they crossed the low divides on the north end of the Simpson Range.

Aleksandra's mouth formed an O at the expanse opening up before her.

'That's where we spend the night, all going well.' Xavier nodded his head south-westerly towards the most distant range.

'Where?' Searching the horizon, other than some isolated buttes, it seemed to be only flat desert nearly to infinity, sprouting mountains at its edges.

'At the top of Dugway Pass.'

She sighted along his finger to a narrow gap between the heights of a towering range spreading as far as the eye could see.

'That little valley with the high bit on its right?'

'Yes, it's the Dugway Range on the north and the Thomas Range to the south. That's Pyramid Peak beside it.'

'Good landmarks for riding the Pony, especially when everything is covered in snow.' Aleksandra shook her head.

'It's a straight and level trail from Simpson's to the mountains, with plenty of landmarks: the Simpson Buttes,' he pointed due west, 'and Table Mountain,' he nodded at the massive hill's treeless cone between them and the Dugway Range.

'Doesn't Simpson's have a few different names?'

'The Express contractors call it Simpson's Springs, but the Mormons call it Egan's Springs and still others call it Lost Springs. Take your pick.' Xavier grinned.

A few miles on, the trail bent west and the pale stone walls and log roof of Simpson's Springs Station appeared, outlined in relief against the darker backdrop of the distant mountains and desert.

'You'll like old George. He's a great old sourdough and a real hand with a horse,' Xavier said with smile.

Sourdough...

She let her breath out with a big sigh, remembering.

The first time she'd heard it used as a title, she was just a little girl. Returning home from clearing traps on a snowy December afternoon, Papa met an old prospector riding east, leading a pack mule. He invited the man home to share the fire and Mama's hot supper. Though he smelled like he needed a bath, she liked the grizzled and wrinkled Mr. McIntyre. His eyes glinted merrily when he grinned through his bushy beard, but most especially when he thanked Mama kindly for the antelope stew. Aleksandra thought he looked like Father Christmas, but Papa called him an 'Old Sourdough'.

As little girls were meant to be seen and not heard, especially before company, she couldn't ask the questions she was dying to ask, squirming on the bench seat beside Papa and wringing her skirt in her hands. Just when she thought she would burst, they stopped talking and looked at her expectantly.

'Whatever can the matter be, Aleksandra?' Mama said.

'Isn't sourdough like *zakwas*?' she blurted out.

'Yesss ...' Papa said slowly, brows furrowed, then tilted his head and waited.

Looking first at the *zakwas* pot on its shelf above the stove, then back to their visitor, finally Aleksandra looked at Papa. 'Well, Mr. McIntyre doesn't look anything like *zakwas*!'

Mama, Papa and her brother laughed, but Mr. McIntyre's forehead wrinkled as he looked at her, then grinned.

'Aleksandra,' Mr. McIntyre said, 'the prospect'rs that raced out

West durin' the California gold stampede of 1849 were called "49'ers." They called 'em "Sourdoughs," too.' He reached into the neck of his buckskin shirt and pulled out two leather pouches. The biggest one he placed before Aleksandra.

'Open it and take a sniff,' he said.

She sniffed the bag, wrinkling her nose at the smell of the sweat stained, filthy leather, and Mr. McIntyre laughed. 'Open it, I said, child, 'n take the packet out!'

She plucked at the drawstrings and slowly drew the top of the bag open. Cautiously peeking inside, she saw an object the size of her fist wrapped in waxed muslin. Pulling it from the pouch, she looked at the prospector, eyebrows raised.

'Ga'wan, open it up, see what's inside!'

Folding back the cloth, she found a soft lump of bubbly, thick dough and gave it a sniff. '*Zakwas*, but white!'

Mama laughed. '*Zakwas* is made with rye flour, Mr. McIntyre, but I imagine it would be a similar culture to your sourdough,' she said. She reached up for the crock and showed him. He took a little sniff, then closing his eyes, inhaled deeply.

'Mmmmmm, Ma'am, that is one lovely sourdough. *Zakwas*, ye call it?'

'Yes, it came all the way from Poland with us.' Mama puffed up like a mother hen.

Mr. McIntyre offered Mama half of his sourdough to make her own sourdough pot. She jumped from her seat to find a suitable vessel, while Aleksandra continued to badger Mr. McIntyre.

'But why do they call the prospectors "Sourdoughs"'?

'Well, Missy, yeast bein' mighty hard to come by out West, and wimmen who could cook fer us even harder, we menfolk needed an easy way to make our biscuits n' flapjacks light 'n fluffy, and sourdough was it! Guess we got called Sourdoughs 'cause it was the only livin' thing most of us had in our lives out there to care fer. We had to keep it warm 'n fed, or it'd die, so it lived with us, in our shirts 'n on our minds, much o' the time! Sourdough—it was a way o' life.'

Mama told him about *zakwas* and its place in a Pole's life, while she "fed" both her and Mr. McIntyre's cultures some fresh flour and warm water from the kettle on the stove. She promised him some *zakwas* to take along with him when he left in the morning.

'Much obliged, ma'am, much obliged. Now, for ye two young-uns, I've got a li'l surprise.'

Aleksandra and her brother sat, wide eyed, as he opened the smaller pouch and tipped out part of its contents. It looked like big river gravel, but it shone brightly yellow in the lamplight. Mama inhaled sharply.

'Gold!' Papa said.

'Yer ma and pa won't take anythin' from me fer their kindness to me tonight,' he glanced at them, smiling, 'but I want ye two to have a little somethin' from me that'll mind ye t' have a care fer those what need it. Ye can save it fer somethin' special when yer grown.' He picked out two small lumps from the pile and handed one to each of the children, who sat dumbfounded, too surprised to answer for a moment.

'Oh, thank you, Mr. MacIntyre!' they finally both shouted and ran to hug him.

He hugged them back, looking a bit embarrassed at the affectionate display, but smiled with a twinge of wistfulness. Aleksandra saw tears in his eyes. A few months later, a letter came from him, telling how he had lost his wife, son and daughter many years before in the gold fields. He was grateful to have been included in a family, if only for one night. Aleksandra had never forgotten.

'ALEKS, are you asleep on that pony?' Xavier said with a grin, eyebrows raised. 'We're at Simpson's.'

Her thoughts still warming her, she smiled up at him as she fingered her papa's medicine bag, now containing both her and her brother's gold nuggets.

'Just remembering another Old Sourdough. I'll tell you about him sometime.'

The station keeper appeared at the door, holding a rifle.

'Welcome back, Xavier,' he called, resting the gun on his shoulder when he recognized him.

'George, it's been a long time, good to see you've still got your scalp!' Xavier said, dismounting. The two men clasped hands.

'Only just barely, not a lot of hair left,' he patted his balding pate, 'but 'specially thankful for havin' what I've still got after t'other day.' He stared through them with haunted eyes for a moment as the smile ran away from his face, then he shook his head. Taking a deep breath, he looked at them again with an attempt at a smile. 'Seen any Injuns today?'

'Indian trouble?' Xavier's eyebrows shot up.

'Mmmm.' He looked towards Aleksandra. 'Now who's this young'un?'

'A new rider, Aleks. He'll be riding out of Fish Springs. I imagine you'll see a fair bit of him.'

'Well then, I'd be pleased if you'd stay for dinner, and I'll tell you 'bout it. Tether your horses there by the spring where they can have some real grass, eh?'

Aleksandra smiled her thanks. Dzień was already heading for it as she reached for his rein to lead him there. 'Just a minute, Bucko! Let me take your bridle off!' Aleksandra slipped the headstall over his ears. He promptly spit out the bit and reached out for a huge mouthful of the tough, blue-green, desert grass. Easing his cinch a little, she hung the bridle on his saddle horn and patted him on the rump. Dzień wouldn't go far from the grass and would return to her whistle, so she needn't tie him. Charro, however, would certainly find trouble if he wasn't tied, so she helped Xavier put up a picket line for the stallion.

They followed the wiry old man as he ducked beneath the low stone doorway. While he dished up their midday meal, ladling big spoons of the bubbling-hot beef stew, they seated themselves at the table, and looked about the room.

'Nicely made, George, quite defensible,' Xavier said, examining the stone walls and cedar log roof.

'Aye, for the most part unburnable, with the dirt over the roof, and we've pretty good visibility, luckily.' He nodded toward the two doors and window as he placed their bowls before them.

'Do you grow herbs out here, or do you collect them?' Aleks inhaled the heavenly vapors steaming from her bowl, enraptured.

'Oh, I find a bit or two out 'n the desert.' His eyes twinkled at her.

He turned to Xavier. 'As to defensibility, we had a spot o' bother, day b'fore yest'day. A party of Injuns came visitin' and demanded I hand over all of the station's provisions. Since we're built of stone here, and we were prepared for their visit, I figgered we might be able to hold out against 'em, so I told 'em they couldn't have what they wanted without a fight. Yellin' and screamin', they shot plenty of arrows and a few bullets, but we answered 'em in kind, and they went away.' Xavier and Aleksandra exchanged a swift worried glance.

'Bet you were thankful for that, George!' Xavier said soberly, his eyes on his horn spoon.

'Well, yes, I was. The news isn't all good, though.' George closed his eyes and sat silently for a moment. Looking up at them, he crossed his arms tightly before him, fists clenched. He took another deep breath and continued. 'When they left, they swore they'd burn all the stations and kill all they could b'fore the summer was through.'

11

With plenty to think about, Aleksandra and Xavier said their goodbyes, then soberly mounted up and headed west for Dugway Pass.

'This trail is so straight you could shoot an arrow—,' she began, then she noticed Xavier's narrowed brows as he stared at her, and reconsidered. 'Mmmm... probably not the ideal way to put it.' She pursed her lips and screwed up her face. 'Sorry.'

'Not your best, under the circumstances,' Xavier agreed. 'How about a different subject?'

'Okay…' Aleksandra hesitated. 'Ummm…how much is it to post a letter with the Pony?'

'Much safer. It's five dollars to post a letter. Mind you, that's for a half-ounce.'

Aleksandra raised her brows at him. 'Few people could to afford to send one at that price.'

He nodded. 'Mostly only businesses and the government.'

'Even if they wanted to reduce the price, they probably couldn't.' Aleksandra glanced at him. 'It would cost plenty to keep the stations running, much less pay riders twenty-five dollars a week.'

'For all it costs, the Pony is vital right now. With the menace of

Southern secession, the Federal Government needs fast communication that runs through only free states.' Xavier's mouth tightened as they exchanged glances. 'Pity the government won't get behind the Pony.'

'Are the Southern states really serious about seceding from the Union?'

'It's looking like it. The situation between the North and South is heating up.' Xavier took a deep breath and went on. 'In February, Southerner Jefferson Davis lobbied the Senate, insisting that Congress safeguards slavery. Most important to us out West were his demands about slavery in new territories.'

'Slavery is legal in Utah Territory, but it's not common where I grew up. Do the other territories allow slavery?'

'That's the question. As common property of the states of the Union, territories are open to all states' citizens, with all their "personal possessions".'

'Which, of course, to the Southerners, includes their slaves.' Aleksandra scowled.

'Yes. Since the Kansas-Nebraska Act, these territories not only allow slavery, but worse, lets white male settlers in each area determine, "by popular sovereignty" voting, whether the territory will be "slave" or not.'

'So Southerners would have occupied or bought a lot of land north of the Mason Dixon Line since then, wouldn't they?' she muttered.

'And that was the start of the Bloody Kansas Wars.' Xavier brushed his hair back with one hand. 'The slave states want to secede, and they want California, not only for its prestige, wealth and immense acreage—'

'—with the sort of soil,' Aleksandra interrupted, 'and climate that would suit the institution—'

'—Yes, but even more so, they see the state as the perfect strategic war base against the North.

'Pardon? War base?'

'There are rumors of a conspiracy,' Xavier said, 'by Southern sympathizers to draw California out of the Union, after which it would join the Southern states in their plans to secede from the Federal Government. The South already has Texas. After annexing the rest of the Southwest and northern Mexico, with the westernmost state in their bonnet...' he hesitated.

'They could block the Federal Government on the Western half of the continent,' she finished, her jaw dropping as she stared at him.

'Yep, which would be the Union's most vulnerable point of attack.'

'Oh my God.' Aleksandra whispered, looked down at Dzień's mane. 'But how could that happen?'

'About a third of the population of California is of Southern descent and favors the state joining their Southern brothers.'

'But they don't make up the majority,' she said, rubbing her eyes.

'No they don't, thanks to the influx of Northerners and foreign immigrants who came in '49 for the gold rush. They don't have to be a majority to be powerful. Ever heard of the Knights of the Golden Circle?'

'Noooo...' Chewing on a fingernail, she peered up at him.

'They're a secret society, pro-slavery, which rather forcefully "assists" those who are not vehemently pro-Union to assist with the Southern cause. There are probably at least sixteen thousand Knights in California. Rumor also has it that guns, ammunition and heavy ordinance are arriving in California and being distributed to them. Many, *many* guns. Thousands.' Xavier reached across the space between their horses and touched her cheek. 'We're helping.'

'How can we possibly make a difference?' Her voice was barely audible.

'By the Pony providing fast communication between California and the rest of the Union back east over the shorter Central Route, traveling only through Northern territories and states. The old Butterfield Route runs through Southern states and would give them control over the mail, in the event of secession and war. They could isolate the state for months, allowing them time to complete the secession and annexation of California, whether by conspiracy or force.'

'Well, I guess we're doing something, then,' She gave him a hint of a smile, 'Helping preserve the Union by maintaining the communication they need. The South loses the control they had, plus the Pony is faster.'

'That's my girl. Funny thing is,' Xavier's brow creased, 'for all the good it is doing the Federal Government, they won't help foot the bill for it.'

They continued west, watchful for any sign of movement. Table Mountain loomed larger and closer, silhouetted against the Dugway Range like a misplaced volcano rising from the desert floor. The Simpson Buttes were the only other relief in sight to the vast emptiness of the Great American Desert around them.

Aleksandra was watching the approaching mountain when the trail before them disappeared.

'Where'd it go?' She and Dzień stopped dead. Xavier chuckled beneath his breath, then held a finger to his lips.

'I forgot, you've not been here before,' he said under his breath. 'Wait here while I take a look.'

Xavier slowly walked Charro forward to what seemed the end of the road, then cut hard left and abruptly descend downhill. He stopped, only the top of his head visible as he scanned the area, then spun Charro around on the steep slope and returned.

'What is this place?' she whispered, when he drew abreast of her.

'Old Riverbed. It's a good place for ambushers and a particularly bad place for those they would rob. It's dangerous both on entering and leaving the riverbed—no visibility, so I like to take a good look.'

'The road seemed to just stop. It surprised me.'

Xavier turned the gray and started down the steep track into the gorge.

Aleksandra stared at the odd panorama opening before her. The channel cut into the desert, stretching as far as the eye could see from north to south, a full mile across and a hundred feet deep.

'This is a *riverbed*? What sort of river makes a chasm like this?'

'An ancient one. I'm told it runs out into the Great Salt Lake Desert, then disappears.'

'Is that Old Riverbed Station over there?' Aleksandra pointed across the gorge to a few small structures near the base of the opposite bank.

'Yes, just before you climb out the other side.'

'Whyever would they put a station in a flood plain?'

He considered for a moment. 'Perhaps it's the only place they could find water?'

'Hmm … yes, but what happens in a flash flood?'

'The dugout's still standing, but I agree. I've heard someone was nearly caught in one here. Plenty of stories about Old Riverbed,' Xavier said. 'Some of the men think it's haunted by "Desert Fairies". Perhaps too much *tequila*, no?' He rolled his eyes. 'They have trouble keeping station tenders down here, though, so who knows?'

'With the Indian threat, not to mention highwaymen,' she counted on her fingers with a wry grin, 'living in a river bed that flash floods *and* being unable to see danger coming until it's upon them, I see why they'd drink.'

'When I last rode through here in a thick fog, I have to admit I had little trouble believing in their Faeries,' he flashed her a sheepish look, 'and that was *without* the *tequila*.'

They crossed the riverbed without mishap and he introduced Aleksandra to George, the station tender.

'*Another* George?' she said.

'We like it,' he said, with a crooked grin. 'It confuses people to have two Georges in a row.'

Aleksandra laughed as she led the horses away to a water trough while Xavier shared their news.

Dzień turn up his nose at the brackish water from the station well and the keeper laughed. 'Tell that pony to drink it now, it's worse after we haul it to Dugway, and there's none better until Fish Springs.'

Dzień eventually drank. Having crossed this desert before, Charro knew the score and drank deeply when it was offered. It smelled bad enough that Aleksandra thought twice about refilling the canteens, but common sense prevailed. Even with full canteens and water bags, they'd only have just enough water to get them and the horses across the desert, *if* nothing went wrong.

Climbing the steep track from the riverbed, Xavier went ahead to check the exit. Motioning to Aleksandra that the coast was clear, they climbed up onto the desert floor.

'This is Riverbed Flat, between here and Dugway Station, just before the pass.'

Table Mountain loomed close on their left.

'That flat terrace goes all the way around it,' Aleksandra said, her gaze following it as they trotted past in the cooling afternoon.

'Different, isn't it? I never saw anything like it before I came east from California.'

'The Buttes, Table Mountain, all those other little peaks and cones... I've never seen the likes of them either,' she shook her head.

'They're from the old and extinct Lake Bonneville, which they say covered a big chunk of the Great Basin from the Wasatch Mountains near Great Salt Lake City to about 120 miles west of there. A few lakes remain from it, including The Great Salt Lake.' Xavier looked around them. 'As the lake levels changed over time, erosion would've carved the mountain slopes within the lake, leaving these strange formations.'

The terrain gradually became more desolate than before, if that were possible. There were plenty of rocks, but little else.

'We've been heading southwest since Lookout, haven't we? I thought Ruby Valley was due west.'

'It is.'

'So why doesn't the trail go west? There's nothing in the way.'

Xavier laughed. 'A few weeks ago, Major Egan's son thought he was smarter than Captain Simpson, who surveyed the trail, and tried it. He took his Express pony straight west from Simpson's to Willow Springs for a shorter ride. He made great time for the first half, then the ground became softer and softer, until an inch of water covered the desert surface as far as he could see in every direction.'

'Oh no.'

'His pony struggled through five miles of that, sinking into the alkali mud up to his fetlocks, until they found some higher ground.'

'Poor beast. I'll bet the Major wasn't impressed.' Aleksandra shook her head, her mouth tight.

'You'd be right there.' He smirked. 'The mustang's okay now, but I think young Mr. Egan might just stick to the trail from now on.'

Xavier pointed north. 'That's Granite Mountain over there. The Indians say it's sacred and cursed at the same time.'

'Both?'

He nodded. 'Yes, they won't go up there at all.'

She pointed south. 'What are those?'

'Slow Elk Hills. The rounded summit next to it is Keg Mountain.'

The Dugway range loomed closer, but Aleksandra still couldn't see station.

'I see smoke,' she pointed, brow furrowed, 'but where's the station?'

'Look again.' He chuckled at her, eyes merry.

She peered forward between Dzień's ears, and finally saw the chimney rising from the ground. Hunching her shoulders, she grinned at him from under her brows 'Oh, a dugout.''

'*Sí, Querida.*'

Dugway Station was made from a four-foot deep hole in the ground, covered by split cedar trunks and dirt, with a rough adobe chimney.

'It might be nice if it were in the foothills,' Aleksandra remarked, 'but I guess the keepers can see trouble coming for miles, just by sticking their heads out!'

Xavier hallooed to the keeper, who climbed out onto the desert floor.

'Any good news?' he asked, after they'd exchanged greetings.

'Not much, and the bad's pretty dismal.' Xavier dismounted, wiped the sweat from his brow and relayed the latest news.

While she listened with half an ear, Aleksandra cut a leather thong from the fringe of her buckskin shirt and tied it on to Xavier's saddlebags to replace a broken lace.

Brows drawn together and lips tight, the old man sighed. 'We knew what we were in for when we signed on with this outfit, can't say we didn't. I'd just hoped the peace would last longer than a month.'

'We all feel that way.' Xavier bit his lip. 'I'm on my way to Fish Springs to keep the station there myself and young Aleks will be riding from there.' He glanced at her, his brows lowered.

'We're all in it then, are we?' He let out his breath and smiled with an effort. 'Change of subject?'

Xavier agreed.

'I'd be thinking you'd like some water for these fine horses?' the keeper said over his shoulder at Aleksandra as he disappeared into the dugout.

'We'd be much obliged,' Aleksandra called after him, remembering just in time to lower her voice.

Rolling a water cask up the stone steps into Xavier's waiting hands, he climbed out of the dugout and uncorked the barrel.

'Just got this a few days ago from Simpson's. It's not too bad a'tall!' He tipped out a bucketful of fresh-smelling water. They each drank a dipperful, then offered water to the horses.

'Dzień is used to pristine spring water, but he's getting over his fussiness,' Xavier said with a laugh as the pony shoved his muzzle, well past his nostrils, beneath the surface for a long drink.

'Fresh water's nice when you can get it. Three times we tried for our own well, down more than 150 feet, but they were all dry. Our water comes from Simpson's, or when we're desperate,' the keeper made a sour face, 'from Riverbed.'

'We had a drink there,' Xavier grimaced, 'but as you said, it's water.'

'Yep.' He grinned. 'So what are your plans for tonight?'

'We could probably press on and get to Fish Springs tonight, but we're pretty loaded up. I'd rather keep a little in reserve in case we need to make a run for it,' Xavier said, glancing at Aleksandra. 'We'll find a defensible spot on top of the pass where we can see trouble coming before it gets to us.'

'Yep, good choice. Keep those horses fresh.' The keeper raised his eyebrows and nodded.

'Take care, then and thanks for the hospitality.' Xavier said, swinging up. 'Can you please warn the west-bound Pony rider we'll be up there? We'd hate to spend the night digging bullets out of our pelts!'

'I'll see you soon on my route.' Aleksandra smiled her thanks, waving as they headed for the gray peaks of the Thomas Range, dead ahead.

She looked behind her at Indian Peak's snowcap shining in the late afternoon sunshine when Xavier pointed it out, then returned her attention to the trail before them as it entered a steep valley between high mountains.

'Big climb coming up.' Xavier nodded towards it.

'I thought I'd seen good ambuscades,' Aleksandra gulped, but this ...'

'Dugway Pass is probably the most dangerous part of the whole trail.'

'I can see that,' Aleksandra said, staring at the track ahead, with its horseshoe-shaped switchback. She could almost feel the wind from imagined arrows on the back of her neck as they flew from behind one of the great boulders flanking the wagon road. Each rock and sage bush concealed eyes, while gooseflesh riddled her arms. A bank rose steeply to their right, and to their left was a sheer drop to the gully far below.

Aleksandra grabbed a handful of mane as Dzień stumbled on a patch of loose rock, nearly slipping into a deep trench.

'What is that ditch doing in the wagon trail?' she growled.

'It's a dugway.'

The trench in the top side of the angled wagon track ran whole length of the climb.

'The uphill wheels of the wagons are anchored into it,' Xavier said. 'They keep the wagons from rolling down the side of the mountain, but they can trap a leg too, so have a care on your rides, especially in the dark.' His brows lowered and lips tightened.

'So *that's* a dugway.' She looked down, then gazed back up at the sweeping curve ahead. 'I can just imagine a line of tilted white Conestoga wagon tops creeping up the mountain.'

'It's hard on the stock to draw wagons up with the trench, but it's better than tumbling to the bottom if it tips over.' He glanced over the edge of the trail. 'They often use dugways in the *sierra nevadas*, where the hills are much steeper than this.'

The silence in the deathly-still valley was unnerving. The horses were tiring and they walked beside them, conserving their energy.

Aleksandra's brows drew together. 'How high do we climb in this, say, mile to the top?'

'About five hundred feet. You'll also need to watch for landslides along here, so take care.' He reached out a hand and squeezed hers briefly. 'The emigrants carved this road into the side of the hill and it's none too stable in places.'

Charro's hoof dislodged a loose stone and it rolled over the edge then rebounded, again and again, in a rapid descent. They glanced at each other, eyebrows raised. She shuddered, thinking of bouncing wagons, emigrants, pots, pans and screaming horses, mules and oxen.

'We turn off here.' Xavier indicated a small track to their right, just before the summit. The trail went straight, then turned abruptly upward, ending at an open level area. It was just big enough for them and the horses, sheltered on the north side by several trees. Wide panoramas to the east and west offered advance warning of anyone's approach.

'Oh, it's lovely,' Aleksandra breathed. Cedar-dotted valleys filled the pass to the west, and further on, snow-topped mountains dominated the horizon.

'Fish Springs Range?' She nodded at the lofty heights, raising an eyebrow at him.

'Yes. The station's just this side of it.'

'Nearly home then.' She smiled.

Whatever that will turn out to be.

Dismounting, he handed his reins to Aleksandra and climbed the rocks to a vantage point just above her head.

'We can even see down the east side of the pass from up here.' He grinned as he jumped back down to the ground.

Xavier's hideaway was the most welcoming place she'd seen in days. Heaving a grateful sigh, Aleksandra slid from the saddle and untied her bedroll. She loosened the cinch *latigo* as Dzień nosed at wisps of grass beside a boulder. Pulling her saddle off, she stood it on its end atop her saddle blankets, then slid the bridle off and replaced it with his halter.

She poured water into her hat.

'There you go, Boy.'

Dzień drank, then continued foraging while she curried and brushed him down. He flexed his body around her hand and reached out to try to scratch Charro's withers when she found his favorite itchy spot.

'WHEREVER DID YOU FIND *CHEESE*?' Xavier's grin lit up his whole face.

'I made it last spring, when we still had a cow.' She smiled, scoring the wax and peeling it from the round of cheddar. Paring off a curling slice with her sheath knife, she placed a bit of the hard cheese onto her tongue. It was rich and tangy, perfectly aged.

'Mmm …' she murmured, handing him a golden-hued, crumbling arc.

'The smell was enticing, but the taste...*Dios mío...*' Rolling his eyes, he licked his lips. 'Beautiful, thank you. Did you say you're not married yet?' He grinned at her, then his brows lowered and he crossed his arms across his chest, wide eyes staring at the ground.

Aleksandra sighed softly, sad at his discomfiture.

Xavier shook his head and took a deep breath.

'So what happened to your cow?' he asked in a gravelly voice, tearing off a chunk of bread and offering it to her.

'It was hard for Papa and I to run traplines and get home in time to milk, so we gave her to a family that lived nearby. Their children needed the milk more than we did and they gave us milk and the occasional cheese when they had spare, so it worked well for everyone.'

'I cannot remember having better cheese, ever,' he said. 'Thank you for sharing it with me.'

Aleksandra beamed. 'It's probably been awhile since you've had it.'

He reached for her and she smiled, letting him pull her onto his lap. She rested her cheek on his shoulder, silent, for long minutes.

'I'm getting to like having you with me, *Querida*. Please be careful out there. I'd miss you more than you know if anything were to happen.'

From beneath her lashes, she watched him close his eyes as he held her tight.

I like this. I don't feel like running.

The thought surprised her.

'Be careful of fallen riders.' His words reverberated from his chest where her body touched his, giving his words more impact. 'Thieves lie on the ground next to their horse and attack, gun pulled, when someone dismounts to help.' Xavier's countenance darkened as he spoke.

'I promise I'll be careful. You know this,' she said with a smile. 'Papa taught me to care for myself and I'm enjoying you too much to not return.' She looked into his dark eyes and he bent his head to lightly kiss her forehead.

'You were telling me the story of your family's exit from Poland.' Xavier's words were soft. 'Just how *did* the son of a physician end up married to the daughter of a Count?'

'It's a long story, and you probably won't sleep after hearing it.' She winced.

'Try me and see.' His eyes glowed above a gentle smile.

'Mmm...Poland.

'As I said before, my grandfather was physician to a great *szlachta*, or noble, house. Papa was only small when the Countess nearly died in childbed, but my grandfather saved her life. A short time later, the Count found my father playing at stick swords with his sons. Out of gratitude, the Count insisted he be trained with his children, so my father grew to young adulthood with the children of the *szlachta* family.'

'What about class divisions? How did they end up married?'

'Class lines were strongly drawn. The Count was liberal in his thinking, but he would never have countenanced marriage between my father and his daughter, under normal circumstances.'

'And I take it they weren't normal.' He left off playing with Aleksandra's fingers and looked her in the eyes.

'No. Poland had the dubious honor of lying between the Kingdom of Prussia, the Russian Empire and Habsburg Austria, the "Three Black Eagles." Between 1772 and 1795, they "partitioned" the Polish-Lithuanian Commonwealth, and essentially eliminated sovereign Poland and Lithuania.'

'How...how could that happen?' Xavier's brows furrowed.

'The Three Eagles claimed Poland was in a state of unrest and unable to rule itself, so they stepped in as "protectors," incrementally seizing the land and apportioning it between them. Although they wouldn't publically recognize it, the Commonwealth began making reforms long before the first partition.

'Poland's improved state may have threatened the partitioning powers, and it seems too many Russian peasants were escaping to Poland, plus Prussia wanted Poland's north coast to control the Baltic grain trade. So, they kept dividing it up until they essentially eliminated it completely. Perhaps they simply wanted the territory and knew they could just take it.'

'Why did the rest of the world allow it?' Xavier frowned. 'Didn't anyone else step in? The Polish people must have had some support from other countries.'

'They used the excuse of instability, but the Black Eagles were major powers. Who could have stopped them? Persia and the Ottoman Empire were the only two countries that didn't accept the partitions. The Ottoman Empire even continued to reserve a place in its diplomatic corps for a Polish Ambassador, but no one stepped in to stop the partitions.'

Xavier shook his head and took a deep breath.

'So they divided the country by 1795,' he said, 'but your parents weren't even born then.'

'I'm getting there, be patient.' Aleksandra shook her head at him. 'The partitioning countries allowed the *szlachta* to retain their hereditary titles, but their ruling powers were limited to those of manor lords.

'My family's manor was in the south of Poland near Tarnów, under Austro-Hungarian rule. It was near the Free City of Kraków, which was allowed a sort of self-rule, but when Papa was still a young man, everything changed.' She stopped and sat for a moment. 'Are you sure you want to hear this?'

'Absolutely.'

Taking a deep breath, she began.

'One sunny winter day, Papa and two of the Count's daughters rode to visit friends on a neighboring manor, lying a few hours' fast ride away. The young woman who was to become my mother was one of them.

'On the way home, they were detained by several hours when my father's horse threw a shoe. Although it became late and bitterly cold, the night was clear and the moonlight reflecting off the snow showed their way across the fields while they travelled cross-country, as was their wont.

'Entering the last dark wood between them and the manor, Papa smelled smoke. They thought it was only the gamekeeper's cooking fire, until they saw the glow above the ridge before them. As they approached the summit, they heard shouting and screaming. Dismounting, they tied up the horses and crept through the shelter of the trees until they reached the crest of the hill. There, in horror, they stood frozen at the sight of the flames and torches of a mob milling against the backdrop of the burning mansion.

12

_____

'In silence,' Aleksandra said, 'Papa held the shaking girls, watching the scene below. By the light of the fire and the mob's torches, they saw my mama's other sisters and brothers thrown into a heap near their mother, whose lifeblood already stained the ground in a dark puddle.

'In stunned disbelief, Papa saw peasants from their own manor in the mob. When a big, burly man chopped off the Count's head with his own jeweled dress sword and paraded it about before the mob, the crofters roared.

The shaking youths hiding in the trees clung to each other, choking on their tears. Mama's sister pulled away from Papa and he let her go, thinking she needed to be alone, then the two of them sat together, arms around each other, while they waited for her sister to return.

'A movement far below them at the edge of the house clearing caught their attention. It was Mama's sister, running out of the wood and straight for the manor, into the thick of the mob. She managed to stab two of those nearest to her father with her sheath knife before she, too, was killed.'

Xavier's arms tightened about her when she stopped talking, and he swallowed hard.

'Mama fainted in his arms and he held her until she awoke. For the rest of the night, they sat wrapped in their cloaks, backs against a tree on the frozen ground, watching the smoking manor and the barns. Papa couldn't see his parents anywhere. In the flickering light, the revelers struggled to haul heavy items from before the house and heave them onto a wagon before moving off, the peasants singing loudly behind the wagon as they marched.

'The *szlachta* cattle and sheep were driven before them and the horses led behind. After the last looters drifted away, dragging their spoils on blankets, Papa saw no more movement as the fires died down.

'In the dawn light, he and Mama were dumbfounded. Only a few bodies remained where they'd seen a great pile in the firelight. Unsure whether anyone watched from the sheds, they waited a few hours more before leaving their hiding place. While they climbed down towards the smoking ruins, a pack of huge wolves slunk into the front yard, sniffing and licking at the bloodstained snow and then at the remaining bodies. Papa and Mama stayed hidden, trying not to watch the carnivores eat their fill. When the shaggy beasts melted into the wood, as silently as they had come, they continued down the hill.

'To their misery, they found the bodies of Papa's mother and father and the half-eaten corpses of two young serving girls from the house, but were bewildered to find no one from Mama's family.'

'What happened to them?' Xavier whispered, his face glowing white in the dusk.

'I'm getting there, just a moment.' Aleksandra gulped. 'They realized that while others from the household were killed, only members of the *szlachta* family had disappeared completely. They didn't know what to do next. Desperate as they were to bury Papa's parents and the two girls, they feared the mob might return or seek them out if they knew they yet lived.

'Painful as it was, they decided to leave everything as they'd found it. Mama held blankets over Papa to muffle the steel-on-steel noise while he replaced his horse's shoe, then they collected travelling food and blankets the looters had missed from Papa's cache at the back of the barn. Praying for their beloved ones' souls, they slipped back into the woods the way they'd come, farewelling their families and home forever. With three horses, they travelled by night toward Vienna, a huge city where they could disappear and make a new life.'

'Aleks, what *happened* to them?'

'In their travels, they heard that over a thousand noblemen died and more than five hundred manors were destroyed in the two days and nights of that peasant massacre.'

'That couldn't be possible.' Xavier's emotions warred in his face, jaw dropped and a look of horror in his eyes.

'But it was. It was the "Galician Slaughter," a direct result of an uprising of the noble *szlachta* and patriotic Polish intellectuals in the Free City of Kraków. They encouraged the peasants to revolt with them against the Austrians controlling their partition, in an attempt to reestablish an independent Poland.

'The revolt began in the Free City and spread to Tarnów and beyond. The District Officer in Tarnów panicked and enlisted the help of the peasant leader Jakub Szela to use the peasantry for a counter-revolution. Urging the peasants to support the Austrian Empire, Szela promised them an end to their feudal duties if they helped put down the rebellion of the Polish noblemen.'

'How did they convince them to go against their own countrymen?' Xavier's eyes narrowed.

'I'm not sure. Perhaps the living conditions of the serfs under the Austrians were better than before the Austrians had come, but more likely the peasants saw their own feudal lords, rather than the Austrians, as their oppressors. Not every peasant participated, but certainly enough to slaughter 2000 people, between nobles and their households.' She closed her eyes for a moment. 'Anyway, between the District Officer promising the crofters money and salt for the heads of nobles, and the partitioning authorities offering the Tarnów City Council coin for the corpses of nobles, you might imagine where the bodies of Mama's, and my, family went.'

'No—they couldn't have—' Xavier held his breath and stared at her in silence.

'The Austrians wished to be freed of the Polish nobility. The Polish peasantry did their work for them. A lot of good it did the crofters,' she muttered sarcastically. 'Szela was given money and a land grant, but the rest of the peasants were forced, some flogged, back to their feudal duties.'

He said nothing, but his arms pulled her in even tighter.

Our Indian situation seems mild by comparison tonight.

She shuddered.

Aleksandra's thoughts flicked to Papa's secret drug, stashed carefully away in one of her saddlebags. She didn't mention that in addition to the supplies Krzysztof retrieved from his hiding place in the barn that fateful night in Poland, he also took his own papa's store of the secret drug and its makings before they fled.

Krzysztof had wondered if the massacre was related to the drug. Vladimir had previously hinted that the tsar was interested in learning how Krzysztof could make long horseback trips at the speed he did. It was lucky they lived in the Austrian partition, rather than the Russian, or the arms master might have done more than just questioned. Vladimir was in Russia on family business for the week prior to the attack, but Papa suspected he'd return and be on their trail, once he discovered Mama and Krzysztof weren't listed amongst the dead.

Aleksandra sighed and relaxed back against Xavier's shoulder.

I'll have to tell him about the secret soon. As risky as my new profession is, I'll have to entrust someone else, and Xavier looked to be the best candidate.

'Well, you were right about one thing,' he said.

'About what?' Aleks looked up at him, eyebrow cocked.

'I won't be sleeping anytime soon, after that bedtime story.' He hugged her close again. 'Would you like to share my *serape*, tonight, *señorita*?'

She was silent for a moment, holding her breath, then let it out slowly.

'Don't mind if I do, *señor*,' she said softly and rose to collect her blanket, returning to lie beside him on the ridge, where they could see and hear anyone moving through the pass. They took turns sleeping, but this time they were curled in each other's arms under Xavier's blanket. Drifting off to sleep, Aleksandra wondered why she couldn't always have this feeling of contentment with him. Even more puzzling, what made him freeze whenever they began to get close? Tonight, being wrapped in each other's arms just seemed right.

IN THE MORNING, they made their way down the track to the main trail, gaining the summit of Dugway Pass as dawn broke. Xavier stopped his stallion and turned. Aleksandra's face lit up when she first saw a smaller set of mountains, and beyond it the immense Fish Springs Range rising above the fog layer.

'Oh,' was all she could say.

He smiled too. 'Those dark hills between here and Fish Springs are the Black Rock Mountains.

'They're lovely,' she breathed.

'Yes, lovely from here, but a bit bleak once you get there.' He glanced sideways at her. 'The only things that grow well there are rocks and mud, depending upon the time of year, of course.'

Sparsely scattered mountain cedars dotted the landscape on the grade out of the pass. It was gentler than the ascent and after a good night's sleep, Aleksandra bounded down the trail beside Dzień. Xavier smiled at her changeability. Rabbits hopped over the trail before them, scattering when she laughed at them. He shook his head, but she just grinned back.

He thought about the night just past, and her willingness to lie with him. She'd been pliant in his arms, but he made a point of merely holding her, as anything else seemed to frighten her. He sighed, wishing she would tell him of her fears.

As for his own, he was terrified to lose her to an attack or accident on the trail. Although Aleksandra was, hands down, the best rider he'd ever seen, as the time approached to send her out into the dangerous canyons and deserts of her first Express ride, he became ever more certain it was the worst idea he'd ever had. He'd tossed and turned at night, thinking about it. Even without the Indian danger, innumerable other things could befall a horseman travelling the rough trail at speed during the day, much less at night.

She was tough and persistent, he'd give her that, but was that enough to keep her alive on a trail ridden with increasingly hostile Indians bent upon killing the racing Pony riders?

'I really want you to be careful out there.' Xavier frowned.

'Doc Faust said Messrs. Majors and Waddell picked only the fastest and fittest horses they could find for the Express,' she said lightly.

'Mustangs are fast, generally,' he shook his head, 'and ours have the advantage of better feed, something they wouldn't get in an Indian village, but they still can't outrun arrows.'

She isn't taking me seriously at all.

'Are we using Mustangs all the way back to St. Joseph?' she asked.

She was on a roll and wouldn't let his fears stop her. He gave in with a sigh and just answered her question.

'East of Utah, where the trail is easy and flat, we use the faster, but softer, thoroughbreds and crosses. Through the Rockies and further west we need Mustangs and Indian ponies because of the terrain. A thoroughbred simply wouldn't survive the punishment.'

'How did they find that many Mustangs and Indian ponies so quickly? They're usually only caught and broken in one or two at a time.'

'It was a bit of a rush. Some of them are, shall we say, a bit rough,' he admitted. 'They bring the Mustangs in to the keepers pretty wild, almost straight off the range. Once they've been ridden four or five times, they go onto the route.'

'That green, eh?' She raised a brow at him.

'I used to think it amusing, but it doesn't seem so funny anymore, now you'll be riding them.'

'Are they shod?' she asked, nonplussed. 'Covering the terrain and distance they do, at speed, with a rider, and without shoes,' she inhaled deeply, 'Mustang or no Mustang, their feet would be torn up in no time.'

'Yes, they're shod, though it's a bit tricky to shoe them.' He grinned, despite himself. 'There's one half-tamed Express Mustang that takes the station keeper and farrier all day to shoe. He's so wild they have to throw him and tie his legs together to get the shoes on, *every* time, but they think the effort is worth it. He's nigh unstoppable.'

Despite Aleksandra's confidence, as her first ride approached, Xavier's apprehension intensified.

HALFWAY DOWN DUGWAY PASS, Aleksandra gazed at the mountain summit north of the trail. 'Pyramid Peak?'

'*Como*? Pardon?' Xavier looked up, seemingly lost in thought.

Aleksandra pointed. 'Is that Pyramid Peak? '

'Yes, it is.'

'It's so much bigger when you're right beside it. Yesterday it just looked like a little hill next to the pass.' She smiled, then looked sideways at him. 'Are you okay?'

His eyebrow lifted and he took a deep breath. 'I just can't stop thinking about your papa's story.'

'That makes two of us,' she added softly.

They descended into the wispy, low-lying fog, and the cold inveigled itself between Aleksandra's skin and her buckskins. Visibility was minimal, but the trail was still clear enough to follow. They travelled in silence, not knowing who might be in the mists along with them.

As the mists thinned, the Black Rock Mountains appeared on their left.

'You're right,' she said, 'they're different. Lovely from far away, then mid-range, they're gray-brown and dead-looking, but close up, they're interesting. I like the layers of ebony and gray rock, all crumpled and folded together,' she said, looking at the steep hills beside them. '

'The black stone is basalt. It's layered with other volcanic rocks. Not much green out here, but some plants manage to survive down on the desert floor,' Xavier said, pointing out patches of yellowed grass dotting the landscape.

'The eternal optimist,' she said with a shake of her head. 'There's almost no grass, definitely no trees, and not even any sage-brush.'

An hour later, the last of the fog dissipated as they rounded the end of the Black Rock Hills.

'There it is, Black Rock Station, otherwise known as Rock House.' Xavier waved a hand toward the cabin beside the trail, flanked by a large ebony outcropping rising from the desert floor.

Looking off to the north, Aleksandra shook her head and blinked…then blinked again.

I must be getting too much sun.

She pulled her hat down over her eyes and looked again at the lone mountain sitting on the surface of the desert. Well, it wasn't exactly sitting, that was the problem. It seemed to be *floating* over the surface of the desert. She frowned.

'That mountain over there,' Xavier flicked the end of a rein north, toward the offending peak, 'is Granite Mountain. When I first saw it, I thought it was floating over the desert.'

Aleksandra giggled and he narrowed his brows at her.

'You laughing at me again?'

'No, just glad it's not only me. I thought I'd had too much sun.' She tapped the side of her head with a forefinger and smiled at him.

'I thought so too,' he said, with a wry grin, 'but later I heard people often see this mirage from here.'

'I guess people would often "see things" out here—with the lack of water, dehydration's a danger.' Uncapping her canteen, she scanned the area around the station and drank deeply. She saw only the jet station house and some horses in three log corrals, staring at them intently. 'They won't have a well here, will they?'

'No, all of their wood and water are shipped in.'

'This has to be one of the most desolate places we've seen so far,' she whispered into the stillness.

Entering the yard, Xavier opened his mouth to broadcast their arrival, but before he could speak, they were hailed from the corral behind the station house by a tall man tightening a sorrel Mustang's cinch.

'Xavier? I heard you were gonna be a neighbor!' A big grin creased the old man's face as he checked the pony's bridle and saddle.

'Sure is, James!' Xavier said. 'This is young Aleks.'

'Nice to meet you, Aleks, I'll be right with you both. Just need to have this pony ready for the rider. He's due any second.' The station keeper led the pony out and tied him to the rail in front of the station house.

'There, all ready to go.' Patting the sorrel on the rump, he strode up to Charro and rubbed his forehead while Xavier dismounted. 'Water's over there,' he indicated with a nod of his head.

'Thanks. Good to meet you James,' Aleksandra said, leading Dzień toward the trough. She was remembering, more often than not, to lower her voice.

'Aleks'll be riding this run sometime in the next few days,' Xavier said to James.

Aleksandra's heart jumped into her throat and she glanced in his direction. Although it was planned, somehow she'd begun to think it wouldn't really happen. While Xavier watered Charro and exchanged news, she wandered over to the black outcrop they'd seen from afar. Picking up a little piece of the black rock from the ground, she examined it closely and returned to the horses.

Its frothy structure grated at her fingers as she rolled it between them. Pocketing the stone, she scanned the surrounding area and saw nothing but the same black basalt scattered across the desert floor beneath a big blue sky. Even the station house was made from the same stone.

I couldn't live here.

She shuddered and looked around again.

Farewelling the station keeper, they set off on the last leg of their journey. As they left the station, a pony loped towards them and the Pony rider bugled. As the puffing, sweating pony neared them, he looked tired, but not exhausted. He flicked his ears at them as he passed. The rider saluted them and began pulling his *mochila* out from beneath his seat, then he was gone. Aleksandra and Xavier turned around in their saddles to face west again. The deadest looking desert they'd yet encountered spread out before them, with the backdrop of the Fish Springs Range beckoning the travelers home.

13

Aleksandra inhaled sharply as they topped a small rise. 'Oh, Xavier, look at the color!' From north to south, the surface of the earth before them might have been splashed with a purple brush.

'It's the sheen off the Fish Springs sloughs.' He smiled. 'The warm springs let the wildflowers grow early.'

'I've heard of the flowers, but no one mentioned the color.' She flashed him a grin. 'The springs have been important to my *Shoshone* family and other Great Basin tribes for as long as anyone can remember.'

'They would have been. They're an oasis in this big desert. Migrating birds stop here and others live here year 'round—muskrats, rabbits, coyote, deer, lizards, snakes and even the occasional otter. The whites named the marshes for the little fish that live there.'

'Can you eat them?'

'Yes, they're good, just little dark colored, speckled things about six inches long. As for the water, it's a bit brackish and warm, but there's plenty of it!'

'Something to be said for *any* drinkable water in the desert. Is the station right on the marshes?'

'The station's a few miles past the slough, so it's not too damp.'

The surface of the trail became increasingly uneven as they

approached the springs. Five miles past Black Rock, the sucking sounds started. Turning to Xavier, she made a sour face. It was the sound of the horses pulling their hooves from the mud as they walked, a thick sludge which became deeper as they progressed toward Fish Springs.

'Major Egan calls this the worst part of the desert.' Xavier laughed, then sobered, his brow furrowed as he went on. 'Watch out for the mud. Depending upon the season, it's one of the most bumpy, soggy or dusty places on the trail. Some riders divert south nearly ten miles to go around the mud flats here. It's dry today, but take care on your runs.'

'Will do, Boss,' Aleksandra drawled.

He regained his humor and grinned. 'Egan's thinking about making a "mud wagon". With a strong team, you could make a good living pulling emigrant wagons out of this muck and carting their goods around it.'

The sloughs spread out before them as far as the eye could see. Everywhere, birds flew in, landing on the water with a great flapping of wings.

'That air off the water is so moist and cool.' She stretched and breathed it in deeply. 'It feels lovely. I'm looking forward to a good soak in a warm pool.' She rubbed at her dry cheeks.

'Yes, but you could probably imagine it in late summer…'

'Mmmm.' She grimaced. 'The swampy stench and the mosquitoes might put you off a bit.'

'The mosquitoes have carried many a man away.' He laughed.

'That must be the station.' She pointed to a long shed in the distance. 'How charming, the thatched roof against the mountains.'

'This is probably the only place in the area with enough grass to *make* a thatched roof!' He raised his eyebrows at her as they rode their sucking way toward the station.

Xavier called out and the keeper's dog set up a racket. A sandy-haired man in one of the corrals glanced up, then dropped the Mustang's hoof he was trimming. Picking up the discarded horseshoe and nails from the ground, he placed his hands on his hips and straightened up with an effort.

'I'm gettin' old!' His grimace became a wry grin as he slipped a hoof knife into his back pocket. 'Xavier, welcome to your new home. I thought you'd be along soon. This must be young Aleks.' Striding to where she held her pony, he firmly gripped her hand with one smelling distinctly of horse hoof, then turned to reach up and shake Xavier's.

'Good to meet you. Mr. Smith, is it?' Aleksandra used her gruffest voice and smiled at him.

'That's Dave, to you, young man. How's about a coffee? I was just finished with that horse. Me back's just about done in, but he had a hoof infection and I wanted to take care of it before I left him to you.'

'Real coffee?' Xavier swung down from Charro and bowed to Dave with a flourish of his hand, grinning from ear to ear. 'My appreciation. I thought you'd never ask.' He led Charro toward an empty corral. 'How'd you get real coffee?'

'I've got friends!' Raising an eyebrow, he chuckled at the Californio over the rump of the gray.

She led Dzień into the next pen, then untacked and rubbed him down. Dave had already filled their water troughs. She smiled her thanks as he forked a pile of hay to each horse from the stack between the station and the barn.

Holding her warm mug between her hands, she sat at the rough table of the station kitchen, savoring the heavenly aroma.

'Which station will you be manning?' Xavier leaned on his elbows, playing with the handle of his steaming cup.

'I'm off today for Smith's Creek Station, out west by Dry Creek. They've had some problems lately. They need a new keeper—a live one.' He shook his head with a grimace. 'A bit daunting, but we'll make it work. I'll be headin' out as soon as you two can take over, so make yourselves at home while I pack up. There's food in the cupboard and water a-plenty, if you can stand the smell. It's not so bad once you get used to it and the hot springs make up for it. I'll show you the best one for a swim before I go.'

'Sounds great. I might just melt right onto the table at the thought,' Aleksandra said, rubbing the back of her grimy neck. 'Mr. Smith, ah, Dave, would you mind showing me that Mustang's hoof and telling me what you'd like done with it?'

Dave raised his eyebrows at Xavier, then looked at Aleksandra. 'You good at doctorin' stock?'

'I do my best, I've had lots of—'

'He's a pretty good horse doc, Dave,' Xavier butted in with a grin. 'He's already made a name for himself on the route helping Ephraim Hanks save a pony with an infected arrow wound. Seems the Mustang would've died without the care he gave it. Aleks learned about healing from his pa.'

'That's good learnin' to have, Son. I'd be happy to show you what I've done, especially if you can teach me a thing or two,' he said with a smile.

Aleksandra ducked her head shyly at the compliments. 'Thanks.' Remembering her new job, she looked up at him, eyes wide. 'So when do I start riding?' she said in a rush.

He grinned at her enthusiasm. 'You're on in a couple of days, maybe three, at around six or seven in the morning. Did you two see a rider today?'

'He flew past us just this side of Black Rock!' Aleksandra could hardly contain herself.

'Right on time!' Dave chuckled, then he sobered, brow furrowed. 'I imagine you've been warned about keeping your hair?'

'—AND THIS,' Xavier handed her a leather sheet with two slots in it, 'is your *mochila*. It—'

'It fits over—' Aleksandra blurted out.

Again. *Dios mío!* He adored this *chica*, but she was driving him mad with her impatience and dogged determination about everything. '—it *fits over* the saddle,' he resumed, glaring at her.

She looked down at the ground. 'Sorry,' she muttered, sounding anything but. Scowling, she stood with arms crossed, her fingernails digging into the sides of her buckskin shirt.

'Aleks, there is a list I need to cover with you before you ride. I still have serious doubts about letting you go, but if you'll listen, you might survive just that little bit longer.'

She stared down at the toe of her boot tapping the ground, then lifted her eyes to his. He could swear she rolled her eyes.

His own narrowed. 'You can ride this portion of the trail because it's safer out here. All the Indian trouble is more than a hundred miles west of here. You'll be right out of it.'

Raising an eyebrow at him, she smirked and seemed about to make some comment, but held her peace.

I wonder what I'm missing here.

'Look, Aleksandra, you seem to think this is a joke. Station keepers have been dying out there.'

Her face fell. 'Yes,' she said, with a little less certainty.

'I haven't told you about "What?" yet, have I?'

'What? ' She frowned, but uncrossed her arms and left off wringing her buckskins to listen, raising one eyebrow and looking at him from beneath her lashes, jaw tensed.

'You don't seem to understand my concern,' he spoke slowly, word by word.

'What is a "what"?' She still looked annoyed, but curiosity got the better of her.

He held his breath for a moment.

'Young George Scovell, an Express rider, nearly died a few weeks ago in an ambush,' he growled. 'What? was an Express Mustang named for his question mark-shaped blaze. Going through the aspen bottoms west of Chokup Pass, What? was uneasy, flicking his ears back and forth, when swarms of arrows flew out of the brush beside them. They were chased by more than thirty Indian braves for over three miles into Diamond Springs Station. They got there, despite two arrows in Scovell's leg and poor What? full of eleven more.'

'Oh.' Aleksandra's attitude and scowl melted, her eyes pooling tears.

'That pony delivered Scovell safely, then collapsed. When they got rid of the Indians, Scovell put him out of his pain with a shot to the forehead and *buried* that pony, right next to the station.'

'He *buried* him,' she whispered. Eyes glowing through wet lashes, she gave him a crooked grin.

'That was his last ride for the Pony. Dead horses are usually left for scavengers, but young George felt pretty strongly about What?. On his way back East, George showed me his journal entry for the day, complete with a photo of the good horse that saved his life.

Aleksandra's brow furrowed. 'How did they protect themselves from the Indians?'

'Willie, the station keeper, dragged George into the station and defended it from the gun ports until the Indians left. Luckily the cedar post stockade and stone station house were difficult to set alight, so they survived.

'Now do you understand why I want you to listen?' He pulled her into his arms and tugged on her braid. 'It would be nice to keep your hair, no?'

Aleksandra looked down at the ground, finally still. 'I am ready to listen.' Xavier had to lean down to hear her whisper. 'I apologize for making this difficult when you are only trying to keep me safe.'

'It's okay,' Xavier held her tightly. 'Shall we continue?' He raised an eyebrow at her and released her.

'I'm all ears,' she said, turning to face him.

'Like the rider we saw just outside Black Rock, some of the boys have been pulling the *mochila* out from beneath them before they get into the station and tossing it to the station keeper to save time.'

Aleksandra nodded.

'The cantinas,' he indicated the compartments on the corners of the *mochila*, 'are kept locked. Three of them can only be opened at military posts along the trail, but all station keepers can open the fourth pocket, which holds a time card and mail for the stations.'

'The *mochila* stays with the rider as he passes from horse to horse?' Aleksandra raised a brow at him.

'Yes, and at the end of his run, he transfers it to the next rider, continuing on until the *mochila* reaches the end of the line.'

'And how much weight will my horse carry?'

'It will be twenty pounds or less, plus the *mochila* and you,' Xavier said.

'With all the rain, water crossings and horse sweat,' she frowned, 'how do we keep the letters dry?'

'The letters are wrapped in oiled silk,' he answered. 'And now,' he turned to an Express saddle sitting on its front skirt, leaning against the wall, 'your tack.' Placing it over a corral rail, he slipped the front hole of the *mochila* over the saddle horn, then dropped the wide slot in its other end over the cantle.

Lifting it up by the horn, Aleksandra peered beneath it. 'It's really just a wood and rawhide tree with stirrups, isn't it?'

'They *were* designed to be lightweight.' He chuckled.

'Without a *mochila* and a thick saddle blanket, they'd be pretty uncomfortable, for both horse and rider.' She grinned.

Unseeing, Xavier fumbled with one of the locks on the *mochila* before him.

She looked askance at him in silence, waiting. As little as he liked it, he had to administer the Oath.

'And finally, the swearing-in,' he murmured, pulling a folded sheet from inside his shirt.

'Oh, it's really going to happen, isn't it?' Her eyes glowed up at him.

'Don't look so pleased, Aleks. I'm still not happy about this.' He gritted his teeth for a moment. 'Swear after me:

'I, Aleks Lekarski, do hereby swear, before the Great and Living God, that during my engagement, and while I am an employee of Russell, Majors, and Waddell, I will, under no circumstances, use profane language, that I will drink no intoxicating liquors, that I will not quarrel or fight with any other employee of the firm, and that in every respect I will conduct myself honestly, be faithful to my duties, and so direct all my acts as to win the confidence of my employers, so help me God.'

'I do so swear,' she replied, stars in her eyes. Irrepressible.

That completed, Xavier stood still and looked at her. Taking a deep breath, he slowly let it out, then waited a few moments more, but finally he could avoid it no longer. 'The official line,' he said clearly, 'is that the mail must go through. If it comes down to the survival of you or your horse versus the mail, the mail is to go through. Official orders.'

He stared at her, his jaw tight, until she looked up at him. Her eyes widened and the color and smile drained away from her face. He reached for her, pulling her hard against him, his heart leaden, sunken down to his boots. He had no desire to let her go out on that dangerous trail, not now, not ever.

He just plain didn't want to lose her.

14

'What *are* you doing, Aleks?' Xavier walked in the door from feeding stock. Staring at the small pile of dry goods unearthed from her saddlebag, he tossed a juniper log into the glowing woodstove and shut the damper.

Turning to face her, he smiled, warming his backside as he surveyed the domestic scene of Aleksandra in the kitchen. She had washed and changed while he was outside and was actually wearing a calico dress, which suited him just fine.

'Making *zakwas*.' She sighed with a contented smile. 'Finally.'

Unwrapping a lump of dough from a piece of waxed fabric, she broke half of it into little lumps and dropped them into a bowl on top of a few cups of dark-colored flour. She cooled a measure of boiled water from the kettle with a splash of cold, and tested it on her forearm, before adding it to the flour.

Her eyes sparkled, her cheeks softly glowing, as she worked.

'You look like the cat that ate the cream,' he grinned, 'but I worry if all it takes is a bit of flour and water to do this to you.' His brow furrowed and he waggled an eyebrow in her direction.

Picking up a wicked-looking kitchen knife, she hesitated for a moment before replying.

'Remember when I told you about sourdough and *zakwas*? And

how you make *żurek* from *zakwas*?' She placed two cloves of garlic beneath the flat of the blade and crushed them with her fist in an abrupt chop, then pulled the garlic skins from the macerated pile of garlic.

He raised his eyebrows at her maneuver. 'Yeeeesss...' he said, making a mental note to watch his comments to her in the kitchen. Glancing up, she caught the look on his face and laughed, then tossed the garlic into the bowl, adding a handful of crushed oats.

'*Żurek* means "home" to me,' she smiled, 'like, the end of travel... family...home. It means...being cared for. It is the very best of Polish comfort food. Finally, I will be living somewhere for long enough to make it,' she said, dropping what looked like a piece of dry rye bread into the bowl with a flourish and stirring it all up with a wooden spoon.

'Will it be ready soon?' Pulling up a bench, he sat down as she covered the bowl with a striped cloth, which had also somehow appeared. It was like watching a magician pull an impossible number of items from his hat.

'It takes four or five days for the *zakwas* to ferment, then you can make the *żurek*.' From the magic saddlebag, she removed a stonewear crock by its handles and crumbled the last of the lump of *zakwas* into it, adding some of the warm water and a handful of the dark flour.

'That's your *zakwas*, your rye sourdough starter? You're feeding it, right?' That earned him a warm smile. He shook his head, wondering how she got the crock to Fish Springs in one piece.

'Yes on both.' She glanced at him beneath her lashes. 'I've made extra so we can make biscuits for breakfast.'

'Mmmm...okay, next step?'

'Done for now,' she replied, fitting the lid onto the crock.

'*Mi madre*, sorry, my mother, had crockery with the same blue flowers. Her head shot up and she stared at him for a moment in silence.

'Your mother? You've not spoken of her before.'

He didn't reply.

She seemed to drag her eyes from him, returning her attention to the jar. 'Now it sits in a warm place until the morning for our sourdough biscuits. Truthfully, we could have just made *żurek* from the old starter, but it's a special ceremony to make a new batch of *zakwas* for a new home.'

'So how do you make *żurek* after the *zakwas* is fermented?'

We add kielbasa sausage and other meats, marjoram, and,' she patted her saddlebags, 'potatoes and other vegetables, if we can find any. If we had chickens and cows, we would have sour cream or yogurt in it and serve it over quartered hard-boiled eggs. Mushrooms are good too, but I think we're out of luck there.'

'Oh,' he said, disappointed. 'I was ready for more kitchen duty. Now what?'

There were many things he could do with her in the kitchen. Taking a deep breath, he dragged his thoughts back to where they belonged.

For once, they didn't need to be anywhere or do anything…until she embarked on her first of many dangerous journeys. He didn't want to think about that now, either.

He couldn't help himself. When she turned away from him to place the bowl and crock on a shelf high above the stove, he caught the back of her skirt and pulled her onto his lap. He wrapped his arms around her as she twisted to face him. 'What am I to do with you, my wayward *Chiquita?*' he murmured into her hair, holding her close.

She gazed up at him with a luminous smile. 'Kiss me again,' she whispered.

He didn't need to be told twice. While her lips melted against his, he released the *latigo* restraining the end of her braid with a little tug and ran his fingers through her hair, slipping it loose from its fetters.

She whimpered and he lifted his head.

'What?' he asked softly.

'It was Papa's pride and joy, my hair.' She gave a little sob, glancing away, then looked into his eyes, a single tear escaping and running down the side of her face. 'Papa spent whole evenings before the fire combing it for me, especially after Mama died.'

'I think *you* may have been your papa's pride and joy.' He smiled into her eyes. 'Will you do me the honor of letting me help you with it now?'

She nodded, her lips finding his once more.

Cuddling her body against him, he stroked her hair again and again, scooping the golden strands into a coil in her lap. Tentatively kneading the muscles of her back, Xavier kissed her more deeply. She didn't take fright, so he began to softly rub lower and lower.

When she responded, opening her mouth to his and tightening her hold about his neck, he broke into a sweat, barely able to draw a full breath. Emboldened, he slowly opened his hand and circled it around her belly, gradually stroking upwards until his thumb brushed the tip of a nipple through her cotton gown. He swallowed hard and stilled his hand.

She wore no bindings over her lovely breasts tonight.

Gasping, Aleksandra's head jerked back, eyes wide. She squirmed against him, but made no attempt to break free.

'*¿Esta bien?* Are you fine with this?' Xavier whispered against her hair, his heart hammering against his ribs.

She nodded, blue eyes darkened to black locking onto his as he took her mouth again and held her close. One by one, he undid the buttons of her bodice down to the waist. Her breathing became ragged as his fingers ran up and down her belly and slowly circled her breasts. All the while he held her mouth with his, their tongues continuing their dance. Lifting his head, his gaze slowly moved downward.

'So lovely—' He brushed his fingertips over one of her nipples. Her abdominal muscles tautened against his other hand.

Drawing a deep breath, she stared at his fingers, open-mouthed. They shifted to the other nipple, and her eyes followed, then she reached up to grip the back of his neck.

He captured her mouth again, and kissed her before pulling his shirt over his head and placing her hand upon the warm, curling hair of his chest. As she stroked him with long fingertips, she shivered and looked into his eyes. He shifted her on his lap as the tightness of his buckskin trousers became unbearable and kissed his way to her ear. She breathed faster as he nibbled its edge, whimpering when his teeth found her neck. His mouth slid down its length and beyond. Taking a nipple into his mouth, he sucked until she dug her fingernails into his back and struggled for breath, pulling him closer, if it were possible.

She startled when he gathered her in his arms and stood. Staring at him as if she didn't quite know where she was, Aleksandra stilled when he smiled into her eyes and bore her to the adjoining room. Laying her on the bed, he left her, returning to place a flickering candle on the bedside shelf.

'We can stop anytime you want,' he said slowly as he sat beside her, pulling her into his arms again.

'I don't want to stop, but know I must,' she said in a faint voice, though she still panted, her color high in the candlelight.

It took many breaths for his pounding heart to quieten.

'Are you ready to tell me why?' he said into the silence.

She tucked her head into his chest. 'Please hold me, just hold me, Xavier.'

He sighed and pulled her hard against him. She must understand how he felt about her. How long would it take for her to trust him?

Then it dawned upon him.

'Is it that we're not married?' he asked, in a voice he didn't recognize as his own.

She didn't lift her head from his chest, just shook her head, no.

'So it wouldn't make a difference if we were married?'

Another negative response from her left him bemused. He had no idea where to even start. Taking a deep breath, he closed his eyes for a moment. 'Let's just hold each other tonight, then, shall we?' he asked, when his speeding heart had slowed.

'Please,' she whispered, a tear running down her upturned face.

Pulling back the covers, Aleksandra slipped beneath the sheets and waited in silence. Yanking his shirt over his head, Xavier slid in beside her, spooning her soft body against his, holding her long into the night, until they both slept.

ALEKSANDRA'S THOUGHTS raced as she bounced out the barn door into the early morning sunshine. She was to ride tomorrow and Xavier seemed determined to ensure she knew the ropes by then.

'*Bien*. Hop on this pony and get a feel for the saddle.' He walked around the other side of the pinto to check the cinch.

She glanced at his tight, compressed lips, over the back of the pony.

'None of these ponies have ever had anyone vault on, so you'd better try it gradually, *Querida*.' Xavier legged her up and stepped back as the pony started to jig. 'They were chosen for speed and endurance, not manners. This boy probably only knows 'go' and probably not even 'whoa', so have a care. It's a good thing you're used to stallions. There are quite a few of them on the route.'

Aleksandra trotted off and returned after a few circles of the yard, vaulted to the ground and slid the *mochila* off, throwing it to the waiting keeper. He replaced it and Aleksandra took the reins, grabbed a handful of mane, clucked to the pony and gave him his head.

As the colt leapt forward, she vaulted into the saddle and he sped to a gallop.

'No problem, he's—' Her over-the-shoulder reply was cut short as the pinto shied violently. Two Indians waited beside the corner of the barn, materialized, it seemed, from nowhere. Managing to keep her seat, she rode straight back to Xavier, watching the visitors all the while.

They sat their wiry horses like statues, silently watching them. Xavier's hand slid towards the revolver at his hip, but Aleksandra caught his eye and shook her head.

'No—they're *Shoshone*. They are not from my tribe, but they mean us no harm.'

'*Pehnaho,*' she called out to them in *Shoshone* and nodded at them.

After a brief second's pause, in which the Indians glanced at each other with raised eyebrows at her speech, the taller and older of the two spoke.

'*Behne.* We have come for flour.'

'What you have to trade?' Aleksandra parlayed in the natives' language. Custom required honorable exchange.

The same man, his face once again impassive, answered her. 'The winter has been hard, there has been much snow and the white immigrants have cut down the *piñón* trees we need for food and fire, and depleted the animals we need to survive. We would like to trade a finely woven basket and an antelope hide for flour and ammunition.'

As Xavier watched her, Aleksandra was silent, considering. 'How much flour do we have?' she said, in English.

'Four bags, plenty.' His eyes never left the Indians.

'We have one bag of flour we can give to you but no spare

ammunition. We are happy to trade this for what you have offered,' she said.

The younger Indian growled under his breath but was silenced by the other with a curt sideways comment.

Without removing her eyes from the Indians, she asked Xavier to get a bag of flour. When Xavier was inside the station, the older man's eyes bored into Aleksandra, brows narrowed.

'You are the daughter of the trapper Krzysztof?' he asked sharply, in an undertone.

Her heart jumped at hearing her pa's name, but caution silenced her and she steeled her emotions. She raised an eyebrow at him and he went on.

'There are no other women I have seen who ride as you do. You are well known to many of the *Shoshone* tribes,' he said with a frown. 'Is this your mate, your husband?' He nodded at Xavier, just exiting the station with a bag of flour over his shoulder. 'I thought you were to be taken to wife by Dancing Wolf of the *Shoshone*.'

'No, he's not my mate,' she said, squaring her shoulders. 'I have no mate. I am riding for the Pony.'

'Don't they only have boys?' The younger Indian said, smirking.

'Do I *look* like a girl?' Aleksandra asked. The two Indians looked sideways at each other with the hint of a repressed smile. 'No, don't answer that,' she added, with her own attempt at hiding a grin. 'I fool some people, even if not you.'

Xavier observed the exchange. 'Your flour.' He set the bag down and placed himself between the girl and the Indians. The young man took the bag of flour while the older man handed the basket containing the rolled antelope hide to Aleksandra. With a 'thank you' in *Shoshone* and a nod to Aleksandra and Xavier, they wheeled their spotted ponies and galloped away.

At Xavier's quizzical look, Aleksandra filled him in on her discussion with the Indians.

'I'm not sure I like them showing up and expecting food and ammunition. Things could get out of hand.' Xavier frowned.

'They're looking to trade, not coming to take anything. The white man has always traded with them and now people are blowing it out of proportion. The Indians have always been friends to me,'

Aleksandra shook her head. 'We don't take advantage of them like some do.'

'Can't say but I'm relieved that they've gone peacefully,' Xavier said with a sigh. 'Now, where were we?' he asked her, looking up at her on her pony, his voice soft, but Aleksandra wasn't quite finished.

'They're just hungry. This winter was the hardest I can remember. It would have been difficult for them, especially with the settlers' destruction of their food and fuel.' She looked down at her hands playing with the reins, well aware of her own family's contribution to their loss.

'I guess we'll just have to help them as best we can,' Xavier said.

Feeling his eyes upon her, she flushed warm with appreciation for his reply.

'You were saying,' Xavier murmured as she leaned towards him, 'he's no trouble to vault on to, this pony?' He held up his arms to her and she slid into his embrace, their lips meeting while the pinto looked on. The whites of his eyes showed, but he stood like a rock beside them as they held each other, their bodies melded into one.

'YOU HANDLED THAT SITUATION ADMIRABLY,' Xavier said, smiling down at her. 'Did they tell you anything else? Anything that'd give us an idea what else might be going on?'

Aleksandra didn't reply, looking down at the lead rope in her hand as they led the colt to his corral.

Glancing sideways at her, his eyes narrowed at her continued silence. Slipping the halter from the colt's head, she gave him a pat and backed out of the corral. Xavier closed the gate and leaned back, his elbows resting on the top rail, awaiting her answer as she stood facing away from him.

She slowly turned, looking up at him from under her lashes, jaw clenched.

'Ummm...' She took a deep breath. 'There *was* something else, Xavier.'

He waited.

'They recognized me as Krzysztof's daughter.'

His head shot up, eyes boring into hers. 'How?'

'By my riding, and by the fact that they see what most white men don't, that I'm not a boy,' she replied evenly.

'That *could* complicate things, now, couldn't it?' He grinned.

'Mmmm. And there was another thing.' Her voice dropped off into a whisper, and she stared at the ground.

'Yes?' He waited, then as she still said nothing, reached out to stroke her shoulder with his knuckles. Almost imperceptibly, she flinched, and he dropped his hand, crossing his arms.

Aleksandra clutched at the halter in her hands, breathing fast. She looked him straight in the eyes, then squeaked and ducked her head again, but not before he saw the blush and the tears.

Xavier shook his head, crossed the space between them and took her tightly in his arms, blood pounding in his ears. 'Shhh... it's okay, *Chiquita.*'

She gasped, then with a sob, continued in a rush. 'They knew something I have not yet told you. They asked if you were my mate. They knew that the son of my *Shoshone* family, Dancing Wolf, had asked my father for my hand in marriage.' She looked up at him, eyes huge and mouth trembling.

As he stared at her in silence, his body rigid, a metal band tightened around his heart. 'So what have you planned?' he eventually said, his voice like sandpaper.

'Nothing.' She twisted her fingers in the fringe of her buckskins again and again. 'It was several months ago that he asked for my hand, but my father believed I was too young to marry and I was not told of any of this until I visited their village on the day I first met you.'

Xavier scowled, his hands lowering slowly to his sides as he backed away.

Shoulders hunched, she dropped her head. 'As I told you, they sent me away.'

'So do you love this man, whatever his name is?' He rubbed his temples, not looking at her.

'His name is Dancing Wolf,' she said wearily, rolling her eyes. 'My father rescued him as a child from drowning and we've been friends ever since. I think of him as a brother and was surprised when they told me of this, although I was grateful for the honor of the offer they made for me. His father is the chief of his tribe.'

'I repeat, do you love him, this Wolf?'

'I love him as a brother, but not as I feel—' she was silent for a moment, then whispered, '—for you.' She looked up at him with a frightened little smile, tears now running freely.

Xavier wasn't sure just *what* he felt. He wanted her to love him and only him, but even that made him want to bolt, as fast as Charro could take him, far away from this contrary, beautiful, challenging yet beguiling girl-woman.

Truth was, he didn't know why he wanted to run. Compelled to make love to her one moment, then in the next, had to restrain himself from putting her over his knee and spanking the daylights out of her. He couldn't understand her, or himself either, it seemed.

He'd do what he always did when a woman intruded on his heart. Hold her briefly while planning his escape.

Gutless, but it always worked before.

Spinning on his heel, he headed for the barn, ostensibly to feed the stock.

15

A flicker of what could have been longing lingered in Xavier's eyes as he pulled his lips from hers after the briefest of kisses, and she sat up tall in the saddle. His mouth closed tightly in a grimace, he glanced toward the barn door and shoved the packet of Fish Springs mail into his shirt. Sam, the incoming Pony rider, was outside in the yard, unsaddling his horse.

Aleksandra waited as Xavier scowled and rubbed at his lower lip.

'Well, guess you'd better be off,' he said gruffly, looking somewhere in the vicinity of the saddle horn. 'What are you waiting for?'

'Ummm ... my hand?' she softly questioned.

'Oh.' He released his vise grip on her hand like it was red-hot, then shuffled backward, finally looking at her face. 'Be safe, *Chiquita*. I'll see you when I see you.' The smile didn't quite reach his eyes.

Her heart aching for him, she took a deep breath and settled herself. Tears got in the way when she tried to smile, so she just blew him a kiss, spun the horse about and loped off east for Rush Valley.

Other than his goodbye, he hadn't had a friendly word for her since her revelation yesterday. The leave-taking for her eagerly anticipated first Express run broke her heart. She couldn't understand how news of Dancing Wolf's proposition and its refusal could affect him as it did, despite her and Xavier's slowly blossoming relationship. Shaking her head, she wiped at her nose, wondering what the future would bring.

It'll bring trouble if I don't pull myself out of this and pay attention to what's going on around me!

Taking a deep breath, she put it behind her for now. She had a job to do and a pony to protect. She smiled down at the keen bay beneath her, scratching his withers as he loped along. Flicking an ear back as she spoke to him, he broke into a gallop, his black mane flying back into her face as he gathered speed.

Horses, the best things on Earth.

She leaned down to hug him as they raced along, with a real smile for the first time since yesterday.

XAVIER STUMBLED over the sill of the barn as he walked out into the light toward Sam.

'First time rider, eh?'

'Yes, a bit nervous about the trip, but he'll do.' He forced a smile.

'Not a bad little rider, that one.' Sam nodded at the disappearing heels of the pony.

'Nope, not bad a'tall,' Xavier drawled. 'How about some breakfast?'

'Thought you'd never ask!' Laughing, the rider thumped him on the back as they walked toward the door.

Tossing the mail onto the table, he set about frying up refried beans and the salt pork he'd covered with water the night before. The pork was nearly edible if the salt was soaked out of it for a day or two. Aleksandra's leftover sourdough biscuits were ambrosia. He'd have a hard time explaining why he couldn't duplicate them to any riders who thought he'd made them.

Sitting down to read the mail, he was surprised to see the first letter addressed to him.

María Arguello
Rancho de las Pulgas
San Francisco Bay
California

5 April 1860

To my Dearest Xavier,
I hope this missive finds you swiftly. I write from our Rancho de
las Pulgas and will soon set out for Carson City, there to await
you, my son. I have not been well, but desire to see you before it is
too late and explain some things I believe may help you in your
life.

Pedro, the man you knew as your father, has passed from this life
and you, my son, have rightfully inherited these lands that you
loved so well as a young man.

Before you refuse, know that you are not of his blood, but of the
husband of my heart, my Manuel, murdered by Pedro's hand
when you were a small boy. He was consumed by his anger that
you were not his own get on my body and that the Rancho was of
Manuel's family and not his own.

I beg your humblest apologies for not giving you the love you
needed and protecting you from Pedro. When I tried to do so, it
brought his wrath even more fully upon your back. For this, I
wanted to die. He threatened me with your death if I told you the
truth of your parentage or your father's murder.

I dream that you have found a wonderful woman to hold and
trust. I hope you have been able to destroy the barriers I fear you
have built to protect your heart as a boy neglected and abused by
those closest to you. It is especially of this I wish to speak with you.

I leave by coach for Carson City at the end of this week and will
wait there for a month after my arrival. After this time, I will take

ship for España to see my homeland once again, if God be pleased to grant me this time. If I do not make it to Carson City, know that I have gone to Him and will not again see you on this Earth.

I beseech you to come to me that I may see you one last time and beg your forgiveness for our past. What I have done, I have done for love of you, although it may not have appeared so at the time. Your brothers care for your rancho upon your return home.

Sending all my heart to you, my ever-loved firstborn,

Your Mama

XAVIER SLUMPED, his head held tightly in his hands. He had absolutely no idea what to do.

'TIME TO HEAD SOUTH, LITTLE MAN,' Aleksandra straightened up as deep wagon ruts and hoofprints came into view on the trail ahead. Steering him southwards, they detoured around the soft, boggy ground on their way to Black Rock.

The miles flew past as she tried to think of anything but last night. Glancing behind at intervals to be sure no one followed, she saw the Fish Spring Ranges diminish with the distance, while the towering dark bulk of the Black Rock Hills proportionately gained in stature as she neared the station. Blowing her bugle, she pulled the *mochila*, already sweaty despite the cool day, out from beneath her seat. In the distance, James stood ready with a pinto dancing at the end of its reins. She flung the letter carrier in his direction and he caught it with a grin.

'Howdy, Aleks! Good ride?'

'How could it be anything but?' Her grin nearly split her face. 'Sunny day, fine horses, smiling station keepers! Life doesn't get any better.'

'Got enough water?' He laughed.

'All good, thanks.' She tapped her heels together, saluted him and loosed the reins. Clicking her tongue, she vaulted up onto the surprised mare as she broke into a canter and shot out of the station.

Aleksandra glanced over her shoulder to see James staring after them, mouth agog, and laughed into the wind as they flew toward the north edge of the Black Rock Hills. Above the low-lying wisps of fog, she saw Granite Mountain, steady on its base, today, no floating in the early morning chill. The pony shook her head and relaxed into an extended trot. Aleksandra gave her a pat. Pyramid Peak, the grand marker for her crossing over the Dugway Range, soon appeared above the horizon.

Dugway Pass ... what an eventful evening that was. What keeps driving us apart?

She looked around, but nothing moved in the desert about her. Resolve slipped a bit, she finally let herself think about last night. After their talk, Xavier had kept busy and wouldn't look her in the eyes. She finally managed to stop her tears from falling and just stayed away from him.

Papa always said he and Mama never went to bed on a disagreement, life being too short to do otherwise. After her mama died, Aleksandra vowed to carry that on that tradition, so just before bedtime, she took a deep breath and approached Xavier.

'I just want you to know, I didn't tell you before of Dancing Wolf's proposition because I thought it had no bearing upon our relationship, so I just let it go.'

He looked up from where he'd been studying his fingernails and raised a single brow at her, all emotion absent from his visage.

'After it was mentioned by the *Shoshone*, I realized it could become an issue between us in the future, so I wanted to be completely honest with you,' she continued, 'and I told you the whole truth when you asked about it. I can do no more, Xavier.'

He listened to her in silence, glanced at the tears in her eyes, gave her a brief hug and left for the barn. He didn't return before she went to sleep, and wasn't there when she awoke, though his indented pillow betrayed his night-time presence. Her heart ached.

Xavier's demeanor hadn't improved by morning, nor even by the time of her leave-taking. Brushing back a tear, she lifted her chin and took a big gulp of air. She wouldn't think of it anymore, it was past. Tomorrow awaited.

Looking closely about her as she rode up the gradual incline up Dugway Pass, Aleksandra glanced left at the faint path leading to their recent tryst, then gritted her teeth and refocused on the trail before her. Past the summit, they headed down the steep descent, the Mustang negotiating the switchbacks and deep dugway like a goat, then loped on across the flats

Wisps of smoke from Dugway Station's chimney showed against the snowy cap of Indian Peak as she blew her bugle. Slipping the *mochila* from beneath her seat, she looked around for signs of life.

The tender, just climbing from the dugout doorway, produced her next ride from the corral, a palomino colt with a bunchy, fluffy mane. A brief exchange while he caught the proffered *mochila* and she filled her canteen, then she was off with a click and a salute at a canter.

The miles rolled. Table Mountain loomed on her right as she pulled the colt to a halt, then stood listening, before edging to the brink of Old Riverbed's cliff. Peering over, she gave the pony his head. He dashed down the trail, straight for the station and his feed. Another quick swap and exchange of pleasantries, and they flew on across the empty waterway, the fresh pony leaping up the far wall. Willingly pausing while she checked the exit from the steep bank, he bounded up the rest of the way and across the desert, headed for Simpson's.

George, *the old sourdough*. She couldn't help the giggle that bubbled out at the thought, then squashed it as she rode up to him and tossed the *mochila* his way, still smiling.

'How goes it out there, lad?' he asked with a grin.

'Like I told the last three that asked me, how could it be anything but great with a keen mount under clear blue skies on a wonderful day to be alive?' She could hardly contain her enthusiasm.

Life really didn't get much better, as long as I don't think of the mess that I've left at Fish Springs.

'Good to hear you say that, Boy, good to hear it,' he said with a chuckle. Rubbing the wriggling pony's head while Aleksandra filled her canteen, he handed her a filled *tortilla*. Stuffing it into her shirt, she saluted him and vaulted onto the buckskin colt with a little cry and a loosing of the reins. She could hear his laugh as she cantered away.

'*Hasta luego*, George!'

The keen Mustang pulled at the reins, so she laughed and let him fly for a few minutes before she scratched his withers and asked him to slow. Swivelling his ears, he responded and slowed to a mile-eating rocking horse lope around the north end of the Simpson Ranges and along Government Creek. At the station, she switched to a bay mare and headed into Government Creek Wash, climbed up the steep grade and rounded the north end of the Sheep Rock Mountains and into Skull Valley.

Ugh... Skull Valley. The very name made her shudder.

Cantering on through it, one of her landmarks, Davis Mountain, reared its head on her left

The mare never batted an eye at the rough ascent to General Johnston's Pass and scrambled right up. Though she was breathing a bit, she was still going well as they trotted into Lookout Station's cedar valley. Waiting for them before the log cabin, Mr. Jackson held a striking Palouse Indian pony. His jet-black coat was relieved only by a snowy blanket over his rump, patterned with tiny black spots.

The keeper's dogs squirmed around Aleksandra when she dismounted, the little brown bitch's lips drawn back into a toothy grimace of a grin while she quivered and wagged her whole body ingratiatingly. Mr. Jackson took only a moment to slip the *mochila* onto the stallion, sign her time card and check for mail before Aleksandra was off again with a pat for the bitch and a wave.

'I call him Scout!' he shouted, as she rode away.

Scout wasn't tall, but he was a powerhouse. He hit a long trot up that steep and rocky incline to the summit, never faltering, never looking to the side. Her heart sang. She was humbled to ride such incredible horses, and actually get paid to do it.

Lookout Pass, she reminded herself as she neared the summit. Glancing north to the distant white tops of the Onaqui Mountains, she swallowed hard as she thought again of her papa and the fossil he'd fossicked for her from its rocky ledges.

The spotted pony broke into a lope over the crest of the hill and began the mile-long descent. Aleksandra's thoughts filled with memories, she was absentmindedly fingering the fossil inside the medicine bag hung about her neck when she felt the first arrow whizz past her head.

Her heart stopped in its tracks and she flung herself to the left side of the Palouse's neck in a Cossack hang, lying flat against his side.

'Yah! Yah! Let's go, Scout!' she shouted, throwing the reins at him.

He needed little urging to run full tilt down the steep and treacherously rocky trail as the yells of Indian warriors echoed through the narrow valley. The arrows came hard and fast from the southwest, screaming like a mad bunch of hornets.

Smart. Her lips curved in the hint of a wry grin.

The Indians had placed themselves between the trail and the setting sun. Aleksandra couldn't see her attackers in the glimpses she stole, from beneath Scout's neck, of the world whizzing past. With the ground only three feet from her head, the scent of sage filled her nostrils when Scout crashed through a clump of brush. Briefly considering letting go of one of her death-grip holds onto the racing horse to pull a gun from her holster, something akin to suicide, she tightened her lip in a grimace and stayed put, trusting far more in the Palouse's speed and handiness to save them. Knowing her weight hanging off to one side had to put him off his best, she tried to stay out of his way, keeping as still as possible, tucked down on the side of the skidding and leaping beast. Praying the cinch would hold, she sent fervent thanks to the pony selectors for their choice of horses.

How I would love to have my bow and arrows, but I only need to get us through to Doc Faust at Rush—

The Palouse interrupted her musings as he threw up his head and reared, angrily trumpeting and shaking his head for a moment, nearly dropping Aleksandra, then resumed his headlong rush down the hill. When he carried on, she heard whistling sounds with every breath and turned her face forward to see where the noise was coming from.

Then she saw the arrow.

16

Aleksandra broke into a cold sweat. The arrowhead was four inches from her face, its shaft protruding from the horse's trachea. A fraction higher or to the left and the iron-tipped arrow would have punctured the colt's jugular vein, or her own skull.

Either way, I'd be dead. I wouldn't be able to talk myself out of this one.

As they raced down the hill, the whine of arrows abruptly ceased and she peeked around the front of Scout's chest. Nothing ahead, but when she turned her head to look back, past the heaving flank of her mount, she saw six or seven Indians astride their colorful ponies in a group.

One big man on a fine Palouse horse sat still as a statue. Turned away from her, with his pony across the trail, he seemed to be stopping the others from pursuit. She heard gruff shouts, and saw his hand raised towards two younger braves, whose horses angrily plunged up and down, reflecting the looks upon their riders' faces.

They didn't follow.

Heaven only knows why he stopped them, but it doesn't really matter.

Her brow furrowed, but if salvation was offered, she'd take it. She breathed deeply, glad to be alive. The distance between them and the

Indians was still too narrow for comfort, so she let the stallion run on until they were out of the foothills and a good way onto the flats.

Looking around again and seeing no followers, she swung down from the gasping pony. The arrowhead had gone through the trachea and straight out the other side. Scout cringed away when her hand approached it. Speaking softly to the stallion, she moved as slowly as possible and carefully broke the shaft on the arrowhead side where it protruded from his windpipe. Scratching hard behind his eye with her fingernails, she jerked the rest of the arrow from his neck. He jumped, but soon settled. After running her hands quickly over the rest of his body for further injuries, Aleksandra sighed in relief and tied the pieces of bloodied arrow onto the saddle tree under her *mochila*.

Scout sucked air into his trachea through the arrow punctures, but it could wait until they reached Rush Valley. They only had four more miles to go. Crossing herself, she gave thanks for their escape, then rubbed the horse's forehead while he drank from her hat. She mounted and took a deep breath as they headed off at a strong trot, the Palouse whistling with every breath. It wouldn't do to be found here by the Indians after so narrowly escaping them in the pass.

Bugle at full noise, she rode into Rush Valley Station and flung herself from the Palouse. The eastbound rider was waiting for the *mochila*. Tossing it to Doc Faust, she breathlessly told them about the Indians.

Grimacing, the rider clapped her on the back. 'Glad you've kept your hair, and the *mochila*. Good riding, Boy. I'll try to do so well. Bye Doc, Aleks.' Nodding to them, he mounted and cantered off.

'Aleks,' Doc looked her straight in the eyes, seeming to look right through her. 'Are you all right?'

'I'm okay, it's the pony,' she said, showing him the pieces of arrow, then gesturing at the holes in the pony's skin over his trachea.

'Green. *Verdammt*,' he swore softly in German.

'Green?' Aleksandra stared at him.

'Poisoned arrows. We don't have much time, I'll explain later. Run to the station and get hot water from the stove and some rags. I'll get my kit ready.'

She flew to the station for the water and was cleaning the wounds by the time Doc collected his surgical gear and dragged a box to serve as a makeshift operating table beside to the wobbly, dripping horse.

'We need to remove any tissue touched by that arrow.' He winced. 'The only good thing about the toxin is that it deadens some of the nerves, but it must be done, or he'll be in serious trouble.'

Aleksandra flicked the blanket she'd retrieved from the station over the horse's back. She took a good neck twitch on him, wiggling his head and neck while Doc trimmed as much affected flesh as he could, then undermined the skin surrounding it.

'This is one lucky pony. It went right between the cartilage rings, so I don't think we need to remove any of them. I've done a major debride. I'll just suture the two adjacent rings together. If we don't get too much dead tissue from the poison, he might just pull through. I've got some ammonia. Some think it neutralizes the toxin, so we'll swab it well with that before we stitch it together and pray a lot. The Indians tend to cauterize the area around a snake bite, but I'd like to see it heal with as little scarring as possible, but that won't happen if we burn the tissues.'

'Where is the ammonia? I'm going to the kitchen for some cobwebs to make the stent to stitch on over your repair,' she said.

Doc raised his eyebrows at that. 'You *do* know what you're about, don't you, missy? It's in a box next to the food cabinet.'

Flashing him a smile in acceptance of the compliment, she bolted back to the station as fast as her tired legs would go.

The pony's head was drooping when she returned. Doc struggled to get up from his crouch under the spotted horse's neck, then stood rubbing his knees.

'Can I help? I'm smaller and I've handled a scalpel all my life,' she said with a crooked grin.

'Glad for the help.' He wiped the sweat dripping from his brow, handing her the blade.

Aleksandra made quick work of finishing the job beneath Doc's watchful eye, then he threaded a needle with catgut suture from a jar of spirit and handed it to her. She placed three pieces of suture with loose surgeon's knots around the exposed circumference of the two cartilage rings, then tightened them as Doc pulled the rings together with forceps. The fully awake and sentient horse flinched, but stood like a rock.

'Stallions are tough, God love 'em,' Doc said, rubbing the colt's cheek with his left hand, while keeping a tight hold on a handful of neck skin with his right while she knotted the sutures.

'Yes, he's a champ. Just about done, love,' she crooned. He flicked an ear back at her. 'Just the skin to close, then the stent.'

'I've got it here.' Doc had wrapped her mass of cobwebs with a clean cloth, turning it into a pad. Aleksandra swabbed the edges of the trachea where the arrow had penetrated with ammonia and the colt snorted, picking up his head, but he never moved his feet. Her own eyes watered just from the *fumes* of the ammonia. Closing the skin incision, she dabbed more ammonia on it, then placed four loops of suture through the colt's skin, two inches out from each corner of the wound.

Doc had sewn a long piece of heavy thread through each end of the sausage-like stent and dipped it in a boiling pot of salted water. Letting it cool briefly, he handed it to her. Placing it over the wound, she tied it in place through the skin suture loops and straightened up with a big sigh. 'Now I guess it's just time to pray. We've done all we can for him.'

'Thanks Aleks, that's a good job you've done there, couldn't have done better myself.' His eyes glowed as he smiled at her.

'Least I can use what my papa taught me.'

'He must have been an amazing man,' Doc said.

'He was my…my…*everything*.' She broke down with a sob, tears springing from her eyes she stumbled blindly into Doc's arms. Holding her, he sat down on the box next to the stallion, who snuffled into her hair as she cried.

'There, there, Aleks. Just a bit shocky. First your papa, then people firing arrows at you, and now your precious pony's in danger. At least you're both still alive.'

She cried for a moment more, and then rubbed at her eyes, blood still all over her hands. She looked up at Doc, pursed her lips together and shook her head at herself. 'I'll be okay. Just been a bit of a rough week.' She rubbed her hands together and stood staring at them, unseeing. 'I won't mind being here with you for a couple of days. It will be good to have someone around who'll talk to me.' She looked off into the distance.

'Oh, like that, is it?' he said gruffly. 'And your name's not really Aleks, is it?'

'Mmm...' She turned to him, then ducked her head. 'It's Aleksandra,' she mumbled.

'We can talk about that later. I'll get this pony settled in the hay barn where it's warm, and we can keep a close eye on him. You go in and see what I've got on the stove for you. I'll be in shortly.'

'How 'bout I help, then we can both go in. It's nearly feeding time, anyway.' She looked down again at her hands then smiled up at him. 'I'm grubby anyway, might as well get the farm work done now.'

'Okay, Aleksandra, happy for the help.' He gave her a quick hug and handed Scout's reins to her. You walk him around for a few minutes. It'll do you both good.'

Replacing his bridle with a halter, she slipped the cinch and pulled off his saddle before offering him a few sips of water, and then meandered around the yard with him.

Walking took some of the kinks out of her legs. The spotted stallion seemed to move more freely too, snatching at any tufts of dry grass they passed, to her relief. He took another drink from the proffered bucket, then played with the water for a moment before raising his head high and dribbling water over the top of her head.

'From you, my fine one, I will take even *that*,' she murmured, then put down the bucket to rub under his forelock. When he stepped closer, she scratched all around his ears until Doc called for her to bring him in. Walking into the newly created and bedded stall in a corner of the hay barn, he vigorously shook his head, and then the rest of his body. He didn't even seem to notice the bulky bandage stitched to the skin beneath his neck.

'How's he doing, Aleks?'

'Wants scratches, but otherwise, not worried about a thing.'

Doc offered him some hay and he ripped it out of his hand. 'That's a stallion for you, they just don't fuss about things—unless of course, there's a mare about.'

'They are simply the toughest and most amazing creatures on the planet.'

Doc looked at her more closely and smirked, blue eyes dancing. 'You already had a bath or something?'

She giggled. 'Yeah, Scout thought I needed it. Seeing how he just saved my life, I thought I'd oblige.' She smiled at the pony and kissed the soft nose he lifted to her, inhaling the sweet smell of freshly chewed hay.

'Well, he looks good for now.'

'I hope he looks this good in the morning,' Aleksandra sighed deeply and gave him another hug. 'Thank you for saving my life, little horse,' she whispered into his mane.

He only snorted and returned to his supper, as she and Doc headed for theirs.

'Mmmmm...what smells so good, Doc?' Aleksandra said, shedding her jacket onto the back of a chair in the station kitchen.

'Just wait until you taste it! He was a bit old and tough, but he'll be *ten-der to-night!* Rubbing his hands in time with his words, Doc Faust practically danced to the cooking fire in the corner of the room to rake the coals off the lid of the Dutch oven.

As a delicious aroma escaped, she watched him close his eyes and inhale deeply. 'Now, doesn't that smell heavenly, girl?'

'Sure does.' She grinned, sniffing the air herself.

'Can you bring over two of those dishes, please?' He waved an arm in the direction of a shelf on the opposite wall.

Aleksandra smiled at the blue and white-speckled spatterware plates as she carried them back. Peeking into the cast-iron pot, she saw two small roasts, root vegetables and some unrecognizable greens plus a small sprig of sage. Her mouth watered as Doc dished up.

She didn't recognize the meat, but it smelled fantastic. 'Wherever did you get the nice little roasts? They fit perfectly in your oven!'

'Well, girl, meat's been a bit scarce. We've already eaten the beefies, most of the cows are calving and game's been scarce. Fortunately for us, a few wolves were trying to kill one of the new calves yesterday, and the haunches of one of the wolves made it into my oven this morning. We call it "wolf mutton"'.

Her eyebrows shot up and her stomach flipped. It didn't smell quite so good now.

She must have made some noise, because Doc looked up at her in surprise.

'Haven't you had wolf before? Daughter of a trapper?' He grinned.

'No,' she said faintly, 'but it seems I'm about to.' She took a deep breath and fixed him with a steady look. 'It smells good, and you clearly like it, so it must be good.'

She set the plates on the table and sat down.

Doc offered grace and started in on his dinner.

Aleksandra took her first bite. 'Doc, it *is* good!' She raised her eyebrows.

'Now, do you think I'd feed you poorly, woman?' He laughed.

'Sorry, Doc.' She hunched her shoulders and looked up at him from under her lashes, smiling. 'I had no idea wolf could taste so good. I was so worried about them eating *me*, that I never thought to eat *them*.'

Doc just laughed and tucked in.

After eating most of their dinner in hungry silence, Doc took a deep breath and looked at Aleksandra.

'You've not seen a poisoned arrow before, have you, Aleks?'

'How do you know it was poisoned?' She scrunched her brow.

'The green. You saw it on the arrowhead.'

17

'*Green?*' Aleksandra's brows drew together, her head tilting.
Doc took a deep breath.

'I'm sure glad they missed you today,' he said, fixing her with a stare. 'The Indians capture a rattlesnake and let it bite into a piece of antelope liver, which they carry, wrapped around a stick. They thrust arrowheads into the green, poison-stained meat to coat them with a layer of the venomous slime, and *voilà*,' he grimaced, 'poisoned arrows.'

'Oh, the poor Palouse,' she whispered, a tear rolling down her cheek, 'he could die.'

Her breath caught when she thought of the danger to her own life. Accustomed to being in the inner circle of an Indian tribe, she was finding it difficult to get used to the idea they might want to kill her.

'I'm just glad,' he said, reaching for her hand, 'they didn't stick an arrow in you, darlin'. Just how *did* you get away from them, and only take one arrow between the two of you? I'm sure they shot a whole lot more of them.'

'That's a bit of a mystery.' She frowned, chewing on a fingernail. 'I was going to ask you about that.'

'I've never heard of such a thing,' he said with a frown after she recounted the tall Indian's act of salvation, 'but it sounds like they were firing plenty of arrows at you *before* they stopped. How did you avoid getting hit?'

'I was doing *džigitovka*, the one I call my "disappearing act".'

'Pardon me, your *what*?'

'Cossack military show riding.' She laughed, her eyes lighting up. 'I was hanging down on one side of the Palouse with my head a hand's breadth from that arrow.' She shuddered. 'I'll show you sometime.'

'Like a Cossack trick-rider? I've seen them in San Francisco! They're unbelievable!' He stopped dead. 'You can *do* these things? How … how do you know this *dzig* … how do you say it?

'*Džigitovka*. My papa taught me,' she said, looking down at the table, uncertain for a moment. Doc waited.

It's now or never. I need this man's advice.

Her breath caught in her throat. Aleksandra sat up straight in her chair looked him in the eye. 'It was taught to him in Poland, by the same man who may have killed Papa. I dress as a boy so he cannot find me.'

He sat for a moment, then took another deep breath. 'Would you like to talk about it?'

She finally finished her story, down to the last bits about Xavier and Dancing Wolf. The relief of sharing it was a cleansing, like standing beneath a cool mountain waterfall on a hot summer day.

'Oh, Aleksandra.' Doc sighed and put another log on the fire, rubbing his hands clean on deerskin trousers. Sitting down, he rested his elbows on the table, chin on fist. 'I can keep your secret for you, but Xavier may be a difficult row to hoe. I can tell you what I know about his past and try to help you understand what it might mean to you.'

'Anything would help.' Aleksandra swallowed hard and looked down at the table.

'He's not told me much about his past, but what he *has* said wasn't good. Do you know anything about growing up in an abusive family?'

She shook her head, eyes wide.

'They usually don't let people close easily. Imagine taking a young foal and every time it came near its mother, you hit it with a stick. How do you think that foal would grow up?'

'I think it wouldn't trust its mother.'

'Yes. Since its mother is the one it was meant to trust more than any other, do you think it will have faith in any other horses, or people, for that matter?'

'Probably not,' she said in a small voice.

'When parents abuse a child, what do you think it thinks about those who are supposed to care for them the most?'

'I would imagine they don't believe in them, or anyone else, for that matter,' she whispered. 'Is that what happened to Xavier?'

'From the little he's let slip, I think he was abused by his father and his mother did nothing to stop it.'

'How could any parents do that to their child?' she breathed, tears rolling down her cheeks.

'Hard to imagine, isn't it? Unfortunately, it's common.'

'Sometimes Xavier seems close and loving, and then suddenly he pushes me away and becomes distant and won't talk with me. It usually happens when we've been close, when everything seems like it's all working out.'

'That sounds about right.'

She hesitated, then winced. She had to know. 'Will it always be like this, or can it change?'

'It isn't easy, but I've seen people make the changes they needed to have a good relationship with someone they cared about.'

'"Where there's a will, there's a way", Mama always said.' Aleksandra roughly wiped the tears from her eyes and set her jaw.

'Just warning you, girl, it might be a rocky road, but I've got a lot of time for Xavier. He's pretty special to me. Maybe, with time, if he sees the real problem and chooses to work through it, you two can make a good life for yourselves.'

'I hope so,' she said, past the lump in her throat.

Doc sat up and looked straight at her. 'Don't take it too hard if he doesn't come 'round. It's got to come from him, and it won't happen overnight, if ever. If it means keeping you, though, it might be worth his while to try. I hope so.'

'Thanks, Doc,' she murmured, glancing down at her hands gripped together in her lap.

'Now, miss, enough talking.' He reached over and mussed her hair. 'You'd better get to bed before you fall asleep in your plate.'

Dragging her weary eyelids up, she grinned. 'Other than the last little bit, today was a glorious ride. Lovely, keen ponies, beautiful weather, what more could one ask?'

'What more, indeed? Shot with poisoned arrows? I just don't know about today's youth!' He snatched a pillow from his bed and threw it at her, pointing out her bunk. 'Bed, young lady. We'll talk more in the morning. I'll go check Scout.'

'Goodnight, thank you for taking care of him and talking with me, and … everything.' Heading for her bunk, she gave him a sleepy smile. She'd never forget her first Pony Express ride.

'GOOD MORNING, SLEEPYHEAD,' Doc called out. 'Hotcakes nearly ready! Time to be up and about!'

''Mornin' Doc!' Closing her eyes again for a moment, Aleksandra let the aroma of sourdough pancakes fill her whole being, the best of all possible morning smells. It brought with it a pang for her lost family, but she resolutely opened her eyes and threw back the blanket.

The blanket?

Her brow furrowed. 'Doc, I don't remember covering myself up last night.'

He chuckled. 'Nope, by the time I returned from the barn, you were on top of it, dead asleep in your clothes. You never stirred when I covered you up with a couple of Indian rugs.'

'I must've been tired, thanks. Do I have time to check on Scout before breakfast?'

'Sure do. I'll be glad to know what you think of him.'

'Be right back,' she threw over her shoulder as she jogged away, long braid bouncing.

The Palouse stood with his rump to her, head down. His coat, so smooth and glossy yesterday, stared roughly and was warm to the touch. He lifted his head a little when she touched him, but lowered it almost immediately. He'd eaten only a fraction of last night's supper and wasn't interested in the handful of feed she offered.

Doesn't want water, either.

She shook her head. The wound was painful to her light touch, but not overly so, and the color of his gums was still good. He didn't have the stench of death, yet.

One of Papa's lessons flooded back as she absently stroked the stallion's forelock.

'This plant, Aleksandra,' Krzysztof held up a shrivelled plant with dark, yellow-brown frayed bits on one end, 'in addition to the features that make it so desirable to those who would seek us out, can you tell me what else it can do?' Wistfully, she watched as he faded from her vision.

Thank you, Papa, for that gift from Heaven. Would that you were here to help this Palouse who saved my life. Her lips formed a lopsided grin. *If you were here right now, I'd be in serious trouble, but there'd be no need to save him, for I certainly wouldn't be riding for the Pony.*

'JUST IN TIME.' Doc handed her a full plate of dollar-sized pancakes when she entered the station, the hotcakes crispy on the edges, light and airy in the middle, wafting their tangy aroma all the way to her taste buds. 'I was about to eat them all!'

'Ooh, just the way I like them!' She gulped, trying to smile, then in response to the question in his eyes, sobered. 'No, I don't like how he's looking, either. The wound looks okay, it must be the toxin in his bloodstream, or something else altogether.' Pressing her lips together, she looked out the open door toward the hay barn.

'What would you do next?' he asked.

'Papa's "secret" I mentioned last night is a plant extract. It has properties that some people would kill for, but Papa taught me it's always been used against depression, tiredness and nerve weakness.'

'Really? What is it? Sure wish we had some of it, then.' Turning back to the griddle, he flipped the hotcakes. 'It might just have helped this horse.'

'Weeeeel,' she stretched out the word, 'I can't tell you what it is in English but I do have some extract we could give him, if you'd permit me to try it.' She looked up at him and bit her lip.

'You *do*?' He spun around, eyes wide, then returned to the griddle, whipping it off the fire onto one of the bricks edging the fireplace.

'Why didn't you say so? Pancakes'll wait,' he said, hustling out the door.

Aleksandra pulled the syringe from her belt pouch and a precious bottle of the liquid from its buckskin bag hung about her neck beside Papa's medicine bag. Dropping the syringe into a pot of steaming water on the back of the stove, she headed for the barn.

'I'm just boiling the syringe on the stove,' she told Doc when she found him checking the horse's gum color.

Smiling at her, he shook his head. 'I am constantly amazed,' he said, 'that one so young has so much skill.'

Her cheeks warmed at his compliment while she ran to get the syringe. Pouring off the steaming water covering the instrument, she carried the hot pot back to the barn. When it was cool enough to touch, she filled the syringe with amber fluid from one of her precious vials. She closed her eyes, stomach churning, at the smell of vodka wafting from the opened bottle, thinking of the last time she'd tasted the spirit. She shook her head to clear it.

'Doc, could you please hold his head for me?' She held off the horse's jugular vein with her thumb. 'Give him a hard scratch right here.' She pointed to the tender area just behind his eye. Scout never moved while she slowly injected the solution. After he was released, he took a deep breath, shook his mane and walked around his stall a few times. He played in his water bucket then settled down to listlessly lip at some hay, but didn't eat it. They gave him a small measure of grain to tempt his appetite and left him to rest.

By evening, Scout had improved. For whatever reason, he was eating and drinking. They talked again until late that night and she spent most of the next day fussing over the horse.

'You'll be spoilin' him, young lady,' Doc said at lunchtime. 'He's probably never had so much attention in his entire life.' He smiled and looked out the door at the Palouse. Later that afternoon, they turned him out into a corral next to the other horses. Though he was alone in his pen, he was nearly back to his normal stallion self, trying to herd the other horses from his side of the fence and eating everything in sight.

Aleksandra's next ride was saddled up and ready to leave for Fish Springs around midnight.

'Doc, I want you to know how much I've appreciated your friendship,' she said, leaning on the railings next to the station tender, watching Scout. 'It means more to me than you'll ever know.' Her voice wavered as she reached out to give him a big hug, which he heartily returned.

'Well, you know, you do just as much for me,' he said gruffly, holding her at arm's length before him. 'Now you remember all I've said about you and that man of yours. He might need your love and care, but he doesn't know it yet, and it may be a long time before he figures it out.'

'Okay, I will. I promise to back off a bit.' She smiled up at her friend.

'In the meantime, missy,' he said, brows drawn together, 'you need to take especially good care of yourself, for your *own* sake. I'd sure hate it if you went out and did something foolish on a horse and never came back to see me,' he tilted his head, brow furrowed, then snorted, 'but I guess that's what you do every day, riding for the Pony.'

She laughed, and a bugle sounded through the midnight darkness of the desert. The horse and rider were still invisible, but soon the trotting hoofbeats of a single horse came to them on the breeze and the pair materialized before them.

Standing ready with her pinto mare, she accepted the *mochila* and exchanged a brief greeting with the incoming rider, then turned to Doc.

'Take good care of Scout and your hair!' Aleksandra said, vaulting onto the pinto mare as she struck off at a canter.

'You watch yourself in those passes!' He shouted, as she headed for Lookout.

Don't think they'll catch me sleeping again, Doc. I'm not bound to forget an ambush any time soon!

The narrow rocky canyon leading up Lookout was quiet. If anyone was there, she was relieved to find they weren't shooting tonight. As they rose above the fog wisping about the desert floor, the moonlight showed the trail clearly and they made good time over the top of the pass.

At Lookout Station, Mr. Jackson's mouth dropped open when she told him about the ambush, and he inhaled sharply at the news of Scout. He'd heard nothing from the Indians for several days.

'The Indians have been my friends for many years,' he said softly, shaking his head and swallowing hard. 'They've always come here to trade. I'm so sad this is all coming to pass.'

'I understand how you feel,' Aleksandra said, tears filling her eyes. 'The *Shoshone* were my second family, and now their way of life is changing, probably forever, because of the settlers.'

'Aye, lass, and it looks to not be ending any time soon,' he murmured.

The news of Scout's recovery heartened him and he smiled as she rode away on a new pony. On full alert throughout the long trip home, thoughts of Xavier warmed her heart. Maybe, just maybe, she could help him through this.

18

'What do you mean, you forgive *me*?' Aleksandra said, through gritted teeth, staring at him, fists clenched at her sides.

Just what is she so furious about?

'Well, I've been thinking,' Xavier looked at his feet, then back up at her. 'I was so angry with you for not telling me you were promised to Dancing Wolf, when I wanted to—'

'You can *not* be serious!' Her mouth dropped open. 'I didn't even *know* about it until the day I met you!' Spinning on her heel, she turned away, breathing heavily.

'I hoped we could let bygones be bygones and start over.' Placing his hand on her shoulder, he turned her around and looked into her eyes, beseeching her. Tilting her chin up with his forefinger, he leaned across the space between them to kiss her lightly on the lips. 'I'm just trying to say *lo siento*, I am sorry for it, all of it, but I seem to be making a poor job of it.'

She took a deep breath. 'I appreciate that, Xavier, can we start over?'

'*Ven aquí.*' He closed his eyes and shook his head. 'Come here, *Querida.*' He waited for her to come, then wrapped his arms tightly about her.

'Thanks,' she mumbled into his shirt.

'Good sleep?' he queried, enjoying the feel of her in his arms. She seemed to fit just right.

'My bed was heavenly soft after being in the saddle for nine hours.' She smiled up at him, then rubbed her face against his chest above the buckskin laces.

I could definitely get used to this.

'So, how was your first Pony ride, *Querida*?' he asked into her hair, and kissed the top of her head. She'd returned to Fish Springs early this morning and stumbled into bed, while he kept himself busy around the place.

'Mostly, it was fantastic, right up until the last six miles...we had a bit of a close call.'

'What sort of close call?' He looked at her sideways, eyes narrowed.

'We ran into an ambush on the far side of Lookout Pass.'

Xavier's blood froze in his veins. Gripping her shoulders, he held her at arm's length. 'What do you mean?' Xavier growled.

'Ouch, you're hurting me!'

'Sorry.' He swore softly in Spanish. 'Please go on.' Taking her hand, he sat down on a bench against the station wall and pulled her onto his lap, wrapping his arms about her.

'Indian attack. I think they were *Pah-Utes*,' she turned to look at him, 'going down that narrow canyon on the far side of Lookout,'

'Are you okay?' he asked, searching her eyes for more than she was telling him.

'Yes, but the stallion took a poisoned arrow. I'd never seen one before. Doc and I treated him. He was okay when I left Rush Valley.'

'You weren't hit?' He still wasn't satisfied.

'No, the first arrow whizzed straight past my head and I dropped into a Cossack hang. Luckily, they were all on the southwest side of the canyon, so I stayed down low on the left, opposite them. I was on Scout, a little Palouse stallion.'

'Oh, Scout! What a blessing you were on him.' He hugged her tightly. 'He's a great little horse. So you really didn't get hurt, at all?' He kept peering around Aleksandra, seeking hidden wounds.

'No, but the arrow went through Scout's windpipe and we had to cut away any muscle and skin that might have touched the poison.'

'Oh no.' Xavier's stomach turned over.

'He looked pretty bad the morning after, but he's pulled through, so far,' she said with a tremulous smile.

'How did you get away with only one arrow?'

'That's what we couldn't figure out.' She told him about the big man stopping the others from pursuing her.

'I wonder what that was about.' He looked at her sideways, his forehead wrinkled tight.

'Hopefully we won't need to find out.' She smiled at him and squeezed his arms with hers.

'All that matters is that you're safe. I don't want you riding anymore,' he stated flatly. 'I want you with me, where I can keep you safe, with you as a woman. Stop all this pretense. There is no need for you to work, especially at something this dangerous.'

'It's a little late for that,' she said, one eyebrow raised. 'You know that better than I.'

He had no good answer for that, though everything in him screamed to keep her close. He tried again. 'I can protect you. What's so bad that you have to continue this masquerade? Come out of hiding.'

She hung her head and said no more.

In his chair before the fire that night, he held her on his lap, stroking her hair as they watched the fire lick at the logs. She finally sighed, brushed her lips against his cheek and headed for her own little bunk, alone.

Xavier cooled his heels, staring into the flames for an hour until her breathing become regular and he heard no more of the little sobs she tried to keep to herself. Climbing into bed, his thoughts circled.

Whatever am I to do with the woman? Dios mío, *she's close and loving one moment, cold the next. Perhaps I'll go to Carson,* a mi madre, *before it's too late. I need to get away for a while, maybe even for good, but I really don't want to leave her ... ever.*

Grooming her third horse for the morning, Aleksandra stole a glance at Xavier over the pony's back, watching as he repaired some shattered corral rails.

When he was finished, he walked slowly toward her, his gaze darting at her face with a question in his eyes. She smiled when he took the hand she proffered. It wasn't his fault, all of this confusion between them. It seemed they both had secrets they weren't getting past.

'Looks like they broke a colt in there.' She nodded at the damaged poles.

'Could be. I think it was that little pinto,' he glanced over his shoulder at a piebald Mustang in another corral. 'He's not keen on having his feet touched. I had a time of it with him yesterday.' He smiled ruefully, rubbing at his upper thigh. 'He got me. Luckily, he only caught me with *one* of his hind feet.

'You be careful of these sweet little ponies.' A giggle escaped her as she let go of his hand and moved towards Dzień. It felt good to laugh after the ups and downs of the past week.

She'd missed her Indian pony while she was away riding, and set about giving him an extra-special grooming. She was nearly steaming from her exertions over his coat when he pulled his head away from her hand and spun around. His little ears pricked, he stared out across the desert, neighing loudly. Through the early morning mist, a horse and rider came toward them, fast. Aleksandra and Xavier turned to look at each other, eyebrows raised.

'They're coming at a pretty good clip across that soft ground. You're not expecting anyone, are you?' She squinted into the distance.

The oncoming horse whinnied back. Dzień ran to the corral fence and screamed, switching his tail and spinning on his hind legs, racing back and forth along the fence line.

'He knows that horse. Sounds familiar to me too,' she said to Xavier, who had just returned with his rifle.

As they came closer, she recognized the pair. Taking a deep breath, she looked at Xavier. 'It's Dancing Wolf,' she said, as lightly as possible, her heart in her throat.

His face clouded over. 'What does he want?'

'You know as much as I do. I don't know why he's come, but we're about to find out.' Glancing up at the Californio, her heart sank at his set jaw and lowered brows as they watched the pair approach.

Aleksandra walked towards her friend as he slowed his pony to a walk.

'*Kwahaten*, are you well?' he called, his brows nearly touching, the Indian's jaw as tight as Xavier's.

'Yes, of course, why wouldn't I be?' Reaching up, she squeezed his hand. 'But please, come and meet Xavier.'

The keeper's eyes shot daggers, his body taut, knuckles white on the rifle.

Dancing Wolf slid from his horse and approached the other man.

She shot off a rapid stream of *Shoshone*, explaining that she was now riding for the Pony, as a boy, and that she and Xavier had become close friends. He looked at her, and she saw in his eyes a brief flicker of sadness before he sighed, then smiled.

'I'm glad you have found someone special with whom to share your time, ' he said in *Shoshone*.

'Thank you, Dancing Wolf.' She replied in his language, her heart in her voice.

Xavier looked hard at her, his gaze steely, then turned to the Indian and extended his hand slowly. 'Hello, what can I do for you?' Though polite, his words were as stiff as his spine.

'I heard about the ambush,' he glanced at Aleksandra, 'and I wanted to make sure she was truly unharmed.'

She started and looked sideways at the Indian. 'How did you hear about it?'

'A *Pah-Ute* runner came to me yesterday, saying an Express rider with a girl's voice and your riding talent was attacked at Lookout Pass. I am a friend of the son of their chief. My friend recognized you at Lookout from my stories in the past.'

Xavier muttered under his breath.

Aleksandra and Dancing Wolf glanced at him. His lips made a hard line as he stared at the Indian and fingered his rifle.

'You were known to have been at Fish Springs, Aleks,' Dancing Wolf continued, with the hint of a smile, 'by two *Shoshone* who visited. They have been telling everyone how you fool many white settlers, pretending to be a boy.'

Aleksandra and Xavier looked at each other and the Californio's face softened a touch.

'The Indians who visited.' She turned to Xavier. 'Yes, they recognized me,' she said, over her shoulder to Dancing Wolf.

'It's a lucky thing for you that they did.' The Indian's voice was edgy.

'That would explain,' Aleksandra nodded her head slowly, 'why they stopped firing arrows at me.' She told Dancing Wolf about the Indians she saw after the swarm of arrows stopped during the ambush.

'Yes, the "big man on the good horse" was my friend, the son of their chief. I am thankful he was on that raid,' Dancing Wolf sighed, 'and that they didn't use rifles. When the runner came, I feared, because I knew that they were on the warpath—' He stopped.

'—and using poisoned arrows?' she finished.

'Yes.' He looked her hard in the eyes. 'I went to Rush Valley to find out what happened to you and met Doc Faust. He showed me Scout, and told me what you two did for him. I'm proud of you, *Kwahaten*,' he said, rubbing Dzień's forehead over the fence.

She looked down and blushed. 'It was Papa's doing. He taught me everything.'

'After being reassured by Doc Faust,' Dancing Wolf continued, 'I rode more slowly. He said you were fine, but I wanted to be sure you arrived home safely.'

'Thank you for your concern, but she'll be fine,' Xavier said, his voice flinty. 'I can protect her.'

Dancing Wolf raised a single eyebrow at him, the corners of his mouth twitching.

'You can't protect me!' Aleksandra gritted her teeth as she spun to face Xavier, fisting her buckskins at her sides. 'How could you possibly? I'm riding for the Pony. You can't save me, you can't tell me what to do and you certainly can't control me.' Turning on her heel, she pulled the reins from the Indian's hand and stalked off to feed and water his pinto.

The two men held their breath and looked sideways at each other.

'THANK you for coming to check on her,' Xavier said from between tight lips. 'I care for her very much and will keep her safe.'

'You have my blessing to try,' Dancing Wolf said, 'but I have known her since we were children. Trying to protect her is like trying to protect the wind.'

The Californio raised an eyebrow at him.

'She has told you of our past?'

'Yes,' he said abruptly, and looked away.

'Good. She cannot be mine, but I would be happy to see her safely protected in marriage to a strong man, so I thank you. Care for her well.' He nodded. 'I will go to say goodbye.' The Indian turned and went to find Aleksandra.

Leaning back against the barn wall, he watched his tired pony sip water from a bucket, then turn to munch hay while Aleksandra brushed him vigorously, using two currycombs at once. The pinto preened as she rubbed hard in circles. Beneath her breath, she muttered words he'd never before heard coming from a woman's mouth.

He raised his eyebrows, wondering if it were safe to approach. She kept grooming when he walked up beside her, though the curses stopped.

'You know, his color might come off if you keep doing that,' he said dryly.

She stopped and leaned over the colt, laying her cheek against his rump. 'I feel so alone and unloved.'

'You are neither.'

'But you don't know the truth of it.' Aleksandra slid down the pony's leg to the ground and sat with crossed legs. She haltingly explained the problems between her and Xavier, staring, but not seeing her fingers, tying knots in a piece of hay.

'It sounds like you need to talk together, as is always the case with mates.'

'I keep thinking if I hold on and keep trying, everything will work out, but every time we start to get closer, he runs away and won't let me close.' Her head sunk to her chest. 'I've only done what I thought was right and best for him '

'You must give him time,' he said. She shrank back from his glare. 'And, you have no idea what is right for him.'

'But will we ever get past it? How long will it *take*? And then...and then,' her breath caught on a sob as she stood up, 'he treats me like a *child*,' she wailed and tossed her brushes to the ground, bursting into tears.

He looked at her, eyebrows raised.

She turned and flung herself at the man, wrapping her arms around him, sobbing.

He stiffened. Disentangling her, he held her at arm's length.

'If he treats you like a child, perhaps it's because you act like one,' he growled.

She looked at him without speaking, mouth rigid. 'What do you mean?' she spat, beneath narrowed brows.

'Stop acting like a spoiled infant. That man loves you enough to want to protect you, despite your behavior and unwillingness to act like a female. It would not have been accepted in our village, nor by me. What I didn't tell you in front of Xavier was *why* my friend, the one who saved your life, sent for me.

She looked up at him, head tilted and eyebrow raised, silently waiting.

'His words were: "Go and get your woman sorted. Stop her from doing dangerous things, things like riding for the Pony."'

She stood in sullen silence, glaring at the ground before his feet.

'So you see? It's not just Xavier.'

She still didn't look up.

'You say he won't let you close, do you let *him* close?' the Indian asked. 'Go back and let him know how you feel. Give him time to fight his own demons. For my part, I just wanted to make sure you were safe.'

She hung her head for long minutes.

'I have been acting like a child,' she finally whispered. 'I appreciate your coming so far to check on me and I apologize to you. I will now do the same to Xavier. I guess it's time I grew up.'

'That is a good idea.' He reached toward her and touched her cheek. 'Go to your man,' he said, turning her around and giving her a little push.

IN FRONT OF THE STATION, she stood before Xavier, biting her lip. 'I am sorry, Xavier,' she looked up, 'for accusing you of not letting me close, and then not letting you near me, either. Dancing Wolf pointed out a few home truths to me just now.'

'What does he have to do with us?' Xavier growled.

'He cares enough to try to help us work out our problems,' she said. 'I'm going to invite him in for a meal. Other than you and Scotty, he is the only friend and family I have left. He's just ridden for days to get here, just to check on me. Think about it.'

They dined with polite conversation, if tight lipped on Xavier's part. As Dancing Wolf stood to leave, the Californio asked him to please drop a letter to Mr. Egan at Salt Lake House. When he left the station, Xavier shook the Indian's hand as if he meant it and Aleksandra let out the breath she'd been holding for what seemed hours.

She followed Dancing Wolf to collect his mount. The brown and white pony and the buckskin were scratching each other's withers over the gate, and she squeezed in to give the pinto a hug. He and Dzień had been foals together in the *Shoshone* herd and were especially close.

'He's as happy to see Dzień as I am to see you. Thank you again for seeing to me,' she said, past the lump in her throat. 'You're very special to me. Please give your family and *Newe* my love. They are always in my heart.'

'And you in mine. Now go to your man, he cares for you. Be patient, *Kwahaten*, everything worth having takes time.' With a quick hug, Dancing Wolf swung up onto the pinto, spun him about and was gone.

A STONY SILENCE persisted between Xavier and Aleksandra.

'What did you send to Mr. Egan?' she asked, later that evening.

'I asked for leave. I need to go to Carson City to meet with my mother,' he said, blood pounding in his head.

'Your mother?' She smiled at him. 'I didn't know you had contact with her.'

'I received a letter while you were away, I must go to her.'

She let her breath out slowly. 'When will you return?' she asked softly.

He was silent for a moment. 'Does it matter? You seem to have other suitors calling.' He was drowning in darkness.

'Suitors?' she whispered, her face falling.

'Dancing Wolf, for one."

She shook her head slowly, then stood very still, her mouth dropped open. 'He did nothing but try to help us, telling me I needed to grow up and give you time, and you insult him. His only concern is that I treat you well so we can get along,' she said quietly, but with an edge of steel.

Truth be told, Xavier didn't know what he was doing, either. Closing his eyes, he retreated to the barn for some mindless work. His head was spinning as he grabbed a pitchfork to clean stalls. Until Dancing Wolf went behind the barn to speak with Aleksandra, Xavier had made no decision about going to Carson. Fearing he would lose her to the Indian made him want to run and never let anyone close again.

The feelings were too strong. He cared more deeply for her than he'd ever let himself care for anyone else. He was embarrassed, no, disgusted to his core, at his failure to protect her and his inability to stop her riding for the Pony. His mother's letter offered him an escape, and maybe some answers. He welcomed the excuse to leave.

Might just be easier to distance myself.

AFTER HE BANKED the fire for the night, he went to her. 'Aleksandra?'

She turned, her face drawn. 'Yes?'

'*Lo siento*, please forgive me,' he said dully, drawing her into his arms and burying his face in the hollow of her neck. 'I know not what I do. My mother has asked for me, so I will go to her. Perhaps she can help me figure out my life.'

She held him tightly.

'It's the best I can do right now,' he murmured.

'Will you return?' she whispered.

'I cannot promise anything.'

'Will you hold me tonight?'

He couldn't deny her. He craved her touch, and nodded his assent.

'Tomorrow, I have something to tell you,' she whispered into his shirt.

'What is it?'

'Tomorrow,' she promised, and they curled up together and slept the sleep of the emotionally exhausted.

19

'Remember I told you Scout was ill the morning after he'd been shot?' Aleksandra took a halter and lead from Xavier and hung them on their hook. 'Fearing he would die, Doc and I treated him with some of my secret drug. Whether or not it had anything to do with his recovery, he got better.'

'Your secret drug?' He turned away, reaching for a pitchfork

'Papa's secret. The reason Vladimir sought us, and killed Papa ... That's what I wanted to talk with you about.'

She had his attention now. He froze, then turned on the spot

'I was afraid to tell anyone about it, but after the ambush, I saw how easily I could be killed in this war. Our secret could be found by Vladimir, or whoever else might still be seeking us.'

'I'm afraid I don't understand.' He slid down the wall to sit on a box of horseshoes. 'Have you eaten yet?'

'No, I came straight out to see you.'

'Well, let's go in for some breakfast, then we'll talk.'

Xavier, to his credit, said not a word while she went through her whole story, explaining how many years ago, Krzysztof's father extracted the drug from a plant growing on the Polish steppes. A well-known folk remedy, Krzysztof experimented with it and discovered it also gave a person incredible endurance. He tried it on some horses while serving as a courier for his papa or the count to faraway manors and cities. It let him travel long distances at incredible speeds without exhausting the horses.

'Sounds useful for the Pony.' Xavier's eyes lit up.

'Well, as I told you already, Vladimir noticed and questioned my papa. Soon thereafter, Vladimir was called back Russia with his wife and young son, just a week before the Galician Slaughter. Upon his return, he couldn't find Papa and Mama's names in the lists of dead *schlacta*, so he tracked them, finding them three years later in Vienna. Luring Papa to an abandoned warehouse, he interrogated him about the secret, as only a Cossack could.' She growled beneath her breath, stabbing her eating knife into a crack in the board serving as a table. 'Papa bore the scars until the day he died.'

'Oh, Aleksandra,' Xavier murmured.

'Vladimir taunted him that the tsar would use the drug for his cavalry, allowing them the speed to overrun Poland, and then the rest of Europe before they knew what hit them. He gloated that he would get his wife and son back from the tsar, though Krzysztof would never see his own family again. Although badly beaten, Papa managed to elude Vladimir and escape to America with Mama and me, still a young baby. Nothing more was heard from him until Papa's death. We'd hoped he'd given up, but never really believed it.'

Silent for a moment, she fumbled at the ties of her papa's medicine bag and withdrew her father's signet ring.

'Xavier, would you hold the secret for me, and my papa's ring, so they cannot become lost if something happens to me?'

'I can do that, if it's so important to you,' he said with a sigh.

'It is. I'll keep these bottles of the drug with me.' She pulled a lumpy pouch, hanging around her neck by a cord, from inside her buckskin jerkin, and waved it at Xavier. 'I'll leave the dried herb from my saddlebags, but the rest is in a secret cache behind Rogan's feed bin in our stable at Echo. I haven't seen the live plant, though I can write down what I remember of Papa's illustrations and description.'

'Aleks, consider this. Let's go back to the Vladimir question. Perhaps you made a mistake. Maybe it wasn't Vladimir who killed your papa.'

She stilled, the pulse pounding in her head as she held her breath.

'We have no proof,' he said, reaching across the table to touch her cheek. 'It could have been anyone with a narrow blade, a bayonet.'

She looked at him across the table, dumbstruck.

'I mean, Russia is a long way away, so is Poland,' he said softly.

He stared down at her hands, held tightly between his own on the table between them.

It dawned upon her that he took her silence for acquiescence.

'Don't you think this is a little far-fetched?' he said, reaching out to stroke her hair, 'I mean, the leader of Russia taking over the whole continent with the help of a plant that someone told him about nearly two decades ago? As you say yourself, it's been a long time.'

'Xavier, I—' she stopped when he held up his hand.

'Just hear me out, Aleksandra, please. You and your papa have vigilantly focused on keeping this secret from Vladimir and the tsar for many years. Who's to say you're not imagining the danger here?' He smiled at her. 'Can't you just come out of hiding, then we can be together and I can protect you properly? You'd have to stop riding for the—'

Glancing back at him from the door as she fled the room, angrier than she'd been in her life, she saw his mouth drop open as he mutely stared at her, brows drawn together in confusion.

How could he want me to come out of hiding, knowing it could mean Russia ruling Europe, and the millions of deaths that would ensue?

LEANING against the railings of Dzień's corral an hour later, her chin resting on her folded arms, Aleksandra sensed him behind her. His arms encircled her waist, pulling her back against him.

How have we ended up this way?

She closed her eyes and slowly turned in his arms to face him

'I'm sorry I didn't take you seriously,' he whispered. 'Europe seems so far away to me—like it's another world. I'll try to understand.' He looked down at her and kissed her forehead.

'Xavier, I care for you very much,' she stared at his shirt buttons and gripped the lapels of his vest, leaning her elbows against him, 'but I don't know what to do. When we begin to get close to each other, it seems you fly backwards and run away from me. I don't know how you feel about me and I can't begin to understand your intentions. The closer we get, the more you seem to shut me out and try to escape.

He let her go, then put his face in his hands, elbows on the top rail. She waited.

'Yes, Aleks, I do,' he said wearily, looking at his hands gripping the fence before him. 'I don't know why, but I just want to run. I honestly don't understand it. You're the best thing that's ever happened to me.' He pulled her to him again, rubbing his forefinger along the side of her jaw.

She smiled, reaching out to touch his lips. He kissed her palm, then looked back into her eyes.

'I love being near you, watching you, holding you, talking with you. I love kissing you. I would love to do much, much more with you.' He hesitated, then brushed the hair off his forehead with one hand, 'but then *you* run.' He gave her a lopsided grin.

'Yes, I do, I'm sorry.' She looked at him through her eyelashes with a lopsided grin and a big sigh.

'What are we to do with ourselves?' He shook his head and sighed.

She shrugged and giggled.

'Now it's my turn.' Xavier smiled. 'Do you know why you evade *me*?'

'Yes.'

'*That* easily?' He raised an eyebrow at her. 'Would you care to elaborate?'

Aleksandra took a deep breath. 'It's because my mother died in childbed.'

'*Una vez más?* Pass that by me again?' His brow wrinkled with the hint of a smile. 'I don't understand.'

'Okay,' she said, then hesitated.

'What does that have to do with not returning my—oh...' He stopped.

'I was afraid to let myself go any further, no matter how right it felt, or how I felt about you,' she started, her cheeks heating as she looked at a fence rail, 'risking pregnancy and death in childbirth.'

'Aleks,' his brow crumpled, 'women have babies every day. Not all pregnancies end in death.'

'Many do, Xavier, and few have secrets such as Papa and I shared. If I were to die, there would be no one to keep Papa's and my secret from Vladimir, and it could fall into the tsar's hands.' She gripped her fingers together.

'You've already shared the secret with me, Aleks.'

Their eyes met and held.

'Does that change anything between us?' Xavier spoke slowly, as if to a frightened horse.

'It does,' Aleksandra gave a little sob, 'but...'

'But?' Xavier tilted his head, brow furrowed.

'Although I know you are honorable and you care about me, I'm still frightened. I need to understand what is actually between us.' She looked up. 'Whatever your intentions, Xavier, I cannot make love, and perhaps a baby, with you if you panic when we get close, and perhaps leave me. That would be no life for me, or for a child.'

'I don't know why I run ...' Xavier murmured, looking lost.

'What was your life like growing up?'

He glanced up at Aleksandra's voice.

'Was your family close?' she persisted.

'My family wasn't a family,' he said sharply.

'Do you want to talk about it?'

'I'm not sure—' he paused, then sighed deeply and continued. 'I'm not sure, because I don't want to tarnish what we have.'

'It can only help.' She waited in silence for him to speak.

'Let's just say,' he finally went on, 'my father was abusive and my mother didn't care—' He turned away from her, clamping his lips together for a moment, then continued, '—didn't care enough to stop him, or wasn't strong enough to leave,' he said firmly. 'It seems she now says otherwise.'

Reaching out to him, she took his hand. He went rigid and began to pull it from hers, then with an effort, he relaxed. Taking a deep breath, he let it lie there, enveloped in her warm grasp.

'When you want to talk, Xavier, I'm here.' Her vision blurred with tears she prayed wouldn't fall.

Xavier glanced at her, then looked away.

'You said your mother now says otherwise? Have you spoken with her?'

He detailed the contents of his mother's letter.

'You *are* going to go, aren't you?'

He was silent for what seemed an eternity.

'I wasn't sure before Dancing Wolf came, but now I think I must.' He pushed away from the rails. 'The way we're going, I might just wreck your life, too, if I don't figure out my own.' Leaning toward her, he kissed her on top of the head, turned and headed for the barn.

STANDING TOGETHER INSIDE THE BARN, the bay pony beside them saddled for Aleksandra's ride east, Xavier and Aleksandra turned their heads toward the sound of approaching hoofbeats.

'Will you return?' she asked in a small voice.

'Yes, I will,' he said, glancing away from her and gritting his teeth.

The incoming Express pony slowed to a walk outside the barn door.

'And yes, I will miss you, more than you know,' he whispered, looking down at her, then wrapped his arms around her and gave her a swift kiss. Releasing her, he turned and led the pony outside.

'Hello Josh, all good on the trail?' she heard Xavier ask as she slipped into the daylight to catch the *mochila* the boy was already tossing in their direction.

'Good morning, Josh,' she managed, past the lump in her throat as she slipped the *mochila* onto the bay's saddle.

'Xavier, Aleks.' He nodded, eyelids drooping. 'Trail's quiet. I was glad for the sunrise, bit cold last night,' he mumbled, leading his tired mount to the water trough.

She stood motionless. Only a breath away, the Californio extracted the Fish Springs packet from the local mail cantina, signing the time card with a flourish, then faced her. He touched her cheek, his heart in his eyes, gazing into her own.

'*Que le vaya bien, Querida,*' he whispered.

'*Vaya con Dios,*' she returned.

Go with God.

She sincerely hoped it wasn't for the last time. Clucking to her pony, she swung up as he broke into a lope, tears streaming down her cheeks. Turning for a last wave, she saw Xavier staring after her, emotions warring in his face. Her heart stopped at the sight, but she could do nothing for him now. Turning her head to the east, she rode away, into the rising sun.

HER PONY, fresh as the wind this chilly morning, snatched at the low willow branches beside the track as they left the station. She gave him his head and he took the bit in his teeth, speeding along the grassy edge of the marshlands, the last real green they'd see until Rush Valley.

Probably the last moist, cooling breeze I'll feel until then, too.

Aleksandra thought of Xavier fleetingly, but stopped herself, determined to enjoy her ride, leaving the "what if's" of their relationship behind for now. It was a beautiful day and she was free, really free. What other employ would allow a young woman this kind of freedom?

Hmmm…this employ didn't even offer *a young woman a job here.*

She laughed out loud and the pony flicked his ears back at her, then shied violently at the explosion of a flock of waterbirds startled by his hoofbeats. Grinning at his high jinks, she clamped herself deep in the saddle and rode on. They passed scattered furniture and wagon bits abandoned by emigrants as they rounded the soft portion of the trail south of the slough.

In no time at all, black-streaked mountains rose high on her right. Slipping the *mochila* from beneath her seat, she rode into Black Rock. After a brief exchange of pleasantries, James sent her off on a little sorrel mare. The trail between Black Rock and Dugway was mainly flat and straight. At thirteen miles long, it was further than the normal ride between stations out West. The long twisting uphill grade, followed by the treacherous downhill dugway, was a killer.

Pa always said "It pays to keep a little horse in reserve."

Now more than ever, it seemed.

Taking a deep breath, she slowed her ride to a trot, returning her attention to the trail. Climbing, it wove between steep sided hills with only forty or fifty yards of visibility ahead and behind. Cresting Dugway Pass, she scanned the scrub for any movement, carefully negotiating the track's rutted surface and avoiding the precipitous drop on her right. The dust, already thick at this high altitude, tickled her nose. Sneezing, she pulled up her bandana, glad she'd remembered it today. At the bottom of the long decline, they loped across the plain to Dugway Station, changed horses and rolled on.

Table Mountain rose sharply on her right and she slowed the mare, edging toward the riverbed. Checking the descent was clear, they trotted down, blowing another bugle blast for the Riverbed keeper. No reports of trouble this time, and she rode out on a glossy Palomino mare.

'Watch her Aleks, she's a little green,' George said with a grin, letting go of the bridle. 'They only pulled her off the range a month ago.'

'Thanks for that, *amigo*.' She laughed as the pony bolted off with a buck. Sitting down and driving the golden horse on, Aleksandra laughed into her mane as she ran like the wind. By the time they neared the top of the climb out of the waterway, she was content to slow to a trot, then a brief walk. Aleksandra checked the surface of the desert floor above them, then the mare was off again, less enthusiastically this time, settling for a ground-eating canter.

Flying along the flats, Aleksandra saw some trees ahead, high on a hill and a flash of green on the valley floor.

Simpson's Springs.

Close by on her left, a stallion trumpeted and Aleksandra whipped around. The huge, rangy bay, his sides scarred by years of combat, raced toward them, intent upon the mare she rode. The Palomino spun toward him, her whinny frantic and high pitched as she tried to go to him.

She hadn't even considered the possibility, but the stallion wasn't about to give her time to think this one out. She gulped, her heart in her throat.

20

S creaming for all she was worth, Aleksandra flapped her hat towards the stallion as he raced up behind them and drove the mare forward toward the east with legs and heels. The palomino crow hopped, then laid her ears back and galloped at full tilt. Ramming her hat back onto her head, blonde braid flying out behind, Aleksandra sounded her bugle at top noise, hoping to scare the stallion.

When she dared to look behind, the big horse stared after them, head up and ears pricked, stopping and starting a few feet at a time, but he gave up pursuit. His herd of a dozen mares plus the assorted foals and yearlings stood at attention behind him.

Looking ahead, Aleksandra saw the Simpson's Springs keeper heading their way at a gallop and stuffed her rein-ends beneath her seat, praying the pony would stay straight while she hastily jammed her braid back under her hat.

George raced up to Aleksandra, rifle at the ready. 'Aleks, you okay?' he shouted as soon as he was within earshot.

'Yes, it was a near one. That big bay,' she turned and pointed, 'thought he'd add her to his band.' She nodded at the palomino's head.

'I heard your bugle from way too far out,' George puffed, his face red. 'The wild ones usually ignore the riders,' he said, shaking his head. 'First time I've seen that happen out here.'

'Riverbed George says she's only been off the range for a month. Could it be she was from his band?'

'Couldn't tell you that, but I'll let the other riders know to take care. Let's get back to the station. I'll put her in the strongest pen tonight in case that old man changes his mind.'

'Thanks for coming out.' Aleksandra wiped her brow with her bandana. 'I was hoping that stallion would stop before he got to us. I didn't fancy being underneath him. You got saddled up pretty fast!'

'No problem, Aleks. This guy was already saddled for you,' he said. 'I've got salt beef and dumplings for you, then this colt's ready to go!'

'Even *that* sounds fantastic after half a day in the saddle,' she said with a wry grin.

'I'm hurt,' he pouted. 'I've become rather a good cook, after a fashion, even if it's out of necessity rather than interest!'

After what truly was a "rather good meal", the pinto dashed away as she vaulted on, and Government Creek Station appeared soon enough, where he was swapped for a gray mare, who ate up the climb to Lookout Station.

'Good afternoon Aleks, any news on the trail? The keeper switched the *mochila* as she slid off.

'All good, Mr. Jackson, other than a Mustang stallion who wanted the mare I was riding, just out of Simpson's!'

'Well, if that's all,' he shuddered, 'don't think I'd want to be out there. You sure find yourself some pretty scrapes!'

'Whatever do you mean?' Aleksandra could only stare at him. 'Your job is more dangerous than mine! You live out here like a sitting duck—at least I have a fast horse under me!' She shook her head and checked her cinch.

'Some get all the breaks,' he said with a chuckle. 'Be off with you now!' he slapped the pony on the rump as Aleksandra prepared to vault on.

'Goodbye!' Turning, she waved and continued up to the top, thinking of her ride on Scout through this valley, looking all the more closely about her as they trotted carefully down the far side of the pass. The lengthening afternoon shadows added another, larger, dimension to the cedar, sage-brush and boulders above the track. Although the large dark areas shrieked ambush, no Indians exploded from them today. Aleksandra gave thanks while constantly scanning the steep canyon walls crowding the trail.

Leaving the foothills, Aleksandra loosed the reins and the mare broke into a lope towards Rush Valley Station, its vast hay fields greening up with the early shoots, shoots that would become hay to feed the Express horses and stock in the year to come.

ALEKSANDRA BREATHED A SIGH OF RELIEF. Riding into Rush Valley felt like coming home. Ready to be done with riding for the day, she looked forward to spending the next few days with Doc. He was giving a last downward jerk to the cinch *latigo* on a pinto colt as she rode up.

'Hello Doc, all good out on the trail,' Aleksandra sang out, 'well, except for one keen Mustang stallion, who—' She stopped as he turned to her, the cleft between his eyebrows deep.

'Aleksandra,' he said in a subdued voice, 'we've got a problem.'

She waited, silent, head cocked to one side. Then her heart stopped.

Someone knows. Someone knows I'm not a boy…or maybe Vladimir's been here.

In a rising panic, she reached for the bag tucked inside her shirt.

'The boy's too sick to ride.'

Aleksandra started breathing again.

Doc Faust looked at her, eyebrows drawn together in a frown.

'The eastbound rider for Salt Lake House,' he said slowly.

'Oh!' She was too relieved to do anything but grin like an idiot.

'Are you okay to go on?' He stared at her out of the corner of his eyes, his brow wrinkled as if she'd lost her senses.

'Of course.' Smiling probably not being the most appropriate demeanor, she schooled her face to a caring look. 'Is he going to be okay?'

'I'm not sure exactly what's wrong with him, but I suspect he's just too scared to go on, with the Indian trouble. Says he can't stand nor ride. If you can take the ride, I'd be much obliged. I know you've already had a long ride today and it's as far again—'

'No problem, Doc,' she interrupted. 'If you get me some food, I'll fill my canteen and leave. I can sleep at Salt Lake House. Really, I'm fine, lovely night for a ride. I'll be back soon.'

Smiling gratefully at her, he trotted toward the station, returning soon with a food parcel wrapped in a kerchief and a fur coat.

'That buckskin you're wearing isn't enough for riding through the night. This should keep you warm, girl,' he said gruffly.

Taking a bite of delicious roast beef tucked between sourdough biscuit, she grinned at him, then stowed the remainder in her shirt.

'You know I hate to ask this of you,' his brow creased again and he offered her a lopsided grin, 'but there's no one else.'

Looking around to ensure no one watched, Aleksandra gave him a quick hug. 'Any time, for you. Thanks for keeping my secret and letting me live my life, Doc—oh, how's Scout?'

'He's much better, you can see him when you return.'

Swinging up onto the pinto, she waved and headed for Salt Lake.

The eastbound trail was easier and they made good time as the light fell, changing mounts at East Rush Valley's dugout, then at Camp Floyd. Wary for drunken blond giants as she rode through the darkened outpost, Aleksandra heaved a sigh of relief when she finally passed the last sleepy soldier posted on the outskirts of the settlement. The bright moon and clear skies showed the trail clearly, but everything became more blurred as the night wore on. Thankfully, her pinto was fresh and keen, trotting on surely through the chill night. She barely remembered to pull up her kerchief to keep her face just that little bit warmer.

Stumbling as her legs hit the ground at Joe's Dugout after so long in the saddle, she followed Joe into the station. A steaming stew waited under the coals of the Dutch oven, its mouth-watering aroma only a hint of the luscious repast to follow.

'That is one of the best meals I've ever had.' She smiled at Joe, then gulped, realizing that in her fatigue she'd forgotten to lower her voice.

'Me mum always said hunger is the best seasonin' of all!' Joe grinned at her. 'That voice of yours not breaking yet, is it? It'll happen soon, Boy!'

'Thanks, Joe.' She chuckled and ducked her head. 'I'll be on my way now.'

'Take care out on the trail. Good thing ye've got a moon to guide ye!' he said as she rode off.

BEST THING about riding long distances is that you get a lot of time to think.

Xavier felt like he'd been released from bondage and could be his own man again. Charro was keen to go, so Xavier let him trot his heart out at his easy, ground-eating pace for twelve hours through that first day. The weather held and they slept rough that night in a sheltered gully off the trail, heading off as soon as it was light.

In the morning, he reconsidered his original thought about distance riding. Nonstop riding lets you think *too* much. What would he find when he met his mother? A woman who didn't care enough about him to keep him close? Who took abuse instead of leaving, and taking her children with her? A woman beaten-down by life? Who was she, really? He'd avoided thinking about her for years. It was easier to detest her than to look deeper and risk feeling the fear and inadequacy, the constant shadows beneath which he'd lived during his younger years, and indeed, to this day. One item mentioned by his mother in the letter, the fact that the man he previously knew as his *padre* wasn't actually his father, changed a few things. Xavier always hated to think the blood of the abusive bastard ran in his veins, just waiting to come out against those he loved. Whether it was the "Southern Institution" of slavery, a child being abused or forced to work harder than one ever should, women reduced to whoring for reasons out of their control or just general bully-bashing, they all had the same effect upon him. The merest hint of human subjugation by others made him ill, freezing his brain so he could scarcely think, feel or function—and usually sent him into an out-of-control, blind rage.

Charro brought him back to the present, flicking his ears back and forth.

'Yes, Charro. I should just stick to you. You never interrupt and we don't disagree on everything.' He chuckled, looking smugly between Charro's ears.

And he won't warm your bed or make you dinner, either, nor smile at you as she does, intruded a little voice on his shoulder.

MAJOR HOWARD EGAN sat at the Fish Springs Station desk sorting the local mail. Three notes for him and one for Xavier, who'd left a few hours ago. Shaking his head, he grinned at the rough scrawl on the envelope from someone at Echo Canyon. The missive had done the rounds—originally sent to Camp Floyd, it was forwarded on to Fish Springs. His brows lowered as he chewed on his mustache, thinking. The boy had seemed reluctant to go deal with his family problems in Carson City.

He smiled. What a good idea.

He scribbled on the envelope, dropped the letter into the westward mail slot and stepped, whistling, out into the morning sunshine. Getting a bit of mail might be a nice surprise for Xavier when he arrived at Carson.

ROCKWELL's and Traveler's Rest flew past in a blur of new horses and faces.

'Is that young Aleks?' The Salt Lake House keeper peered into her face, as she slid from her mount in the yard, long after midnight. 'We met when ye come through here lookin' fer Xavier and Mr. Egan. I'm Johnny. Where's young Richard?' he asked, his brow furrowing.'

'He was apparently "indisposed" and unable to ride.'

'Where've ye ridden from today? Aren't ye stationed at Fish Springs?' The furrows deepened.

'Yes, Fish Springs,' she mumbled, and took a few tentative, painful steps.

'Well then, ye get yerself to bed, Boy. Ye can have a sleep-in tomorro'. We'll see ye when ye waken. Ye won't need to leave back west 'til late afte'noon.'

She smiled her thanks, somehow finding an empty bunkhouse bed and falling down dead onto it.

Aleksandra awoke, still in her clothes and boots, to the late afternoon sun filtering through a window.

'Mornin' sleepyhead, you've been out all day,' said a grinning lad, freckles covering his pert, upturned nose and a shock of red hair sticking out in all directions.

Blinking a few times, Aleksandra struggled to sit up, then realized she was covered by a heavy Indian blanket she'd never seen before. Someone must've covered her up, once again.

'What time is it?' she asked, stomach growling.

'After three. You're due to go out in an hour, keeper says.'

'Thanks.' She climbed out of bed, every muscle screaming as she got to her feet and shook her head.

Johnny had food ready for her on the table when she stumbled into the stationhouse.

'Thanks for covering me up last night, Johnny.'

'You weren't likely to do it, so thought I'd better,' he said, with a grin.

She winced as he thumped her on the back, but by the time she'd eaten and walked around the station for a half hour, she felt ready to ride again. Hearing a bugle call, she ran back to the bunkhouse to grab her canteen and *pemmican* bag, pocketed her pistol and headed outside at a trot.

Johnny held the gleaming palomino stallion by his bridle, his coat glowing like burnished gold as he danced, impatient to leave. *Mochila* already in place, he was more than ready to go.

'Hey Boy,' Aleksandra called to the horse and he turned to her, then quieted as she cupped his muzzle in her hands for a moment. Checking his cinch, she clicked her heels, saluted Johnny, then called to the stallion and vaulted lightly into the saddle as he struck off into a canter.

Riding away, she shivered as goosebumps raised on the back of her neck—along with an eerie feeling that someone was watching her.

21

Vladimir sipped his whisky, wishing for the hundredth time that it was a good Russian or Polish vodka. By force of habit, he sat in an isolated corner seat with his back to the wall, facing a window the only window commanding a view of the entire main street of Great Salt Lake City. Hearing a short spurt of notes from a far off bugle, he vaguely wondered who might be bugling out here in this God-forsaken hellhole that was Utah Territory.

Perusing the muddy central boulevard of what passed for a city hereabouts, he raised his lip and one eyebrow in a sneer as he thought of his beloved *Moskva*, its cobbled streets impeccable since 1700. Already, Moscow was lit by gas lamps throughout much of the city.

Looking past the serving girl placing his supper of the ever-present biscuits, beef and gravy before him, he saw the reason for the bugle call as a lithe figure, crouched over a galloping pinto colt, flew around the corner. Vladimir looked up and nodded to the woman, his tight-lipped smile of thanks not quite reaching his eyes. Through the smudged windowpane, he watched the rider slide from his heaving pony as the Mustang skidded to a halt. The boy whipped a leather pad with compartments at each corner from atop his saddle and flung it onto a fidgeting palomino. A grizzled old man gripped the golden horse's bridle while the incoming rider led his tired mount away.

Another slim rider, this one relatively clean and wearing the huge hat favored by these Westerners, emerged from the station. Walking swiftly to the palomino stallion, he cupped its muzzle in his hands for a moment. The horse quieted and the boy moved back to slide his hand beneath the girth to check its tension. Clicking his heels together, he saluted the ostler and with a cry to the pony, vaulted into the saddle as it broke into a gallop from a standstill.

Something tugged vaguely at his memory.

'Is that rider exchange,' he said to the girl as she was about to walk from the room, motioning with his knife, 'part of the new Pony Express I have been hearing about?'

'Sure is,' she said, puffing out her already ample chest. 'It's the fastest mail out, bar none!'

Returning his gaze to his whisky, Vladimir grimaced and prepared himself to sample his supper. Doubtless, it would have the flavor of every other salt beef stew he'd had since coming West. What he wouldn't give for a trencher of *żurek* and to hold his lovely Tatiana and Nikolai in his arms. By now little Niko would be approaching manhood, if he yet lived. He shook his head, brutally yanking his thoughts from this vein. Sawing at a chunk of the meat, his heart gripped with despair of ever finding this elusive boy of Krzysztof's. Taking a deep breath, he dragged his gaze back up to stare out the window again.

Across the street, he watched the Pony Express ostler run gnarled hands over the pinto's legs and body and then sponge him down, while the dusty rider dunked his head in the trough. Handing the tired pony over to a stable boy, the old man went inside the Express station. The horse's tail swung from side to side as they walked off up the street.

The double doors swung open a few minutes later, interrupting Vladimir's musings, as the bowlegged ostler clumped into the saloon. Glancing toward Vladimir, he bobbed his head in greeting.

'You care well for your mounts,' Vladimir remarked in his heavily accented, but precise English.

'They're a rough lot 'n we don't spoil 'em. They work hard for their oats.' He sounded nonchalant, but Vladimir had already caught him absently rubbing the itchy spots around the colt's ears as he gave instructions to the young stable boy.

'Your young riders are obviously well taught. I haven't seen the likes of the young lad who just rode through since I left Europe,' Vladimir raised an eyebrow and inclined his head, his nod almost a bow to the ostler.

'Well then, yer lucky to've seen *him*,' the old man continued ruefully. 'Few 'nuff of our boys can ride like that *and* take care of the ponies too—reports are, his mounts always come in without a mark and they're tired but never thrashed. He's quiet with 'em, for all his heel-clickin', salutes, 'n vaultin' on like that at a gallop!'

Tugging at his memory, indeed.

Vladimir's face grew red-hot and he broke into a cold sweat as he realized what, or rather whom, he'd just seen—the salute and vault— the same click of the heels, salute and vault he'd learned during his training at the *Moskva* Military Commander's Training School. The same he'd taught to the young boys and men under his tutelage at the houses of the finest nobles in Russia and Poland—and the same he'd taught to Krzysztof Lekarski.

'Nice riding,' he managed, past the lump of clay in his throat. 'Would you care to join me, sir ...' Willing his pounding heart to stillness, Vladimir rose from his seat.

'Johnny', he extended his hand. 'Johnny Keating. Be happy to join you.'

'Count Yuri Moskvina, at your service.' He shook Johnny's hand. In the formal European manner, Vladimir waited until Johnny's drink was served, then continued. 'So, you're the ostler for this Pony Express station, are you?'

'Yep, I'm the station keeper fer Salt Lake House, right across the street.'

'An impressive changeover. Do they change horses and riders at every stop, and how far is it between stations?'

'The ponies'r changed at each station, an' it's 'bout ten miles from station to station, d'pendin' on the terrain. We call this 'un,' he nodded across the street at the big white building, 'a Home Station, 'cause riders stay here b'tween their runs. In b'tween the Home

Stations'r swing stations, where riders swap their mounts fer fresh ones.'

'Impressive, ten miles at speed.' He raised an eyebrow. 'Do you get many local riders or do they usually come from afar?'

'Most come from here'bouts, but some even come from the East Coast, what with them advert's Russell, Majors an' Waddell posted from New York clear t'San Fran.'

'And what advertisements might those be?'

'Have you got one of them Pony Express bills here, Kip?' Johnny shouted to the barkeep, then he rattled on. 'Oh, here's one, thanks.' Picking it up off the bar, he handed it to Vladimir.

The Central Overland California and Pikes Peak Express Company seeks:

Young, skinny, wiry fellows not over eighteen. Must be expert riders, willing to risk death daily. Orphans preferred. Pay: 25 dollars a week.

'They come from all over these parts fer twenty-five dollars a week, what with most buggers working the hard slog fer *two* dollars a week,' Johnny mumbled through his mustache. 'Must be pay fer the dangers they run up against. Can't say I'd wanna ride all night alone out there, over that rough trail or be ambushed by robbers'r Injuns, never knowin' where them rabbit holes wait fer your pony's feet and your neck! No, siree, it's no wonder they want orphans to ride! No kin to raise Cain when they disappear! One pony showed up a ways back, riderless at a swing station 'n they never found the rider again. He were pr'sumed dead.'

'Sounds a dangerous life indeed, especially for boys so young.' Vladimir averted his eyes. 'So would many of your boys be orphans?'

'Some of the first ones weren't but a lot of 'em are now. One boy come through here t'other day, looked no more'n eleven years old!'

'So, for example, what about that young lad? Surely a rider of that quality has been well-raised by a family?' Vladimir's voice was steely.

'Well, now, that young'un lost his family, trappers they wuz, east of here somewhere,' Johnny's brow wrinkled and he sat back in his chair, arms crossed over his chest.

As Vladimir wolfed the last few bites of his supper, a tic started up in his jaw. 'So how far does each rider ride?'

'Well, now,' Johnny paused, one eyebrow raised at the stranger, 'that depends.'

'Depends?' Vladimir's own eyebrow raised, and he fixed the old man with a hard look.

'Depends on if the next rider 'n horse'r where they oughta be. Ye just never know what happens out there.'

SOMETHING' creepy about this guy, for all his fancy manners.

Johnny wondered where this rather pointed conversation was leading. People out west pretty much lived and let lived. Suddenly he wasn't sure he wanted to tell this odd stranger any more about one of the friendliest and best lads who rode for the Express.

'Depends on,' Johnny continued 'whether or not the next rider's been injured or killed in an ambush.'

An astute horseman, Johnny read animals like he breathed, and this man worried him. As the tall, powerfully built foreigner clenched his chiseled jaw, his gunmetal eyes seemed to miss nothing as they bore into him. His strong, Slavic features emanated power, but the sudden alertness and edge of malice he'd heard in his voice for a moment added an air of savagery to boot. He shivered.

That steely gaze gave him the heeby-jeebies and he had no desire to give this man any more information. He started as the Russian's sharp voice intruded into his thoughts.

'Can you tell me how to get to Carson City, along the Pony Express trail? I hear it's the best and the fastest route,' he asked with what sounded like forced casualness.

'It might be the fastest, but it's far from the easiest.' Johnny said, trying not to grit his teeth at the sudden scent of anxious sweat from the stranger.

Johnny figured anybody who'd found their way out West had a basic idea of where the Express route ran, including Carson City. He was also pretty sure he wasn't about to give him any more help.

'I could make ye a map and drop it by later,' Johnny said with a smile. 'Where're ye stayin'?'

'At the boarding house down at the end of the street. Not as nice as your Salt Lake House. Wish I'd know about it when I arrived.'

'Ah well, next time, then.' Johnny stood to leave. 'See ye soon.'

The count let out a breath and the corners of his mouth turned up, but the dangerous glint in his eyes remained.

WHEN JOHNNY KNOCKED on the dingy door of the boarding-house room a few hours later, the count opened it, his eyes averted. His mouth was set in a firm line that wasn't quite a smile.

'You've brought me a map, have you?' He reached for it, then visibly relaxed for a moment. 'Thank you. I'm in a bit of a hurry to get to Carson, so I'm leaving tonight.' He patted his saddlebags, already slung over his shoulder. Closing the door behind him, he walked across the street with Johnny, toward the Express station.

'My horse is just past your office, at the livery stable,' the Russian nodded in that direction.

'I've given ye the directions fer the safest route to Carson City.' Johnny's heart thudded in his chest, but he kept his cool. 'It shortcuts 'round the desert an' keeps ye out of the way o' the Injun trouble we're havin' along the trail, b'tween here an' Fish Springs. It goes up the California Trail a ways, then cuts down after the desert. Matter o' fact,' he paused, closely watching the blond man, wondering if his hunch might be right, 'this trail meets up with the Pony Express Trail at Fish Springs, the Home Station where that rider ye was commentin' about works.'

'That's great. Thank you for the map.' Vladimir clamped his jaw again, his hand clenched on the map, and his pace quickened.

'No problem, Count.'

Once around the side door of the station, out of view of the street, the count glanced around, then turned to Johnny. 'Would you be so kind as to point the way out of town to me?'

The Russian held a revolver, aimed straight at him.

'Better yet, I believe you might wish to accompany me,' he continued smoothly.

22

Other than the sheer pleasure Aleksandra gained from riding keen young horses that knew their work, the trip to Rush Valley was uneventful. Doc waited in the station yard with a lantern held high. This time, he was his usual, jovial self.

'You're right on time, girl. Young Richard seems to have recovered,' Doc muttered under his breath. He nodded in the direction of the boy, who stood hunched over, staring at the ground. 'He'll take your *mochila* when its time for him to go, next time,' Doc continued, in a louder voice.

'He doesn't seem terribly excited about the idea,' Aleksandra raised an eyebrow at Doc as the boy hugged his arms about his body.

'Well, I think he prefers it to the chores I put his way last night, and those he'll do until you return from Fish Springs with the next mail. Right, Richard?' he shouted in the boy's general direction with a wry grin and a wink.

Dragging his feet, the lad led Aleksandra's pony off away to cool him out.

'And remember the rest of the water buckets in the corrals when you're done, lad.' Doc waggled his eyebrows and grinned. 'He's been doing it most of the day.'

'He's in for a long slog, by the looks of things.' Aleksandra chuckled as they turned and headed for the station house and a late supper. 'Anyway, Doc, I'm looking forward to a good sleep tonight.'

'Sounds good. He opened the station door for her and flashing her a smile. 'Plenty of time to see Scout and ride home to Fish Springs at first light.'

'Oh Boss, your coat!' She shrugged out of the fur. 'Thanks, it was a lifesaver.'

'After your supper, we'll go see Scout.'

THE COUNT MOTIONED toward the livery stable with his pistol. Moving in the direction indicated by its muzzle, Johnny was silent, grateful he'd thought to warn the young stable lad to make himself scarce if the stranger should come sniffing around. Glad, too, that he'd given him a letter for Xavier and one for the sheriff.

Inside the livery stable, the Russian directed Johnny to saddle a big, powerful bay horse while he led out a saddled chestnut mare and mounted, indicating the bay with a wave of his pistol.

'Mount up, quietly,' the count hissed.

Johnny said not a word as they rode out of town. It might be too late to save his sorry old hide, but at least he might yet save Aleks. Surely, this must be the foreigner the lawman sought for the murder of the lad's father. With the sheriff out of town, this was the best he could do.

WATCHING the trail ahead in the moonlight, Vladimir led Johnny, his hands tied together behind his back, on Krzysztof's bay.

I can't believe I spent the night there in the same town as Krzysztof's son.

Swearing, he growled at the bay to keep up and ignored the station keeper.

The lake, shining in the moonlight as they travelled north on Hensley Cutoff from Great Salt Lake City, gave way to the flat plain they now traversed. As the rocky Wasatch Mountains rose sharply from the valley floor east of the trail, Vladimir spied the lights of a town.

'Old man,' Vladimir barked.

Johnny's head came up. Sleepy-eyed, he looked around at him, one eyebrow raised.

'What's that town?' He nodded at the lights.

'How long we been goin'?' the station keeper asked.

'About three hours.'

'Cain't see so good in the dark, is there a big canyon openin' up there?'

'Yes.'

'That'll be North Cottonwood, then.'

He's not giving anything away.

Vladimir pulled the bay and his rider off the main trail and up the next goat track towards the mountains, then continued northward, skirting the town. A few dogs barked in the distance, but soon the lights of North Cottonwood were behind them, only the sounds of the night wilderness serenading them on their way.

Suddenly the horses picked up their pace, ears pricked. Vladimir glanced around, peering into the darkness ahead. He sighed in relief as the tinkling of a creek tumbling down its bed came to his ears.

'Heh he he, it's no'bbut a bit of water, young man,' the old man chuckled, his eyebrow raised again, as the horses slid down the bank and buried their muzzles in the cool water.

Vladimir scowled and jerked on the bay's lead, dragging him from the creek and back to the main trail. He kept looking up into the hills for just the right place.

He finally found it, about a mile and a half past the town. Riding off the wagon trail, he forced the reluctant mare through the dense oak brush on the ravine floor, hard twigs snapping like shots as she passed through, then pushed her up into the scrubby little box canyon. The anxious bay, his reins held by Vladimir from atop the chestnut, kept trying to shoulder past the mare with great leaps as the brush tickled his belly and the rocky walls rose ever higher on either side of them.

After traversing two bends, Vladimir jerked on the colt's reins and he swung to face him, startled. The old man still looked at him, his annoying eyebrow raised, without a trace of fear. The ostler made him feel like an untried boy playing a game, and not a good one at that. He pointed the gun at Johnny's head.

'Down,' he growled. 'Off the horse and onto your knees.'

Johnny flicked his right leg over the horse's head and slid off onto a clear patch between bushes, hands still tied behind his back. He looked up at Vladimir enquiringly, then kneeled amongst the rocks.

'Now Johnny, is this indeed the shortcut to Fish Springs? Tell me the truth or I'll shoot.' He lowered his aim to the level of the man's heart.

'Yep.' The old man looked at him steadily in the moonlight. 'The best way and safest. It's 'round the desert and like I said, it misses out the Injun trouble part.'

Colt revolver still trained on Johnny, Vladimir swung down. He let the ostler stand up, which he did, albeit stiffly, then marched him further up the ravine. Tying him, he stuffed a dirty bandana into his mouth, wrapped another around his eyes and left him there.

He probably won't survive the wolves tonight, poor old beggar. He didn't really do much wrong, but the town's close by. He'll make it if he tries.

Thankful for the clear, bright moonlit night, Vladimir rode on, eyes drooping, until he nearly toppled from the saddle. Picketing the horses, he rolled up in his blankets and slept on the banks of a deep creek with clear water and plenty of grass for the horses. They moved on northward at daybreak.

After stopping at midday to feed the horses and let them rest awhile, he carried on for another six hours, the rolling sage-brush-littered hills posing no worry to the horses as their big strides ate up the miles. He kept thinking of the old man, wondering if he'd made it to town alive, and hoping he had.

I'd make a terrible crook.

That night, he slept soundly on a soft bed of sage-brush, thinking, not for the first time, that using a saddle for a pillow wasn't all it was cracked up to be. By his reckoning, he figured they'd covered a hundred miles so far, by switching horses every hour or so and spending half of the time at a trot and half at a walk.

Dawn found them on the trail again. According to the map, he should have seen a fork heading west yesterday. His brows drew tightly together as he began to wonder about old Johnny's map. No, he wouldn't think of that yet.

With the sun high overhead on the following day, he rounded a bend to find the terrain completely changed. The rolling country gave way to flat, sage covered valleys edged with pine and cedar. In the distance, a few rocky outcroppings showed, and before him, the trail seemed to end at a huge gray boulder. The trail circled left around it, diving into a valley of countless granite formations, creating a rocky wonderland as far as the eye could see. The many forms: rounded, angled, and even spire-like, reaching for the heavens, seemed to have tumbled from the skies above to populate the valley. At the edge of the trees, several Indian women and children looked up from their pinecone-gathering beneath the *Piñón* pines.

On the valley floor, the wagon road curved around the huge obelisks. Aspens filled the ravines and ran down onto the flats before him, their light green foliage lush against the sage-green brush on the flats below.

Rubbing his hand over his eyes, he shook his head as his feeling of unease intensified.

A valley like this, as unique as it is, should be on the map.

And it isn't.

His chest tightened as he came to the full realization that the map couldn't possibly be correct. They were nearly out of food and grain, with no trading post in sight.

Two days. Right.

The westward turnoff around the desert was meant to have been only two days distant from Salt Lake House. Blood pounding in his ears, he forced himself to relax his fist on the reins, thinking of the hopes he'd had, waiting in the dingy boarding-house room for Johnny's arrival with his map, the map that would lead him straight to his goal. This was a setback, but there was no doubt he would find the boy. God wouldn't have let him come so far to snatch it away from him again.

Riding past an eerie rock formation, he ran over his plans again. After extracting the secret from the boy, he would take the main California Trail to San Francisco. There he could find a Russian vessel, perhaps one purchasing supplies for Fort Ross, upon which he could book passage to Russia, and Tatiana.

Tatiana, although you are still in Russia, I feel so close to you now. I am coming for you, my love. Soon. Just hold on a little longer!

THEIR SHADOWS STRETCHING out before them, Aleksandra and her mount left Rush Valley in the early dawn and headed for Lookout Pass. Sniffing the breeze, the sorrel mare set off at a lope, dropping to a brisk but steady trot up the first slopes of the pass. No sign of human life showed as they climbed toward the heavens then over the top to drop down into Lookout's juniper valley, where new shoots of grass heralded the onset of spring and little wildflowers were beginning to bloom, their sweet scent on the breeze.

Pricking her ears, the mare looked up the hill above the station. Young Mrs. Rockwell, out walking her precious dogs, waved. This daughter-in-law of Porter Rockwell, along with her husband Horace, had just come to run the stage stop at Lookout. Smiling, Aleksandra waved in return.

Mr. Jackson replaced her mare with a bay colt at Lookout. At Government Creek, he was replaced by a green horse, who tried to pull Aleksandra's arms from their sockets for most of the way to Simpson's.

'I'm tempted to ride her on to the next stop just to see if she ever gets tired.' Aleksandra looked at George and laughed.

'No one's seen her get tired yet.' The Simpson's keeper smiled, swapping her *mochila* onto a Palomino colt, 'but then, we've not taken her on to the next station, either.'

They rode off at a lope, soon dropping into a long trot across the straight, flat desert towards Riverbed.

In the distance, she saw the wild Mustang band and hurried on a bit, giving thanks the stallion didn't look their way. Aleksandra held the colt back while she checked the entrance to the riverbed, then gave him his head. He leapt over the top lip, slid his way down and dashed across the bottoms until they reached the dugout station.

'No, no news of trouble from the east.' She shook her head at the keeper, wondering once again, how anyone could live in a riverbed flood plain.

Guess it just goes with the territory.

'Three more stops, then home,' she said, between sips of a dipperful of the rank, barrel-stored water and refilled her canteen.

'Off with ye, then, an' watch yer hair!' he shouted after her as she vaulted on.

Dugway and Black Rock flew by, and before she knew it, she was cutting left to veer around the sucking mud, heading for the green that meant home, Fish Springs...but a home without Xavier.

THE LANDMARKS on Johnny's map had led him here. Vladimir took yet another deep breath and closed his eyes, swallowing hard.

This tiny outpost, consisting of only a trading post and saloon, wasn't even mentioned on his chart. Dismounting, he stretched his stiff legs and looked around. A bonneted, red-haired young woman coming out of the trading post doorway caught Vladimir's attention as she carefully stepped down onto the road, lifting her skirts high. Noticing him standing before her, she ducked her head and looked at the ground.

'Excuse me, madame,' he said, sweeping off his hat and bowing to the girl.

Covering her mouth to hide a giggle, she peered up at him, her eyes sparkling. 'Yes?'

'Could you please tell me what this place is called and how far it might be to Fish Springs via the shortcut around the desert?'

'Around the *desert*?' She frowned, brows creasing, then tilted her head, the trace of a grin beginning. 'I ain't never heard of a shortcut around the desert, but anyways,' her face lightened and she smiled at the stranger, 'this is City of Rocks. Don't you have a map? You could get one if you was to ride up north a ways to Fort Hall, Mr....?' She raised an eyebrow at him.

'Mr. Novokov, at your service, ma'am,' he replied somehow through gritted teeth, his worst fears becoming rather more real.

'Well, Mr. Novokov, to get to Fish Springs, hmmm...' She placed the tip of one slender finger against her lips, considering. Counting on her fingers with the other hand, she grinned and announced, 'It will probably take you about four or five days, at a good pace.' Looking back the way he'd come, she pointed the same finger back south and *east*. 'Just follow that trail through North Cottonwood, that's where my husband and I live, he's a farmer. Folks are even starting to call the village "Farmington" because so many of us are starting to farm there.' Her eyes glowed over an expansive grin when she paused for a breath.

'Oh really? How lovely for you.' Vladimir's breeding and training kicked in to offer the girl a polite reply. He thought he might be smiling as he arched an eyebrow at her, but he wasn't sure. His thoughts reeled.

'Oh, but you don't want to know about that, sorry, sir! Anyways, carry on to Salt Lake House, then south a wee ways, then west. You follow the trail that the Pony Express riders use!' The words kept flying from her mouth as she stared southwards. Turning back to him, her face was lit with a rosy glow.

Normally it would have made Vladimir smile.

This was not one of those times.

Glancing up at the look on his face, she froze. Her eyes grew wide as she took a sharp breath, her mouth forming a small 'o'. 'You can't miss it,' she stammered, 'sir.' Ducking her head, she bolted across the road between the trading post and the saloon like a hare pursued. Bundling her skirts into one hand, she leapt like a chamois onto the wagon box, where a grizzled man waited in the shade of the saloon, scowling first at her, then at Vladimir. He whipped up the horses as soon as the girl's feet hit the floor, growling at her in a low voice. She didn't look back, clutching at the strings of her sunbonnet with one hand and the wagon seat with the other, as the conveyance lurched away.

Head spinning, Vladimir's only clear thought was that, in a civilized world, the little girl to whom he'd just spoken couldn't *possibly* be old enough to be married to the angry old man in the wagon. The saloon was looking more inviting by the second. A drink and a good meal might let him face the return trip with some form of equanimity.

Sitting at the rough wooden trestle table in the saloon, head down and speaking to no one, he considered going to Fort Hall for a real map, but as it turned out, it was a hundred miles to the Fort, and time was not on his side. He'd just have to get by on his own wits, not a plan he liked, being the exacting sort of man he was, but unfortunately, a necessity right now.

He finally had to concede he'd been duped, royally duped. He grinned ruefully. He had to give Johnny credit for a stunning acting job. The old man should've been on the stage.

Amazed at what a good meal and a stiff drink, or three, could do for one's attitude, he paid up and left. He pushed the horses for another half day before he slept, exhausted and depressed, in what would have normally been a lovely setting on a cottonwood creek with plenty of grazing for the tired and hungry horses.

THE EASTBOUND RIDER into Fish Springs Station was expected last night, at the latest, but by this morning, still no rider had appeared. Jaw clenched, Superintendent Egan drummed his fingers on the gate as he let the stock out into their day pasture, deep furrows marring his forehead.

The riders were never this late.

23

'Aleks, I'll need you to go west, Son.' Major Egan handed her a plate of beans and biscuits as she came in from grooming her neglected Dzień.

'West?'

'I know you've not been that way, but it's well marked and the *mochila* you brought from Salt Lake has to go on. The eastbound rider hasn't come in yet, so he can't take it...'

'How late is he?'

'Nearly two days already.' His brows lowered over pursed lips.

'Of course, Boss, when do I leave?'

'Your mount is saddled.'

'Oh, *now*.' She blinked.

'I'll bring this out,' he said, as he reached for her canteen.

'I'll just eat and be there in a moment.'

'Good boy.' Egan sighed. Smiling his thanks, he strode out the door.

Grabbing her coat and gloves, Aleksandra stopped to refill her *pemmican* bag from the stash in the kitchen and a grabbed a small sack of grain from the feed shed. She'd doubtless be fed by the station keepers, but she was happier carrying food on an unfamiliar trail.

They headed north along the base of the Fish Springs Range and Aleksandra turned the pinto off the trail for a drink from a little spring, North Spring, she recalled Major Egan calling it. The perky pony cantered on, eyes forward and ears pricked. Rounding the northern point of the barren Fish Springs Range, Aleksandra watched the new grass abruptly disappear as the rocky plains turned to salt flats. Wheel ruts and the spade marks of travellers digging their transports out of the mud were the only undulations visible between her and the Deep Creek Range ahead. The tallest snow-capped peaks she'd yet seen stretched before her from north to south, towering toward the sky. She remembered someone in Running Wolf's village talking of Ibapah peak, the highest one, with its aspen, conifer and game-filled ravines.

As she passed some wind-carved rock formations on a low knoll, Boyd Station came into view, the mortared stone cabin complete with rifle ports. Behind the station stood the biggest hay barns she'd ever seen, still holding the remains of the winter's hay and firewood.

The keeper appeared around the corner of the station, rifle in one hand, hat in the other.

'Halloo! You must be young Aleks. Egan said you'd be riding along here sometime!'

'And you must be Bid.' Aleksandra smiled at the keeper's grip-of-steel handshake and handed him the *mochila*.

'That's me, pleased to meet you.'

'Aleks,' he turned to slip the mail carrier over the saddle of a dancing bay colt, then glanced back at her, his forehead creased, 'have you heard anything at Fish Springs from the overdue eastbound rider?

'No, that's why I'm here. Major Egan's pretty worried.'

'Show's got to go on, I guess.' He winced. 'Got enough water, young man?' he asked, as he unlocked the cantina.

'Could use a little, thanks.' She headed for the well.

Bid looked up from the time card with a start. 'No Boy, not there! That well's nearly pure salt. Great for preserving meat, but not for drinking. You want that barrel over there.' Laughing, he pointed. 'It's from our tiny spring—brackish, but drinkable.' Finishing his sift through the local mail, he locked it and held the reins out to Aleksandra.

'Thanks, Bid.' She slung her canteen over the saddle horn and took the reins with a smile. Saluting him, she snapped her heels together, clicking to the horse as she loosed the reins. The bay responded with a snort and she swung up as he cantered away. Glancing over her shoulder to wave, Aleksandra saw him staring after her, eyes wide. 'Goodbye! Hold on to your hair!' she called as Bid disappeared in a cloud of dust.

Rocking along on a loose rein at an easy lope, they passed a trail heading north into the Salt Desert.

Who would possibly want to go out there?

In the distance, juxtaposed to the salt, sand, dust and sage, was a tall stand of cottonwoods, which grew into a whole valley of spring-fed lush grass, willow and cottonwood as they drew nearer. Smiling at what had to be Willow Springs Station, she pulled out her bugle.

Looking up from the horse he was grooming at her bugle call, the keeper untied a saddled horse from beneath a big willow and led it past a dugout toward her.

'Good morning, you must be Peter.' Aleksandra grinned as the colt, still dancing after ten miles, neared him.

'Hello, Aleks, is it? We were told we'd meet you soon.' He smiled at her, catching the *mochila* she threw.

'Yep,' she said. 'You haven't seen the eastbound rider come through here, have you?'

'No, and it's a worry.' His brows drew together in a frown. 'I've had no word from either direction.'

She held up her canteen with a lift of her eyebrows.

'In that barrel by the door.' Nodding toward it, he slid the *mochila* onto a gray mare, who pricked her notched ears at the colt, whickering softly.

'You take care out there through the canyon. Horses and riders don't just disappear by themselves.' Peter shook his head, his lips a firm line below his furrowed forehead.

'I promise.' Thanking him, she vaulted on and the mare laid back her ears and fairly flew on toward Overland Canyon.

The trail entered the canyon from the flat valley floor, meandering gradually upward in a wavelike fashion, sage-brush and early sprouts of grass growing along the creek next to the trail. Aleksandra was just wondering why everyone thought Overland Canyon was so dangerous when the trail became abruptly steeper and began to twist and turn tightly as the hills closed in. Sitting straighter, the blood beginning to pound in her ears, she picked up her reins and scanned the mountainsides flanking the track as they rose higher and higher, ensnaring the pathway within a narrow gorge of exposed strata and tumbled stone bluffs.

Bluffs just meant for ambuscade, with caves big enough to shield a man.

Aleksandra gulped. Giving the little mare her head, they raced on through the canyon.

She glanced left up the mouth of a small ravine as they surged past it.

Blood Canyon.

She shuddered, remembering its name from stories in the Indian village, glad she didn't have to ride through that even narrower defile winding its way to the top of Blood Mountain.

The trail finally opened up into rolling sage-brush covered flats, Canyon Station dead ahead.

Feeling faint, Aleksandra gasped for a breath, wondering how long she'd held it through the last gauntlet. Laughing shakily, Aleksandra leaned forward, giving the puffing mare a heartfelt hug, then sat up and mumbled sweet nothings to her, scratching her withers as they trotted slowly into the station.

Aleksandra left there on a gray colt, keen and ready to run. The keeper, his jaw set and a frown deeply embedded in his lined face, hadn't seen the Eastbound Express rider either.

The trail ran gradually uphill ahead of her along the little creek, then left it, rising up the center of a long, open valley. On her left, two prospectors looked up from working their rocker in the creek to wave at her. She reined in for a moment.

'Good afternoon gentlemen!'

'And to you! Safe through Overland, are ye?' shouted a big bear of a man.

'Yessir!' she shouted. 'You haven't seen an Eastbound rider in the past few days, have you?'

'No.' He turned to the other, who shook his head. 'No, we haven't, sorry, lad!'

'Okay, thanks. Having any luck?' She smiled at the pair.

'Luck's all good, Boy! All good!' the other one added in a shrill voice.

'What are these workings, please?' Aleksandra remembered to lower her voice this time.

'This here's Clifton Flat, best gold workin's in the territory!' He puffed up his chest. 'Major Egan found gold here a few years ago and we're in his employ, workin' it for him!'

'Excellent, thank you, enjoy your day!' she replied with a wave and loosed the reins. The colt, needing little encouragement, shot off like an arrow from a bow.

'Hold on to your hair!' The burly prospector bellowed over the wind in her ears, as the horse bolted on up the valley, then over the top of the next ridge.

Hopping off at the top, Aleksandra looked out over the expanse spread out before her in awe. The track arced steeply down the mountainside for several miles, with good visibility in every direction, before coming to rest in a huge, fertile-looking wash that seemed to go on forever. Her papa had called the place by its Indian name, *Ibapah*.

'That'll be Major Egan's ranch down there, but then you'd already know that, wouldn't you Boy?'

Without doubt, the horse had eaten the lush grass between runs at Egan's Deep Creek Station. He picked up his head, sniffing the wind.

'Guess we'd better start down that hill,' she said, and began running down the track beside the colt, who snorted and skittered beside her until he became accustomed to trotting alongside her.

The Deep Creek Station keeper had no word of the missing rider either. Feeding her well, he sent her out on a pinto Mustang, who loped across the flat valley floor, heading for Prairie Gate. Only four more stations until she was done for the day.

On a keen horse and free to enjoy the day.

She finally let her mind wander back to Xavier and her heart sank, the only shadow in her day. She wondered how he fared with his family and if he missed her as she missed him.

With a gulp, she realized was time to face it. Ahead was a good three hours of open and clear trail to ride. It was time to work through it.

She took a deep breath to try to dispel the anxiety that immobilized her when she thought too hard about their relationship. Every time they seemed close, it all slipped away. She feared nothing she could do would ever hold it together.

Her thoughts circled throughout the day as they traversed the dry sage-brush flats, passing Prairie Gate and Antelope Springs Stations. She repeatedly gripped the buckskin bag beneath her shirt, desperate for guidance.

In the distance ahead stood the Antelope Range. The pass they needed to traverse wasn't particularly high, but the rocky divide lined by cedars and *piñón* pines was still challenging. The fresh scent of the evergreens tingled in her nostrils when she brushed them in passing, clearing her head.

AT SPRING VALLEY STATION, the worried keeper handed her two thick sourdough muffins filled with salt pork.

'Hope it don't spoil yer supper over at Schell, but it's a long slog over that mountain.'

'Always enough room for more food,' she said with a grin.

'Anyways, I'm givin' you the best little horse I've got, Aleks.'

'Thanks, Patrick.' She took a deep breath and looked at the little black Mustang. Her eyes shone with a quiet intelligence. She was evenly muscled and solid, her legs clean.

'She's the toughest horse I've ever known. She'll take good care of ye over Shellbourne Pass and get ye to Schell Creek in no time!' He puffed his chest out as he stroked the mare's neck.

'I'm thankful for all the good horses and the men of the stations. They've always got a smile for me and a pat for the horses when we ride out.'

His brows drew together and he tried for a smile. 'You take care out there, won't you? We don't want another missing rider.'

'I'll see you on the way back. We'll be fine.' Aleksandra gripped his hand firmly, then vaulted onto the mare and set off for Schell.

Aleksandra wasn't sure which of them she was trying to reassure.

Her heart sang as the nimble mare climbed up through the trees to the top of the 7000-foot high pass. As the sun neared the horizon, the air began to cool and she hopped off, jogging down the descent to warm up and get some feeling back into her feet.

As she prepared to mount again, a movement back down on the flats caught her eye. Spinning toward it, she saw only a herd of antelope, now motionless, eyes staring and ears perked to scrutinize her passing. She gave a shaky laugh and the antelope disappeared into the dusk.

ALEKSANDRA SWAYED and jerked back upright, coming awake from drowsing.

Not a good idea.

A station showed, about a mile away.

Must be Schell Creek. Think about something to stay awake.

Her mind flicked back to Xavier and she cringed.

And stop avoiding the challenge with him. Think it through, focus. Try to resolve something, before we get to Schell.

She shook herself.

It finally clicked. In her impatience, she'd driven him away by asking for more closeness than he could give. The emptiness in the pit of her stomach overwhelmed her, and the thought she might never have a chance to see him again, much less get the opportunity to make, no, *let* this relationship work.

Life is indeed short in the West.

As they neared the station, her choices suddenly became clear as a mountain lake.

How did I miss them before?

It was as if they were written on a wall before her.

You can't make someone love you,

you can't fix anyone,

and there's nothing you can do to change it.

Fervently she vowed to offer Xavier, and others in her life, the time they needed to learn to trust, fully knowing she might never get the chance to try again with Xavier. Her desolation ran deep and tears poured down her cheeks as she rode into Schell Creek Station.

It might have been the mare that did it, stopping dead in her tracks, nearly dropping Aleksandra over her shoulder, or maybe it was the flies that buzzed around the blood pooling beneath the butchered man in the Express station doorway. Whichever it was, it got her full attention.

24

One more night sleeping on the ground and two nights in Express stations brought Xavier and Charro to Carson City. Putting the stallion up at a livery, he found his mother's lodgings down a quiet side road. Despite his ambivalent feelings about her, he was pleased her hotel was new and looked comfortable.

María received him in the dining room, empty at this mid-afternoon hour. She rose to her feet when he entered the room, looking at him with wide eyes, shifting her feet as she waited in silence.

Astonished at how small and frail his previously robust mother appeared, he strode to her, bowed over her hand and kissed it.

'*Buenos días, Mama*,' he murmured, then at the tears in her eyes, pulled her into his arms. They stood thus in silence for an eternity, then she leaned back to look up at him and smiled.

His lips bent a little, uncertainly at first, then he gave in to it and chuckled. '*Mama*, how I have missed your smile, for far too many years.'

'And I yours, my son. And see how you have grown into *un hombre magnífico*.'

His face grew warm beneath her gaze. 'But what is this of ill health? I see you looking well before me.'

'My heart is not what it should be, but I wanted to see you again before ill befell me. My doctors wish me to put all in order, and you are at the top of my list.'

Xavier flinched. 'Do you find me in order?' he asked, his whole body stiff.

'My son, it is our relationship I would see in order. I could not leave this earth without righting the wrongs which have been done you, so you may go forward in your life, if you haven't yet.'

'I find you lied to me about my father, or my stepfather, as it were.' Turning his head, he stared out the window as he spoke.

'I apologize for that, Xavier, but it was solely to protect you from him. I didn't want him to kill you. He knew he wasn't your father, but any reminders put him into an insane fury. Manuel, your true father, loved you with all his heart. He was killed by your stepfather, who took his place in our lives by force. I had no say in the matter, though I nearly died for my efforts several times.' She shuddered and looked at the ground.

The ice around Xavier's heart began to melt, just a little bit. In silence, he took a deep breath. Memories flooded back, unbidden. The images were blurred, as if they were from a long time ago and he was very young.

'I have some hazy images in my mind of you smiling and dancing, and of a man, a huge man, clean-shaven, black-haired, who picked me up and swung me around.' Xavier looked at her, his heart in his throat. He inhaled deeply. 'Was that my father?'

His mother softened and she let out a breath.

'Oh yes, you do remember him, then, Xavier. I am so glad,' she said, clutching her hands together over her heart. 'You were nearly three years old when we lost him. I continue to hold to my memories as to gold.' Her eyes glowed with a soft light.

Xavier's knees turned to jelly. Shaking his head to clear his blurred vision, he sat down on a bench at the long table.

'Over here, Xavier, they have laid a meal for you.' She smiled, indicating the single place setting. 'You must be hungry after your long ride.'

'Yes, thank you,' he said, moving to sit before the plate heaped with cold roast pork, eggs, fruit and to top it off, a piece of chocolate cake with sugared icing. A whisky shot and glass of water rounded out the offering. 'Food's a bit sparse in the desert; I've not seen such a feast in months.' He smiled his gratitude.

'It sounds as if you've done well for yourself, my son. Station tender for the famous Pony Express? It sounds glamorous, but also a little lonely?' She gazed at him while he carefully ate his dinner, her eyes always upon him whenever he glanced up from his plate, as if she were memorizing his features.

They spoke of the Pony and of what his *mama* had been doing in her life. He winced at the mention of the *Rancho de las Pulgas*.

'It is yours, my son.' She raised an eyebrow at him. 'Your brothers hold it for you in your absence, but you are my firstborn. They would see you well and await your coming, whenever, if ever, you see fit to return.'

'I'm not sure I'll return, *Mama*,' he replied in an even tone as he pushed the whisky away to the opposite side of the table.

'Well then, it will be there if you should someday wish to claim your birthright. You could visit sometime and see if you still feel the same way,' she said softly.

'I might do that when we have a break from the Pony, if that ever happens.' He took a deep breath. 'I thank you, *Mama*, for coming here to see me. I really didn't think I mattered enough to you for you to bother.'

'I can see how you might have thought that, *Querido*,' her gaze on her fingers turning her wedding band, 'but it's not true at all. Shall we walk outside, now that you've finished your meal? Your whisky remains, Xavier.'

'Thank you for the meal, *Mama*, but I don't drink.'

'Not at all?'

'Not a drop. A hangover from my stepfather, I believe,' he said with a smile.

He rose with her and the solid sheet of ice between them thinned a little more as her warmth ate away at its strength.

Crossing the quagmire of a street, Xavier helped his *mama* to the boardwalk and motioned her into the livery stable to see Charro. His Spanish mother had always been one for fine horses, and she didn't disappoint. Shaking her head, she sighed in appreciation at the stallion pressing his nose against her hand. 'Xavier, he's the most glorious horse I have seen since leaving *España*.

'I've trained him in the high school movements you taught me, *Mama*.'

'You were always gifted with horses, I merely gave you some tips,' she whispered, glowing.

'If you think I am gifted, you should see Aleks.'

'Aleks?' his mother questioned, eyebrow lifted.

SUPERINTENDENT HOWARD EGAN found another letter for Xavier in the mail, this time from Johnny at Salt Lake House. Knowing the letter would miss Xavier if he forwarded it to Carson now, he tipped the envelope against the inkwell for Xavier to find upon his return.

XAVIER SQUIRMED BEFORE his *mama's* scrutiny. 'Aleksandra. She… ummm…she…well, she rides for the Pony,' he said in a rush. 'I'd probably better not talk about it, no one knows…no one knows he's a she…someone might hear…' His words drifted slowly to a halt.

'Oh, like that, is it?' His mother bit her lips together with an effort, containing her mirth.

'Let's go check for any messages at the Pony Station.' He looked at her out of the corners of his eyes. 'It's just across the street. I'd like to know if there's any news.'

Xavier took his mother's arm as she held her skirts high above the mud, helping her onto the boardwalk on the other side.

'*Gracias*.' María smiled, preceding him into the station while Xavier held the door.

The station keeper jumped up from his chair with a grin as Xavier introduced himself and his mother.

'Mrs. Arguello.' The blond man smiled, nodding to her, and then turned to Xavier. 'Nice to finally meet you in person, Xavier.' He turned to shuffle through the papers on the board he used for a desk.

'And here, I thought you two knew each other.' María grinned at them. 'Thank you for your information of my son's posting, *señor*.'

'You're welcome anytime, madam. Xavier and I have corresponded for the Pony, but we hadn't met,' he explained in an aside to María, then turned back to Xavier. 'A letter for you just came in.'

Xavier raised his eyebrows at his mother.

'Two letters in a week? That's a record.' He raised an eyebrow and gave them a crooked grin.

'Never say the Express isn't efficient,' the tender announced, producing a letter with a flourish. 'Oh yes, and Xavier, did you notice anything amiss when you came west? We haven't had a rider come in for a few days. This hasn't happened before.'

'Everything seemed fine,' Xavier said with a frown, 'but now that you mention it, I've not been passed by a rider for at least the past day. Let me know if...'

Xavier's head swam and the sun disappeared as he glanced down, sighting his name and address in Scotty's rough scrawl on the envelope. Scotty wasn't much for writing. He only wrote when things were dire. Thanking the keeper, he opened the door for his mother, then excused himself as he turned away to open the letter, fear clutching at his heart.

The blood froze in his veins as he read the brief scrawl.

XAVIER,
VLADIMIR WAS HERE TODAY, LOOKING FOR "SON" OF KRISTOF, URGE YOU TO SOMEHOW KEEP ALEXSANDRA CLOSE TO YOU AND SAFE.
GODSPEED YOU BOTH,
SCOTTY

Dated eleven days ago.
More than forever.

25

Shocked out of her self-pity, Aleksandra stared at the bloody horror in the doorway, then twisted wildly from side to side, seeking perpetrators, but they were long gone. The mare snorted, wild-eyed, at the smell of blood and death. Staying mounted, she tried to control her own heart and breathing as she urged the spooked horse to walk around the station house and barn.

No one, and no animals either. The corral gate rails, ripped from their hooks, lay askew on the ground before the pens.

Slowly dismounting, revolver in hand, Aleksandra crept toward the station. Biting her lip, she approached the door for a proper look. She had to ascertain the man in the entrance to the cabin wasn't still alive, while keeping her eyes peeled for any movement within the station.

No question, her stomach lurched, *he was dead.*

His body was stuck full of arrows, his jugulars severed and his head…she vowed not to look there again. Seeing no movement inside, Aleksandra swallowed noisily and forced herself to step over what was left of him into the station. Two more dead men full of arrows, these two looking like they'd seen the wrong end of a tomahawk. Shuddering, she spun back around and peeked out the door before returning to the yard. The black stood where she'd left her, quivering in the stillness.

Nearly everything in the barn was gone or destroyed. Collecting the single bucket not shattered into kindling, she led the mare around the back of the barn, out of view of the station. Grabbing her canteen, Aleksandra sank to her knees, and the mare nuzzled her hair as she began to shiver uncontrollably.

Shock, water.

The words crept into her brain, as if from afar.

Get food.

She managed to take a deep breath. Slowly, her shaking hands uncapped the water vessel and she drank, hands and canteen quivering. Struggling to her feet to pull the bags from the saddle horn, her wobbly legs barely obeyed and she returned to slide down the adobe wall and sit against its warm support. After chewing a little *pemmican*, she could think clearly again.

It took a drink from the water bucket and a few handfuls of feed for the black's eyes to quiet, too. Aleksandra rubbed around the pony's ears and ate more *pemmican*, the only dinner Schell Creek Station would provide tonight. There was clearly no one to replace her or the mare. She gulped. She couldn't very well stay here.

Not a lot of options, then.

Company policy, if nothing else, dictated that she continue west. The riders knew what they signed on for. Aleksandra just wouldn't think of the man's head again, gagging at the thought.

Mounting up, she said a prayer in the direction of the dead men, hoping she would find something different at Egan Canyon, hoping hard.

At this rate, I might as well become a priest, I'm saying so many blessings for the dead.

Pushing the thoughts away, she sobered. Her strict Catholic mother wouldn't have been impressed.

Despite having already done her stint, the keen mare's trot ate up the miles. Aleksandra's stomach churned after she'd gone less than a mile. She had to dismount and vomit, sweat pouring from her body despite the falling temperature as the sun slid behind a distant mountain range. Wiping her face, Aleksandra took a small sip of water to rinse her mouth.

Her heart constricted when she recalled her talk with Xavier last week.

'All the Indian trouble is more than a hundred miles west of here, you'll be right out of it,' he'd said.

Aleksandra had raised her eyebrows at him, well aware a hundred miles was nothing to an Indian. Many of them could *run* that far in a day, if need be, *without* a horse. This was one time she'd much rather have been wrong.

The black mare checked her stride abruptly, shooting sideways as Aleksandra heard the rattle of the snake, sluggishly crossing the trail.

Sitting deeper in the saddle, she returned her attention to where it should be, smiled and patted the tough little mare. She'd started out on her second run like she was just leaving her first station, loping along the sage-brush flats until they reached the Cherry Creek Range, then up the gentle ascent of Egan Canyon. Aleksandra didn't know how she would've survived without the game little horse.

The openness of the valley, a half-mile across either side of the stream, surrounded by rugged mountains, was a relief after the tight canyons of the past few days, but she wasn't in the mood for scenery tonight.

It was nearly dark when they trotted into Egan Canyon Station, stopping to observe the station from some distance away, then cautiously walking toward the buildings.

The door opened and she stopped the black, ready to spin the mare about if all was not as it should be.

'Hello, is that Michae—' the station keeper cocked his head. 'Hello, I don't think we've met, where's Michael?' The crease between his brows deepened at the look on her face.

'Things aren't good at Schell,' she said, somehow remembering to lower her voice as she slid off. 'Everybody's dead and stock are all gone.' She looked at him, her wide eyes reflected in his.

SCOTTY'S LETTER must have gone to Camp Floyd, then Fish Springs. Egan would have sent it to Carson. The writing blurred and swam before his eyes as he broke into a cold sweat.

How could I have been so stupid?

Aleks knew the danger, told him about it, asked for his understanding and help—and he'd laughed, scorning her fears as nothing.

Scotty didn't fear ghosts.

Xavier, you are the worst kind of idiot.

He closed his eyes and shook his head.

How could I have not believed that someone who tracked Krzysztof and his family halfway around the world, AND killed him, might not be a real threat to Aleksandra's life?

Vladimir was nearer to Aleksandra than he was, several days nearer.

His mother moved close to his side. 'Is everything alright, Xavier?' Her concern was alive in her tremulous voice.

In a flash, he remembered that voice, remembered how she always tried to care for him, despite the pain that invariably resulted.

'Let's find somewhere to sit and I'll tell you about it,' he said faintly as she took his arm and led him towards the kitchen garden behind her hotel.

Sitting together on a log bordering a garden bed, Xavier absently broke off a sprig of rosemary, its scent wafting over him as he crushed it in his hand, while his mother silently waited.

'I've let someone down, someone for whom I care very much, although I've been afraid to let myself care,' he said, slipping into Spanish.

His *mama* waited…She always had, hadn't she? Why hadn't he understood? How many years had he wasted? He gazed down at her graying head as she sat beside him, watching her hand lying still on his arm.

When she looked up, there was love in her eyes. No one could have missed that, but he had.

Her scent, forgotten, for how many years? Jasmine—the memories it held.

Playing with a beautiful, smiling, raven-haired woman and a big, strong, laughing man who threw him up in the air and caught him just before he hit the ground—he could barely picture the face of the man, his *papa*, now in shadow. He wasn't the same man who he knew later as his father, who always seemed to hate him. His mother's letter had finally answered that question.

So many years of burying the memories, so many questions, so many regrets, but it was too late to change the past. If only he could take back the words spoken to his *mama* in anger so long ago, the day he walked out of her life. She still loved him, had always loved him. He tilted his head, eyes wide, staring at her in wonder.

'Of course, I love you, Xave,' she murmured, nodding at him with a soft smile. 'I have always loved you and always will. Everything I've done was to protect you and keep you as safe as I could, although it mustn't have appeared so, then.'

Tears welled in his eyes as he looked at the woman who had taken beatings to protect him and his siblings for many years until Xavier had left in disgust at her "weakness".

'How could I have been so blind?'

'You were only fourteen, my Xave,' Her voice was honey on a wound.

'I was afraid to get close to you, so I pushed you away. I didn't want to let you in then, but maybe I'm being given a second chance. Perhaps it isn't too late, and maybe it's time.'

Was he thinking of his mama or Aleksandra? Was it the same thing? Was letting someone into his heart the key he had been missing all his life?

'I didn't want to let you in, *Mama*,' he whispered. 'I was afraid to let her in too. Now that I see what I might have lost, I can see that I should have…let her in, believed in her, and now it might be too late.'

The words came out in a jumble, but his *mama* smiled up at him, wrapping her arms around him.

'I was also jealous,' Xavier swallowed hard, 'that she was close to someone else before we met. I was too proud and, truth be told, probably too afraid to accept her love and believe her when she said it was me she cared about.'

María sat up and looked at him. 'I have found happiness only by letting people, the *right* people, into my life, and by letting myself believe I am worthy of love. Only by this can we break the cycle of abuse which otherwise binds us and blinds us. Pride has no place in a relationship. It only tears people apart. Jealousy, likewise. Belief and trust in oneself and in each other are essential. There *is* no other way, so far as I have seen.'

'This I begin to see.' Xavier looked at his hands, enfolded in his mother's.

'Only love, especially love for yourself, is the real answer. It was not your fault your stepfather beat me. It was *never* your fault. You are, and always have been, worthy of love,' she said, looking into his eyes intently.

'It will take time for me to believe that, but I'm working on it.' Xavier shook his head. 'Did the bastard keep hitting you after I left?'

'Nothing but death would stop such a man. Why do you ask?'

'I thought he hurt you to get at me, so I thought my leaving would solve the problems for you.'

She took his face in her hands, shaking her head, tears streaming down her face. 'I thought as much. My Xave... no, it didn't solve any problems. I was heartbroken for many, many years to think you left because you believed I didn't love you. I was afraid I would never be able to tell you or show you how much I cared, but you have come to me and offered me the chance. For this, I am eternally grateful.'

He squeezed his eyes shut as tears welled from them. 'I have to admit something I am even more ashamed of,' he whispered. 'I believed, then, that you were weak for staying. I see now how wrong I was.'

Closing her eyes for a moment, she took a deep breath, and with a ghost of a smile, nodded her head. 'Where could I have gone with all of the children? Who would have protected those living on our lands? I had no way to get the money to escape with the children to our family in *España*. I considered every option. I am a woman, a chattel. I knew he killed your father, but I had no proof, other than my word. When he forcibly took me to bride, he took me, the land and our people. The men in his employ were no more than guards for his interests and they watched my every move, reading every letter I wrote.'

'This I see now.' Xavier hung his head. 'I beg your apology for even thinking it.' He looked up to see her head held high, her eyes smiling at him.

'No apology is needed, nor desired, *mi querido*,' his mother said.

'We all only knew what we knew. I have learned much since then and I see you have as well. I am proud to call you my son, as always.' Her eyes glowed.

'I now understand the courage it took to stay and protect all of us. You are a wonder and I am proud to call you *mi madre*. I'm sorry it took so long for me to understand.' Xavier looked her fully in the eyes and clasped her to him. 'It seems it is not too late, after all.'

It was a long while before he let her go. When he did, a huge stone had been lifted from atop his heart.

'I never doubted this would come to pass.' Her smile brightened the late afternoon sunshine. 'You are my son and will always hold a special place in my heart. I am so thankful to have found you.' She inhaled deeply, let it out, then gave his arm a little shake.

'*Ahora, mi querido*,' she said firmly, 'who is this person that you feel you have let down?'

The fullness of heart burst as if stuck with a blade, and he suddenly couldn't breathe.

THE NEXT DAY DAWNED EARLY. Vladimir's days were becoming rote.

Keep going, switch horses, find feed, find water, walk-trot-walk-trot, watch for dust, travellers and Indians.

It became his mantra. Always the goal kept him driving on, but he was tired after another seventy miles. A good day's ride, all in all. He sighed, and then lifted his chin. Rogan pricked up his ears as they approached the deep cottonwood-filled creek bed where they'd stayed on the way north. The horses wouldn't have let it pass by, not with its shade and good feed.

They ate their fill and stood dozing, hobbled in the long grass.

'Soon, my Tatiana, Niko,' he raised his eyes heavenward, 'soon we will be together again.' His heart ached as his eyes closed and he slept.

'A WOMAN, *sí*?' Xavier's mother prodded, when he sat frozen.

He took a deep breath, and rubbed his chest.

'*Sí, Mama*,' he began slowly, past the lump in his throat. 'She is a beautiful young woman, who has only recently been orphaned after her father was killed. He was a Polish trapper in Echo, near the Weber River.'

'*Echo*, I just heard of Echo, it was…oh yes, I shared a coach from San Francisco with a lovely woman and her son who were headed there to find someone. I think she was Russian.'

'Small world *Mama*. It's only a tiny settlement,' Xavier brushed the hair off his forehead with one hand as he returned to what he had begun to tell her.

'But no, my son, I have interrupted you. Please go on about your young lady.'

He gulped and started again. 'She has been given trials beyond her years. I neglected to take her fears seriously and now could lose her to someone who would stop at nothing to possess a secret her family has protected for many years. She won't relinquish it willingly and her life is in danger.' He closed his eyes, his fingers gripping hers. 'I could have protected her, but I did not. Her name is Aleksandra,' he whispered.

'Worse, she has given me her love and I was afraid to open myself to her. It may truly be too late, for everything … everything.' He managed a deep breath with difficulty.

'Did she send news in that letter?'

'*Sí*, or rather, *no*, the message was a warning from a mutual friend. He said the man who killed Aleksandra's father for his secret is seeking her, and is getting close. It was dated eleven days ago. I don't think she knows he is so close.' He ran his fingers through his hair and gripped it tightly.

María jumped to her feet and pulled at his hands. 'You must fly to her, now, *Querido*. You understand what love can do, and what happens when one is denied it. Think on it, *mi hijo*, my son, my life.' She gripped his hands in hers and he looked up to see her heart, and a tear, in her wide, sparkling eyes.

'I thank you for not giving up on me, *Mama*, even when I pushed away you and everyone else in my life.' He rose to his feet, pulling her with him, and held her close once again. He inhaled her scent. The jasmine infiltrated his being like a talisman.

He would remember.

'I will remain here and await word from you before I leave town.' She smiled at him. 'You'll need provision for your trip. The general mercantile is on the way to the stables.' Her quick steps led the way.

Entering the cool darkness of the livery stable, the traveling food in Xavier's saddlebags restored, they walked down its wide aisle. The rows of heads nodded at them, stirring up the rich, beguiling scent of horses and hay. Yes, he would remember.

Xavier reached out to take his mother's hands. 'Thank you again, *Mama*, for giving me your love and helping me see I needn't fear it as I have.'

'Be safe, *mi querido*. Go protect your young woman.' She shook her head at him, smiling, as he deftly saddled and bridled Charro. 'Never let love go without a fight. *Recuerda*. Remember, *sí*?

'*Recuerdo, Mama*.' He hugged her, then swung up. The lump left his throat and he wanted to shout, his heart was so full. As he had done so many times as a child, he blew her a kiss. Charro rose, lifting his forefeet from the ground in a motionless *levade*, then flew like an arrow released, away down the street.

26

Seeming to sense his master's urgency, Charro picked up the pace, frequently breaking into a canter and loping along until he tired, then dropping back to his ground-eating trot. They ate on the run, Charro grabbing any grass he found as they moved along and Xavier nibbling *pemmican* and hardtack from his packs. They stopped at a spring in an aspen thicket near Cold Springs and sheltered there for the night.

The spring's crisp, fresh water was a refreshing change from the musty liquid they usually found at desert springs or stations. The stallion munched contentedly from his feedbag while Xavier, wrapped in his *serape*, dozed fitfully, half-alert for Indians. He awoke in a cold sweat, his heart trying to bang its way out of his chest, dreaming of a blonde wraith fleeing a cloaked and hooded man. Charro nuzzled him, blowing his sweet, oatey breath in his face. Xavier managed to draw a deep breath, his pounding heart gradually slowing, and forcibly relaxed his muscles as he rubbed the horse's nose. Stars still twinkled overhead. It wouldn't be daybreak for hours yet.

'Well *hombre*, you ready to go?' he asked Charro. The horse shifted his weight from foot to foot and swung his head around toward the trail.

'Let's go on, then, neither of us are getting much rest.' Xavier stood and stretched.

THE EGAN CANYON Station keeper shook his head at Aleksandra's announcement, eyes wide, and his mouth dropped open.

'This mare's come all the way from Spring Valley today.' She stroked her neck after she'd dismounted. 'She was pretty upset by the...the blood,' she tightened her jaw and continued, 'but she drank some water and had a little feed from my bag.' Aleksandra's head drooped.

'I'm sure you've taken good care of her, sorry, what's your name?'

'I'm Aleksan—Aleks, from Fish Springs.'

'Good to meet you Aleks,' he said gently. 'Can you tell me what you saw?'

'He was ... he was ...' She couldn't go on.

'Dead?' The keeper's low, calm voice and his hands clamping her shoulders steadied her.

'No, I mean yes. Three men were dead. The man in the doorway, he was dead, but he was ... scalped.' She shuddered. 'I've seen people dead, which is bad enough, but never ... scalped.' The tears squeezed from her tightly-shut eyes.

Strength flowed through his hands to her shoulders and she picked up her head and looked at him, tears falling in earnest now.

'It's okay, lad, you're here now,' he said gruffly. 'Come into the station.' He led Aleksandra by an arm around her shoulders.

'The blood,' she winced, 'was still wet, though clotted and dark red. It can't have been long since they left.' She looked at him. 'You haven't heard of any more attacks?'

'No, Aleks, I haven't.' He shook his head. 'You're one lucky boy. If you'd happened upon that, or been caught sleeping there ... I hate to think what might've happened to you, too.' He gave Aleks a brief hug. 'Anyways, glad you're here now.'

'You've no idea how happy I am to find someone alive here, after that,' she said with a sigh.

'Can't say but I'm glad too. I've got no one here who can relieve you, can you go on?'

'Course I can, but I need another horse. The black is amazing, but she's tired, after twenty miles at that speed.' She gave him the ghost of a smile.

She followed him into the station.

Odd, how love and care for a stranger becomes a simple matter in the face of conceivable impending death.

The keeper's voice pulled her back.

'Sit down, I've got some supper and a good pony ready for you. I promise to take good care of the little black for you.' He winked at her as she smiled her thanks.

Supper done, she waved her goodbye and rode out on a bay Mustang who seemed to know the ropes, setting off at a strong trot through the desert and keeping them true, even when Aleksandra could see no trail. The moon rose, making huge, stretched-out shadows from even the smallest sage bushes. She watched all about her, frequently starting at the long dark figures on the ground.

The colt never faltered, but loped straight on to the station at Butte Creek, where the keeper took the news in silence. He asked a few questions, skirting around the topic of the dead men, once he saw how Aleksandra reacted to it. He described the upcoming trail to her, mounted her onto a pinto colt and shook her hand.

'Proud of you for going on, son,' he said, like he meant it.

'My job's easy,' Aleksandra said, shaking her head, her face scrunched up. 'Like I told someone the other day, at least I'm on a horse and can try to get away. You men aren't. You take care of yourself too, sir.' She gave him a grim smile as she rode away.

They traveled west down a long valley and through a little low pass. In the distance, the Maverick Springs Range rose before her, its snowcap shining white in the moonlight. On the eastern slope was Mountain Spring Station. Even in the darkness, she could see the station keeper pale at her news. Wishing her well, he sent her off over the top of the high pass into Ruby Valley on a chestnut Mustang.

The Ruby Valley keeper didn't relish the news any more than the others and frowned as he patted his pocket. 'Just makin' sure I've got enough ammunition,' he replied in response to her questioning look.

He gave her some salt beef and biscuits to eat on her next mount, a beautiful leopard Palouse named Christmas.

Aleksandra's mouth went dry at her first sight of the snow-covered Ruby Mountain range looming tall before her. As they climbed, her breath turned the bandana over her mouth and nose into a patch of solid ice. She didn't like their chances of scaling the pass, but breathed a sigh of relief at finding only a foot of well-packed snow at the summit. The moonlight reflected off the snow and lit it like day.

Taking a breather at the top, Aleksandra scanned the descent and the valley far below for any signs of movement, clutching the bags hanging from her neck like the talismans they were. Cold again, she dismounted to run the downhill slope, Christmas snorting and bouncing in the brisk air.

Lovely pony. Friendly too. She smiled as the pony nuzzled her hand while she unscrewed her canteen, vaguely noticing it seemed quite tight. She gasped before she took her first sip of the icy water, jerking her lips away from the frozen metal. Still shaking her head at herself, she mounted and carried on down the trail to Jacob's Well.

'Halloo, young man,' the keeper called. The light from his lantern swung as he strode from the cabin, wiping his mustache on his forearm. He led the way to the saddled palomino, wearing a blanket over her rump.

'I'm sure she appreciates that, sir.' Aleksandra nodded with a smile at the horse standing warm in her quarter rug in the chill night.

'She's a special one and feels the cold,' the young keeper mumbled. He smiled a little and ducked his head, caught out coddling the Mustang.

While he signed the time card, Aleksandra took a deep breath and told him about Schell Station.

Eyes narrowing, he straightened up and thanked her for the news.

'You've not been west before, have you? This mare knows the way well, so you should be okay. You'll go across Huntington Valley a bit further on,' he said, 'then it's a fairly easy crossing over the Diamond Mountains to Diamond Springs Station. Likewise, on to Sulphur Springs is a fairly easy ride. After that is where it gets a bit interesting.' He winced. 'It's pretty rugged between there and Robert's Creek, but you'll get a rest once you get there.'

'I'm starting to think I need it.' She rubbed her grimy forehead. 'I've been on the trail since early this morning.'

'They'll take good care of you at Roberts's. It's a long trail in the dark if you've never been over it, even more so if you've done two runs in a day!' He grinned and shook her hand. 'I usually ride this run, but the regular keeper is away for a couple days. You take care,' he said as he slid the quarter rug off the golden horse's rump. Aleksandra vaulted on and loped away. Much as the keeper described, the pass over the Diamond Mountains was easy, but the night became a blur.

Riding a pinto mare between Diamond and Sulphur Springs, on one of the easiest portions of the trail she'd yet seen, the horse suddenly staggered, her head dropping as Aleksandra saw the ground coming up to meet her. Frantically tucking into a ball, she slipped over the mare's shoulder and the big brown and white body followed. Aleksandra managed to roll free as the pinto flipped over and lay still. The wind knocked out of her, Aleksandra wasn't so keen to move either. Finally, turning her head, she looked at the motionless mare, then peered into the darkness around them, seeking attackers. No one was there.

Just a fall, then.

Aleksandra inhaled deeply, then gagged at the coppery taste of blood filling her mouth. She slowly pulled herself to a sitting position as her head and knee begin to throb. 'It's okay, mare,' she said to the pony in a soothing voice. She wasn't sure which of them she was trying to reassure. The pony whickered softly in reply and struggled to rise on one foreleg. Aleksandra limped the few steps to her side and steadied her head as her mount got to her feet on three legs. The pinto stood shaking and nodding her head, her right foreleg held flexed, not touching the ground. Aleksandra's stomach turned over, her hands clammy at the sight.

'Oh, my poor lady,' she whispered, sucking in a rapid breath at the pain in her knee when she hunkered down beside the mare and took the injured foreleg into her hands. Beginning at the hoof and working upwards, she deftly felt for each bone and tendon, gently rocking each joint to ascertain the damage.

'Hoof, pastern and fetlock all fine,' she murmured, then her hands reached the back of the cannon and she stopped dead. The mare flinched as she slid her fingers over the already swollen, soft knot in the normally rock-hard fibrous band of flexor tendon between knee and fetlock. Aleksandra shook her head. The mare had bowed a tendon.

'My poor angel.' She started breathing again, realizing that she needn't shoot the mare, as she would've had to if she'd broken the leg. Unlike a fracture, a pulled and torn tendon wasn't a death sentence, but she wouldn't be going fast for months, if she recovered soundness at all.

Pulling off her extra shirt, she wrapped the leg to support the injured leg. She wished she had more padding for it, but there simply wasn't any.

She looked around again, listening, but only the sound of the breeze stirred in the night. Wondering how such a surefooted pony had flipped, she retraced their steps. Two lengths behind the pinto was a badger hole. Peering down at it in the darkness, she saw the caved-In edges. The pinto's hoof must have gone down the hole, with disastrous results. Turning back to the pinto, she stroked her head. Walking on the leg would damage it more, but it was better than being eaten by predators.

'We'd best get walking, it'll be hours before we get to the next station,' she murmured. Hoping they had a horse for her and a stable for the game little mare struggling beside her on three legs, they limped their way to Sulphur Springs. Fortunately, the terrain was gentle and they reached Sulphur Springs Station just as the sun rose over the next mountain range.

Aleksandra was exhausted and her knee and head still throbbed, but she got the pinto into a pen and sent the keeper for some wadding, blanket strips or anything he could find to pad the leg bandages.

'Can you keep her bandaged and in a small pen for the next couple of months?' she asked the keeper when he'd returned with the bandaging.

'Sure can.' He handed her a torn blanket from his bed.

'And then she'll need gradually increasing hand-walking to get the leg mobile again after it's healed.'

'Okay, can do. Show me how to do it, please.' He knelt beside the mare.

Aleksandra nicked most of one edge of the blanket at four inch intervals and tore it into strips for its full length to make the bandages. For the 'quilts', or under-bandage padding, she cut the remaining piece of blanket into rectangles, with their long side the length of her whole arm.

She showed him how to roll the bandages and quilts down the surface of her own thigh, like a snail shell, in preparation for bandaging.

'You need plenty of padding beneath the bandages, with no creases, like this,' Aleksandra said as she wrapped a rectangle of thick blanket around the mare's leg from knee to hoof. Slipping the end of one of the bandage rolls beneath the edge of the quilt, she unwound the bandage against the padding, laying it smoothly, snugly and evenly from knee to hoof.

Aleksandra stood up, sweating with the pain of her bent knee. 'Here,' she managed. She drew a deep breath to forget the pain in her own leg. 'You try putting the bandage on this leg. You saw how I did the other one.

'Okay,' he said, ducking down beside the mare's good foreleg. 'Why do we bandage the other leg?'

'It's to support the good leg, which will bear most of her weight while she's so sore on the other one.'

'Makes sense. You overlap the bandage strips halfway each turn, you said?'

'Yes, that keeps the compression even and doesn't damage the tendons any more.

The pinto, who had stood like a rock the whole time, sighed when they were finished. She softly whickered at them, glancing their way briefly from her pile of hay.

'I'll get you a bite to eat. Are you able to go on?'

'Yes,' she said briefly, and he headed for the station.

Aleksandra sank to the pile of hay beside the mare. She bandaged her knee with one of the remaining bandages, then closed her eyes.

She awoke to the smell of food.

'Wakey, wakey, Aleks,' the keeper smiled. 'I've got food for you.'

'Oh, um, food?' Aleksandra blinked as she struggled to a sitting position.

'Thank you for your help, Aleks. Your knowledge will help a lot of horses.'

'I wish I could do more,' she said, reaching over her head for the plate.

He smiled, handing her a veritable platter of eggs and salt beef rolled up in a big sourdough pancake.

'Eggs! And pancakes!' Aleksandra's eyes opened wide.

'I keep a few hens here. Thought you deserved a treat after your walk and lack of sleep.' He chuckled.

'Thank you!'

'No problem. You've done more than most could have for this horse. I'll change her bandages daily and keep her locked up. Hopefully, she'll be good as new.'

'I hope so. Walking on it for four hours couldn't have helped it.'

'These Mustangs are tough. I'll bet she makes a full recovery, thanks to your care. Now you'd best be off, your pony's waiting. There'll be a bed ahead at Roberts Creek. On your horse, young man!' he sternly barked, then grinned as he lifted her into the saddle, taking care not to jar her bulky knee.

The dawn's early light showed the trail clearly, but riding the big-striding gray Mustang was tricky with a throbbing knee and a brain seemingly stuck in a fog. Luckily, the track continued relatively flat until they neared Robert's Creek Mountain.

Loud metallic clanging rang out somewhere before her on the trail, accompanied by shouting, and Aleksandra pulled the mare to a halt. She slowly walked the gray forward to the top of the ridge before her, peering over the edge. She began breathing again when she saw it was a large troop of US Army soldiers.

The men were at various stages of breaking camp. Some stood about in loose formation on the trail while others hadn't even rolled their blankets. Heaving a sigh of relief, she sent the mare toward them at a lope.

One of the lounging soldiers saw her and began shouting. Others joined him, all of them grabbing for their rifles at her approach. Aleksandra suddenly realized they didn't recognize her as an Express rider, so she yanked the mare to a halt as a few dozen rifles pointed in her direction.

'PONY EXPRESS!' she screamed at the top of her lungs. When the sound reached them, several of the men cheered and knocked the muzzles of their slower companions' guns toward the ground. Smiling, she loosed the mare's reins and the Mustang fair galloped past the troop while Aleksandra waved to the cheering men and let her run, her long strides eating up the miles.

Aleksandra smiled wearily as the horse slowed down to a slow canter when they entered the steeper foothills of Robert's Creek Mountain. Soon enough, she'd be asleep in a bed and resting her head and now-stiffened knee. A grin flashed as she realized the pain in her knee might be a blessing in disguise—it was probably the only thing keeping her awake.

Topping a rise, she saw smoke just a few miles away, and thought of the warm fire and breakfast she was going to have before falling asleep.

'Close, we're close, mare,' she ground out, with more enthusiasm than she'd thought she could muster. They loped on.

Suddenly off to her right she heard, and then turning her head, she saw a band of Indians in war paint, whooping and screaming, racing toward her down the mountain. She drove the mare off the trail, further down the hill, hoping upon hope they weren't coming for her. Her heart stopped and her breath caught in her throat as their cries grew louder.

27

The faintest light was beginning to show on the eastern horizon and another day of hard riding began. Xavier prayed he wasn't too late.

He made Dry Creek Station just after dawn. No one answered his halloo and he pulled Charro gradually to a halt. The station door stood ajar and the gateway poles were scattered before the empty corrals.

Scanning the surrounds, he saw no movement, so he rode closer, then circled the cabin. He gulped, feeling the blood drain from his face as he sighted the bullet holes and arrows riddling the walls and sills. Moving closer to the cabin, still looking for any sign of life, he slid from the saddle and quietly cocked his rifle as the rusty tang of blood filled his nostrils. Keeping flat against the side of the building, he looked well about him, then slipped through the doorway.

Xavier stopped dead. His breath caught, spots swimming before his eyes at the sight of the two station tenders lying still as clay, askew in pools of their own blood. Ralph and John were riddled with arrows, bright red lifeblood barely clotted around the ragged bullet holes ripping their skin. Xavier shivered and flicked a glance over his shoulder, realizing the men couldn't have been dead for more than an hour. His eyes darted about as he filled his canteen and gave Charro a long drink from the water barrel. Hating to leave the men unburied, yet fearing for Aleksandra, he wedged the broken door shut, praying for the departed men as he rode, hard and watchful, to the east. He gave notice to the keeper at Grubb's Well in a shaky voice and cantered on towards Robert's Creek Station, the mountain looming large on his left.

A barrage of gunshots rang out from the direction of the distant station. Xavier's heart thudded wildly in his chest. He could almost smell the blood as he dragged Charro to a jerky halt.

VLADIMIR'S JAW CLENCHED, his mouth set in a firm line, when he saw the landmarks that told him he was nearly back at Great Salt Lake City. It felt like forever ago he'd left Salt Lake House on his wild goose chase around the desert. The flat plain before him narrowed between the mountains and the marshy edge of the lake as a string of cottonwoods came into view. Turning the bay's head toward its dappled shade, they passed clusters of Gamble oaks, their stiff leaves making no movement in the light breeze. The cool air in the gully welcomed him as he rode down a bank into a branching creek. The horses tore into the lush grass beneath the leafy thicket, eating their fill before lying down for a night of well-earned rest.

Half an hour down the trail the next morning, Vladimir spied North Cottonwood in the distance. Soon, the entrance to the ravine where he'd left the old man came into view.

DISMOUNTING, Xavier tied Charro to a small bush and crawled to the crest of the small rise before him. He was hoping beyond hope that he would see the Robert's Creek keeper "Colonel" William Rogers, or "Uncle Billy", as Xavier knew him, at target practice.

His heart constricted at the sight of the puffs of smoke coming from the station gun ports and the Indians, resplendent in war paint and feathers, circling the building at a gallop on their painted ponies.

As he watched, several of the Indians broke away and raced north up the steep side of Robert's Creek Mountain. Forcing down the nausea, Xavier took his eyes off the scene below and scanned the horizon for the reason. The wave of relief washing over him made him want to cry and shout for joy at the same time.

From the west, a sea of blue uniforms, their metalwork glinting in the sun as they galloped toward the besieged cabin, revealed itself as a sizeable troop of U.S. Army Cavalrymen.

He returned his gaze to the station. Most of the Indian warriors, not about to retreat, remained to continue their assault until they either turned to engage the uniformed men or fell from their ponies. Xavier glanced around him, brow furrowed and knuckles white on his rifle. He'd be in a bad place if any of the fleeing Indians or soldiers came this way.

'They seem to have it well in hand,' he murmured to the gray as he mounted up. 'They've got all the help they need, but Aleks doesn't, so let's go find her.'

The horse spun on his haunches and they headed off the side of the trail, leaving a wide berth around both Robert's Creek and the next station, Sulphur Springs, riding ever east.

As darkness fell two hours later, he reached Diamond Springs Station. Charro's head was drooping

'Would you like a meal and a bed, man?' the keeper asked.

'No, I've got to go on,' Xavier whispered, but then looked at Charro. His head, usually so proudly erect on his arched neck, drooped, and his ears flopped to the sides like a carthorse.

Xavier sighed.

The keeper nodded at him. 'Yep, I know you're keen to get out of all this, but your horse needs the rest, even if you don't. Come on in when you're done, we've got good stout walls,' he said, thumping the logs of the cabin with his fist.

'He'd give till he died. Yes, I know, thank you.' Xavier tugged at the stallion's forelock and offered him another sip of water. Cooling him out properly, he settled him for the night, then bunked down inside. He wasn't actually sure he wanted a roof over his head, under the circumstances.

Sighing deeply as he lay on his mattress, he thought of Aleksandra out riding in the middle of this mess. He had to get to her in time, he just had to. He refused to believe he would never see her again, and get another chance at winning her love. He prayed for her safety, and his own, as well as that of all those on the trail before and behind.

The cold, blue metal of his rifle lying beside him was scant comfort. Xavier was well aware just what safety rifles and stout walls had afforded the unlucky men of Dry Creek.

'NOTHING.' Vladimir slapped his hat violently on his thigh and ran his hands through his gritty hair, biting the inside of his cheeks. The chestnut mare behind him threw up her head and took a step backwards, while the colt he was riding ignored him completely, other than tugging at his reins to reach a clump of dry grass beside the narrow trail. He took a deep breath and peered at the ground again. No sign of the crusty old sourdough, no blood, no rope, no scraps of fabric nor hair. Brows lowered as far as they could go, he mounted. Swearing in Russian, he rode on south.

Knowing what his life would be worth if he made an appearance anywhere near Salt Lake after the old man found his way back, Vladimir steered clear of approaching wagons and riders. He detoured far around Great Salt Lake City and further westward, Camp Floyd. The Russian kept a close look about him, holding the mare tightly on a short lead in case they needed to make a run for it when they rejoined the main Express trail at Five Mile Pass. As they exited the pass, a strip of fast-moving dust appeared to the west. His heart pounded, his hands becoming clammy, when the lone horse and rider materialized and rapidly approached. Backtracking and dragging the horses into a concealed ravine, Vladimir placed his hands over his horses' noses to prevent their calling out to the horse loping past them. His heart fell when he realized the Express rider wasn't Krzysztof's son.

A short while later, just after crossing a creek, he spied what looked to be a Pony Express station. Darkness was falling, so he reluctantly turned the horses back to follow the meandering stream north until they were out of view of the main trail, camping there for the night.

Vladimir's thoughts rolled on and on as he made his final plans. With the cooling of the night air, fog invaded in wisps, gradually obscuring everything except the tops of the horses, rhythmically cropping the tough grass beside the softly tinkling stream. Between the proximity of the station and the anticipation of apprehending Krzysztof's get, sleep evaded him until deep into the night.

LEAVING Diamond Springs Station early the next morning, Xavier saluted the grave of the plucky Express pony "What?" that saved George Scovill's life, and continued east. As he rode down from Overland Pass, he saw the Ruby Valley Station and Camp Ruby ahead. The new U.S. Army outpost had just recently been installed to protect the mail and settlers.

Xavier went to the camp to report what he had seen at Robert's Creek, and was led to the Sergeant's tent.

'I understand you saw the attack upon Robert's Creek Station, and Dry Creek as well, young man,' the uniformed man barked. 'Your name, please?'

'Yes, sir, I did,' Xavier replied, offering his name and employment.

'Oh, so you're a station keeper yourself.' His eyebrows shot up. 'Fancy you not going in to help!'

'Well, sir, I didn't see I'd be much help, under the circumstances. Your men had already engaged the Indians and they appeared to have it under control. The Robert's Creek men were the lucky ones. Regretfully, I was too late to do anything for the boys at Dry Creek,' he said, as his guts tightened.

'I'm sorry about the men of Dry Creek,' the sergeant said, in a softer voice. 'A messenger arrived just after you rode into camp.' He hesitated for a moment. 'You were wise to stay clear at Robert's Creek and you'll be pleased to know that Colonel Rogers is fine, along with the hands who were there with him.'

'That's a relief.' Xavier let out his breath. 'How long was it going before your men arrived?'

'Apparently, it began early in the day. The Indians showed up and asked for flour, then demanded that the men make bread for them. While the men cooked as fast as they could, the Indians told them how they were going to torture and kill them. Rogers got his men alone into the building and started firing on the attackers. They somehow managed to hold on until the Army showed up.'

'What luck the troops were on hand to help!' Xavier smiled as he shook his head, raising his eyebrows at the commander.

'Luck? It was more than luck, it was a Pony rider!'

'Really?'

'It seems a young Pony rider, usually stationed at Fish Springs Station—'

Xavier's heart froze in his chest.

'God Almighty,' Superintendent Howard Egan swore over the barking dogs to the farrier standing beside him in his long johns as he watched the Palouse stallion amble into Fish Springs just after midnight.

'Who *is* that?' the horseshoer squinted into the darkness.

'What a day.' Egan scowled as he slapped a lead rope against his boot and turned to the man. 'First Jason shows up with an arrow in his leg from Dugway, and now Aleks deigns to amble in, days after expected, in the middle of the night, probably drunk. What is this world coming—'

'Major Egan!' he interrupted, 'he's asleep. Keep your voice down or he might tumble off.'

'Serve him—' Howard Egan rushed over to the pony, then stopped and spoke to Aleksandra softly, putting a hand on her knee to steady her.

'Ouch!' she yelped. The horse flung up his head as she grabbed for the saddle horn, reins still clamped tightly in one hand. She came awake, staring in horror at the man gripping her knee.

'Aleks, it's me, Egan,' he said softly.

'Le'go my knee,' she mumbled, eyes closing. 'Hurts.'

Egan pried Aleksandra's fingers from their death grip on the reins and pulled her from the saddle.

'Hurts,' she said again. 'Horse flipped, tendon, sleep.' Her chin fell to her chest as he carried her to a bed and covered her.

'The horse's fine, but there's no *mochila*.' The farrier frowned at

Egan as he pulled the saddle off the Mustang, his mouth in a firm line. 'Aleks isn't one to just lose a *mochila*.'

'We'll let him sleep until morning.' Egan shook his head as he led the colt off for a drink and a rubdown. 'The boy's shattered, we've got no other rider who can ride and no *mochila* to go east. Go back to bed, man. Tomorrow's soon enough to sort out this whole mess.' Egan closed his eyes and rubbed his forehead with a sigh. 'You've had a hard day shoeing that big bronc. You could probably use the rest too. Goodnight, Jake.'

'Best idea I've heard all day,' the farrier said, rubbing his back as he headed for the bunkhouse.

'MAJOR EGAN,' someone called loudly and pounded on the station door. 'Major Egan!'

Pulling on his dungarees, Egan stumbled to open the door in the early dawn, rifle in hand.

When he saw a U.S. Army officer standing at attention before him, holding a *mochila*, he knew today was going to be interesting.

'*FISH SPRINGS? DIOS MÍO*!' Xavier spat out, eyes bulging. He checked himself abruptly and gulped. '*Lo siento*, sorry to interrupt, sir.'

The commander arched one brow and carried on.

'Seems this rider had just come in from the East and saw the Indians attacking the station. Luckily, before they saw him.'

Xavier felt himself go cold and willed his clenched hands to straighten while he waited, not daring to breathe.

'Seems the rider'd passed the Army units heading home to Camp Ruby some miles back near Sulphur Springs, so he hightailed it back to the troops and they raced to help the station keeper. You know the rest.'

'Lucky for them!' he managed. His mind spun as he brushed back his hair with the back of one hand.

What was Aleksandra doing out in the middle of all this?

'And the rider from Fish Springs?' He tried for nonchalance.

'I think his name was Aleks. A good little rider, that! He was about to drop, seems he'd been riding non-stop for two whole days,' he said with a chuckle.

As the blood pounded so loudly in his ears he thought his head would burst, he tried to draw a breath and failed.

'Was the rider hurt?' he finally blurted out. He managed a deep breath and held it.

'Far from it. Exhausted, but after he'd been assured that the station master would be protected, his only concern was that damned leather thing, that *moochie, mochie*—'

'*Mochila*?' He managed a ghost of a smile at the inanity of the girl.

'Yes, *that*. He was determined to go on West, but we wouldn't let him, had to force him to give us that blasted piece of leather. He pulled a sword, a funny short one, on the man who tried to take it, stroppy lad! Just about had to throw him into the clink!'

Xavier couldn't hide a wry grin, remembering their first meeting. Yes, it was Aleksandra, and yes, she was very much alive.

'He wouldn't let go of the weapon until we promised to deliver his *mochila* to Robert's Creek Station after it was secured, and to bring any *mochila* we found at the station back East to Fish Springs for relay.' He gave a belly laugh and shook his head, eyebrows raised. 'Have to admit, I offered him a place in my troop when he stopped by here to report. Wish I had more men of that caliber under me here!'

Despite the gravity of the situation, Xavier couldn't help a deep chuckle at that. Wouldn't the sergeant be shocked when he learned a bit more about her?

'Thanks again for your report.' The commander turned to go. 'You'll find dry rations for you and your horse at the picket lines. Much obliged, Xavier.'

He fairly flew out of the sergeant's tent, headed for Charro. Caching the waiting packet of food and grain into his saddlebags, he thanked the private who supplied them and swung up, his heart in a vise.

What was she doing this far West, embroiled in the middle of the Pah-Ute war … when she was only to be riding east of Fish Springs, where she would be safe, at least from the Indians. Where was Vladimir now?

Charro raced on, caught up in Xavier's urgency.

XAVIER SMELLED the smoke long before Mountain Springs Station came into view. His heart banged against his ribs while he considered returning to Ruby Valley, but his concern for Aleks overrode any sense of responsibility he had to the army or anyone else. They'd know soon enough anyway, so he went on, carefully checking the area around the station before he approached the buildings. The station was still on fire, but he didn't find any people nor animals, dead or alive. Perhaps they'd received word of the attacks and cleared out. He fervently hoped so.

At Butte Creek Station, Xavier's stomach rolled at the sight of the keeper stuck full of arrows, blood spilling over the earthen floor, but the man was past his help, or anyone else's, for that matter. The stock must have been driven off, for there was nothing alive on the place, so he rode on.

Egan Canyon was just as bad, but there were two dead men there and one dead cow. She looked like she'd been used for target practice. Xavier wasn't sure he could handle finding more bodies, but couldn't pass by any stations without checking for survivors.

Xavier skirted Schell Creek Station, as the commander at Ruby had told him it was gutted and there were no survivors, so he proceeded to Spring Valley.

Charro remained keen to go on, so he gave him his head and let him set the pace. As Xavier's spirit sunk further with each of the next three destroyed stations, his worry for Aleksandra escalated. Sick to death of finding burned out stations and dead men, Xavier tried to prepare himself for the inevitable, that Aleksandra couldn't have survived the onslaught of violence he saw before him. He refused to believe she was dead, for he still felt her in his heart. He held on to this certainty as the hours wore on.

He heaved a great sigh and slid from his horse at Egan's Deep Creek Station, hugging the keeper who looked at him askance until he told them what he'd seen. When he asked after Aleks, the keeper grinned.

'So he's from your station, eh?' He chuckled. 'He left Robert's Creek in strife, as you know, but probably saved all their bacon, then shot straight here on a pony he rode all the way from Mountain Springs. There were Indians attackin' most of the stations he passed and he didn't have a *mochila* anyway.'

Xavier looked at him aghast, his pulse pounding in his throat. 'He went on?'

'Ever tried to stop that boy doin' something he wanted to do? He was dead on his feet, but still had a little smile for us and the new pony. We're still treating that pony he rode in on like glass. We'd be afraid he might hear of us doin' otherwise!

'Thanks to his warnings, we're all packin' up the most important farm equipment and headin' east. Take a meal and have a sleep here tonight?'

'I'd be grateful for a feed, as would Charro,' he nodded at the stallion, 'but we'll move on. We're in a hurry to catch someone ...' Xavier's murmur faded away.

The man glanced at him, his brow furrowing, then looked sideways at the clearly exhausted gray horse.

"I'll get you both something and you can go on,' he said, looking down at the ground as he walked slowly toward the station.

As the great Andalusian ate a feed, Xavier sighed and wrapped his arms around his neck. 'I'm sorry, Boy, but we've got to get back. Aleks is still out there,' he whispered into his mane.

Half an hour later, he took a deep breath and headed the tired but willing stallion up the long, steep grade towards Clifton Flat and Overland Canyon.

As they reached the summit, Charro stumbled and stood still, breathing hard. Xavier dismounted and watered him, rubbing his withers where he liked it best. He couldn't ask any more of his friend. He led him down through Clifton Flats and on to Canyon Station, taking up the Canyon keeper's offer of a bed and corral for the night. Though he chafed at the delay, Charro needed the rest. Unlike an Express rider, he didn't get to switch horses every station and they needed to get to Aleksandra in one piece. The dawn found Charro ready to go on, shaking his head and bouncing as they left the station, heading for home and Aleksandra.

AWAKENING WITH A START, Vladimir peered around and sat up in the dense, early morning fog, willing his heart to stop its insistent pounding. The troop of horse that awoke him was probably only a beaver, out for his morning ablutions, distorted and amplified by the mists. Despite the cold morning, he wiped the sweat from his brow and chuckled softly to himself at his jumpiness, then sobered. Who knew how many people might be out seeking him if Johnny had already made it back alive and sent the dogs out after him.

Krzysztof's son rides out of Fish Springs, less than a day from here.

Stomach clenching at the thought, he followed the stream back toward the trail heading west.

Vladimir skirted what appeared to be Rush Valley Station, by the description he'd been given. He stayed far north of its hayfields and horse pastures stocked with impressive Thoroughbred mares, but kept a close eye out for Pony riders. A steep and rocky mountain range blocked his way west. The only way he could see over it was the main trail through Lookout Pass—he'd just have to keep his head down and his mouth shut in hope of finding the rider from Salt Lake House.

'ALEKS, BREAKFAST!' Howard Egan put his head through the bunkhouse door. Aleksandra picked hers up from the pillow and dropped it again, bone-tired. Heaving a great sigh, she tried again. Her head thumped and her muscles weren't listening to her brain, what there was of it, but she swung her legs off the bunk and managed to stand. Her knee throbbed as she limped out the door, blinking in the early morning sunshine.

'I don't remember getting here, nor going to bed.' Her brow wrinkled as she eased herself onto a bench before the fire in the station house.

'That's because you were asleep.' Egan raised an eyebrow at her as he placed a plate heaped with aromatic potatoes and beef before her.

'Then you won't have heard the news,' She sat with her head bowed.

'News?'

'First, everyone at Schell Creek was slaughtered. On the way home, seven stations were razed, keepers killed, and stock driven off or killed. I rode the same horse all the way from Ruby to Deep Creek on the way home, because all the stations in between were burning or under attack.' She took a deep breath and swayed as her stomach lurched, then pushed her plate away. Egan was quick to remove it from sight.

He sat down beside her and put an arm around her shoulders. 'And I hear that without your warnings, many more would have died. Did you really ride from here to Roberts Creek and back?'

'Yes, sir. On the way home I rode one pony all the way from Ruby, oh yeah, I already said that...oh, and,' Aleksandra whispered, not lifting her eyes from the floor, 'Major Egan, I'm so sorry, but I lost a *mochila*.' The keeper leaned close to her as tears blurred her vision. 'Or rather, the Army took it off me,' she looked up, 'but they promised to bring any *mochila* they found at Roberts Creek—'

'—Aleks,' he waved his hand before her face, 'stop. You mean *this* one?'

Her head shot up. Egan held a *mochila* in his hands.

'Where...who...?'

He laughed. 'Aleks, the men of Mountain Springs Station thank you for their lives. Your warning saved them. An officer from the army delivered the *mochila* at first light this morning.

She took a deep breath and beamed at him, nearly hugging him as he continued.

'He was quite concerned that you get the *mochila* immediately. Said you'd have their guts for garters if they delayed.' He gave her a crooked grin. 'I think he was a bit afeared of you, Boy!'

She looked at the ground again for a moment, started to speak, then clapped her mouth shut, then opened it again, like a fish out of water, but no sound came out.

'Out with it, Aleks, what did you do?'

'Well...ummm...I pulled my *shashka* on them when they tried to take my *mochila*.' She hunched her shoulders and peeked at him from under her lashes.

Egan gave a belly laugh. 'We've already heard all about that. Sounds like they want you on staff there.' He shook his head and clapped her on the shoulder and she gasped, nearly falling off her seat. 'What have you gone and done now, Boy?'

'A mare stepped in a badger hole and flipped. She's bowed a tendon. I rolled clear, but my head, shoulder and knee haven't been great since then.'

'We'll get you fixed up, Aleks. How are you feeling now? Do you think you can ride?'

'Sure, I can ride.' She grinned at him and gulped. 'Just feed me.'

'Do you feel good enough to go east with this *mochila* you've fought so hard for? Truth be told, we're having so much Indian trouble, we might keep more people alive by sending them east for now, and putting the Pony on hold until it's all quieted down.' He shook his head and closed his eyes. 'That's the most important message I want to send east with you. The *mochila* needs to go and our other rider is incoherent from a festering arrow wound.'

'No problem. I can ride, as long as I get this knee rebandaged. Is the other rider okay?'

'He's not good, you can take a look at him, if you would, please. Your healing skills are becoming legendary,' he said, smiling, as she tucked into her breakfast.

'Have you heard from Xavier? And how is Dzień?'

'No, sorry lad, haven't heard a thing from Xavier, but your pony is fine. Gettin' fat, but fine.'

ALEKSANDRA LEFT FISH SPRINGS, for the East. She'd told Superintendent Egan she could go on, but six hours of sleep apparently hadn't been enough to un-muddle her brain.

Maybe it's concussion from my fall.

The scenery she passed blurred into a gray mush, but the pain in her knee kept her on track. Thinking back over the previous day, she gave thanks for the few stations that were still functional, Butte Creek, Spring Valley and Deep Creek, where she could change a tired pony for a fresh one. She just had to take especial care of her mounts until she was able to find stations the Indians hasn't yet razed.

XAVIER RODE into a quiet Fish Springs Station at midday to find the peace broken only by the snores of a rider he'd never met, who upon closer inspection, sported a clean, but foul-smelling bandage on his leg. Egan was nowhere to be found, but the stock were in the corrals and everything looked in order. Finding a letter propped against the inkwell on his desk, he roughly ripped it open with a scowl. Letters seemed to bode no good lately.

Xavier—

Some silver-haired Rusky was here asking mighty odd questions about young Aleks who rides for you.

I met him in the saloon. Aleks had just ridden out and the guy saw him leave. I have to apologize to you both, I told him that Aleks rode out of Fish Springs, before I realized there was something fishy going on. After that, he got pushy and wanted to know the way to Fish Springs, so I've made a map, which will take him far to the north before he figures out he's been fooled.

On the possibility that something sinister happens when I deliver the map tonight, I will leave this letter with my stable boy to send on to you in case I cannot.

I just have a bad feeling about him and wanted to warn you both. I hope this reaches you in time. He's a good lad and doesn't deserve whatever this evil-seeming man might plan.

Best regards,

Johnny Rand, Keeper at Salt Lake House

Xavier closed his eyes and tried to breathe deeply before the dots swimming in front of his eyes coalesced into a gray fog, letting the anger settle before he went mad.

28

Vladimir grudgingly admired the huge buttes to his right as he skirted Simpson's Springs, still staying as far away from the trail as possible. Every few minutes, he scanned the horizon before him.

He shook his head and looked again, but it was still there. Running from north to south as far as he could see, a straight line stretched before him across the desert. Beyond it, an odd, flat-topped mountain, dominated the background to the west. As he drew nearer, the line revealed itself as a deep chasm, and then as a riverbed. He stood on the brink and stared. It had to be the widest one he'd ever seen, many miles across. He turned the horses to follow the trail and descended to the bottom, repeatedly looking up and down the ancient watercourse.

Vladimir recalled a story an old man in Great Salt Lake City told him a week ago about an ancient riverbed in the area, and how flash floods came when they were least expected. Sighing, he raised an eyebrow and shook his head. The same gentleman also said it was haunted by desert faeries, of all things. Probably delusions from the sheer volumes of whisky they consumed just to stay sane out here.

He imagined a rolling wall of water racing toward him, wiping out everything in its path. Fortunately, though, the temperature was dropping and the late afternoon sky stayed blue and clear, though.

Against the far wall smoke appeared, then the roof of a dugout beneath it.

Must be the Express station. It should be down here somewhere.

He took in the steep wall of the riverbed ahead of him. A narrow trail snaked its way up it, from the Express station to the desert floor far above.

He'd found it—the place where he would lie in wait.

He tried to control his racing heart. No use getting excited now.

According to Johnny's map, his quarry would ride through here if he rode the eastern run out of Fish Springs.

'That is, if,' he said to Rogan, rolling his eyes, '*this* part of Johnny's map is to be believed.' The bay ignored him and walked on.

'Halloo!' Vladimir shouted, as he rode up to the station. A dusty young man sporting the inevitable big hat stepped out of the dugout, wiping his mustache with the back of his sleeve.

'Afternoon, sir, can I help you?'

XAVIER DROPPED Johnny's letter onto the floor of Fish Springs Station as he spun around and strode to his bed. Fighting the darkness threatening to overwhelm him, he dumped the contents of his saddlebag and repacked bare essentials, returning to the kitchen corner for more travelling provisions.

Egan came in with his rifle, carrying two jackrabbits slung by a twine over his shoulder. 'Lookee, I've got dinner, how goes it, Xav—? *Xavier?*' His eyes widened at the look on his face. 'Are you okay, man?'

Xavier stood still, mouth open. He had no idea where to start, but he sure didn't have time to explain.

Egan glanced at the letter and picked it up. 'Oh, this came four days ago for you.' He reached out to hand it to Xavier.

Xavier stared at it like it was a rattlesnake.

Egan's brows narrowed. 'I'd have sent it on, but thought you'd be back soon. Did you get the other one I sent on to Carson?'

Xavier gave no answer. He was afraid he'd blow up if he spoke.

'Look, son, what's this about?' Egan asked him softly.

'Have you seen Aleksan—' Xavier said abruptly.

'Yes, of course.' Egan raised his eyebrows, mouth quirked. 'He rode for Rush Valley a short while ago. He was pretty tired. He came in after midnight last night, asleep on his pony, having just ridden about 280 miles with very few pony changes, but I thought he might be safer heading east.'

Xavier closed his eyes and counted to three. 'Can you stay awhile yet? I haven't time to explain, but she's in danger. Please read the letter. I have to find her before he does.'

'She? What's going on, Xavier?' The creases in Egan's already-furrowed brow deepened.

'If we all survive this, I'll fill you in. I need to go, but I'll be back as soon as I can.' Xavier raced out the door, saddlebag slung over his arm, heading for Charro.

'YES, I HOPE YOU CAN,' Vladimir said smoothly to the station keeper. 'I was heading across this desert of a riverbed and saw your smoke. Would I be able to buy some water from you, mayhaps?'

'Sure can. It's a bit brackish, but you should try it by the time we ship it to Dugway!' The lad tipped the lid off a water barrel standing against the adobe wall of the shed and scooped out a dipper for Vladimir.

'Ship it? To Dugway? Thank you.' Dismounting, he smiled and took the dipper.

'Dugway's got no well. At least we have that. Water for your horses?'

'Yes, please. The Pony Express horses and the riders must drink a fair bit. I take it this *is* a Pony Express Station?'

Vladimir took a bucket from the tender and nodded his thanks. The colt turned up his nose for a moment, then reconsidered. He took a long draught, then promptly sloshed the rest of the bucket down Vladimir's chest and leggings, taking a quick step backwards and flinging his nose up high.

'He's done that a few times before, hasn't he?' The young man laughed. 'That's some colt! What do you call him?'

Brows drawn together, lips pursed, Vladimir muttered something about dog meat.

'Ahem.' Stifling a chuckle, the keeper tightened his lips as he ducked his head. 'Sorry.' He backed away and hastened to the chestnut's head with another bucket. She drank quietly until the bucket was empty. 'Would you like any more water for them? No? okay, that'll be fifty cents, thanks.'

'Let me get it.' Vladimir went to the other side of his mare and fumbled in his saddlebag.

'Thanks. I just need to get a horse ready, be right with you'

Haltering a little pinto Mustang, he led her toward Vladimir from the pen next to the shed.

'Is an Express rider due in here soon?' Vladimir mumbled excitedly from under the flap of his saddlebag. He turned to the station keeper with what he hoped passed for wide eyes and a delighted smile. 'I've seen a Pony rider race past me, but haven't seen a change of horses yet! How soon are they due and where are they coming from?'

'The eastbound rider should be here in the next half an hour or so,' he glanced at his pocket watch and picked up a metal curry, 'but I like to have my mounts ready early, just in case.' He turned to the pony and began knocking the worst of the dust out of her coat.

'Can I help you with that?'

'No, that's all—' The young man looked around with a raised eyebrow and a smile, then his mouth dropped open at the sight of the gun in Vladimir's hand and he turned slowly to face him.

HER BRAIN still in a foggy haze, Aleksandra rode through Black Rock, changed horses, then raced through Dugway canyon, taking the descent as fast as the palomino would go. She saw neither Indians nor arrows, and gave thanks to whoever would listen. Changing horses at Dugway Station, she struck out across the desert towards Old Riverbed. The boulders at the edge of the gorge wavered in the afternoon heat as she slowed to check the descent. She glanced down the cliff toward the station. Riverbed George held a saddled pinto for her.

No dangers evident, Aleksandra gave the pony her head and she bolted down the steep bank.

I MUST ADMIT,' Vladimir said aloud, with a grim smile and a shake of his head at the unconscious young station keeper, 'like everyone else out here, you've got guts.'

He also had good aim.

The metal curry cut Vladimir over his cheekbone when the lad threw it, but the boy was unfortunately no match at hand-to-hand combat with the Cossack-trained, heavier man. Vladimir eventually hit him over the head with the butt of his gun and he went down in a heap. Still, he was no murderer. He just needed him out of the way for awhile. The boy stirred lightly when Vladimir spoke to him.

He'll do.

He dragged him down the steps into the dugout and tied him to a bedpost. Someone would find the boy soon enough. This route saw more traffic than most places out here.

Vladimir left the colt and his chestnut out of sight in the pen behind the barn, finished currying the little pinto, then saddled and bridled her. They quietly waited for the incoming rider, the pony yawning as Vladimir absently scratched her rump.

The pinto's ears pricked, her head swinging around, just as Vladimir heard the bugle call in the distance. A puff of dust rose from the top of the bank near the descending track and a lone palomino and rider slithered down the precipitous trail toward him.

By his riding, Vladimir was certain this was the same boy he'd seen at Salt Lake House, although today he drooped with exhaustion, his face nearly black with dust and sweat, and his legs loose on his horse. As they approached, the rider gave him a brief look of surprise as he lifted a hand in greeting, then turned his attention to his saddle as the pony slowed. Yanking the mail pouch from beneath his seat, the boy tossed it to Vladimir and performed a creditable flying dismount. With a curse, the rider stumbled as his feet hit the ground, hopping on one leg for a few steps.

Vladimir greeted him, asking the boy how the pony was doing…in Polish.

Krzysztof's son answered automatically, then started, alarmed. He grabbed for the mail carrier while racing toward the pinto. Vladimir had a firm hold on it and wasn't about to lose the boy attached to it. Calculating, Vladimir released the leather, with an extra push, and dove for the pony. The boy lost his balance and hit the rocky ground rolling, then reached for his hip. As the youth drew a *shashka*, Vladimir dove on him, crushing his wrist and twisting until he dropped the weapon, then aimed a punch at his head. He went down hard.

Bit soft.

He drew a deep breath and looked the boy over. He weighed almost nothing when Vladimir cautiously rolled him over with his foot. He was vaguely discomfited at the delicacy of the lad's features. Remembering well this boy's mother and father at a similar age, he had no doubt this boy was their get. The young man had the unmistakable features of his mother, though there were touches of his father as well. He gave him a good nudge with the toe of his boot, but the boy didn't respond.

Definitely out cold.

Vladimir felt around the boy's belt and extracted his sheath knife, then found another in a boot. He couldn't help grinning.

Definitely armed.

Too bad he passed out so soon—it might've been an interesting fight.

Checking over the lad's body, he stopped, attention drawn to his neck, where two well-worn thongs were knotted. The first was attached to a buckskin bag nearly covered with Indian beading. He curled his lip. The smell was enough to keep him from touching it, much less opening it. The other cord ended beneath a wide band of soft goatskin, wrapped tightly around the boy's chest.

He yanked at the cord and another, larger and heavier, buckskin bag fell out, and the leather band slipped a little.

'What the…?' The bag had been hidden, carefully tucked in—

'*O mój Boże.* My God.' He sat back on his heels, stunned. The pouch had been tucked between *her* breasts, beneath the soft goatskin strap that bound this *girl's* chest flat.

He'd just knocked out Krzysztof's *daughter.*

Closing his eyes, he shook his head.

That would explain the delicacy.

He scrunched his face into a grimace.

How could I have missed that?

Having come this far, there was nothing for it but to go on with his search, female or no. He dragged his attention back to the pouch while keeping one eye on his captive. The leather bag must hold importance to have been so carefully guarded for safe-keeping, hidden where it was.

It might contain that which he so fervently sought.

Eyeing her while he pulled open the drawstring, Vladimir carefully tipped out three, hard, paper-covered packages.

He unwrapped one to reveal a stoppered glass vial containing an amber fluid. Uncorking it, he inhaled its fumes. Alcoholic, yes, and the hint of an herb that smelled vaguely familiar, but he couldn't quite place it.

Could this really be…after all this time…

His breath caught in his chest and he gazed upward, raising the vial to the sky with one hand.

Tatiana, I am coming for you.

She seemed suddenly so near.

He felt, rather than saw, the girl's sudden movement. At the same time, he noticed a coolness as liquid ran down his arm.

ALEKSANDRA WOKE SLOWLY, blood in her mouth, *again.*

This is becoming a bad habit.

Opening her eyes made her head throb more than before, if that were possible, so she closed them again. After a moment, she remembered where she was and was glad she'd kept her peace. Stiff paper crackled.

He'd found the vials.

Keeping her breathing slow and even, she peeked out beneath her lashes.

Her shashka.

Despite the pain in her head, she had to repress a grin.

Idiot.

Her sword lay on the ground beside her. Vladimir, if this was him, sniffed at the unwrapped vial. Almost of its own volition, Aleksandra's hand crept towards the razor-sharp weapon as she watched him stopper the bottle from the corner of one eye. Her knives lay, seemingly forgotten, on the ground beside him.

Grasping the familiar hilt, she awaited her moment. He raised the golden bottle to the sky and stared at it, his mouth moving fervently.

Summoning all her strength, she slashed at him with the blade, reaching for his heart, but knowing it was a long shot.

Aleksandra jumped to her feet, holding her weapon before her, and leapt backwards, swearing as her bad knee took her weight. Blood flew from the blade and dripped down his slashed sleeve. Striking with the speed of a panther, Vladimir pounced, hitting her hard. The air left her lungs as she crashed backwards onto the hard ground. There was a crunch and a dizzying pain in her wrist as Vladimir mercilessly crushed it until she let go of the *shashka* and it fell to the rocks with a final clatter. The silence was ominous and the darkness welcoming.

29

Vladimir squirmed. A gentleman doesn't strike a woman, but her attack upon him made him forget his manners.

Nonetheless, she would pay.

He gritted his teeth. Despite his growing, albeit grudging, respect, he wouldn't take this abuse. For God's sake, this slip of a girl had actually cut him.

Dragging her behind the stable to his horses, he tied her feet together, then collected bandages and a flask from the chestnut's saddlebag. A few strips of kindling from the station's chopping block completed his armamentarium and he returned to her side, sitting down on his heels to await her awakening. He glanced around, itching to be gone.

Impatience got the better of him.

Grabbing her jaw, he poured some whisky into her mouth. Her eyes shot open. She pulled away, spluttering, and reached for her *shashka*, swinging her head around and growling when she found her scabbard empty.

Her eyes flashed as she struggled to sit up and grabbed her injured wrist, clamping her lips tightly against any sound. Curling wisps of hair, escaped from the long golden braid, framed her delicate features.

Rather glorious, this girl.

'Does it hurt?' Guilt stabbing at him, he crouched down over her legs. Though she'd cut him, he knew he was in the wrong. Tatiana would've had his guts for garters.

The girl looked down her nose at him and his sympathy slipped away.

Quite a feat, as I'm sitting above her.

He shook his head, his lips tight in a line. The girl's stoicism in the face of certain pain annoyed him.

In silence, he splinted and bound her wrist snugly. 'I wouldn't bother, but I don't want you to slow us down.' He jerked the last tie for emphasis, almost pleased to see her wince. 'The whole territory will be after us when you're discovered missing.'

She raised one eyebrow at him until he looked away.

He glanced at his forearm wound, still bleeding and now beginning to sting, then glared at her. The gash was superficial, but infection would slow him down, if it didn't kill him. He pulled out his hip flask again. The whisky's bite in the open wound was infinitely worse than the cut itself. At his sharp intake of breath, Krzysztof's daughter smiled through gritted teeth. She looked like a she-wolf.

She'll bear watching.

The girl stared at him, her eyes steely.

He raised his brows at her. 'What?'

'That blade.'

'Which blade?'

'My *shashka*, not my father's, which you *stole*.'

'What of your blade?' he spat out, his already short patience all but disappearing.

'Did you bother to check it? Did it have dried blood on it? Perhaps greenish blood?' Her laugh was pure evil.

'I don't know what you're on about, but you're obviously going to tell me, so why don't you get on with it?' he said, through clenched teeth.

'I was raised with Indians and learned their ways. They capture a rattlesnake,' she dropped her voice to a whisper, 'and squeeze the venom from its fangs into a piece of antelope liver. They carry the meat with them to rub onto their arrows—and my *shashka*. Alcohol doesn't affect the poison.' She smiled at him as she held tightly to her injured arm.

Vladimir schooled his features to aloof stillness. The girl was likely bluffing, trying to frighten into making a mistake. If it was true, then he might die. It didn't sound as if he had much choice about it now, so he would carry on.

He avoided looking at her face, since her stare could melt ice, and busied himself shaking out coils of cord and rope from his saddlebag.

'Well, young lady, I see I taught your father too well, and he,' Vladimir sent a brief nod of acknowledgement in her direction, 'you. No one else has cut me in twenty-five years.'

'That didn't stop you from butchering him, did it?' Rancor dripped from every word.

Vladimir tied the girl's wrists together, then untied her legs, glaring frequently to the east and west. They needed to get away from this trail.

'We'll talk while we ride.' He dragged her to her feet by an elbow. She limped and seemed weak, but he wouldn't make the mistake of letting his guard down around her again.

He fairly threw her over the colt's back. Binding her hands to the saddle horn, he tied her feet together with a rope running beneath Rogan's belly.

'Your problem if he falls on you,' he said coolly.

'Thanks, I appreciate your concern,' she mumbled.

He led Rogan around to the front of the station and pulled the bridle and saddle off the pinto and the tired palomino, filling a bucket for them from the water barrel.

'You'll founder her with that much water, she's hot,' she growled.

'These Mustangs are tough, and the pony might as well not die of dehydration.' He looked at her askance. 'With your father, I'd have thought you were a horseman.'

'And you're stupid as well,' she snarled. 'Now they'll know where I disappeared.'

'They'll be looking for you anyway, girl. Not hard to figure out where you went missing.' He peeked at her from out of the corner of his eye. She gazed after the Express pony sadly, then she started and spun her head around to face him, wincing as she put weight on her bad leg in the stirrup.

'What have you done with George?' she menaced, looking around toward the dugout.

'Who?'

'The station keeper, you ignorant—,' bitten off as he jerked her arm.

'Be still. What's your name, anyway?'

She glared at him, lips in a rigid line.

He gritted his teeth and shook her by the arm. This wasn't getting him anywhere. He let go and swung onto his mare. With the bay on a short lead, they headed north up the riverbed at a trot, seeking a place where he could properly interrogate the saucy chit without fear of discovery.

The sun slipped below the horizon as they crossed the floodplain, the sky swirling with blue and red clouds. Vladimir scanned the horizon in all directions every few minutes.

'They'll find you, you know,' she stated flatly, staring straight ahead as she stood in her stirrups.

'I'll try to prevent that.'

'You won't see them,' she whispered eerily, looking at the sky. 'The Old Riverbed is haunted, everyone knows that.' She smiled at him, eyes huge and teeth showing in a grimace. 'Besides, it flash-floods, all the time. The faeries do it to evil people.' The girl glanced at the sky.

The wind suddenly began to blow. A dust devil formed and swirled away. The air felt charged. He scanned the skies for lightning.

'You're heading us into the Great Salt Lake Desert, I hope you know.' She was relentless. 'Not a lot of water out there.' She raised a brow and her eyes bored into him.

The hairs raised on his arms and the back of his neck. He looked sideways at her and began to cross himself, but stopped before she saw.

I don't believe in ghost stories.

He tried to ignore her comments, but glanced north, up Old Riverbed. It was an understatement that the middle of this ancient watercourse was a bad place to be caught by a flash flood, but he needed to get away from the main trail, unless he wished to be apprehended, and this was the best way he could see, under the circumstances. He pushed them on. Even with her injured wrist tied to the saddle horn, the girl somehow gracefully kept time to the bay's big trot.

She was still smiling woodenly when he looked at her again.

'Perhaps Papa will come to haunt you,' she whispered softly.

'Your papa's death was an accident, girl, I didn't kill him.'

'Accident by *shashka*, how convenient for you, *Vladimir*,' she said between clenched teeth.

She knows my name. What else does she know?

His chest tightened.

Face hard, she betrayed no emotion whatsoever, and kept her eyes forward. He would try again soon.

'If you've already killed him, what do you want with me?' Her voice intruded on his thoughts some time later.

'You *know* what I came for, or you wouldn't have been hiding it in your, er—, shirt.' He watched her eyes as he pulled her pouch from inside his shirt, where it hung from his own neck. Her eyes flashed and a low growl escaped her throat.

'What's in the bottles, girl? How is it made? How is it used? I have tracked your father many years to learn this. I need to know now and you *are* going to tell me.'

She looked at him calmly, brows lowered, mouth rigid.

'When we took Polish prisoners back to Russia, some didn't want to cooperate either. Many of them continued in their insanity. We dragged them behind horses or wagons until they talked or died.'

She raised an eyebrow at him and turned away, unmoved. Stopping the horses, he glanced around again as he slid from the chestnut's saddle and pulled a large coil of rope from his saddlebag.

'Are you that stubborn?' he asked, as he untied her feet from beneath the horse, holding tightly to the bay's lead. 'Will you die too? Your father would not have been pleased to see his last remaining family die. It's just a matter of time before I figure out how to use the bottles. You may as well tell me the rest. You are too young to die today.'

And too beautiful.

He was met with only silence. Grimacing, he untied her hands from the horn and yanked her off the bay. The colt snorted at the rough treatment. She stumbled when the foot of her bad leg hit the ground, biting off a cry as she grabbed her splint. Vladimir hauled her to her feet and lashed her wrists together before her, trying to ignore the bandage.

She'll give in soon.

He measured out a long piece of rope. Lashing one end to the leather binding her wrists, he tied the other to the chestnut's saddle horn.

'First, what is your name?'

Silence.

He mounted his mare and started her away at a walk. The girl walked a length behind the mare, limping and tripping over loose rocks in the sand. She held her head proudly, eyes straight ahead, lips set in a firm line as she gripped her injured sword arm with her other. A quarter of an hour passed and darkness began to fall.

'You ready to tell me your name yet, girl?'

She ignored him and kept walking. Her head was beginning to droop as the mare walked faster. He pushed the mare to a trot. She ran along, stumbling, behind the mare until she fell and was dragged by the rope at her wrists. She made no sound until she lost hold of the splint and the full weight of her body jerked on the injured wrist.

'Stop, you son of Satan,' she shrieked, then was silent as he stopped the mare, backed her to release the tension, vaulted off and hurried to the stricken girl, shaken that she had taken so much abuse, and at his own hands.

She held the splint tightly, eyes closed, mouth moving silently, as he untied the rope. Her face showed white where the tears streaked their way through the dust on her cheeks.

'What is your name,' he stated flatly, hardly a question anymore.

'Aleksandra,' she ground out.

'What is in the bottles?'

'An extract of a Polish plant.'

'Can we be a bit more specific? What plant?' he spat.

'I don't know.'

'You must.'

'An alpine plant, that's all I know. I've only seen the dried leaves, broken into pieces or dust. How simple are you?' She rolled her eyes. 'Papa's had them since he left Poland. By rights, they should all be dust.'

'How much do you give a horse?' he barked. 'How?'

'By mouth, one bottle, makes it go fast.' She hung her head and swayed.

'Okay, where are these mysterious dried leaves, and where did they come from?'

'In our old cabin. From Poland.'

'Poland…the leaves are in your cabin at Echo? Where in the cabin? Don't lie to me. I searched the entire place.'

'Under the eaves in a box, with the instructions for extracting the drug from the dried leaves. Leave me. You'll find them there.'

'Oh no, Miss Lekarski, you're coming with me.' At this, her head fell to her chest and she finally sobbed.

He wanted to comfort her, but it couldn't possibly help his situation. Guilt kicking him in the guts, he dragged her dusty body back to the colt, tossed her onto his back and tied her hands behind her back, not worrying about her feet this time. If the horse fell, at least she would be able to roll free. Finally she'd given in. She was cowed, and too sore to make any more trouble.

The colt took a vicious nip at his shoulder as he stepped back from tying Aleksandra's hands. Vladimir, itching for a fight after dealing so abysmally with this far-beyond-annoying wisp of a girl, was more than ready to retaliate. He sent a punch to the horse's muzzle, but the colt was too quick, dancing out of the way, jerking the rope from his hands.

Vladimir's heart hit his boots. It didn't do to forget the kind of horseman Krzysztof had been.

Of course, the colt could be ridden without a bridle.

And certainly, Krzysztof would have taught this girl everything he knew.

EVEN WITH HER hands tied behind her back, Aleksandra had no trouble guiding the well-schooled young horse as they escaped across the riverbed towards the track rising to the desert floor. Hadn't Papa taught her to ride without reins since before she could walk?

She'd bypass Riverbed Station and send someone back to help the tender, if he yet lived. It wouldn't help either of them if Vladimir caught them. Lying low on the colt's neck, she glanced back. The Russian pursued, but the mare was struggling. Rogan seemed fresher, and Aleksandra was perhaps half of Vladimir's weight.

With a rush of excitement, she laughed into the bay's mane. They might get out of this yet. Rogan bucked once, as if from sheer pleasure, then put his head down, ears back, and flew. She could scarcely see for the watering of her eyes, but she couldn't hold back a grin as the wind whipped the bay's mane into her face and she breathed in the exhilaration that always struck her at speed. She was escaping from Vladimir, back towards safety, and hopefully, Xavier.

Reveling in the awesome strength of the young stallion's hindquarters as he climbed the steep wagon track out of the riverbed in great leaps, she faintly wished she could hold on to the colt's mane. She was shocked out of her reverie by a vision of Xavier on his stallion before her on the trail ahead. She shook her head and blinked, but he was still there. With a cry, Aleksandra urged Rogan on, calling desperately to Xavier, hair flying behind her, screaming out a warning.

'Hola, *Poquita*,' Xavier laughed coldly, grabbing Rogan's trailing reins and the end of the leadrope as the colt rammed into his horse.

'Run, Xavier! It's Vladimir!' she screamed at him, looking wildly behind her, kicking at Rogan's sides. The colt danced on the spot, his reins held in an iron fist. Vladimir was just a breath away behind her.

Xavier regarded her and calmly turned to watch Vladimir's gasping chestnut leap the last yards between them. The mare barged into Rogan's hindquarters on the narrow track and the colt bucked again, then quieted.

'Aleksandra, is it?' Xavier raised an eyebrow at her, a faint grin touching his tightly set lips.

Aleksandra's mouth gaped as she stared at him in shock.

'Lost something?' Xavier called out, lifting the reins he held toward Vladimir.

The Russian had pulled a gun and now held it trained on Xavier. The Californio glanced at Aleksandra briefly again before returning his attention to Vladimir.

She stilled abruptly and continued to gawk at Xavier. He wasn't even looking at her.

30

'Y̶ou can put the gun away. Mighty pretty catch, but if she's yours, you can have her after I'm done with her. Can't trust 'em, women,' Xavier commented.

Aleksandra's heart plummeted. He acted like he didn't even know her. Could he still be angry over Dancing Wolf? What would it take for him to believe that he was all she had ever wanted? Would he ever forgive her?

'The girl goes with me,' Vladimir growled, his gun still trained on Xavier, who ignored it.

'I think not,' the Californio said, as if he hadn't a care in the world.

Vladimir looked around them and up the trail, then waved the gun at him. 'Shall we go down to where we can discuss this like civilized men?'

They turned the horses down the hill, Xavier first, leading Rogan. No one spoke. Aleksandra stared at the ground, not daring to look up, her heart aching. Her wrist screamed and her skinned elbows stung. She pushed away the thought of her aching knee. Dust, not noticed before, filled her mouth and eyes.

No matter, the tears will wash it away.

Reaching the riverbed floor, they turned north. When she risked a glance up, the Express station was on their right, but no light showed there in the falling darkness.

'In there.' Vladimir indicated a small patch of scrub oak showing dark against the pale wall of the waterway.

'It should suffice.' The Californio raised an eyebrow at him.

'You can start a small fire while I watch the girl,' the Russian barked, motioning with the gun. He stayed atop the chestnut while Xavier gathered kindle-dry twigs and started them glowing with a flint and steel. The temperature had fallen with the dusk. Numbness clouded Aleksandra's brain. She shook so hard her teeth rattled, but now it was not only from shock, but cold. Her world narrowed to a pinpoint as she drew into herself, her only focus the flames licking again and again at the logs Xavier added to the fire as it grew.

'Put the gun away!' Aleksandra started as Xavier snapped at Vladimir, who stood right next to her. 'As I said,' he continued, 'you can have her. First, however, I need to extract a little information. She knows something my friends from the South want.'

Xavier dragged her off Rogan and shook her, hard.

Aleksandra wobbled, but he held her upright as she stared at him, eyes narrowed and jaw dropped, then he shook her again.

She wanted to crawl into herself and disappear. There seemed to be nothing else to do. No life with the man she loved, no use for the new understandings she'd found. She hung her head. A flash of her papa before her eyes made her grit her teeth and she slowly shook her head.

This time she fought back. She bit at the hand that held her and swung at him, but she was no match for his strength, especially tonight. Xavier grabbed her and threw her over his shoulder. She kicked as he walked with her toward the fire.

'I already know what she knows,' Vladimir said. 'You can stop with the girl.'

'Why didn't you say so?' Xavier slowly turned to face Vladimir, dumping her unceremoniously onto the ground.

Everything blurred around her. Aleksandra could make no sense of anything they said now. Tears ran down her face. Someone was sobbing. She became faintly aware that it was herself. Desolation overwhelmed her and all she wanted was to sleep. Xavier or Vladimir tied her to some sage-brush at the base of the riverbank, where she lay huddled, knees tucked up to her chin. The smell of smoke drifted to her on a breeze and the sound of a fire snapping, then footsteps. The rope binding her hands suddenly tightened and she screamed as pain shot through her wrist. Someone half-dragged, half-carried her into the circle of light cast by the fire and dropped her there. She fitfully drifted in and out of consciousness, catching fragments of men's voices, but nothing she could firmly grasp.

'My superiors in California,' Xavier said, over the crackling of the campfire, 'have ordered me to return here and collect the secret, whatever it is, off Krzysztof's daughter.' He ignored the muffled whimpers coming from the girl. 'I was given leave to "obtain" it if someone had gotten to her first.'

'It is *mine*.' Vladimir's eyes narrowed, his accent thickening as he spoke, hand straying towards the inevitable *shashka*.

'It is in our interest that we have it,' he added coolly. 'We are willing to pay a considerable sum.'

'How did you hear of it?' Vladimir raised an eyebrow.

'It's relatively common knowledge. Lekarski or the girl must have spoken of it to the wrong people.' He stood to throw another branch onto the flames. 'You're a long way from home, why are you so intent on having this drug?'

After a long silence, the Russian seemed to come to a decision. 'The tsar holds my wife and child upon its return.'

'Oh, a worthy cause, to be sure.' Xavier raised both eyebrows, with the hint of a grim smile. 'Just how long have you been searching for it?'

'Nearly two decades, and the wait is almost over. What is your purpose?'

'Well, as you've been frank with me, those of California's Southern cause will use it to ensure our victory in the war that is soon to come between the North and South,' he said with a sly grin. 'The Union boys will never know what hit 'em, we'll move so fast across the land.'

Vladimir raised an eyebrow and looked down his nose at Xavier. 'Petty squabbles in a primitive land. I'm talking about all of *Europe*, under Russian rule. No comparison is possible.' He turned his head to glance at the barely moving girl at the end of his rope. 'Why are you alone?'

'There is a whole troop of us.' Xavier gave him a hard look. 'We've split up to find the girl, but they should be here soon.'

Vladimir flicked a glance around into the darkness, his hand tightening on the rope.

'We were looking for a girl, but she wasn't known as one in these parts. Fortunately for me, she was riding Lekarski's colt, who *is* renowned throughout the territory. I merely put two and two together.'

'And came up with a million. That's what it will cost you,' the Russian said, his voice icy.

Xavier raised an eyebrow. 'We will pay half of that, and you will live to return to Russia.'

Eyebrows raised, head tilted to one side, Vladimir stared at Xavier for long minutes.

'Okay, what do you say we share the information?' A hard glint in Vladimir's eyes showed by the light of the fire. 'You pay me now. When we get back to the cabin and unearth the recipe, you get the information and half of the dried plants from which the liquid is made.'

'All of it,' Xavier said, steel in his voice.

'Half, or no deal,' the Russian stated flatly. 'You have your uses, so do I.' He looked away and into the fire.

'Deal, partner.' Xavier held out a hand.

'Deal.' They shook on it, but the brittle look of Vladimir's face left no room for doubt the Russian planned to arrive at the cabin without him. He smiled coldly in return.

'The money, if you please,' Vladimir said sharply.

'*Un momento*. I will get it.' He rose and went to his horse, glancing down at the now-quiet girl on the end of the rope.

Returning, Xavier tossed four leather pouches to the ground beside Vladimir, which landed with heavy jangling clunks. 'Four hundred thousand, final payment at the cabin upon transfer of instructions, as we trust each other.' Xavier gave him a hard look.

'The whole lot now, if you please, or no deal,' he said, loosening his *shashka* in its sheath.

The Californio considered for a moment.

'You drive a hard bargain, *hombre*, but okay.' Xavier returned to his mount for another pouch. 'Gold straight from the California goldfields and silver from the Comstock Lode in Virginia City.'

Vladimir grunted and loosened the drawstrings, peering inside each bag by the firelight. He hefted the bags, as if estimating their weight and value.

'Pretty bit of fluff, that,' Xavier nodded in Aleksandra's direction, 'despite the dirt, the boys' clothes and her reputation. Apparently, she'd sleep with anybody.'

'Reputation?' He looked at the girl and curled his lip. 'Lekarski would turn over in his grave to see a daughter of his become a whore.'

'I expect you've enjoyed her already.' He looked slyly at Vladimir, then at the tangled mass of curls about Aleksandra's face at the edge of the firelit circle.

'I'm above that,' the Russian sneered, 'but as I'm feeling magnanimous, you can have her tonight.' He grinned evilly. 'Just don't plan on leaving without me, I'll hunt you down.'

'Fair comment.' Xavier leered, reaching for the rope Vladimir threw in his direction.

They sat for a moment more, anticipation palpable in the air, then Xavier stood up, pointedly yawned, and looked at Vladimir. 'Don't wait up, we'll be busy for a while,' he said with a lascivious grin and jerked on the rope. 'Get up, girl, he shouted, as he hauled her to her feet, swaying and supporting herself mostly on one leg. 'You're mine tonight. Haven't had a woman in months.'

She looked at him in despair as he dragged her from the firelight, making no sound. He tugged the lead and she whimpered.

'Not too far, Xavier, I want to know where you are.' Vladimir looked into the fire.

'You shouldn't have too much trouble hearing us.' The Californio laughed lecherously as Aleksandra stumbled after him into the darkness. From his saddlebags, he pulled his *serape*, shook it out and dropped it. He untied her hands and tucked the thong away in his shirt. Twisting his hands into her tangled hair, he dropped to his knees, pulling her down beside him on his *serape*, making her cry out.

'You can't be a virgin anymore, so what's the point of fighting?' Xavier barked loudly into the darkness as he pulled her hard against him.

She stiffened as he buried his face in her hair, then struggled and lashed out, crying, but he just rolled on top of her and her frantic movements ceased. He continued to hold her tightly, but said nothing. She eventually seemed to give up and went limp in his arms, her breathing regular. She slept.

FROM THE TIME Xavier dragged Aleksandra to her feet in the early dawn, the usually beautiful scenery of her route passed by in a blur. Whenever they broke into a trot, her vision blurred from the pain in her wrist. Standing in her stirrups lessened the pain, but the difficulty of trying to balance in her stirrups with hands lashed to the saddle horn made her beg Xavier to tie her hands behind her back instead.

Aleksandra sat, staring but unseeing, in the direction of the Simpson Ranges, waiting while Xavier left her with Vladimir to fill their canteens from the springs. When they passed Lookout Point, she caught a glimpse of the panorama. Tears fell as she thought of the last time she'd been there with Xavier. Her heart was leaden.

She lost track of the times her mount was dragged off the main trail and through rough country when dust heralded an oncoming rider or an Express station showed in the distance. A gag would be stuffed into her mouth and her bonds checked. The wrist throbbed. They skirted Rush Valley Station, and her heart ached for the companionship and help that waited only minutes away.

Could her talk with Doc Faust have only been a few days ago? She held to her memories against certain insanity. Doc Faust was one of the few to have seen through her farce, but more importantly, understood what drove both Aleksandra and Xavier, including what pushed them apart. The wise old man's advice had challenged, then comforted her. What would he think now, to see Xavier? What could have happened to make him change this much? Was this the real

Xavier? A thought dawned. She slowly filled her lungs and settled deeper into the saddle.

Could he be playing a game with stakes higher than her momentary discomfort? She resisted the urge to turn and look for him. While her body hurt so much, it would be a simple thing to withdraw into herself and just hold to her heart. She knew he had begun to love her once, and could hold out for just a little while longer. If he was gambling with their lives, she'd just have to give him the space to work and a little time. With more peace than she'd felt in weeks, she relaxed. Her world went black and she knew no more.

31

Aleksandra struggled for a moment when she awoke in the darkness with Xavier's arms around her, then stilled as he kissed her forehead in silence. He placed his fingertips on her lips.

'*Dios mío*, but I thought you were trying to kill yourself when you pitched off Rogan,' Xavier whispered into her ear.

She froze.

'Vladimir wanted to leave you behind.' He stroked her hair and the tension in her body lessened.

Xavier turned her and pulled her backside against his belly, holding her close. Sliding his hand down her arm, he slipped Krzysztof's signet ring onto her finger, then felt for her bandaged wrist and held it steady. She turned to look at him, eyes wide and doubtful in the moonlight.

'Where are we?'

He barely heard her words.

'In a little canyon in the foothills, just past Joe's Dugout.'

'But ... we were just at ... how ...?' She stopped, her brow wrinkling beneath his hand.

'You passed out and fell off Rogan. I carried you on the front of my saddle for most of the day.'

'Oh. I'm sorry, Xavier,' she whispered.

'*Dios*—no, *Querida*, it is I who owe the apology. Please believe me, Aleks, there was nothing else I could do. To my dying day, with every fiber of my being, I will regret my treatment of you, especially not telling you what was going on. It was the only way I could see to convince him to deal with me. We both know I could have never have beaten him in a fight. This was the only way I could see of saving you when you two galloped up to me at Riverbed.'

She lay stiff in his arms. He waited without speaking.

When she finally relaxed, he took a deep breath and opened his mouth to speak, but her fingers pressed against his lips. She clung to him, then rolled over onto her back and pulled him atop her. She kissed him hungrily, whimpering when she bumped her sore arm.

'What has he *done* to you?' he whispered hoarsely, lightly gripping the splint with one hand and feeling over her dusty shirt and trousers with the other. His heart rate shot through the roof and the old familiar darkness threatened to overtake him.

'Nothing that can't wait until we're out of this,' she breathed against his neck. 'It's splinted and pretty well stablized. We've done all we can for now.'

She let out a long breath and he reined in his temper with everything he had in him.

'So you believe me? I love you and we'll get out of this alive, *Querida*. We have too much to live for.' He drew her tightly against him.

'Yes, I believe.' She swallowed. 'What are your plans?'

'Well, to start with, let's build some belief.' He kissed her eyelids, 'You'll need to scream, *loudly*.'

Aleksandra stilled, then Xavier whispered 'Scream!'

Xavier slapped himself on the thigh, several times and she shrieked hysterically.

There was a growl from Vladimir in the darkness. 'So she wakes. Watch your knife around her. She's quick.'

'Lie still, you'll soon learn who's boss here! Think you can cut a man and get away with it?' Xavier growled.

'I know how we might escape him.' Aleksandra pressed her lips against his cheek.

'Mmmm ...'

'One bottle in the vein makes a horse go fast, faster than he should ever be able to, but two bottles in the vein can cause a heart attack if the horse is pushed too hard.'

'How certain are you of those outcomes?'

'Not certain at all, just what Papa told me, but it might be our only chance to get free of Vladimir before he kills both of us.'

She sounded deadly certain. He'd made the mistake of not listening to her before, he'd not do that again.

Xavier slapped his leg again, loudly, twice. She took the hint and screamed wildly.

'Shut up, and keep your teeth to yourself!' Xavier shouted. Her wail was bitten off as he clapped his hand over her mouth. He replaced it with his lips and she melted into his arms. Her lips curled into a smile against him as they kissed.

'That's more like it!' Xavier said aloud, slapping his arm for good measure and Aleksandra whined.

'Leave enough of her to help us find the herbs, eh, Xavier?'

Sparks flew into the air as Vladimir threw more fuel on the fire.

'She's tough, there'll be plenty left of this girl. Maybe she'll even learn to be a proper woman instead of a boy. About time somebody taught her a lesson,' Xavier shouted back at the Russian.

He stilled as the tip of his own knife pricked him beneath the ribs.

'Just for his benefit, eh, *Querida*?' He silently took his knife from her, replacing it into its sheath. 'You know I don't feel that way.'

'Yes, I know,' the corners of her mouth lifted slightly, 'but I suspect you'd prefer the proper woman.'

'I can't deny that I might have once, but I seem to be changing my mind,' he breathed, pulling her close again.

'Mmmm.' She kissed him softly.

'I'm pretty sure he's planning to rid himself of both of us as soon as he's sure of getting what he wants. He doesn't seem the sort of man to share.'

'I have a plan.' She snuggled down into his arms, holding him tightly beneath his warm *serape*.

'Can't wait, *mi amor*.' He kissed her hair.

'Remember that shortcut from Weber Station at Echo, near our cabin, the one over Forney's bridge?'

'That bridge that goes underwater when the river floods?'

'The same. It takes ten miles off the trail, and misses out Heneforville.'

'And it hasn't rained for weeks ...'

THE MORNING SUN found them riding ever eastward toward the cabin on the Express trail, Aleksandra's horse on a short lead held by Xavier, with the Russian bringing up the rear.

'Oh Vladimir, by the way,' Xavier leered at her as he turned backward towards the silvery-blond man, 'I managed to *drill* a bit more information out of her last night. She was pretty useless the night before.' He laughed harshly and reached out toward her dirty buckskin shirt.

Hands tied firmly to the saddle horn, she twisted away, then held her body rigid, eyes sparking. Her lips remained tightly in a line, her hair now just a dirty matt down her back.

'She didn't want to talk, but she got over it,' Xavier said, and glanced sideways at Vladimir.

Vladimir looked at them for a moment, eyebrows narrowed and lips pursed, then pointedly looked away from the grubby girl and glared at the Californio.

'Well, what is it?' Vladimir barked.

'The fox *does* know how to make the drug. She told me how *and* exactly where she's *really* cached the herbs. All we need to do is get the herbs. We don't really need her anymore. She's too much trouble, plus with that wrist, she'll slow us down. Like yesterday.'

Aleksandra's eyes widened and she trembled, hunched over Rogan's withers.

'But she's a nice bit of fluff, so guess I'll keep her around a bit longer.' Xavier licked his lips in her direction and laughed.

She stared at the ground, quivering.

'Oh yes, and of course, Vladimir,' Xavier said sarcastically, 'the last little details—it takes *two* bottles *into the neck vein* to make a horse run like the wind.' Xavier raised an eyebrow at Aleksandra. 'Not one, by mouth, as she told you,' he finished flatly.

'Interesting information to omit, girl' Vladimir's brows narrowed, his teeth bared.

Slinking lower in the saddle, she gripped her bandaged and tied wrist as best she could.

'She knows how to inject a horse and has an instrument for injecting it. Good thing for us to know. How 'bout we keep that little secret to ourselves?'

The tic in Vladimir's jaw quickened, but he just glanced at Xavier and scanned the horizon in both directions. 'We haven't seen your friends yet, Mr. Arguello.'

'Don't you worry, they'll be along soon. They had a few loose ends to tie up with someone who talked a little too loudly about some of our plans.' He gave Vladimir his best evil eye.

SHE WAS MORE alert today and knew exactly where they were. Seeing no point in showing she'd regained her faculties, Aleksandra swayed as Rogan ambled along.

Going home.

What sort of a home would it be now? She shook herself mentally. She had more pressing things to consider, like trying to stay alive. Given her lack of sleep this week, it was easy to appear exhausted. Keeping her head down, she surreptitiously noted the landmarks they passed.

Rogan's head came up, ears pricked forward, and his strides lengthened. She tightened her lips to keep from smiling. The big horse was finally at a place he recognized, and he was on a mission for home.

Near Dixie, with the roar of the river in the distance, she nodded to Xavier. He took a tighter hold on Rogan's lead to keep him heading straight past the shortcut over Forney's Bridge to his familiar stable, and they continued toward Hogback Summit, heading for Henneforville. Another mile on, she tumbled from the saddle and lay still as death.

'She's out again,' she heard Xavier say. 'Guess it's as good a time as any to make camp. We can still make it to the cabin before dark tomorrow.'

Vladimir didn't reply. He looked carefully about him, and dismounted.

～

'THINK YOU'LL R'FUSE *ME*, will ya, *Chiquita*?' Xavier shouted in anger. There was a deep thud, then nothing.

Vladimir startled and leapt to his feet. He must have dozed, his eyes still half-glued to the dying campfire.

Xavier strutted into the firelight, wobbling a little as he shook his head and rolled his eyes at Vladimir.

'*Sí, sí*, she'll learn! Gave 'er a bit of m' whisky, thought it might warm up 'er *corazón, un poquito*, a little bit, but it di'n't.' His face fell.

'Where is she?' Vladimir spat out. Whisky fumes emanated from Xavier as he approached.

He went on like he hadn't heard him. 'She won't r'fuse a man 'gain, I vow.' He chortled.

'What have you done with her *now*?' Vladimir growled, peering into the darkness.

'Went *down* like a ton o' bricks, she did, *la poquita*, out *cold*, but she's stirrin' already, don' need t' worry 'bout *her*,' he continued, turning his backside towards the fire and hunkered down near the dying embers.

Vladimir turned back, plans circling in his head, then smiled. This was help he hadn't expected. The lad was clearly drunk. It was time.

'This fire's warmer'n she is,' Xavier mumbled, 'an it don't bite.'

'I'll check the horses,' he remarked evenly, and walked away.

Xavier nodded his head a few times, chin sinking to his chest, grinning like the village idiot.

Now is my chance.

Once out of the firelight, Vladimir moved away from the horses, towards Xavier's bedroll, swearing under his breath as he stumbled over a saddle lying in his path. In the moonlight, he could just make out the figure of the girl, huddled half on, half under a blanket.

'Aleksandra, get up,' Vladimir muttered in an undertone and shook her by the shoulder.

The girl stirred, and lay still again, the scent of alcohol wafting from her floppy body.

He saddled his mare and the bay, keeping one eye on the man before the fire and the other on the semi-comatose girl.

Returning to her side, he dropped to his knees, grabbed her arms and pulled her to a sitting position and shook her. She shook her head.

'No more,' she groaned. 'You can do what you want with me, I don't care.'

'Aleksandra, *wake up*. Where is your hypodermic syringe?'

'*Wha—*?' Her eyes opened and she shook her head, then turned her face toward him, squinting. She tilted her head as she stared at his face.

'Aleks, wake up.'

'Oh, it's *you*.'

'You are going to inject my mare and your colt,' he enunciated carefully, word by word, 'then we are leaving.' He shook again for emphasis, then dragged her by the arm toward the horses.

'But I can't!' she wailed. 'We don't have one.' Her eyes narrowed and she seemed to focus on his face.

'I have the drugs.' He waved the buckskin bag before her eyes.

'But not a *syringe*.' By the way she said it, he knew she was rolling her eyes at him.

'Where is the syringe?'

'You broke it.' She scowled. 'It was in my belt pouch inside my trousers when you dragged me behind your horse. I threw the remains of it away last night.' Her eyes shot daggers at him.

'You must have another one,' he persisted.

'It's at the cabin,' she said wearily, gripping her splint and closing her eyes.

'Well, then, we leave for the cabin.'

'Where is Xavier?' She looked around, eyes wide, and turned toward where Xavier crouched before the fire.

'He's staying behind.'

'*Please* take me away from him!' she whispered, grabbing at his coat, her eyes wide.

'So now you *want* to come with me?'

'At least you don't rape me,' she faltered, 'or haven't yet, anyway. I don't know. I don't know what to think anymore.' She hung her head.

He repressed the urge to hug her. Instead, he tied her wrists before her.

'Are you going to be quiet or do I have to gag you again?'

'Do you think I want to alert *him*? Can we go, *please*?' she begged in a frantic whisper, glancing towards the man in the firelight.

Lifting her back into Rogan's saddle, he lashed her ankles beneath the horse again, tied the horse to a tree, and left her.

He watched Aleksandra's face as he walked towards the man before the fire and smiled. The Californio sang himself a little ditty, half Spanish, half English. He swung before Xavier could react and the younger man hit the ground with a thud.

As he returned to the girl, she was peering toward the fire, eyes wide.

'He won't bother us ever again,' Vladimir said in a smug voice.

'You didn't kill him, did you?' Her voice rose on a wail.

'Of course.' He smiled at her, turning his face into the light so she could see it, his voice honey-sweet. 'Is there some reason I shouldn't have killed him?' he snarled.

'There was no need to kill him, you could've just left him tied up,' Aleksandra growled, then she began to cry.

'You'd have both done the same to me. I saw your little game and wasn't about to play.' Yanking the slipknot on Rogan's rope, he swung up on his chestnut and looked back at her. 'I haven't lived this long by being stupid.'

32

Why didn't I just kill Xavier?

He turned around again to look at Aleksandra, the campfire behind her diminishing in the distance as they rode away.

'Which way now?' he snapped.

'Keep going over Hogback Summit, the next one, and straight on for Henneforville.' Her eyebrows dropped and her forehead furrowed. 'You should know the way, that's where you murdered Papa.'

Her glare cut through the darkness.

He looked away, not willing to apologize, especially as they'd just tried to trick him. A shiver ran up his spine. How difficult her life must have become with Krzysztof dead.

And I'm certainly not making it any easier for her now.

The guilty feelings surfaced again, more strongly than before.

'But I did not—,' he said shortly, but softly, and stopped, shaking his head.

They rode in silence for hours, trotting where the track would allow, with Vladimir constantly checking behind them. Xavier's Southern sympathizers hadn't appeared yet, but no doubt they'd be along soon. Who knew how long the Californio would take to realize he was alone? Perhaps Xavier didn't even know where the cabin was at all. They hadn't discussed it, so maybe this was his lucky night.

The girl remained silent.

Must've frightened her, thinking Xavier was dead.

She was, he hoped, cowed now—perhaps this time, anyway.

'How far to Echo?' he asked her.

Aleksandra lifted her head and sighted the trail around her. 'Fifteen minutes or so.'

He stopped his horse, and with Rogan still tied to his saddle horn, stuffed the gag back into her mouth, tying it in place with a second bandana behind her head. He prided himself on the fact that she hadn't quite bitten *him* yet.

'We've come this far, can't have you waking the natives,' he muttered, increasingly uncomfortable at making this harder on her than he had to.

No lights showed from the outlines of the Express station or other buildings in Echo. He preferred to go around the town, but between the river crowding too close on one side, and the sheer canyon wall on the other, there wasn't room. The towering red-pink obelisks showed tonight as black and white sentinels in the moonlight. He shuddered as something ran over his grave.

With a sigh of relief, he passed the last house of the village, then they rode up Echo Canyon and turned left into the big canyon, the last leg on their journey to Krzysztof's family home.

Vladimir peered ahead of them before they rode into the cabin clearing. No sign of life showed in the breaking dawn. He glanced at the drooping girl on the bay as he tied Rogan to a ring in the cabin wall. He removed her gag, looking away from her face, wet with tear streaks below flashing eyes.

'I'll be right back, then I'll get you down to inject the horses,' he said, turning to pull the latchstring.

She ignored him.

The blue-black sheen of light reflecting off metal flashed on his left as he entered the log house, and he spun to avoid the rifle stock heading for his skull. It struck a glancing blow across his shoulder.

Vladimir grabbed at the gun and it went off with a loud report, echoing in the tiny cabin. The combatants gripped the rifle between them, each fighting for their life. Passing before the doorway, the dawning light caught them and Vladimir's assailant was revealed. He nearly dropped the gun in shock.

Xavier? How did he get—?

The Californio shoved hard and twisted the gun when Vladimir paused, forcing him backwards over the foot of the big bed, his breath a snarl as he fought to bring the long barrel down over Vladimir's throat.

He heaved with all his strength and rolled, taking Xavier with him, but he overcompensated and they crashed side-by-side, on the wooden floorboards. Rolling over again, they managed to rise together, still locked on either side of the gun.

The younger man gripped his rifle for grim death as Vladimir whipped him around. Xavier's head crashed against the doorway with a sickening thud. For the second time tonight, he slumped to the ground, his body sliding down the door and over the threshold.

'Xavier!' Aleksandra screamed.

Rogan reared, fought his rope for a moment, then stood, still tied. Vladimir grinned, one eyebrow raised, at Aleksandra's stricken face, her despair clear.

'Should've killed him when I had the chance,' he said, panting. His hunch had been correct, but they'd not gotten away with it. He leaned back against the wall of the cabin for a moment to get his breath back, then entered once more, eyeing Xavier and nudging him with a foot as he passed.

The box was where she said it would be, but it only contained a small handful of powdery green plant material with a few larger pieces. He growled beneath his breath.

Aleksandra was staring with wide eyes at Xavier when Vladimir stepped over his still form and shoved the container beneath her face.

'Is this it? You said there were whole leaves that would let me identify the plant.' He squeezed her arm, then spun away, looking back at her over his shoulder. 'So Xavier means nothing to you, eh?' He shot her a sly grin.

'There *were* whole leaves, the last time Papa showed the box to me,' she said faintly, dragging her eyes back to Vladimir, 'but it's been a while since we had it out.'

'Well then, you come with me until they are identified and I board a ship out of this country.' His jaw was set. 'Better yet,' he smiled at her, 'I'll take you with me to Russia and let the tsar keep you in exchange for my family,' he said, stowing the box of powdered plant in his saddlebag.

'Please, just leave me here.' Her face was ashen in the early morning light. 'I won't make any trouble. Even if I wanted to, you'll be too far away for anyone to catch you with the drug in your horse.' Her voice quivered, rising toward the end.

'Do as I say and you'll live to see another day, Aleksandra. Where is the syringe?'

'It was in a case next to the one in your hand.'

Turning on his heel, he hopped over the prone body and rummaged in the darkness beneath the eaves until he found it. He sighed, letting out the breath he didn't know he'd been holding. His heart squeezed tightly as he carried the wooden box to the doorway and opened it. Lying on its bed of dark velvet, the polished surface of the glass and steel instrument gleamed in the faint light.

Finally.

Then a thought occurred and he shook his head.

There must be more than one syringe—and no one else must be able to catch me.

'One is here. Where are the others?' His eyes narrowed at her.

'There's only the one now.' She raised an eyebrow at him. 'You broke the other.' She looked away as he pulled the bag from around his neck and set the bottles down on a stump near the door with the glass instrument in its case. Untying Aleksandra's legs from beneath Rogan and her hands from the saddle horn, he pulled her roughly off the stallion, supporting her as her knees buckled. He still held the end of the rope attached to her wrists.

'What's the fastest way to Henefer?'

'Over the mountain. It's shorter, but rough. Probably too rough for you,' she added, glancing at him sideways, her brows narrowed and jaw tight.

'I can certainly manage it, if you can.' His brows dropped into a glare. 'Right, inject the mare with two bottles and yours with the last one and we'll be on our way.'

ALEKSANDRA'S HANDS shook as she uncorked the bottle and sniffed its open top. It smelled as it should, so she inserted the needle into the liquid and drew back on the plunger, filling the syringe with the vial's clear amber contents.

She turned her body to surreptitiously glance at Xavier past the syringe as it filled. Her heart was in her throat when his hand moved. Stopping her gasp in its tracks, she calmly turned and limped to the horse, then exhaled slowly as she stepped the chestnut mare around to block Vladimir's view of the doorway.

'Just turn her head so I can get some light on her vein here,' she mumbled while she held off the mare's jugular vein with her thumb.

'Like this?' he said, brow furrowed.

'Yes. Watch her eye closely,' she said, as the vein filled, 'and hold the noseband with your left hand. Scratch her here with your right when I tell you,' she indicated with a wave of her hand, 'This needle is thick and they don't like it much. Scratch hard.'

With Vladimir's focus firmly on the horse, his back turned to Xavier, Aleksandra slowly injected the drug, apologizing in her heart to the already-exhausted mare.

'Keep holding her just like that. I'll be back with the rest,' she said over her shoulder. She hurried to get rest of the dose and stand between him and the doorway. Filling the syringe swiftly, she tucked the third bottle into her pocket and returned to the mare. Vladimir hadn't moved, he was still focused on scraping a hole through the poor horse's skin with his fingernail.

'And the last one,' she said to the squirming horse 'Sorry, girl.' The chestnut was so distracted by the scratching that she never flinched as the needle slid into her vein again.

'Is that it?' Vladimir said, glancing back towards the cabin door.

'Yes.' She moved so he had to look away from the cabin. 'You really would travel faster without me,' she tried again, more calmly this time.

'Without a hostage, I have nothing to bargain with, do I?' He raised an eyebrow. 'Get on with it,' he barked.

She jumped and bolted toward Rogan, who shied violently

sideways as Vladimir raced after her. Aleksandra gulped down a chuckle. Rogan, used to quiet handling, resented rough or forcible treatment.

'You'll have to hold his halter tightly when we inject him.' Looking at Vladimir with wide eyes, she somehow managed to keep a straight face. She pulled the final bottle from her pocket and drew it into the syringe while Vladimir took a firm grasp on the colt's bridle.

'I've been holding horses since long before you were born, girl. Get on with it.'

'Really, you'll have to hold his halter, not his bridle. He'll go crazy if you pull on the bit.' The colt was already staring at him, his ears laid back, showing the whites of his eyes at the tall man who moved his hand to grip the halter for grim death.

Aleksandra stabbed, with rather more effort than necessary, at Rogan's vein. As she suspected he would, the colt objected —strenuously.

Rogan reared high and dragged Vladimir with him. He screamed the throaty trumpet of a grown stallion as he struck at his captor. Usually an exceptional horseman, Vladimir wasn't on his game this morning and the stallion's shod hoof raked his ribcage. The Russian hit the ground, still clinging to the lead of the angry stallion. He hunched over, covering his head with his free hand.

'Damn you all.' Jumping up with a yelp, he jerked both Rogan's lead and Aleksandra's rope with one hand, clasping his chest with the other.

Out of the corner of her eye, Aleksandra saw a movement and flicked her gaze sideways. Her breath froze in her chest when she saw Xavier heading for the Russian at a staggering run.

Warned by her glance, Vladimir dropped the ropes and reached for his *shashka*, but Aleksandra was already clinging to his sword arm like a limpet. Trying in vain to shake her off, the Russian swung his other fist at the oncoming Californio, connecting with his jaw and knocked him flat. He shoved Aleksandra to the ground and reached again for his sword.

Leaping to her feet, Aleksandra crouched, staring at him over the *shashka* she'd just pulled from Vladimir's belt. One jerk of the rope fastened to her wrist flicked it out of the Russian's reach, and she stood, tensed, waiting for his attack.

He looked at her, considering, his brows narrowed and head cocked. Shaking his head, he bolted for the mare and caught her reins. Grabbing the saddle horn, the Cossack shouted at her and vaulted on as the chestnut set off at a gallop, heading for the trail over the top of the mountain.

Aleksandra watched the mare as she flew up the hill, every muscle straining, then disappeared into the trees.

Against the sound of fading hoofbeats, Aleksandra raced to Xavier's side and lifted his head onto her lap. His color was good and his pupils responsive.

He's only stunned, again. Vladimir can sure use his fists.

She began to breathe again as Xavier stirred beneath her hands. Why hadn't he taken the *shashka* from her and finished them both off? She glanced up the hill as Vladimir reappeared above the tree line, the mare still at a full run.

The Russian set her at the steepest part of the grade and she bolted up like her tail was on fire, but then her legs seemed to give way and she crumpled, fell and lay still. In the distance, she appeared to be lying on her side. There was no sign of Vladimir. In the still mountains, they would have heard a shout or scream, but the only sound she heard was the wind through the aspens and Xavier's regular breathing.

There was little she could do for the Russian right now, and she was more concerned for her man.

Vladimir would have to wait.

She sat in the stillness, stroking his hair.

Rogan shattered the stillness, spinning around and calling out to an old roan horse as it ambled up the track toward the cabin, walking beside a young man carrying a rifle. Rogan shook his head and trotted over to meet the visitors. The young man tossed the rifle to the petite older woman mounted on the horse, dressed in fashionable, but dusty and travel-worn, attire. He caught the bay's trailing lead and steadied the horse, crooning to him softly in—

Russian!

Aleksandra nearly screamed.

Leaving Vladimir's *shashka* beside Xavier, she slipped his head from her lap and stood to meet the comers.

'Hallo and good morning,' the dark haired woman called out as she dismounted and hurried towards Aleksandra. 'Is your friend hurt?'

'Yes, but at least he's alive,' she said weakly.

'You look as if you've had a difficult time yourself.' She glanced down Aleksandra's body. 'Is your wrist hurt?'

'Good morning to you,' Aleksandra said automatically, then tilted her head, wrinkling her brow. 'I'm sorry, but have we met?'

'Oh, I'm sorry,' she apologized. 'I'm a nurse and I forget everything else when I see injured people. I was looking for Krzysztof Lekarski and I was told his cabin was this way.' She smiled hopefully.

Aleksandra inhaled sharply and held her breath, letting it out slowly.

'This is his cabin, but he's no longer here.'

'Oh dear.' The woman whispered, standing absolutely still for a moment, then her face fell. She swayed a bit, and the young man came from behind to support her, having tied the colt to one tree and the roan to another.

'*Mama*, everything will be fine. We will find him,' he said anxiously as he looked to Aleksandra with big eyes. 'Would you know where he might be, please, miss?' the young man said with perfect, if heavily accented, English.

'He's in the graveyard over there, sadly enough,' she whispered in return.

'We'll never find your papa, and we've come so far!' the woman said on an exhalation, rising toward the end.

Aleksandra stared. The boy was younger than she was. This could not be.

'*Your* papa? He was *my* papa. What is this about, and who are you, please?' Aleksandra stared at the pair, hands clenched at her sides.

'I am Tatiana and this is my son Nikolai. We were looking for Krzysztof Lekarski because my husband was meant to be seeking him here. You might know of him, Vladimir Chabardine?'

33

Aleksandra glanced up the hill and nodded at the chestnut mare lying still near the crest of the mountain.

'There he is, your husband, the man who murdered my father Krzysztof.' She spoke between gritted teeth. 'He took what he came for and it's probably killed him under that horse. Now, if you'll excuse me, Madame Chabardine, I have my man to attend to, another of Vladimir's casualties.' She turned back to Xavier's still form.

'I don't know what to say, Miss Lekarski,' the woman stepped toward them, 'but I apologize for any injury caused by my husband. Will you let me help you with him, please?'

Aleksandra looked away from her, but moved aside to let her examine Xavier.

She checked his pulse, his gums, and opened his eyes to see his pupils. At this, he stirred.

'Aleks?' he mumbled, his voice haunted.

'It's okay, Xavier, I'm here and Vladimir's gone.' Aleksandra knelt beside him to kiss his brow.

'I think he'll be all right.' Tatiana said. 'Nikolai, would you bring a canteen?'

'It's been a long ordeal,' Aleksandra whispered, and nodded at Xavier. 'Vladimir laid him out cold three times in one day and my wrist might be broken. Add to that, your husband may have killed himself for the damnable secret of my father's—the same one he killed Papa over.' She sighed and rubbed her gritty eyes. 'I just want it to be over, and we have yet to see if Vladimir lives.'

'I'll go up there with Nikolai and see what my husband has done with himself. He was always rather careless with his person,' Tatiana said.

Her bedside manner was impeccable, but Aleksandra could see the strain beneath the surface. 'Your man looks stable enough,' she said brusquely, as she rose to her feet. 'May I see that wrist of yours?'

Aleksandra grudgingly placed her throbbing limb into the woman's hands. Her understanding of medicine went out the window when she or someone close to her was injured, so she was grateful for the assistance.

'I am indeed sorry to have to meet you under such circumstances, but what is your name, my dear?' she asked softly, and began unwrapping the filthy, lumpy bandage.

'Aleksandra, Krzysztof's daughter.'

Tatiana was silent for a moment, then she took a deep breath. 'Well Aleksandra, I should like you to know that Vladimir used to speak glowingly of your father when he was a young man. He was his favorite protégé.'

Aleksandra's heart turned to stone.

'Then why did he kill him?' she muttered.

'This we will ask him if, God willing, he lives.' She closed her eyes.

Xavier groaned and stirred.

'Aleks?' He turned his head toward her.

'Yes, I'm here. How do you feel?'

'Like I've been run over by a train, a big Russian one.' His brow wrinkled and he shut his eyes again. 'How did you escape him?'

'After you tried to stop him, I grabbed his *shashka*. He must've decided we were too much trouble, so he left at a gallop on the chestnut, heading for the top of the mountain. She collapsed, up there.' Aleksandra waved a hand up the hill and he shaded his eyes and looked. 'The mare's still there, but I've not seen any movement.'

He turned his head from side to side, as if his neck was sore, and saw the strangers. Brows narrowing, he turned to Aleksandra with a silent question.

'You'll never believe it in a million years.' She shook her head. 'Xavier, meet Madame Chabardine and her son Nikolai.'

'Please, call me Tatiana,' she said quietly.

'They've come from Russia to find Krzysztof and Vladimir,' she said, looking at him, with a raised brow.

Xavier squeezed his eyes shut tightly and shook his head slowly. He took a deep breath.

'I can see it's time for me to get up,' he said resignedly. 'We have a walk ahead of us.'

'You're going nowhere just yet, young man,' his new nurse stated in a voice of steel, as she looked up from Aleksandra's wrist. 'You may have a sip of water and consider sitting up while I re-bandage this arm.'

'What do you think?' Aleksandra tightened her jaw as Tatiana motioned the joint.

'I suspect my husband will pay for his roughness,' she growled. 'I think it's just sprained, but I wouldn't discount a dislocation.'

Aleksandra let out a long breath.

'Tsk-tsk,' she grumbled. 'If this is his bandaging technique, however, he has even more to learn,' she said, pulling a clean bandage from her kit and wrapping the arm firmly from fingers to elbow.

'That helps a great deal,' Aleksandra sighed as she looked into the eyes of the woman for the first time. 'Thank you for helping me despite my treating you so disrespectfully.'

'Under the circumstances,' the dark haired woman raised an eyebrow, mouth in a grim line, 'it is quite understandable.'

'Thank you, for both of us,' Aleksandra said.

Tatiana smiled at her.

'Xavier, how are you feeling?' Tatiana asked. 'Do you think you can stand?'

Xavier stood up, swayed for a moment, then shook his head. 'I am fine now, but I plan to ride. Walking would be difficult.' He gave them the ghost of a grin and rubbed his hand over his forehead, wincing.

The woman glanced at Nikolai. He stood beside Rogan, shifting his weight from foot to foot, staring up the hill to where his father waited.

'I would have sent my son to check on Vladimir right away,' she added in an undertone, 'but I didn't want to send him alone in case the unthinkable has happened, but we can go up now.'

'I'll get Charro.' Xavier got to his feet and turned away.

'I'll get him for you, sir.' Nikolai spun and leapt for the barn, barely able to contain himself in his anxiety to seek his father. He collected the Andalusian, returning from the barn staring with awe from one massive stallion to the other.

'Obsessed with fine stock, just like his father, though he's not seen him since he was an infant,' Tatiana said with a smile, as she placed her foot into the roan's stirrup.

The rest mounted and set off at a trot to find the Russian, Nikolai already racing ahead on foot.

'I believe you were being held by the tsar against Vladimir's return with Krzysztof's secret,' Xavier shouted over his shoulder to Tatiana, 'but what I don't understand is how you're here today. How did you escape from Russia and find us here?'

'That, Xavier, is a long story, one which I didn't know until recently. I was not permitted much contact with the outside world.'

'How about we make a start?' Aleksandra raised an eyebrow at her.

'To understand how this came about,' Tatiana took a deep breath, 'you must understand the Tsar Nicholas I. He was a severe autocrat, suppressive of any liberal thought or action. His success in gaining Armenia, the Caspian Sea, the east coast of the Black Sea and the mouth of the Danube, as well as his brutal suppression of the Polish uprising whetted his appetite to possess all of Europe. He saw your father's invention, whatever it is, as a means to that end and knew he would only attain it by holding us against Vladimir's return with his secret.

'Nikolai and I were "under the protection" of Tsar Nicholas I for twenty years. In the beginning, I believed my parents petitioned for our release many times. My father hoped managing the tsar's Training School might afford them some influence with Tsar Nicholas, but apparently this was not the case.' She shook her head as the roan stumbled.

Aleksandra and Xavier rode abreast of Tatiana now, letting their tired horses walk as the trail dwindled and they had to clamber over rocks and fallen timber on their way to the summit.

'Excuse me for interrupting, madame, sorry, Tatiana,' Xavier looked sideways at her, his brows furrowed, 'but you say you 'believed'?

'Early in our captivity, after one such petition, my stepmother gave my father a letter from the tsar's secretary—they were threatened with exile of the entire family to Siberia if they attempted to query it again. My papa was too frightened to put it forth again. He believed her for many years. It turns out,' she gulped, 'she lied to him for those many years, fabricated stories, forged letters, you name it.'

Aleksandra's jaw dropped.

Xavier stared at her in horror, then leaned forward as Charro hopped over a large log.

'A little more than a year ago, my father received hope in the form of a letter from Vladimir, which said he was leaving Poland to find a place in America called Echo, Utah Territory, to talk with Krzysztof and find that which the tsar sought.'

'Talk with him,' Aleksandra growled low in her throat. 'Is that what he calls talk?'

Xavier reached for Aleksandra's hand and gave it a little squeeze, and she dropped her head and desisted. 'Did he say how he discovered Krzysztof's whereabouts?' he asked.

'No, hópefully he can answer that himself.' She scrunched her brow, then carried on. 'A Danish Count and sea captain friend of my father's, Kim Petersen, whom he hadn't seen in twenty years, took lunch with him last year in St. Petersburg. Captain Petersen mentioned he was acquainted with the new tsar, Alexander II, from his cadet days in the Royal Danish Naval Academy, when the twenty-two-year old Tsesarevich Alexander visited Denmark on a European tour with his governor. As the only, albeit minor, royalty resident on the sparkling new ship of the line *Christian VIII*, the young Count Petersen served as escort for the emperor-to-be on his naval ship sojourn.

'Captain Petersen offered to speak with Tsar Alexander the next day at his planned audience. My parents were fearful, but the Count reminded them that Alexander II, who had become tsar upon his father's death only a few years before, was a different man from Nicholas I. Tsar Alexander was raised with a poet for a governor, and since he'd come to power, he'd been implementing governmental reforms, such as the elimination of serfdom, rather than making war.'

'That *would* make a change.' Aleksandra raised a brow at the others.

'Yes, and for the next day,' Tatiana stopped and peered up the hill as they came out of the trees, 'my father waited in fear for the shouting and pounding on the door portending their exile.'

VLADIMIR SWAM upwards toward a spot of light, red pain screaming in his head and leg, then he felt no more. A white stillness surrounded him and a fleeting image of Tatiana, dressed in flowing white gossamer, slipped closer and closer, holding the hand of a little boy, then they were gone.

'ARRRGGGGHHH,' Vladimir screamed with the anguish of losing them yet again, and the agony of his broken body returned. The pain in his leg was slowly diminishing, and he soon could not feel it at all. Awake now, he saw the horse's heaving barrel lying atop him, her twitching legs surrounding his head and body.

She would never be able to rise without kicking him to death. He was going to die alone here upon this mountain—he couldn't possibly expect help after the treatment he'd meted out to Aleksandra and Xavier.

'Please God, I am not afraid to die, and I never intended to kill. I killed as a soldier because I was compelled, but never have done so since leaving the tsar's forces. You, of all, know Krzysztof's death was an accident. If it is your will to grant me the opportunity to do right by all, I would gladly die to make it happen. If not, please care for my beloved Tatiana, if she yet lives, and my little Nikolai, for I have failed in my duty to them, and to Aleksandra—as the daughter of my protégé, and even to poor Xavier.' His lips curled into a parody of a wry grin. 'Xavier, I would have loved to teach to fight.' The darkness descended until the light was no more.

TATIANA CONTINUED BREATHLESSLY with her story as the horses struggled through the brush, rocks and fallen trees. 'The knock on the door the following day was only Captain Petersen, who told my father that Tsar Alexander had forgotten we were under house arrest and wasn't at all sure why his father detained us in the first place. Having no intention of attempting to overrun Europe, especially after his father's Crimean War fiasco, the "secret" his father sought of Vladimir was superfluous. He seemed pleased to right what he considered a wrong, so we were released and provided safe passage on a Russian vessel carrying his envoy to San Francisco to discuss Russia's sale of Alaska to the United States.' She pushed the old horse to a trot, now they were clear of the tree line, and the rest followed.

'Did you ride that horse all the way from San Francisco?' Aleksandra stared at her, aghast.

'No, we went by riverboat to Sacramento and boarded a stagecoach to Echo,' she twisted her lips, 'a ride I would not wish to repeat soon.'

'Excuse me, Tatiana, but did you meet a woman on the coach, a Californio named María?' Xavier asked.

'Why, yes, we did! Do you know her?'

He grinned. 'She is *mi madre*, my mother. I met with her in Carson a few days ago.'

'She was the loveliest woman. You are lucky to have such a mother.' Tatiana smiled and continued her story. 'We arrived last night and this morning found a horse to hire for the day, so here we are.' She raised her eyebrows at them. 'New friends and,' she took a deep breath and looked up the hill, 'I hope, an old husband.'

Aleksandra looked back. Nikolai struggled up the steep hillside, but he still trotted in their wake.

Topping a rise, Vladimir's horse appeared in the distance, only a few minutes ahead of them. The mare lay motionless, her head down the hill. Rogan whinnied when he saw her.

She raised her head slightly, then lowered it again.

'She moved!' Aleksandra shouted, and loosed Rogan's reins. He shot forward, reducing the minutes to seconds. The chestnut, drenched in sweat, picked up her head and blinked, but didn't try to rise, as Aleks flew from the saddle and ran to her head. Kneeling on her neck, she gripped the cheekpiece of the mare's bridle and lifted her nose up to prevent her from rising.

Vladimir lay white-faced and still, with one leg beneath her barrel. Aleksandra gritted her teeth and looked around to see how close Tatiana was. If the Russian was breathing, it was difficult to tell.

Then Xavier was there beside her.

'We can't let her move yet. God, he's in a bad place,' Aleksandra glanced at the trapped man, his upper body between the chestnut's fore and hind legs.

'Not the safest place, no,' Xavier said, placing one foot on either side of Vladimir's head, in case the mare should begin to kick.

'I'll try to keep her down.' Aleksandra nodded at the mare's muzzle, as she held it pointing straight to the sky.

'Is he alive?' Xavier whispered, as Tatiana slid from her horse and ran up behind them.

'I don't know, but if we don't get the mare off him before she tries to get up, he won't be for long,' she hissed at him, pulling back the mare's lips. 'Her color's somewhere between white and blue, so her circulation's not very good, and her heartbeat and pulse are all over the place. She'll fall on him again if she tries to get up.'

'With her legs uphill, she can't possibly rise without thrashing and destroying—' Xavier glanced around at Tatiana's white face and changed tack. 'We need to roll her over.'

Aleksandra looked steadily at Vladimir's wife. 'Tatiana, we need to get this horse off him before you can get in there, okay?'

The woman nodded and raced back towards her horse.

'Xavier, we need some rope,' Aleksandra said.

He hesitated, looking from Vladimir's head to the mare's feet.

'You'll just have to leave him.' Aleksandra shook her head. 'He won't survive if we don't move her, anyway,' she said, and he ran for his gray.

'I'll take some reins from the horses' bridles,' Nikolai puffed over his shoulder as he bolted toward Rogan.

Tatiana returned and untied the exposed side of the cinch, pulling the saddle as far back as possible, so it wouldn't impede their efforts, then wordlessly handed Aleksandra a stethoscope. Aleksandra smiled her thanks, tucking it into the neckline of her buckskin shirt until she had a free hand.

'She's got the full weight of her guts on her lungs right now, no wonder she's blue,' Aleksandra muttered. 'Xavier, can you get your rope onto her fetlock on the down-side foreleg, and Nikolai, put yours on the fetlock of the lower hind one.'

'Like this?' Nikolai pulled the rein tight.

'Yes. Now you'll both have to pull at the same time, I'll count to three. Be sure you're not downhill from her and let go of the ropes as soon as she's turned over. You won't be able to stop her from going further, and you might get killed if you try. Okay? One...Two... Three!' Aleksandra kept the mare's heavy head from crashing as she rolled over and lay still with her legs pointing down the hill. The mare would be able to rise with less difficulty now. Aleksandra let out a big breath.

Tatiana and Nikolai raced to Vladimir's side, tears rolling down their cheeks.

'He's breathing and his pupils are constricting, thank God,' she sobbed. She collapsed over his still form for a few moments, then sat back and hugged her son. Wiping her eyes, she turned back to her husband and began checking him over.

'Tatiana, your stethoscope. Catch,' Aleksandra raised an eyebrow at the other woman and tossed it to her, then removed the tethers from the chestnut's fetlocks and pulled the now-freed saddle out of the way.

Vladimir's wife finished listening to his chest and handed the stethoscope back to Aleksandra.

'He seems to have several broken ribs as well.' Tatiana frowned.

Aleksandra just nodded, placing the earpieces into her ears. Listening to the mare's heart, she shook her head slowly. After a few minutes, the horse picked up her head, then set it back down and groaned.

'Tatiana, you might want to listen to this horse's heart. She has an arrhythmia—many rapid beats, then none, highly irregular and fast. I've not heard one like this before, but Papa described it to me.'

'No wonder she's blue.' Tatiana looked up from her husband's chest for a moment, then she began to catalog her husband's injuries aloud.

'A handful of scrapes and nicks, a rather nasty cut over his cheek and a broken tibia. From the dried blood on the bandage, a significant wound beneath it, I'd imagine?' She looked at Aleksandra, eyebrow raised.

The girl nodded. 'He ran into my *shashka*.'

Tatiana's eyes widened at that, then returned to her husband. She carried on. 'Several broken ribs and a big bruise on his shoulder—'

'Look out, the mare's getting up.' Aleksandra grabbed the chestnut's bridle with her good hand, and the rest of them stood between the struggling mare and Vladimir's still form, steadying her heavy body as she rose.

'*Lo siento*, sorry Tatiana, I lay claim to the bruise, but in fairness, I have much more damage from him,' Xavier said, his brow wrinkled and the ends of his mouth upturned.

'Fair turnabout for sure, he's given me a lot worse,' Aleksandra said, 'not to mention killing my papa.' She turned back to the mare.

'*But I told you, I didn't kill him,*' Vladimir choked out, rolling his head back and forth, then took a deep breath.

34

All eyes turned to his face and watched his eyes slowly open in the direction of his wife. He blinked, shut his eyes tightly and groaned.

'Oh please, not another vision of her, just let me die in peace,' he whispered. 'I cannot bear it.'

'I'm here, Vladimir.' Tatiana kneeled beside him and buried her head in the hollow of his neck. 'I'm here and I'll never let you go again,' she said, and sat up, looking down at him, tears flowing from her eyes.

Vladimir began to lift his arms, but gasped instead.

'You mustn't move, Vladimir, you've several fractures.' She wrapped her arms around him and kissed his forehead on a spot that wasn't grazed and bleeding.

He pulled his head back from his wife's embrace. 'How ... what ...?'

'I'll tell you all about it after we get you taken care of,' she assumed her nurse's tone. He lay still, smiling at her, slowly rocking his head from side to side.

A shadow passed over his face. 'My little Niko?' he asked in a breathless voice and gripped her hand. 'Is he ... here?'

'Your little Nikolai is no longer.'

'*No, he's not*—' Vladimir cried out, then gasped in pain, reaching for his ribs.

'Vladimir,' Tatiana winced, then forced a smile and looked around at their boy. 'Have you so little faith in me? He is here, he's just not little anymore.'

Vladimir turned his head with difficulty and gazed at his son, then turned his eyes skyward, his mouth moving for a few moments. Taking a careful deep breath, he faced his boy, now nearly full-grown.

'Niko, we meet again, my son. But you are a man now.' His heart in his voice, he reached out a hand to him, and bit his lip.

Nikolai dropped to his knees and kissed his father gently on both cheeks, then sat back, beaming at him. 'We scarcely hoped to find you, much less alive.'

'And that was a near thing,' Aleksandra growled over her shoulder, 'not as if you deserve to—'

'Aleks, not now.' Xavier's voice cut like steel. He shook his head.

She stood still, her tongue between her teeth to keep from shrieking, good hand clenched on the bandaged arm. Taking a deep breath, she turned to the unsteady mare and carefully led her a few yards across the slope to a level area sporting a few tufts of grass. The mare lipped at the green blades, then took a nibble, ignoring the two stallions eyeing her with interest. With no trees to tie up to, Aleksandra hoped the horses' remaining reins would stay where Nikolai had wedged them between rocks.

With her now-pink gums and a near-normal sounding heart, the chestnut appeared to have no injuries, other than a skinned knee, muzzle and hip. Aleksandra sighed, gave her another pat, and returned to kneel next to Xavier, beside Vladimir.

'Aleks, I beg of you, a word please,' Vladimir breathlessly whispered into the profound silence. She slowly turned, holding her breath.

'Aleksandra, please accept my humblest apologies for the death of your papa. I will turn myself in to your authorities, but please know Krzysztof's death was truly an accident, though I am guilty of great stupidity.

'I bragged before the wrong people that your papa could ride great distances in half the time it should have taken and it came to the ears of the tsar, who of course wanted it for his armies to overrun Europe.' He closed his eyes, took a careful breath and gritted his teeth. 'He wanted it enough to hold Tatiana and young Nikolai for many years. I never meant to hurt Krzysztof. I swear to God, I never meant to harm him.'

'You never meant to harm him.' She shot daggers with her eyes. 'How can you lie about this?' Her words cut the chilly mountain morning air, and her voice continued, dripping with sarcasm. 'Your skill with the *shashka* is legendary, according to my papa.'

'I admit, we were sparring, with some intent, but Krzysztof's foot rolled on a stone and he fell upon his own blade. I know it is difficult to believe. An arms master should have been able to prevent the death of his greatest young protégé.' A tear leaked from the corner of his watery eyes. 'And then, like a coward, knowing I would not be believed, I dropped him into a crevice below where we had fought, hoping no one would find him. For this, I am so very sorry, as well.'

Aleksandra stared at him, breathing hard, tears running down her cheeks. She hadn't the slightest idea what to say.

'Please believe me, Aleks, I could never have killed him. I needed his secret to exchange for the life of those I loved. They were to be sent to Siberia if I failed, or if I returned to Russia without it,' he pleaded, brow furrowed and eyes wide. 'Niko, my saddlebags please?'

Tatiana unlaced them from Vladimir's saddle in silence, began to pick them up and nearly dropped them.

'What do you have in them, rocks?' she raised a brow at her husband.

Aleksandra and Xavier looked at each other and grinned.

'I'll take care of it,' Xavier said, 'later.'

Tatiana hefted them to the boy, then moved sideways to stand slightly between Aleksandra and Vladimir.

'What do you need?' Nikolai asked, fumbling with the buckles.

'In the right one, canvas wrapped, long. Please, get it for Aleks.' He closed his eyes tightly and paled as he carefully inspired.

Aleksandra untied the cord and lay the package on the ground. Heart in her mouth, guessing what it contained, she slowly unrolled the canvas cover with her good hand and glanced at Vladimir as she lifted her father's *shashka* from a bed of red silk. Her eyes brimmed again, about to spill over.

'I was going to give it to you when we reached San Francisco and I was safely on a boat,' he said, his lips in a crooked little smile. 'I've seen your skill with yours, and have a hole in my pelt to prove it.' He closed his eyes again. 'I wish to make good the promise I made to your papa, to do my best to see you were looked after. Until now, I've done an abysmal job, but if I survive this, I plan to do so, if you will permit.' He looked at her intently, his face open.

'I'll take care of her, Vladimir,' Xavier raised an eyebrow, 'and to better effect, I hope.'

Aleksandra raised her own brows at the Russian and turned away.

'Your papa said you would never believe me,' he said faintly, 'but I promised nonetheless. When you cut me, and then wouldn't believe me, nor communicate with me, I lost my temper and didn't find it again until now. To you both, I apologize with all my heart. The *shashka* is in your hands to do as you will, Aleksandra. I can no longer fight you, nor will I ever again.'

She shook her head and took a deep breath, then reached for Xavier, kissed him on the chest blindly and headed for Rogan. 'Nikolai, help me get a travois and bandaging for your papa,' she said over her shoulder as she mounted the colt. 'Bring the roan, he should be safer than Rogan for this work,' she added, as she turned him down the hill. The boy scrambled on the loose stones behind her as he ran for the old horse.

'THAT WENT WELL.' Xavier looked at Vladimir, mouth quirked to one side, eyes narrowed. 'You're one brave man, lying there and handing Aleksandra her pa's *shashka*, either that or very trusting in her honor.'

'Or stupid, I might say.' Tatiana's white face said what her words didn't.

'Her papa would've taught her well. I could ask no more of her. In her eyes, I'm sure I deserve to die, but her honor kept her from it.'

'You've got more guts than brains, that's for sure,' Xavier said, shaking his head and turning away, glancing back to smile at the injured man.

The Russian closed his eyes, but returned the smile.

Xavier mounted Charro. Nothing but occasional clumps of dry grass grew up this high, so he headed down toward the tree line to gather sticks to splint Vladimir's leg.

ALEKSANDRA'S ATTITUDE was improved by the time she and Nikolai returned, but Rogan dragged the travois. Xavier grinned, knowing there would be an interesting story to come.

'Your new cart horse?' he called out to her.

'Mmmm. Seems the roan didn't like the travois. Luckily for us, Nikolai is fast,' she said, grinning at young man. 'He caught him before he ran too far.'

Xavier hid a grin, pleased to see Aleksandra smile again. Nikolai's infectious enthusiasm had clearly taken its first victim.

'Your Rogan has been well trained, I should say.' Nikolai looked as proud as if he'd done it himself.

'A good thing it is, or your papa would be out here for quite some time.' She smiled at Nikolai as she unloaded the padding for Vladimir's splint and laid it out beside him.

'Oh, I forgot splints!' she looked at Xavier, her eyes wide.

'Got them.' Picking up the trimmed branches, he caught the grateful smile she sent his way.

Aleksandra knelt beside Vladimir, a whisky bottle in hand. 'Do you want this for the pain? Straightening out that leg will be past excruciating, but alcohol won't help the shock any. Your choice.' She looked from him to Tatiana.

Considering for a moment, Vladimir shook his head. 'I'll live with the pain, but perhaps not with the shock. Go ahead.'

By the time the leg was splinted, all five of them were ashen as the sheets binding his broken leg. It took everyone's fullest effort to accomplish it, both men using all their strength against the injured man's muscles to pull the bone ends apart from where they had overridden. Nikolai pulled towards Vladimir's head on one of

Tatiana's bedsheets placed between his legs while Xavier provided traction and rotation at Vladimir's ankle. Aleksandra and Tatiana reduced the fracture, lining the ends up to their satisfaction, then padded, splinted and bound it with yards of bandages, rolling strips of sheets when they ran out of those. Vladimir, to his credit, did not scream. He kept his eyes tightly shut and bit down hard on a piece of buckskin, and moaned a great deal. He slept almost immediately, beneath the eagle eye of Nurse Chabardine.

'I'm sure I would have yelled, at least.' Xavier shook his head, his stomach roiling at the thought. 'I was surprised how much I wanted to quit, knowing the pain we were putting him through, although I knew it needed to be done.' Xavier took another deep breath and willed his churning guts to stillness.

'Yes, it's always like that,' Tatiana said softly, watching her husband sleep. 'Why don't you two go for a walk? He'll be out for some time and it's a beautiful morning to be alive.'

35

Aleksandra and Xavier unsaddled their tired horses, trading their
bridles for halters, then jammed their leadropes between rocks
near what little grass could be found growing at this altitude.

They left the horses behind and climbed still further up the
mountain to a rocky eyrie out of the breeze, where the sun had already
warmed the dark stone. They sat silently beside each other until Xavier
finally spoke.

'Aleksandra, I apologize for hurting you. It was never my intent.'

As she averted her head, his heart squeezed tight in his chest.

'Making the scenario live was the only way out I could see for us to
escape from Vladimir alive,' he pleaded, cocking his head, then he
kissed her forehead.

'I know.' She looked down at the strip of grass she was shredding
between her fingers.

'What's bothering you, other than the fact that someone you
thought you could believe in totally betrayed that trust?' He gave her a
twisted smile.

She glanced at him, brow furrowed. 'I wanted to believe you
completely, but you were so convincing that I despaired,' she took a
deep breath, then went on firmly, 'like—, like—are you really involved
with the Southerners?'

He hauled her toward him and pulled her onto his lap, hugging her close.

'Do you genuinely think I could condone the abuse underpinning their society? The sight of someone being subjugated has sent me into a killing rage more than once. I couldn't abide it.'

He closed his eyes for a moment, and Aleksandra turned to face him, reaching out to stroke his cheek with the side of her finger.

'After speaking with my mother, many things became clear. Until I left home, my mother, brothers, servants and I were all abused by the man I thought my father. He manipulated me by my uncontrolled anger when I saw someone I loved being abused.' He looked into her eyes for a moment, then away. 'It's always been my Achilles heel.'

'I could never beat Vladimir in a fight, but I knew if we were both convincing enough to fool him into relaxing his guard, we might win. Perhaps it was wrong of me, keeping it to myself and not letting you in on it, but we had no time to discuss it, so I took the risk upon myself.

'Keeping my anger from clouding my judgment while seeing you hurt, and more so, having to subdue you myself without being swayed by it, was the hardest thing I ever did in my life.' He took a deep breath and held her away from him, his gaze intent upon her face.

She pulled out of his arms and sat with her knees tucked to her chin, burying her face in her hands, whimpering as she twisted her wrist.

'What is it, Aleks?' He gripped his hands together to stop himself from reaching out to her.

'So where did all the gold come from?' she choked out. 'You don't just carry that kind of money around in your saddlebags every day—' she broke off, sobbing like her heart would break.

'Aleks, Aleks, Aleks…' He shook his head, then cuddled her into his lap again. 'Is that all? That's the best part,' he said with a grin. 'It was part of my inheritance from my mother.'

'From your mother?' Her mouth fell open and she closed her eyes for a moment, then snapped her mouth shut.

He nodded.

'Really?' She took a deep breath and began to throw her arms about his neck, then froze, wincing. She reached for his hands, instead. 'I wanted to believe you, but that stopped me dead. I knew you cared for me, but I feared I'd pushed you away by asking for more closeness than you wanted. Despite the silly gold, I finally decided to trust you, and what I knew in my heart, despite what I was seeing, hearing and feeling.'

He kissed her lips, but she pulled her head back.

'Just a moment, please, let me finish,' she said. 'For so long after Mama died, other than Papa's decisions, I had to be in charge of so many things in our lives. Since Papa's death, there's been no one to do for me. I am slowly learning patience, and discovering the world would not fall apart if someone makes decisions, or does things for me.' She stopped. 'I needed to let go of control and trust you, though everything except my heart screamed against it. It was the hardest test I could ever imagine.'

His lips found hers again, then he spoke. 'It was your willingness to trust me, in the face of everything,' he waved his hands around, 'that proved I could trust someone besides myself, and even more, trust you. Growing up with an abusive father, I learned to trust no one. Despite desperately wanting to be close to you, I feared being hurt and abandoned if I let you too near. I wanted to put as much distance between us as possible. These feelings are still part of my life, but thanks to my mother, they no longer rule it, and I want to share it with you.'

They were silent for minutes, each lost in their own thoughts.

Aleksandra lifted her chin and squeezed his fingers, fully meeting his eyes for the first time.

'I think we're worth a go,' her voice rang clear and bold. 'What do you think?'

'We'll have to talk with each other, instead of clamming up and running,' he took a deep breath, 'but I'm willing to give it my best shot.'

'Sounds like we've got ourselves a deal.' She smiled.

'Oh, one more question,' he tilted his head as she looked at him with big eyes. He sat silently, the pulse ticking at his throat.

'Mmmm?' She raised an eyebrow at him.

'Would you consider ...' he cleared his throat, then continued in a deeper voice '... would you do me the honor of becoming my wife?'

He held his breath, brushing his hair back with one hand as he awaited her response.

'I'd be proud to, Xavier.' Her heart was in her gaze as she took his hands and their lips met in a promise, then his arms were around her.

He dropped to his knees and lay down, pulling her with him. Aleksandra responded to his gentle explorative kiss, hesitantly at first. Finally, she sighed, and with a tremulous smile, began to stroke his face and hair, her work-roughened hands turning to velvet in a touch.

ALEKSANDRA LAY IN HIS ARMS, caught by the glowing embers of his eyes so close to her, just as she'd dreamed. Running her fingers through his hair, tears flowed softly down her face as her heart brimmed over. A glow began in her core and move downwards as he spoke to her in the same voice he used with frightened horses, his gentle murmur and firm, loving strokes erasing their fears. Her heart had ached to watch him, so strongly did she desire what he gave to them. Today it was all for her, and she wanted it to last forever.

'I've desired this for so long, but I wanted you to trust me and come to me of your own volition.' His voice was husky, his lips against her forehead. 'When I saw you riding up that trail in front of Vladimir, I thought I'd lost you forever.'

'We're both here now.' She touched his lips with her fingers. 'We've fought our demons and we're still here. If we can survive the past week, we can live through anything.'

She fell silent as their lips met, his strong, callused hands running the full length of her body in firm, warm strokes, her cheeks hot as they rolled over, his arm cradling her head. She quivered when his hand slid past her breast, feeling a tightening in her core. Xavier took a deep breath and gripped her good hand, staring at her intently.

'*Do* you want this, *mi querida*?'

She could only nod her assent, her eyes locked on to his, and reached up to touch his nose, his mouth, his hair. Rolling onto his back, Xavier pulled Aleksandra up to sit on his hard abdomen.

'I've missed you so much, Aleks. Your heart, your smile, all of you.' He slowly slid her buckskin shirt over her head and laid it beside them, his eyes moving slowly down her body. 'Oh, your lovely breasts, and the rest of you which I haven't yet dared to touch.'

Aleksandra took his hands and placed them over the soft leather binding her chest flat and he shook his head, with a smile. Teasing her with his fingers, he slowly untied the strap and unwrapped her, releasing her breasts, then sat up and pulled his shirt off, his eyes barely leaving her nipples, hard and erect in the crisp morning air. He turned her to lie with the warm leather shirt beneath her back, her body open to the sun and his eyes.

Her breath came short when he filled his hands. She gasped as his fingers gently squeezed the rosy peaks between them. His head lowered to suckle one taut crest, and she sucked in air as her belly tightened against his hand. He chuckled against her skin as his lips slid to her other nipple, the first wet and tingling in the alpine breeze.

ALEKSANDRA'S BREATH came faster as he touched her shoulder, her belly, her thighs. The pulsing tension in her core grew stronger by the moment. Unable to lie still any longer, she reached for him, drawing him close. As he lowered his hips, his desire for her pressed hard against her thighs and she inhaled sharply.

'I don't know what to do, Xavier,' she whispered.

'You're doing everything you need to, *Querida*. Touch me as you will,' he rumbled, deep in his throat.

Emboldened, she stroked downward from his neck, over his strong shoulders and through the dark curling hair of his chest. Glancing at him beneath her lashes, she ran tentative fingertips over his nipples and he stilled. She lightly pinched them and he groaned and stiffened, his hands frozen on her back.

His glorious, muscular body, flexing gold beneath the sun, captured her eyes as he sat up to slide her trousers off, then his own, and lay back down beside her. Closing her eyes, she relished the feeling of his hands stroking her as she tried to slow the beating of her heart.

'Xavier!' Her eyes flew open and she clasped her legs together when his fingers found her most sensitive part.

'Be still, *Poquita*', he said, smiling into her wide eyes, and stroked her down again, sliding a leg over hers. She took a deep breath and willed herself to stillness as his fingers returned to that place and slowly rubbed until her world melted down. Capturing her mouth with his, his probing fingers slipped lower as her mind whirled. She rose higher and higher on undulating waves of feeling she'd never known, then broke from his mouth and called his name as she went over the top. Gripping him tightly, she sank her teeth into his chest, sobbing ... wanting ... she knew not what, only that between her legs a throbbing she'd never known begged to be appeased.

Xavier held her eyes with his and slowly moved atop her. She felt his hardness pressing tightly between her legs. Black eyes intense, he looked her a question and she nodded, head spinning.

'You already have my heart and my soul, take the rest of me,' she breathed, wrapping her legs about him.

'This will hurt, *Querida*, but there is no other way.' He stroked the wisps of hair from her face.

She nodded slowly, barely comprehending his words, only aware of the need deep inside. Crying out, she froze at the sharp pain as he gave one powerful thrust. Xavier trembled and stilled, face hard, his body like a statue. When Aleksandra smiled and moved tentatively against him, his eyes softened and he glided to meet her. They matched each other stroke for stroke until he stiffened, his body taut beneath her hands. With a great shudder, he called out her name and collapsed, going with her to that place she'd never been before.

They lay entwined for long minutes. Xavier picked up his head, touched her face and kissed her. Lost in the glow from his eyes, Aleksandra closed hers, wrapped in the safety of his arms.

WAKING to the feel of something lightly brushing her lips, Aleksandra turned her head to Xavier. She flinched when she rolled to her side at the soreness between her legs and her arm, and gave him a wry grin.

Her eyes focused on the sprig of flowers with which he'd awakened her.

'Flowers for my lovely lady.' He leaned down to kiss her lips.

The smile ran away from her face and she grabbed his hand,

staring at the yellow blossoms. Her world spun as she remembered her father's words and sketches: "... fleshy leaves; several shoots, five to thirty centimeters tall, growing from the same thick root; small yellow flowers."

She sat bolt upright, eyes wide, staring at the sprig, then shook her head and stared again.

'*Querida*?' Eyebrows raised, he looked sideways at her.

'Where did you get these?' Her eyes narrowed, then darted to his face.

'*Como*? Are you alright, Aleks?' Xavier's brow furrowed at her.

'No, I mean it.' She sat up on her knees, facing him. 'Where did you find these flowers?'

'There.' He pointed at a splash of yellow in the shadow of a rocky outcropping. 'And there. There's plenty of it, I didn't think you'd mind ...' his voice trailed off as she took the flower from his hand and slowly twirled it before her face, examining it intently.

She let out the breath and shook herself, then began to smile. Falling back on the ground, she laughed until he dropped down beside her.

'What is this about? Are you okay?' he demanded, with something between a grin and a grimace, and grabbed her by both shoulders, willing her to look at him.

She winced, then turned to face him, still giggling, her eyes alight, then sobered enough to answer him.

'All this, and it grows right here,' she whispered.

'What are you on about?' He frowned.

'The plant. It's Papa's plant.'

He shook his head again.

'Papa's plant? What do you mean?'

Xavier's eyebrows really *could* touch each other. It made her laugh again and reach out to hug him.

'Yes, the secret plant. Vladimir's plant, what this whole mess is about.' She stopped and glanced at the golden sprays painted all about them. 'Now that I think of it, it's a similar climate and elevation to where Papa said it grew in Poland. I don't think we ever looked for it here.' She shook her head slowly.

'Are you sure?'

'Yep.'

Still shaking her head, she stood up, her still-matted hair swaying about her hips as she walked towards the biggest clump of flowers, in the shelter of a big boulder.

'Where are you going?' Xavier called.

'To see the plants,' she threw over her shoulder and smiled, seeing him pick up their discarded clothing and follow. She climbed higher.

When he caught up with her, she was still staring at the yellow blooms, silent. She shivered as the breeze touched her naked skin, but she scarcely noticed.

'What is it?'

'Xavier,' she said slowly, 'they're planted in rows.'

'Rows?'

'Yes, someone planted these. And he didn't tell me about them.' She gave him a wry grin, her brow wrinkled. 'Papa would've seen the funny side of this.'

'Finding it here?'

'Yes, and our jealous guarding of his precious store of it, when there appears to be an unlimited supply right here.'

'There is…rather a lot of it.' Xavier looked around the hillside above him, seeing splashes of yellow in several rocky recessed areas.

'How could I have missed it?'

'Perhaps it only blooms for a short time.'

'Yes, and this is a busy time for trappers. I've never had the leisure to laze around at this altitude as we've been doing today.'

'Your papa wouldn't have wanted to put you in more danger, but he clearly had a reason for planting them.'

Aleksandra turned and hugged Xavier close. 'I'm sure he did. We'll just have to figure out what that was,' she said as she pulled the buckskins from his hand, dropped them on the ground and pulled him down beside her. 'It may take us quite some time.'

The End

THANK YOU

Thank you for joining Aleksandra and Xavier in
A Long Trail Rolling.

They will be returning in
The Hills of Gold Unchanging
Find it here!
https://books2read.com/HillsOfGoldUnchanging

Enjoyed the story?
If you loved it, a short review on Bookbub, Goodreads and your
favorite eBook retailer would sure be appreciated.
I'd be grateful for your help in spreading the word!

Want to hear more?
Sign up for Lizzi's VIP Club to hear about new releases and specials,
plus get your free sampler gift here!
www.lizzitremayne.com/viplong/

FIND EBOOKS & PAPERBACKS

Find eBooks

at your favorite online retailer via buy links at www.lizzitremayne.com/books/

Find Paperbacks

Signed print books are available in standard (and some in large format) print from the author and and unsigned print books are available from most online retailers.

Contact the author via her website at:

https://lizzitremayne.com/contact-lizzi/

New Zealand Schools

Available from Wheelers and AllBooks (print and digital)

LIZZI TREMAYNE
BOOKS

COMING SOON!

WITH LOVE FROM
NEW ZEALAND, RUSSIA, SCOTLAND, AND U.S.A.

BOOKS DETAIL AND UPCOMING RELEASES

The Long Trails Series

Book One: *A Long Trail Rolling*

A dangerous job. Is it a convenient escape route... or a death trap?

Winner of True West 2016 Best Western Romance, Romance Writers of New Zealand: 2014 Pacific Hearts Award and 2015 Koru Award

UTAH TERRITORY, 1860. *Alone.* Aleksandra has spent her whole life training for the inevitable. So when a brutal Cossack tracks down and kills her father, she knows what she must do. She flees, disguised as a Pony Express rider, in an attempt to keep her pa's killer from discovering their family's secret.

Xavier has kept the world, especially women, at arms-length since he ran from his troubles as heir to his *Californio* rancho family. As a Pony Express Station Keeper, having a girl riding the Pony out of his station wasn't ever part of his plans... but somehow it happened, blackmail being what it is. Curiously, he didn't want to let this one out of his sight.

They begin to let each other into their hearts, but the cards are stacking against them as the minutes tick by and Aleks rides full speed into the Indian Paiute War. Can they learn to trust in time to escape the Indians, evade the killer, and save both their love and Aleksandra's family legacy?

Book Two: *The Hills of Gold Unchanging*

As the Civil War rages, secessionists menace California. The Confederates want the state and they'll stop at nothing to they'll stop at nothing to take it.

UTAH TERRITORY, 1860. On a wagon train headed for the Golden State, Aleksandra makes a dangerous enemy of a gun-running Confederate when she fights her way out of his unwelcome embrace.

After a late-night poker game, Xavier's new friends realize he's heard too much to be allowed to live.

Embroiled in the Confederates' fight to drag the new state from the Union and make it their own, can Aleks and Xavier survive? The secessionists mean business.

Book Three: *A Sea of Green Unfolding*

They set sail for the peace and calm of New Zealand, but they hadn't counted on murderers, mutineers, and a land war in paradise.

SAN FRANCISCO BAY AND NEW ZEALAND, 1863. Aleksandra and Xavier have finally found happiness on their Rancho de las Pulgas, but tragedy and death strike far too soon. Sickened further by the U.S. government's treatment of their Native American friends, they only want out. Of everything.

They are thrown a lifeline by an old friend of Xavier's from the California goldfields. This Gustavus von Tempsky, with his shadowed past, is now a newspaperman in Coromandel, New Zealand. His invitation draws them to a new start, with a part to play in the development of the peaceful young country—but by the time they arrive in Aotearoa, everything has changed.

Aleks thought mutineers and scoundrels aboard ship were the worst of their worries, but she hadn't planned on disembarking into a turbulent wilderness and befriending the helpful local Māori, only to find von Tempsky leading the colonial troops into the bush against the natives who'd saved her life.

Box Set: *The Long Trails Box Set*

Can an orphan, with only her Mustang and a Cossack sword, survive alone on the frontier?

From the deserts of Utah, through the gold mines of California, to the turbulent wilderness of Colonial New Zealand, Aleksandra rides, loves, and fights—with only her Cossack skills to keep her alive.

*** From multiple award winning author Lizzi Tremayne ***

UPCOMING: *The Tatiana Series* (*with links to* The Long Trails *series*)

Book One: *Tatiana I*

Stableman's daughter Tatiana rises to glamorous heights by her equestrienne abilities—but the tsar's glittering attention is not always gold.

MOSKVA, RUSSIA 1842. Tatiana and her husband Vladimir become pawns in the emperor's pursuit of a coveted secret weapon. While Tatiana and their infant son are placed under house arrest, Vladimir must recover the weapon or lose his wife and young son. With the odds mounting against them, can they find each other again—half a world away? *Coming soon!*

UPCOMING: *The Somewhere Series*

(also with links to The Long Trails series!)

Book One: **Somewhere Called Home**

Highlands to Waterloo—can love prevail over fate?

SCOTTISH HIGHLANDS, 1813. Lachlann is disowned for refusing to become clan tacksman after his father and heads for the city, alone, to build a life for himself and his beloved Annis. Annis' waiting turns to despair when her mother buys safety during the clearance of their village—leaving Annis at the mercy of the laird's degenerate son. Lachlann emerges from the hell of Waterloo wanting only to see Annis again... and his father. *To be released soon.*

The Once Upon a Vet School Series

Drama and humor abound as Lena pursues her childhood dream of becoming an equine vet—and beyond—in this upcoming, unique series of

six independent novella sequences:

~Junior Years~

After Lena hears she needs good grades to become a veterinarian, things start to get tricky. Even her pony doesn't get out unscathed. (Middle Grade) *USA 1972-1976*

~High School Days ~

When your high school counsellor says vet school's too hard for you and your HS sweetheart offers you a dream life of farming, writing, and babies, what do you do? Is vet school really the be-all, end-all? (Young Adult) *USA 1976-1979*

~College Nights

How can you have a life when you need an A in every class for four years to get into vet school... on top of 800 hours vet practice work? Something's got to give. (Young Adult and up) *USA 1980-1984*

~Vet School 24/7~

Now they're in, the pressure for grades is off and vet school social life is upon them... there's only the tsunami of 200 years of veterinary knowledge to pack into their heads. Can Lena and her friends stay afloat? (Young Adult and up) *USA 1984-1988*

~Practice Time~

Finally graduated, prima ballerinas of the university, Lena and her vet school classmates disperse to far-flung practices... and real life. What could possibly go wrong? Late nights on-call, mud, blood, and finally, a light at the end of the tunnel... unfortunately, it's only the penlight of a dictatorial vet technician in Lena's eyes after she passed out on the floor. (Women's Rural Fiction with Romantic Elements) *USA & New Zealand 1988-2012*

~Long in the Tooth~

When Lena suffers another catastrophic back injury in New Zealand, what's she to do to feed her family and keep the farm? She can't breathe around cats or birds and what good's an equine vet who can't hold up a horse's leg? Time for Lena to go back to school. Again. (Women's Rural Fiction with Romantic Elements) *New Zealand 2012- ...*

Currently Available Reads:

~Vet School 24/7~

Fifty Miles at a Breath

Horses bring them together and their future looks rosy—it's the present they can't handle.

When equine veterinary student Lena and veteran pilot Blake fall in love, vet school and the past intrude. Add in a long-distance relationship, and things get just plain hard. A grueling endurance race forces them to draw on their strengths and face their fears—together.

Lena Takes a Foal

She needs help... he needs to stay away...

Lena's got a problem—one that might prevent her from graduating. When her horse flips over and lands on her, it has to be the dashing resident, Kit, who finds her. Luckily, she's sworn off relationships after her last debacle and sea-green eyes and rugged good looks are the last things on her mind. Besides, to a veterinary school faculty, relationships between residents and students are like oil and water.

They just don't

mix.

~Practice Time~

Greener Pastures Calling

A new country, a great job, and a good Kiwi bloke. Life couldn't be better.

Until it gets worse.

Newly emigrated to New Zealand, Lena wants a 'good Kiwi bloke', but they're elusive as their nocturnal namesake. Nigel's avoiding females, unless they're cows, horses, or his mother after his first marriage. Sparks fly when they meet—but not the first time, over the dirty instruments in a filthy cowshed. They seem to be made for each other, until Nigel remembers where he first saw her. And then the questions start.

Understanding Modern Vet Med for Owners

The new series of veterinary books for horse owners to let you use what vets know to keep your horses healthier and happier. *First volume due out soon!*

Sign up for Lizzi's VIP Reader Club to hear about new releases and specials, plus get your free sampler gift at

www.lizzitremayne.com/VIPSea/

AUTHOR'S NOTES

This is the first saga in *The Long Trail* series. The succeeding stories are listed a little further on. A few clarifications may be helpful:

Aleksandra's hero Xavier, is a Californio, an old Californian of Spanish descent, and as such his name is pronounced 'HAV-ee-air' in Spanish.

Clifton Flat, the background photo on the cover, did not actually have a Pony Express station. The montage bears my photo of the restored Simpson's Springs Station cabin. The small trail visible before the cabin is truly there, and Pat Hearty believes it to be one of the last parts of the trail appearing as it did 'back in the day'.

The Pony Express poster quoted in the story may not have been written until 1923. I am purposely perpetuating this misconception.

The term 'ostler' is used by Vladimir, as it was in England and Europe at that time, although 'hostler' was the accepted American term.

My main characters are fictitious. Although I have altered a few dates, the events and some other people portrayed are real, presented in this fiction as best I understand them from the historical record. While my research has uncovered no precedent of female riders of the Pony Express, in light of the prevalence of women who followed the guns of the American Civil War in the same year, it is not impossibility.

With respect to the recipe at the back of this book, some controversy exists regarding the difference between *żurek* and *biały barszcz*. Some use it interchangeably. In Poland, I was told they are both called white borscht, but that the latter is usually made with wheat flour. Countless personal and regional variations exist. For a real treat, try the recipe for *żurek*, Aleksandra's favorite comfort food of *Polska*.

I hope you enjoy my first foray into the world of historical romantic suspense. Please leave reviews and comments where you purchased it, on Goodreads, and on my webpage. If you want to pass on a comment, find me via my Connect with Lizzi page.

Warmest regards,
Lizzi Tremayne

GLOSSARY

a charaid (G) a friend

a nighean (G) O girl

basta (S) enough

bien (S) good

cállate (S) be quiet. shut up (command)

chiquita (S) petite one (feminine)

Californio (S) Spanish California colonist or descendent

dinna fash (G) don't worry yourself

dios mío (S) my God

džigitovka (P/R) Caucasian then C & Ukranian military show riding

Dzień (P) Day. Pronounced "Zshen/ Jean/ Jen"

kwahaten (S) antelope

le gusta (S) to please or like

mi corazón (S) my heart

que le vaya bien (S) I hope that you go well

querida/o (S) my darling or my love (fem/masc)

mo nighean bhan (G) my golden-haired girl

moje drogie córki (P) my darling daughter

señorita (S) girl or miss

sguir (G) stop (whatever you're doing)

shashka (R) hiltless Caucasian/ R/ C sword

te quiero (S) I love you or I want you

zakwas (P) rye sourdough starter

żurek (P) white borscht/ a traditional Polish stew

C: Cossack G: Gaelic P: Polish S: Spanish Sh: Shoshone R: Russian

RECIPE: ŻUREK

This hearty stew, typical of the 'sour' soups common and beloved by many Eastern Europeans, is my favorite soup. It is well worth the time it takes to make it. Thank you to the Glinkowski family, third generation owners of Glinkowski Carriages, for sharing with us their love of Poland and *Żurek*. After leaving them, we tasted different versions of it in every town we visited around *Polska*.

Zakwas *("ZAH-kvahss,")* –Sourdough Rye Starter Culture
    2 cups rye flour
    1/2 cup oat flakes
    3-4 cups water, boiled and cooled to room temperature
    2 cloves garlic, thinly sliced
    Crusts of a piece of Polish rye bread (remove after 2-3 days to prevent mold) or a few tablespoons of sourdough starter

Mix in a nonreactive vessel (glass, stainless steel, stoneware) and leave in warm place (70-80 F / 20-27 C) to ferment for 2-5 days until bubbly and as sour as you wish, then use it to make *żurek*.
    The resulting culture: After I use some to make *żurek*, I refresh the rest by 'feeding it' more kibbled/cracked rye or rye flour and water, as Aleksandra's mother did in the story. Leave out, covered, to ferment

overnight then refrigerate. When it hasn't been used for a while, liquid will accumulate on top and be less active. Stir it and replenish as above. With this starter, I can make *żurek* whenever I want and also use it as a starter in sourdough rye bread recipes.

Żurek or zur or biały barszcz ("ZHOO-rek","BYAH-wih BARSHCH")

White Borscht or Sour Rye Soup
Serves 6
1-2 onions, minced
fat or oil for frying
1 lb bacon, chopped (450 g)
1-2 lb Polish kielbasa sausage (pork/beef) in ½ - 1 inch slices (450-900 g)
Spices: 1 T marjoram, 2 whole allspices, 6 peppercorns, 1 bay leaf
6 cups boiling water or stock
2 cups *zakwas*
½ cup cultured sour cream
vegetables (carrots, peas, mushrooms, parsnips) in small pieces, if desired
salt and pepper to taste.
To serve:
5-6 eggs, boiled and cut into wedges or quarters
4-5 potatoes, boiled and hot, cut into quarters or cubes
rye bread or trenchers

In large soup pot, brown chopped onion till translucent, then add bacon and cut up sausage. Stir-fry until browned (some prefer to prick sausages and cook them whole in the liquid soup, then cut up later). Add spices and boiling water or stock. Add *zakwas, while whisking*. This will thicken the soup. If you used oat flakes, you may wish to strain the *zakwas* but I don't strain it, as I also use kibbled rye in my starter. They cook down, .

Bring to a boil and simmer for 10-15 minutes. If it has thickened enough, add the sour cream. If not, stir one tablespoon flour into the sour cream before adding, then bring to boil again and simmer for another 10-15 minutes. I make (at *least*) a double recipe, as it is better the next day or after freezing.

To serve, ladle soup over potatoes and eggs placed into the bottom of individual bowls or make bread trenchers to use in their place! Cheat by horizontally cutting the top off of a large bun to create a lid (or cut a hole out of the top as you would a Jack O'Lantern pumpkin). Hollow the bread out and ladle the soup into it.

Serve with rye bread (what else?) and enjoy!

ABOUT THE AUTHOR

Lizzi grew up riding wild in the Santa Cruz Mountain redwoods, became an equine veterinarian at UC Davis School of Veterinary Medicine and practiced in the Gold and Pony Express Country of California before emigrating to New Zealand. She has two wonderful boys, a grandson, and an awesome partner in that sea of green. When she's not writing, she's swinging a rapier or shooting a bow in medieval garb, riding or driving a carriage, playing in the garden on her hobby farm, singing, cooking, teaching, or looking into a horse's mouth in her equine veterinary dental practice. She is awarded and multiply published in fiction, nonfiction, special interest magazines and veterinary periodicals.

With her debut novel, Lizzi was:
Winner 2016 True West Magazine
Best Western Romance
Winner 2015 RWNZ Koru Award
Finalist 2015 Best Indie Book Award
Winner 2014 RWNZ Pacific Hearts Award
Finalist 2013 RWNZ Great Beginnings

CONNECT WITH LIZZI

I'm looking forward to hearing from you!

Join conversations and find story excerpts, buy links, and more here:

www.lizzitremayne.com/VIPLong
www.lizzitremayne.com
www.horseandvetbooks.com
www.bookbub.com/profile/lizzi-tremayne/
www.facebook.com/lizzitremayneauthor/
www.instagram.com/lizzitremayne/
www.tiktok.com/@lizzitremayneauthor
www.twitter.com/LizziTremayne/
https://www.youtube.com/channel/UCylITovsoX1H1E17lJZTxTQ
www.goodreads.com/LizziTremayne/
https://nz.pinterest.com/lizzitremayne/

ACKNOWLEDGMENTS

Thank you to my son *Elliot*, my rock. He not only persisted in the creation of this cover, kept me fed and helped us through my last injury, but also participated in untold hours of research, visiting museums and historical sites of the hero and heroine's families around the globe. He heard repeatedly 'what they did' as we drove through Utah, and 'what they will do' in Nevada, California and New Zealand in the next books of the series. He is a champion. Thank you to *Matt*, my soulmate and techie. He helped keep me sane, somehow surviving the last six months in my 'mildly' stressed presence.

Keeping horses, entering my veterinary world, and this book would never have become a reality without my mum Kirsten, Jerry, Veronica, Morfar, the 4-H Club and Dad. *Mange tusinde tak*, Mum. Thank you also to the Glinkowskis, third generation at Glinkowski Carriages, Poland, for sharing with us their love of Poland, horses and *Żurek*.

My appreciation goes out to several authors who built my love of history and reading early on in the piece: Mary Stewart, my all-time favorite for history and travel, plus the first writer who showed my beloved veterinary medicine in a story; Walter Farley, for his soul-capturing horse yarns; Laura Ingalls Wilder, who gave to me the American pioneers (My gratitude also to Mary Catherine Sears, the primary teacher who enthralled us with Mrs. Wilder's series annually.); and Diana Gabaldon for her epic writing across genres, giving me the idea, rightly or wrongly, that I might get away with writing the stories residing in my heart.

Finally, one doesn't write a book like this alone. I am indebted to the many people who assisted me in my historical research, especially Patrick Hearty, National Trails Chairman and Past President of the

National Pony Express (PX) Association. Pat's unstinting offerings of his knowledge and love of the PX has given this book many layers it wouldn't otherwise possess. Pat and his family not only showed my son and I over the Utah portion of the trail last dusty July, but took me riding up a lovely aspen valley, always happy to stop to explain the significance of places and people, or for me to take more photos, two of which grace this book's cover. For your enthusiasm, Patrick, I thank you with all my heart. Thanks also to: Linda Hearty for her gracious hospitality and patience with my many calls to her husband; their daughter Kellie for the trail ride; Beth (nee Bagley) and Don Anderson of Callao, Utah, for allowing us to visit and photograph their PX artifacts. Beth is fifth generation at what was Willow Springs PX Station; Tom Crews of XP Pony Express Home Station, the PX website, for introducing me to Patrick, as well as promoting my story during the 2013 PX Re-Ride; Jaromy Jessop for his many XP articles on Tom's site; Jason Wood for his nature craft comments; Randy'L Teton, Public Affairs Manager, Shoshone Bannock Tribes; Kurt Williams of Expedition Utah; and Davy Crockett of Pony Express Trail 100 for his detailed descriptions of the trail through Utah.

Thanks to Amy Taylor (and parents!), Elliot (again), Maya and Sonny, for giving up half of a Saturday for cover photos. Amy lives to compete, but Elliot hadn't been on a horse in years, much less bareback.

My immense gratitude goes to my writing mentor Sophia James, my beta readers, Ngaire, Kate, Matt, Rebekah, Dash (the first YA to read this) and others for the great criticism and ideas. Kate and Matt, you were right, and I was wrong. Another story was needed before the epilogue. Kudos to my critique partners Jen and Jen, Netta, Deryn, Christine, those unwitting victims upon whom I foisted the odd chapter, and too many RWNZ fellow writers to even count. You are an amazing bunch of people.

Thank you to the many others who have helped, not only in my pedantic search for detail, but in so many ways, not the least in your everyday encouragement to finish this story and get it published!

Thank you all. I couldn't have done it alone.

xx

Lizzi

EXCERPT FROM THE HILLS OF GOLD UNCHANGING

J*une 1860, Echo Canyon, Wasatch Mountains, Utah Territory*

HIS BLADE GLINTED in the sunlight as he lunged toward her, but she ducked and spun, her own sword flashing in figure eights while she retreated, and his strike met with only air. He recovered and set himself up for the onslaught he knew would come, coughing as the dust kicked up by their boots thickened.

Blade up, he parried the blows she rained down upon him. He managed to get in one of his own, and retreated for a moment, breathing hard. She stepped back as well, her breasts heaving beneath the thin linen. Blue eyes glittered below brows narrowed with concentration, before her sword returned to action with a vengeance. They circled, dodging and striking in turn. Her skill was far greater, but the girl's injuries from her last fight, combined with his greater reach and fitness were beginning to tell. A movement tugged at the edge of his vision—he glanced up from her sword to see her hat tumble off. Her hair cascaded down in a tangle to her thighs, and his heart surged.

She's mine now.

He offered the ghost of a smile as he moved in to disarm her with a passing lunge and struck at her sword arm.

The air left his lungs and he tasted dirt in his mouth as he hit the unforgiving ground face-first. He groaned and rolled over, expecting the worst.

Above him, her laughing visage met his eyes. Her glorious curls, molten gold, fell around his face like a veil as she bent to wipe his face and kiss his lips. She slid the hilt of his sword from his hand.

"All right, *halte*, hold, you two," their instructor said, in his heavy Russian accent. "There's still work to be done, Xavier, but you've done well."

Xavier Argüello took the hand his opponent offered, hopped to his feet and dusted off his clothes.

"Well done, *Querido*," said his intended, Aleksandra Lekarski, as she returned his sword.

"Xavier, come here, please," Vladimir Chabardine said, from the doorway of the cabin, where he was propped up in his sickbed. "You have worked hard. I am impressed, and it is rare that I am compelled to say that. That *shashka* now belongs to you. Use it in good health."

Xavier stared at him, then at the Don Cossack saber in his hand, its leather grip smooth with years of use. He was silent.

"But it's yours, Vladimir," he said.

"It was one of mine, yes. Now it is yours. Tatiana brought my other two *shashkas* with her from Russia. One is for Nikolai, when he is ready, and this one is for you. It's the least I can do, after my part in," he looked at Aleksandra and grimaced, "your papa's death."

She nodded grimly in acknowledgement.

"Thank you, from the bottom of my heart," Xavier said, shaking his head at the Russian, as he ran a finger from the tooled embellishment on the pommel through to the rawhide bouton and strip they used for their practice sessions. He slid the protectors off and his new shashka whispered into its scabbard. He turned to face Aleksandra, and bowed to her. "Thank you," he said, then turned to Vladimir, "and again, to you."

She returned the bow and smiled at them both.

"You're not quite done," Vladimir said. "Xavier, replace the guard."

"What would you like?" Aleksandra asked.

"One more bout. *En garde*," he said, and they prepared. "*Prêt.*" They nodded. "*Allez,*" he snapped, and they began. Aleksandra feinted, then moved to strike, but Xavier saw a hole in her defense and lunged. She twirled way, with a laugh, then drew back, looking frightened, her body twisted strangely to the right.

Was she injured?

His gaze lifted to her face. What a chance! Her whole left side was open. He went for the opening. Before he could alter his course, she unwound and her *shashka* flashed toward him. For the second time in his life, he froze as he found her blade across his throat.

"*¿Recuerdas?* Remember this?" she said, her eyes merry.

"How could I forget, *Querida,*" he spoke for her ears alone, "our first meeting?"

Hands clapped behind them and they spun as one, hands on their sword hilts.

"No need fer that, no need fer that," said a man, mounted on a chestnut horse. Beside the horse walked a black man, tied by the wrists to the rope in the rider's hands.

"What do you wan—" Xavier began, then clamped his jaw, as his breath came short. Blood pounded in his ears and his face heated. "What can I help you with," he finally managed, past gritted teeth, as he walked away from the house door, toward their callers.

"Well, hello theah," the rider said, his Southern accent heavy. "Good fightin', and fer a girl, too." He looked sideways at Aleksandra.

"Aleks," Xavier hissed, as he felt, rather than saw, her bristle beside him. He glanced at her knuckles showing white on the pommel of her saber. He reached out and covered her sword hand with his own and she took a deep breath and stilled.

"We're yer new neighbors down th'road. Y'all wanna buy a slave? We've jus' done come West 'n now we've done finished buildin' the house, he's," he nodded at the man at the end of his tether, "jus' 'noth'r mouth t'feed. Ca'int use 'im to grow nuthin' in this rock y'call dirt around heah." He stopped and looked at the yard and cabin. "Nice place y'all got here."

Xavier nodded, silent.

The man's brows narrowed, then he continued. "Well, ah

wondered if y'all had a breedin—ah, a woman slave I could trade fer him. The missus wants help in t'house, an' I could use a little...too." The glint in his beady eyes turned his grin into a leer.

Xavier closed his eyes and clenched his fists. "This territory may allow slavery, but nobody holds with it around here."

The Southerner was silent for a moment, then answered with a voice dripping with sarcasm. "Now that's mahty neighborly of ya. Are y'all some o'them ab'litionists we come West to git away from?"

"As you wish." Xavier raised a brow at him, then shifted his gaze to the man on foot, staring at the dirt. "I apologize to you, sir, but you'll have to go home with him again. May you find yourself a better life soon."

The corners of the slave's mouth lifted briefly. His eyes flickered up to Xavier's, brightened, then dulled again as he dropped them to the ground.

"C'mon Jordan," the rider growled, "we're not welc'm here, by all accounts." He jerked his horse around and they retreated the way they'd come.

Xavier stood silent, watching them go, then began to shake. He closed his eyes, willing himself to control the anger, and the deepening darkness. He inhaled sharply. When he opened his eyes, Aleksandra was staring at him.

"Are you all right?" she said, her brow furrowed.

"Yes." Xavier nodded.

"More Southerners," Aleksandra scowled as she wiped sweat from her brow with the back of her sleeve, "running from home before the government takes their slaves away?"

"That'll never happen," Xavier said, from between clenched jaws. "Too strong, too wealthy—cotton—slaves. Poor beggars down South." He peered around. "Even here. I can't believe it."

"Believe it," she said. "They're coming."

He shook his head. "I just wish we could stop it—the abuse, the owning."

Aleksandra wrapped her arms around him, held him close until the tremors quieted. She leaned back in his arms and studied his face, then seemed satisfied with what she saw.

"Having you here makes it bearable, I think," he said, and kissed her.

"I'm so used to you being the strong one...sometimes I forget the demons that still eat at you," she said.

Keen to read on?
Find *The Hills of Gold Unchanging* at
www.lizzitremayne.com/books

EXCERPT FROM A SEA OF GREEN UNFOLDING

N *ovember 1863, East Coast North Island, New Zealand*

"I'M THINKIN' we be in the Aucklan' Current," Jacob confided that evening, over the supper they shared in the hold. "This time o'year it run to the east o'New Zealan', down past Poverty Bay and heads fer th'South Islan'."

"So you think we're headed for New Zealand, then? The captain doesn't know where we—"

"—this 'cap'n' ain'a real cap'n," Jacob interrupted, "and don't know sh—"

"—I understand," Aleksandra cut in, flashing him a grin. Dzień shuffled his feet and even the little rustling of straw sounded loud to her ears.

"Jus' so we understan' each oth'r." He smirked.

"So how would I find Coromandel Town from that coast?" Aleksandra muttered into her salt pork.

"Coro? I don' be likin' yer chances, Mrs. Argüello."

"Jacob, you can call me Aleks, remember?"

"Aleks, then. Some awful big mount'ns a'tween that'n East Coast n'

Coro Town. Y'll need'n t' find a mission house'n ask 'em fer help. They c'n prob'ly find y'a native guide," he whispered, blowing crumbs of hardtack with his words. "There be lots'a boats comin' up'n down th'coast, all a time."

"Jacob, we owe you more than you can ever know. If we get out of this alive, please come find us, wherever we are. We're seeking a man called von Tempsky. He's from Poland, where my family comes from. Xavier met him in California, and he's a bit bigger than life, so I'm sure you can find him, and through him, us. When you tire of the sea, you'll always have a place with us."

The boy's eyes shone wetly in the dimness, and he ran a sleeve across his eyes.

"Thank'ee, Mrs... Aleks." He gulped. "Ain't no one never said nuthin' like 'at a'fore. My thanks. I'd best be goin' now. I'm thinkin' yer land'll be 'ere soon. I seen alb'trosses las' night, an' it smells like land. T'morro', mebbe?"

"Thank you, Jacob, from the bottom of my heart. Now go." She gave him a little push. He turned and dashed up the ramp, his light footfalls barely audible over the munching of many beasts.

Louder feet, heavier ones, irregular, came down the ramp and she looked up, heart in her throat.

"And what was all that about?" Broadhurst strode in, the collar of Jacob's shirt in his clenched fist. "Why did the boy run out of here, and why were you two talking together so quietly?"

Aleksandra looked down at the ground, as her guts churned and her face heated. How could they get out of this?

"Well, sir," she put her hands over her face, "I do believe I embarrassed the lad, being frank with him about a woman's needs..." She rubbed her eyes and whimpered a little. "With my man not available, why, I just wanted a little closeness, but... but the boy's as good as his word and I'm a married woman... a bad, bad married woman. Please, please don't tell my husband I've been unfaithful in my heart," she got out, between sobs.

"That true, Jacob?" Broadhurst growled.

"Well, yessir. 'Tis," he said, in a small voice.

ALEKSANDRA PEEKED BETWEEN HER FINGERS. The boy was biting his cheeks, his lips quivering.

"Aleks." She awoke to Jacob's voice beside her ear and his touch light upon her shoulder.

She bumped into Dzień's muzzle as she sat up in the darkness and reached out to the boy. The Mustang whickered softly at the diminutive seaman, then nuzzled the back of Aleksandra's neck, his whiskers tickling her fully awake.

"Good save yest'day, wi' the cap'n'. He just'n 'bout found ye out," he whispered. She could swear he grinned in the pitch-darkness. "I smell'n land fer sure. It's jus' aft'r midnight, but I smell it and I hear some o' them li'l owls them have, them'r callin' 'em moreporks."

"What do you want me to do?"

"First light, if'n it's safe, I'll knock on th' deck above ye four times. Ye come out 'n ride fer yer life. I'll have m' men ready so's ye don' get shot while yer swimmin', but there won' be much'n time. If'n it gets t' be no safe, I'll bang three times. Ye'll have to do summat else, mebbe use th' two horses'n like we talked 'bout."

"OK. I'll be ready," she said, her stomach already knotting.

"I'll be tellin' yer man how ye went," he whispered, and they clasped hands before he melted into the night.

Sleep came hard, but she got some, in fits and starts, as the ship rocked through the night.

"It must be near to dawn," Aleksandra murmured to Dzień as he nuzzled her hair and shifted his weight to his other hind leg.

She sat with her skirt loosely tied over her short trousers, arms clasped around her knees. Aleksandra's knapsack remained hidden and Dzień's bridle stowed with it. No sound had yet come from the boards above.

At the sound of footsteps, Aleksandra looked between the planks lining Dzień's stall and she frowned. This wasn't their plan.

"Over here," she whispered.

"Expecting someone, were you?" Broadhurst sauntered into view.

"Only wishful thinking," Aleksandra said, and pulled her blanket up under her chin to better cover her fully-dressed frame. Her heart pounded so loudly she was sure he'd hear it six feet away.

"Better get used to the idea your husband won't be coming back to you. He'll be hanged for what he did to Symes. Remember that," he said. His footsteps retreated toward the ramp.

"Thank you for the visit," she said, sarcasm dripping from her voice.

"Just a reminder. I'm watching you," he said, not bothering to stop.

How she wanted to bury her throwing knife between his shoulder blades.

Four knocks came through the ceiling boards and the captain's footsteps stopped.

"What's that?" he growled, his shoes squeaking as he spun around.

"It's still dark, you've woken me up from a sound sleep, you hear noises, and you ask me what they are?" Her voice raised as she railed at him, making sure it reached maximum volume by the end. "Good night, Captain Broadhurst," she shrieked at him, her hands clenched at her sides.

He took a deep breath, then resumed his walk topside.

Two minutes later, three knocks sounded and repeated.

Aleksandra assembled all just beside the door and went for a walk to see the lay of the land. She walked the long way to the privy. It gave her a view all around the ship as she walked, slowly and a bit unsteadily, as if still groggy from sleep. She turned a corner to see the captain headed back toward the galley and Rach's old cabin, then a door clicked closed. Ducking into a narrow space where she couldn't be observed, she strained her eyes to starboard. There, rising from the straight line of the sea.

Jagged lines of mountains, glorious mountains, broke the horizon. She bit her tongue to keep from crying out as she quietly opened, then slammed the privy door shut, and slipped back the way she'd come. No one else was out walking at this hour. As she entered the hold, four faint knocks sounded on the wood above.

Aleksandra smiled. Jacob was on the job.

Dzień took the bit she proffered, then her fingers flew as she slipped the crownpiece over his head, buckled the throatlatch, and flicked the split reins around his neck. Slinging the knapsack onto her back, she strapped it on tightly. One tug on the string of the waistband of her skirt and it slid to her feet. She stepped out of it and shivered, goosebumps raising against the thin men's trousers.

Leading her pony from his tie stall, she swung up and they dashed away, up the ramp from the hold to the 'tween decks. She turned the corner toward the top deck and Dzień slid to a halt as a shadow rose up before them, hands held high.

"Stop," Broadhurst barked.

The captain dropped his hands and walked toward them, shaking his head.

"Stupid, stupid. That's the oldest trick in the book." He grinned as he reached for Dzień's reins.

Next Chapter

Aleksandra's father hadn't spent years training her and her mount in the Cossack ways for nothing. She drew her shashka as Dzień rose up on his hind legs in a levade, tucking his forelegs up to protect his rider and free her to swipe at Broadhurst. He dodged, but not before he received a slice across the inside of his right forearm for his efforts.

The captain's fingers jerked backwards and he screamed.

Desperately hoping Broadhurst shot his pistol right-handed, she called out to Dzień and he swerved around the man crouching before them, holding his arm and screaming.

Dzień galloped the rest of the way up to the deck. She turned her head to sight the five-foot-high bulwark, topped by the even higher gunwale, and lined the Mustang up to give him the longest possible run. Reaching behind her, she shoved her shashka into the pack then loosed the reins and called to Dzień as she aimed him for the solid wall. Her heart sang as he raced toward it like he'd been shot from a cannon. The Mustang gave a great grunt as his forelegs left the ground and he shoved with his hindquarters. Then his hind hooves, softened by the long trip in the damp hold, slipped.

Heart in her mouth, Aleksandra held her breath and kept her eyes up, her legs clamped firmly on his sides. She'd never jumped this high, much less bareback. Dzień swung his hind legs sideways to miss the rail and his hind hooves clipped the top of the gunwale, but then they were over, and falling, falling until they hit the dark water.

Keen to read on?
Find *A Sea of Green Unfolding* at
www.lizzitremayne.com/books

EXCERPT FROM TATIANA

M*id-1842 Moskva, Russia*

BY THE TIME I was fifteen, and Vladimir sixteen, we were inseparable. No longer did he clean stalls as punishment, but to help me before his Training School classes began. This gave us more time to fit ourselves and prepare our combined *džigitovka* performances. We had been selected as part of the team to perform for the Tsar on his next visit to Moskva from St. Petersburg.

The tsar's creepy messenger, who came to our door with increasing regularity, for no seemingly good reason, had delivered the invitation for our group to give the performance. His terse smile showed through the lace curtains as he stood before the door. I managed to talk Papa into answering it, claiming I couldn't leave my cooking pot.

The messenger, whose name I never asked, but he told me anyway, was Sambor Andropov. Due to his frequent visits, I had taken to ignoring anyone knocking on the door when I was in the house alone. His mere eyes on me made my skin crawl, and I felt I was being undressed before his eyes. Although a servant of the tsar could not be ignored without serious repercussion, if he didn't know I was there, all would be well. If the message was important, he would return, or Mrs. Bagrov would get the door if she was in.

I had the grace to be embarrassed when I realized he had carried such a special invitation to our door after I had avoided him. It was just that men and boys in Papa stableyard never looked at me like that, so perhaps I was being overly sensitive. I vowed to be kinder to him when I saw him next. He was, after all, just doing the tsar's bidding.

After this missive, our training intensified. We only had a month to prepare our troop for our presentation before Tsar Nicholas and his Empress Alexsandra Feodorovna.

There were eleven men in our group, plus me. We were drawn from the wider area around Moskva, but bragging aside, Vladimir and I were the stars of the show.

We had a joint act, with a quadrangle, jumping and shashka work, but our own little act was the best one. It began with Vladimir and I standing in Sarda's saddle, with me just behind him, one hand in the air, waving at the audience. We would then do a lift, ending up with my standing upon Vladimir's shoulders—at a full gallop.

It was a truly tricky maneuver, and one that few ever attempted. We lived, ate and breathed *džigitovka*. In any spare time, we worked out together— running, press-ups, sit-ups— we needed all the strength we could muster, and on the day of the performance for the Tsar Nicholas and Tsarina Alexandra Feodorovna, we triumphed.

During our bows to their Excellencies, the Empress Alexandra Feodorovna beckoned us closer.

"Your skills," she said, "for such young people are to be rewarded. I should like to see you both again." She paused for a moment. "Perhaps," she glanced at the tsar, who lifted an eyebrow at her, and then turned back to us, "you would like to attend the ball at the Kremlin tomorrow night?"

I swallowed hard.

"We should be honored, your Excellencies," Vladimir said, his voice smooth.

"We will see you there." The tsarina nodded and turned back toward her husband, dismissing us.

I curtsied as gracefully as I could, holding a pair of reins and wearing jodhpurs and boots, lacking the essential skirts. Vladimir drew me to my feet and escorted me away.

"A ball at the Kremlin?" I blinked and took a deep breath. "However will I find a ball dress before tomorrow night?"

"You have none?" He looked at me, jaw dropped.

I peered from beneath my brows. "How many balls have I attended since we met?"

He stared at me. "Well…"

"Exactly. I attended the end of year cadets ball with you last year, but that dress will hardly be suitable for an audience," I indicated my breeches and boots, "other than this, of course, with the tsar and tsarina. It's easy for you. You simply need your Training School dress uniform."

"Sisters. Yes, that's it." He spun to face me. "Olga and Sonja will have a dress to fit you."

My jaw dropped. His sisters were elegant young ladies. I'd been introduced to them before, but they hadn't seemed impressed by the stable girl performing with their brother. "But they live a full day's ride away. I'd never be able to ride there and return and still take care of my stable duties."

"I'll go. I can get one of the other lads to do my work for me, if your father permits."

"I permit," he said, walking up in time to hear the end of the conversation.

"Thank you, sir. I have three sisters, most of them close in size to Tatiana. With your permission, I will leave as soon as I cool out my horse."

"We'll take care of that and inform the headmaster. Well done, both of you. Your performance was without equal," he said, taking the reins of Vladimir's horse and leading him back toward the barn.

"Papa," I said, and he turned. I reached out for Sarda's reins. "Thank you, for all you've done for me, for us." I glanced at Vladimir's retreating back.

He handed them to me and hugged me, his eyes glistening with unshed tears. "You have made me so proud, both you and Vladimir. What a team you make."

"We could've never done it without you."

"Soon he will be finished here and must enter the tsar's army." He took back Sarda's reins and together we began walking the sweating horses. "Have you considered what you will do then?" His eyes looked at me—through me—and I shuddered, then swallowed and looked at the floor.

"I honestly do not know, Papa."

"A life of horses is hard for a man, much less a woman, and I won't be around forever."

My eyes snapped up to his. "What?" For the first time, I saw his weathered visage, the grayness of his skin at the edges, and my stomach clenched. "Papa, are you ill?"

He took a deep breath. "I'm not sure, but my heart, it does funny things sometimes. Not badly, but it's enough to give me pause—to question and to ensure you are provided for."

The walls of the Kremlin swayed around me. Papa was my rock, although I'd been increasingly leaning on Vladimir as we had become close friends, and now, it seems, something more.

"Have you been to a doctor, Papa?" Knowing he hadn't.

"No, but there is little they could do."

"You don't know that…"

"Trust me, I know. Anyway, *princessa*, you will be going to the ball and dancing the night away on the arm of your prince.

"Will you becoming?"

"The invitation was only for the two of you, but I will be awaiting your return with bated breath." I offered the horse a few sips of water from a bucket then pulled Sarda away and we resumed our walk.

"This will be my first ball without you, Papa…" I searched his face, seeking to know the extent of his sickness, but nothing showed.

"My *solnishko* has grown up." New tears in his eyes threatened to fall. "You will be the loveliest woman there."

Woman.

I'd never thought of myself as that… it would take some time to sink in.

Due out soon!

Sign up for Lizzi's VIP Club to hear when Tatiana I is released at
https://lizzitremayne.com/viplong/

Thank you for reading. I hope you enjoyed A Long Trail Rolling. To join Lizzi's VIP Club and hear about new release and specials, plus get your free book!

It's right here:

www.lizzitremayne/VIPLong

www.ingramcontent.com/pod-product-compliance
Lightning Source LLC
Chambersburg PA
CBHW022242020726
47496CB00004B/1031